The Mechanics of Magic

W.B.J. Martin

Copyright © 2022 W.B.J Martin

All rights reserved.

ISBN: 9798799039530

Special thanks to Amy and Laura, who have been with us every step of the way, as well as Jake Pleshe for designing the artwork for the book. We couldn't have done this without you.

CHAPTER 1

A shiver ran down Roy's spine despite the warm night as his eyes landed on the gun holstered at the guard's side. He instinctively reached for his magic to cast a shield; maybe security wasn't as lax as he'd thought.

Even knowing he could block the weapon, seeing one in person made him nervous. There was a reason people rarely bothered with guns in Ardveld, but he wasn't keen on testing it. At least he was out of sight. For now.

He shifted atop the wall, long legs numb from his perch amongst the sweet-smelling leaves of the overhanging tree. It had been a simple enough climb. Original stonework formed this part of the perimeter and the loose mortar fell away at his touch, adding to the deep indents created by time and weather to make easy footholds for his soft shoes.

From here, he had a full view of the house and grounds. There were no cameras yet; his scouting two days before had confirmed that, but the old place was definitely wired up. Electric light streamed from a set of windows on the second floor, but as he watched they shut off, leaving only the glow of lamps by the staff entrance where the guard stood. Moonlight illuminated the rest, revealing the disfiguring silhouette of scaffolding rising at the property's rear.

Roy wrinkled his nose in disgust. He wondered how the original inhabitants would feel about the building's new occupant, though they didn't deserve the consideration. Whatever great magic family had lived here held as much responsibility for the takeover as its current owner. Arrogant bastards.

A rumble to his left heralded the approaching car before he saw it. Bright headlights lit up the high gate leading to the estate's front courtyard, and Roy watched as a man leant out to tap a password into the keypad embedded in the red-brick entranceway. With a hum, the gates swung open, and the car continued through. New enough; the plates marked the white vehicle as barely a year old, but not something Felix Marek would be seen in. This was a staff member.

The shift change would be his best opportunity. Drawing a little more magic, Roy focussed on forming the illusion that would darken his clothes and red hair. Nothing special, but it had been over a decade since he'd last had to cast one, and it definitely showed. Manipulating light well enough to replicate reality was beyond his skill, but the smudged effect his spell gave him would at least provide some camouflage.

Gravel crunched as the man from the car crossed in front

of his hiding place. Roy slipped down from the wall and followed, keeping sufficient distance to hide both his footsteps and the magic radiating from him. A strong enough mage might sense him, anyway, if they were paying attention, but that kind of power would make them easily detectable by other magic users themselves. With any luck it meant the man was weak, if he was a mage at all, and the waste energy from Roy's crude illusion would go unnoticed.

The guard at the staff entrance raised a hand in greeting, as the new arrival approached. Now that he was close enough, Roy recognised the symbol on their black uniform; the sunburst logo of Sunstone Enterprises.

That answered why he couldn't sense their presence. Sunstone belonged to Aiden Heliodor; completely now that Felix Marek had sold his share and retired to Ardveld, but apparently Marek had brought his security with him. Even after twenty-three years, the few mages born in Vailberg wouldn't be relegated to guard duty.

The two guards exchanged greetings, their conversation carrying easily across the calm air of the courtyard. From his position in the shadows, Roy analysed the staff door behind them. It had what looked like another electric locking system, which blinked with a green light as the first guard swiped a card and pulled it open.

Magic ready, Roy launched his shield spell towards the entrance. Shaped by his will, it wrapped itself invisibly along the narrow edge where the door would lock. As expected, neither of the guards gave any indication of sensing the spell, and Roy retreated against the wall of the house where he was hidden, focussing his mind on maintaining both the shield and his illusion.

After some time, two sets of footsteps passed his hiding place; one presumably to patrol, and the other heading home to their bed. If either had looked closer, they would have seen that the lock's light remained green. The door swung open at the push of Roy's gloved hand, clicking shut behind him as he released the shielding spell.

A chemical smell of fresh paint dominated the little kitchen he stepped into. Small, but fully equipped with sink, stove and kettle, the cupboards shone a glossy white that contrasted sharply with the scuffed bare stone of the floor. Refurbishments were incomplete and whatever flooring was originally there must have been ripped out.

A closed door at the back blocked off the main body of the house. This one was unlocked, and after a pause to listen for footsteps, Roy passed through.

It was warmer inside, and would have been cosy had it not been the height of summer. Instead, the plush carpet had trapped the day's heat, making the air close and heavy. Roy dismissed his illusion, the disguise no longer worth the focus it took to maintain, and drew a deep breath.

The stale air didn't help the sense of confinement, and he unzipped his brown jacket, flapping it open in an attempt to dry the thin layer of sweat forming on his skin. He had entered what looked like a ground floor foyer, composed of a small seating area occupying the vacant space below a spiral staircase that led to the top floor.

Here at least, the house retained some of the elegant, Ardveldian style that would have once defined the property.

Dark green walls were embossed in a wide angular design, extending up to a high ceiling swirled with intricately carved patterns.

Not that Felix Marek wasn't trying to impose his mark. Inside, it was clear to Roy that the scaffolding he'd seen was part of an extensive modification. Dust sheets covered the floor where a large fireplace had been installed, comprising an elaborate mantelpiece over the deep hearth. There would have been no need for fire in the original construction, not when the staff could use their magic to charge the passive spells for heat and cooling.

What had happened to them when the family that owned this place fled?

The familiar heat of rage burned through him, not eased by how simple this break-in was proving to be. He'd come for answers, but all was quiet, security lax. Marek might have something to hide, but if this was his set-up, then any evidence was likely back in Vailberg. In any case, he was here now.

Tall windows lit the stairs with an eerie glow, and Roy headed up. As he turned the corner, the disapproving eyes of a portrait peered down at him from the wall. Whoever painted it must have been in a forgiving mood; Felix Marek's wispy hair looked almost dignified in this depiction, and you could almost believe his width was still the muscle of his youth. He gave the painting the finger as he passed. Unfortunately for Marek's apparent ego, television told a different story.

Honestly, Roy wasn't even sure where he was going. He'd let instinct carry him up the stairs, knowing the building works on the ground floor likely meant nothing of interest would be stored there. The top corridor smelled of fresh paint, like the guards' room below, but he was relieved to see that this floor had carpet to muffle his footsteps.

Still watching for movement, Roy reached out with his magic sense. There was no answering presence of another mage and, though it didn't guarantee the upstairs rooms were unoccupied, it fuelled his confidence enough to move on.

The lights he'd seen from outside had been to the left of the house, so Roy went right, running a hand along the bump where wooden panelling met newly papered wall. He couldn't help smiling as he did so; the satisfying sensation of being in a place he didn't belong, echoing the buzz that had driven him to a multitude of less-than-legal activities in his teens.

Magic flaring against his fingertips brought him to a sudden stop. At first glance, the wall here looked no different from the rest of the corridor. But with his attention drawn, Roy spotted the narrow gap that ran from floor to ceiling. It was a magic locked door, flush with the wall and concealed, with no obvious entry point other than a thin, metallic strip along the gap in the panelling.

He licked his lips as he saw the metal, trained eyes instantly recognising the simple alarm that had been embedded in the wood. It would sound an alert if anyone opened the door, but he had come prepared. Roy reached into the inner pocket of his coat and grasped what he was searching for; a thin rectangular magnet. Alarms like this were common, especially on internal doors that required little security, but the wires inside were easily tricked. Held near the metal connector, a magnet would temporarily disable it. The magic lock, however, should provide a bit more fun.

Magnet ready, he turned his attention to the passive spell that was keeping the door shut.

The moment he extended his power to read the spell, he recognised it. Roy froze, blood beating through his ears as he ran over and over the familiar pattern, his shock tinged with pain and grief.

He'd not encountered a lock like this since he was eight years old. Not since his mother had crafted simple replicas for him to solve; basic imitations of the spells that secured the palace where she'd worked. This was a palace lock.

Fear had swept the country in the days and months following the takeover and, for a brief moment, Roy felt it again. Ardveld's most powerful mages, slaughtered by some unknown means. The royal family and their Champions... All the apprentices and staff who'd been at the palace that day.

There shouldn't be anyone left alive who could craft something like this. Certainly not in the home of someone like Felix Marek.

Roy realised he was shaking and forced himself to focus. He pulled off a glove with his teeth and rested his hand against the rough wallpaper over the door, reading the spell more easily without the physical barrier. As he did, he noticed that it wasn't much more advanced than the practice locks he'd cracked as a child.

Passive spells sustained themselves via a continuous flow of magic imprinted on a physical object. They looped via a framework created from the caster's will, beginning at the start of their intent through to the completed instruction and over again. Further intentions could be layered over the top; in the case of a locking spell, this usually meant adding a pass signature and additional bindings to a door that would each need to be unravelled for the spell to break.

Any spell could theoretically be broken with enough force, but by feeling the weak point in the loop, the point at which the caster's intent began, only a slight nudge of magic was required to unhook the connection and disperse the structure that lay there.

What made the palace locks different from any other Roy had encountered was the introduction of false loops. It took exceptional focus to set up false intent within a passive spell; a lie, to both caster and reader. The false loop lay over the true instruction, obscuring the weak connection point from view.

This lock had three.

With a fevered curiosity about the caster, Roy closed his eyes and worked his way through the spell, unhooking each true loop in turn until, with a whoosh of energy, it dispersed into nothing.

He allowed himself a smug smile, then pocketed his glove, pressed his magnet against the alarm, and pushed the door open.

The room was smaller and darker than he expected, lit only by the moonlit corridor behind him. If there was ever a window, it had been bricked up, leaving the air stale. Roy didn't risk the light switch. Instead, he generated a small magelight that reflected off the glass cabinets lining the walls as he shuffled further inside.

His mage sense immediately picked up the radiated energy of half a dozen spells; small trinkets, faint from behind the glass. Roy directed his magelight towards the nearest cabinet and looked over the contents. A tea set, some metal cylinders, a pair of glasses. Only some had their passive spells still present, though it wasn't like Marek would be able to tell.

Hair pricked on the back of Roy's neck and he jerked around. For a moment, he'd thought someone was in the room with him, but everything remained still. As he scanned the walls, his eyes picked up a faint glow from a cabinet on the opposite side. He moved closer, letting the door to the room swing softly shut. The unsettled feeling grew as he approached.

When he was near enough to peer through the glass, Roy was surprised to find the cabinet empty except for three slim wooden rods, about half the length of his forearm. A handle was carved into the end of each one, reminding Roy of the wands used in the old fairytales. Two were dull and charred, like they'd been taken from the edge of a fire, but the last one glowed; a sickly light emanating from what looked like small marks etched into the surface.

Roy opened the cabinet, feeling out with his magic to read the intent of the passive spell that must be there and realised what was wrong. There was no spell. The magic given off was undirected. Faceless.

Whatever marks were carved on the wand were too difficult to see in this light. He went to pick it up, but as his hand tightened around the smooth wood, a jolt of energy coursed through his body. Roy reeled against the cabinet, stomach lurching as his own magic reacted with the intrusive power that surged through him. In a second it was gone and he was left swallowing the bile that had risen at the back of his throat.

Too hot. He couldn't breathe. Roy's vision spun like he'd just finished a Friday night at the bar, and he staggered to the door, yanking it open to reach the freedom of the corridor. Breathing heavily, he leant against the bannister until his mind cleared enough to realise that the ringing in his ears was coming from outside his own head.

"Shit."

He'd completely forgotten about the electric alarm.

Footsteps from the floor below told him that it had definitely alerted the guards to his presence. He backed away from the stairs, wondering briefly if he should try to force his way down and out the way he came in. The thought was quickly dismissed as he locked eyes with the man rushing up towards him, gun in hand.

Roy turned and bolted. An angry shout followed, but his mind was already focussed on casting the shield that would cover his back. The corridor ended in a wall, but there were more rooms to his left and he slammed through the first door that opened.

Inside was a mirror of the building works downstairs. Dust sheets littered the floor in front of the new hearth, and on either side were windows, through which he could see the bars of the scaffolding beyond.

Without time to think, Roy leapt towards the nearest window, fumbling with the latch. It clicked open just as the first bullet ricocheted off his shield, and he experienced the accompanying wave of exhaustion as he tried to maintain it. Ears still ringing from the gunshot, he threw himself out onto the scaffolding, descending in a half climb, half fall to the garden below.

A second bullet graze his shield, and it took all his focus to prevent it from shattering. He wasn't sure he'd be able to hold it if another shot struck. Whatever that wand had done to him, he was running low on magic, and exhaustion wasn't helping his willpower. So much for guns not working on mages.

Electric lights blazed on in the house behind him, flooding the patio and illuminating a short wall that Roy had been about to stumble over. Instead, he leapt down, dropping onto the grass below. The landing expelled the air from his lungs, but he didn't wait to catch his breath, sprinting further into the gardens until he was lost in the darkness.

* * *

The wall at the end of the garden was as easily scalable as the one he'd used to enter. Roy didn't stop running until the dirt covered country path from the house became a streetlamp lined pavement.

Lungs still burning from the sprint, he fumbled off his jacket and turned it inside out to display its lighter lining. It wasn't much, but it might throw off anyone looking for him. As he did so, he saw the point of the wand poking out from a pocket. He barely remembered putting it there, though thinking back, he must have still been gripping it when he left the hidden room.

Hesitantly, he brushed a finger against the smooth wood, bracing for a shock of magic, but this time it didn't come. Roy pulled it out as he replaced his jacket and noticed that, though there was still a glow from the symbols, it was now so faint he could have missed it.

The sepia light of the streetlamps was enough for him to see the markings clearly. Each was carved into the wood; shapes made of fine lines ending in circles that seemed only vaguely familiar until he saw the last. It was formed of a horizontal line, with two others that fanned up from each end and one striking down through the centre. Small circles marked the joins with a large circle crowning each point, and Roy's hand quivered as he recognised it.

It was the mark of the Ardveldian Royal Family.

CHAPTER 2

Calling it backstage would be generous. The area where Alex sat was hidden by little more than a black sheet, printed with the band's logo, flung down over the wooden beam above. His mother had arranged it through her business; the factory-made fabric imported from Vailberg, along with the T-shirts Eira had ordered for what small fan base existed outside of their classmates.

It was proving to be an uncharacteristically hot summer, and the yellowed grass had not benefitted from the swarm of final year students descending upon the field at the edge of town. Alex's clammy T-shirt clung uncomfortably to his tan skin, the usual waves of his dark hair flattened by sweat. He licked his chapped lips and reached for his magic, intending to at least dry off his clothes, but thought better of it. It wouldn't cost a lot, but he didn't want to risk the over-exertion, not after dumping so much of his power into his generator that morning.

Colourful lights flickered from above as the heavy bass reassumed, bright enough against the darkening sky to be visible through the cloth, but Eira was too skilled for him to sense any radiating magic. It hurt to miss the display; even after seeing countless practices, her routines were impressive.

He sat down, ignoring the dry grass spiking against his jeans, and put a hand on his machine. It could almost pass for a guitar amp; a metallic box with a panel of buttons and wires running out from it towards the stage. The cool metal hummed under his fingertips as the electric generator whirred inside, but Alex explored the device with his magic instead, probing the passive spell he had cast there.

The spell within the machine enabled the turbine to move, and Alex was disappointed to find its power running low. Even with all the magic he had stored inside it, the generator could only run for around three hours. Still, his framework of instruction was holding and it should last one more song.

It was perhaps an indication of his inexperience that he could sense the generator's passive spell so readily. A more focussed will as he formed the spell would have meant less waste energy as it ran; less radiation for his senses to pick up. Alex knew the generator shouldn't have required as much magic as it did. His father would have done better.

With a sigh, He pulled a crumpled envelope from the back pocket of his jeans. It was still sealed and his eyes passed over his name without reading it, drawn instead towards the logo printed at the top left.

Aedemeer City University. The letter had come from the capital that morning. It was the best place in Ardveld to study engineering, almost on par with the great universities in Vailberg. That's if he'd made it in.

A sputtering from the machine behind him broke through his rumination. Shoving the letter back into his pocket, he spun around, sucking air through his teeth in frustration. The spell was dying.

It took only a thought for Alex to draw on his magic. The passive spell within the generator glowed in his mind, accepting the gush of his remaining power. He wasn't sure how much it would need; there must be less than a minute of show time left. But the electric lights, the speakers... Alex cut his connection with the spell and hoped for the best.

Reality replaced the feeling of magic; sharp and loud, as though he had emerged from deep water. His ears rang over the sound of the music, and Alex couldn't separate the thumping of the bass from the beating of his heart. Black dots danced across his vision when he tried to stand, and he sunk down into the dirt as quickly as he had risen, trying to quell the shaking in his limbs.

Deep breaths usually helped to soothe away the dizzy sensation of magic exertion. He leant against the metal casing of the generator and closed his eyes.

A cheer from the crowd startled him back. Blinking up, Alex saw letters shining in colourful sparks over the velvet sky, but it took a moment before he realised they were backwards, clearly directed at those looking at the stage: Thank you and goodnight!

Alex groaned as he forced himself to sit straight. A spot on his right shoulder ached where he had been leaning against the hard surface, and he rubbed at it while summoning the strength to stand. His generator had stopped its whirring, and he didn't need to check to know that his passive spell had expired along with it. Stupid, really. If he'd bothered to add a fail-safe loop, he wouldn't have to recast the framework. Again.

In the absence of what meagre light the electric lamps had provided, Alex saw the bobbing glow of magelights rising from the crowd to brighten the paths out of the field and illuminate those bothering to clean up. Wincing, he rotated his shoulder and pushed himself to his feet, leaning on the machine for support. This time, his vision mercifully stayed clear.

A rustle of fabric told him someone was approaching.

"Alex?" The dark blonde of Eira's hair was hidden as usual by one of her illusions, this time cycling through a rainbow of colours that cast a hypnotic glow over her pale face in the fading light. Like the magelights he'd seen earlier, it was an active spell, requiring constant focus even if it didn't use much power. If it was distracting her, Alex couldn't tell.

"Is it all right to unplug the stuff now? We're packing up."

"Sure." Alex bent down and started pulling the wire connectors out of the generator, hoping the movement would disguise the weakness he felt.

"You had to shut it off in the end then? I thought you'd leave the lights on at least," Eira said as she wound the cables up. Alex passed her another, but this time she paused as she took it. "Are you okay?"

"Yeah, fine!" Alex shook his head and immediately regretted it, blinking away the woozy sensation that rushed back.

To his relief, Eira didn't seem to notice. "You've been quiet all day." She hesitated, then placed her hand on his shoulder. "Did you hear yet? About Aedemeer?"

"Oh." Alex's thoughts jumped to the crumpled paper in his pocket. "Sort of. Well… I mean, I got a letter. Here." Standing up straight, he pulled the envelope from his pocket and held it out.

Eira just looked at him. "You haven't opened it?"

He shrugged, not meeting her eyes.

"Want me to do it?"

"I guess someone's got to."

His weak smile faded under Eira's scrutinising gaze. Then she took the letter, slid a thumb under the flap of the envelope, and tore it open. Alex watched her face out of the corner of his vision, trying not to guess from her expression what she was reading.

"Hmmm, Interesting." He made a grab for the paper, but the wooziness from his magic exhaustion made him slow, and she danced back, laughing. "I thought you wanted me to tell you!"

"Hurry up then!" He grinned. Eira wouldn't tease him if it was bad news.

Her own suppressed smile broke wide across her face. "You got in!" She pushed the letter into his hand, sweeping him into a hug that almost knocked him back off his feet. "You've got to let me be there when you tell your mum. I bet she's gonna cry."

"Happy tears, I hope!" Alex replied. The thought of how proud she'd be almost felt better than knowing he'd been accepted.

"You're still coming to the pub, right? We should head

back to yours afterwards. Maybe just stay for one drink, since we need to tell her. I can't believe you had the letter on you all day and didn't open it!"

Alex listened contentedly to Eira's excited rambling as she collected up the last wire. "You said your dad's got a phone, right? Wanna use mine to call him? Tell him the good news?"

The question broke him from his happy daze. "I—" Alex hesitated before continuing quickly. "I mean, he's coming down at the weekend. For my birthday. We'll tell him then."

"Well, I guess you can do a double celebration." Eira's careful response told him she hadn't missed his deliberate avoidance. She pulled him into another hug, the fruity smell from her clothes reminding him how much he needed a shower. "You should be really proud."

"Thanks." Now that the excitement was wearing off, Alex remembered how exhausted he was. "How about you?" He reached for the strap to lug the generator over his shoulder, but found his limbs shaking as he attempted to lift it. "Did you get anything back from Beriant?"

Eira flinched, and for a moment he wondered if he'd said something wrong. Then she reached across him, laying a hand on his machine. "The spell... You didn't— Alex, I knew you weren't okay. Do you think I can't spot when you're magic sick? Why didn't you just let it die? Or ask someone for help?"

"I'm okay," Alex replied. "And I didn't have time to ask anyone; it only needed another minute. Anyway, I just sat down for a bit and now I'm fine."

"You don't look it," Eira said. "Let's get you home. You should rest." She gently tugged the strap from Alex's hand, but he snatched at it.

"I can carry it!"

"Yeah, if you want us to take half the night." She laughed. "I know it's your baby. Trust me, I'll be very careful."

Alex frowned, but stepped back, allowing her to hoist the generator off the ground, strap over her shoulder and both hands on the handle that stuck out from the top as she leant away from the weight.

Together, they shuffled down the path from the field, Eira's magelight ahead of them. The few stragglers that remained waved as they passed, and Alex focussed on standing as straight as possible.

"They can't tell, you know," Eira whispered beside him. "It shouldn't matter, anyway."

"What about the pub?" Alex asked suddenly. "Karla's going to be there, right?" He might not manage going tonight, but Eira shouldn't have to miss out because of him.

"There'll be other nights." She took a hand off the generator to punch his arm, earning a disgruntled 'ouch!' in return. "Hopefully the guilt will stop you pulling this again."

"It'll probably be the last in a while." He appreciated her words, but most of their peers would leave for a career soon, the rest heading off to university. Either way, it meant a long time until another event like this. That's if the field would even be here when he came back. He'd heard it had been bought up, likely by one of those rich guys from Vailberg his mum was always complaining about. After so long dreaming of leaving, Alex was surprised by how sad the thought seemed.

"Your health is more important than a night out. You need to rest."

As much as he hated to admit it, Eira was probably right. He did need to rest, and he didn't want anyone to see him like this. At least if he slept in tomorrow, he'd be back to normal by the time his father arrived.

CHAPTER 3

The last drops of the recent downpour spattered across the steaming pavement, but the humidity left Matthew as damp underneath his jacket as he was outside of it. Food smells wafted from the undercover market to his right, mixing with the earthy scent left from the rain.

He was early. The trains had run well for once and, given that he had allowed extra time for the journey, it was a good half hour before he was due to meet Oliver. At least it would give him time to settle down at the rendezvous and dry off.

A shout from an overzealous market seller boomed over the roar of cars and chattering shoppers, and he jolted in alarm. Being in the capital always put him on edge.

Sweeping a lock of soaked, black hair from his eyes, Matthew looked around for the name of the road. A drip of water snuck under the collar of his jacket, running a chill line down his back as he saw the sign carved into the stonework above. Practically a historic artefact itself nowadays. The familiar stab of sorrow followed as he noted the faded royal coat of arms inscribed next to the street name. It was a wonder Morgan Heliodor hadn't had them all destroyed.

The well maintained words, at least, told him he was in the right place.

A few shops down, the tea room looked bright and inviting against the overcast afternoon sky. Matthew pushed the door open and bundled himself inside. It was occupied, but mercifully not busy. A couple of people in business dress were dotted around the single tables, and a group of women with prams had taken over a corner, too distracted by a fidgety baby to notice his entrance.

He headed towards one of the rear corner tables, ducking under the low beams, as he passed. A man was already sat there, his well-cut suit jacket open over an emerald green waistcoat. Sandy brown hair fell towards golden eyes that lit up with a smile as they met Matthew's.

"You're early." Oliver rested his half empty teacup back on its saucer, the movement showing a flash of gold cufflink.

"Not early enough apparently." Matthew shook his head in mock disbelief, then dragged a chair around the table so its back was against the wall. His wet jacket began to trickle a puddle onto the floor as he peeled it off, and Oliver frowned.

"Dare I ask why you didn't use a shield?"

"Didn't seem like anyone else was doing it. I don't want to draw attention."

"Well, I'm not sure that looking like a drowned rat is

more subtle."

Matthew laughed and sat down, sodden jeans still dripping. Then, drawing on a small amount of his magic, he heated the water in his clothes and hair until it puffed away in a light cloud of steam. "Better?" It definitely felt better. "How long have you been here, anyway? I thought I might have beaten you for once."

"Not long," Oliver replied, taking another sip of his tea. "I decided I may as well take a half day; I could certainly use one." He gave a heavy sigh and Matthew noticed dark circles beneath his eyes that even the youthful appearance gifted to those with high magic ability couldn't hide.

"What, did Morgan change the tax code or something?" Even in jest, the name burned as he said it. He continued in a gentler tone, "you look knackered."

"Thanks," Oliver replied. Then with a dismissive shake of his head he seemed to appear brighter. "It's nothing to worry about. Just unusually busy for this time of year. Actually, that's probably not a bad thing..." He trailed off, a sombre silence falling over them both.

The sound of Oliver tapping the table snapped Matthew out of his reflection. "Before I forget! This is for Alex." He pulled out a brown paper bag containing a wrapped parcel. "Please tell him how sorry I am that I can't deliver it in person. I don't suppose he's heard back from the university yet?" Oliver passed the bag over to Matthew, who tucked it away by his seat.

"I imagine he will tell me when I'm down." He gave Oliver a sideways glance. "Don't think I've forgotten what you did."

"I just offered him a place to stay for the interview. How was I to know he hadn't involved you?" Oliver's reply was cool, but Matthew could see a tinge of pink around his ears.

"Oh come on. When do you not know what's going on in my life?" Matthew ran a frustrated hand through his hair, but there was no anger in his comment. "I thought I was supposed to be your boss."

"In that case, I thought you are supposed to listen to my advice. He doesn't understand, and I don't blame him. Alex thinks that he isn't good enough."

"Not good enough?" Matthew paused in confusion. "How? You've seen the things he's made, the spells he's done. He's better than I was at his age."

"I have seen them," Oliver nodded from behind his cup. "And that's why he can't understand why his own father wants him to stay wasting away in Couden Cross."

"He said that?" Matthew's gaze fell to the wooden table, and he found himself tracing the scuff marks with his finger. "That's not what I want. It's just more important that he's safe. He can be successful and still have a quiet life."

"He'd be safer if you told him the truth."

The clink of the empty teacup snapped Matthew's eyes back up. "I'm not telling him. Not until he's older. We've been through this." There was an ache in his jaw as he clenched it.

"He's going to be eighteen. He's older than you were when it happened."

"Yeah, and he deserves more time than we got."

Matthew sat up straighter, anticipating a counter argument until he noticed that Oliver's attention had been caught by the tea shop entrance. Concerned, he glanced over in the same direction and saw that the group of women were leaving, struggling to squeeze one of the prams out past the heavy door.

With a small exertion of his magic, Matthew nudged the

door wide. The women departed, presumably unaware of his interference, though the flare of energy obviously hadn't been missed by Oliver, who turned to face him, wide eyed.

"Everything okay?" Matthew kept his voice low.

"Fine." The shock on his face faded instantly to a blank expression, but Oliver's eyes didn't seem to focus.

He's talking to Ewen. Matthew sank back in the chair and waited.

For the most part, he found it easy to forget about the other soul that had occupied his friend's mind for the past twenty-three years. The voice of Oliver's predecessor had, of course, been a great asset, but Matthew couldn't help but feel unsettled when he remembered that two people often looked out at him through one pair of eyes. It must be worse for Oliver, and Matthew thanked whatever luck he had left that whoever had crafted the Champion spell hadn't seen fit to confer the same powers upon the royal line.

"Sorry about that." With a blink, Oliver's attention was back in the room. "Would you like a drink? I should have asked when you first arrived."

Matthew didn't reply, folding his arms sceptically.

"Ewen was advising on tea," Oliver explained. He looked relaxed enough, but Matthew knew better than to trust his outwards appearance. "This place was actually his recommendation. Would you like me to choose you one to try, or will you have your usual?"

The question was half-hearted, but Matthew decided to let it go. Perhaps he'd misread the concern on his friend's face. "Maybe next time. Just grab me a can of something." Unlike Oliver, no amount of education or pressure had ever given him a taste for warm drinks.

Oliver groaned and got up from his seat. "Fair enough.

Though you don't know what you're missing." He left the table mumbling something that sounded like 'sacrilege'.

Left alone to his own thoughts, Matthew let his eyes wander over the room. It was an old building, even by Aedemeer standards, and he wondered how much it had seen over the years. Ewen had been his father's tactician, to use the common term for it, and it was odd to think of the man sitting in this very room. Perhaps he had been prompted by his own mentor, and so on, going back generations.

His musings were interrupted by the return of Oliver, who placed a can in front of him, along with an empty glass, before retaking his seat.

"I'm not saying it has anything to do with us," he began, arranging a teapot and fresh cup in front of him. "However, I have been observing one of the tea shop patrons— Don't look!" He commanded with a sigh.

"I wasn't going to look!". But his heart rate had increased. Matthew tried to focus on the chilled can in his hands rather than the other people in the room.

"Their behaviour has raised suspicion," continued Oliver. "Now, I need you to tell me if the large, fair haired gentleman, seated at the table to the left of the door, looks familiar to you."

Matthew's fingers seemed clumsy as he cracked his drink open, looking far less casual than he had intended. Ignoring the glass, he took a sip and glanced over towards the table that Oliver had indicated. From here, he had a clear view of the man hunched there, face partially obscured by the newspaper he appeared to be reading. He was tall and broad, wearing a hefty black jacket still damp from the rain. Matthew didn't recognise him.

"No, I don't know them," he said, leaning in towards Oliver so that they could keep their voices low. "What's he done that's worried you?"

"He came in earlier, when the women left." Oliver responded, "He's passed the front of the shop three times since you arrived, along with another man, but entered alone."

"That's not hugely suspicious," Matthew said, though he didn't relax.

"I agree," Oliver replied, "However he hasn't ordered a drink, nor removed his coat, and I have watched him continue to take glances in this direction from the moment of his arrival, despite the fact he's attempting to appear engrossed in a newspaper."

Matthew made a noise of agreement. He didn't want to be paranoid, but experience told him Oliver wouldn't have mentioned anything unless he had a genuine concern. As if sensing Matthew's thoughts, Oliver continued.

"I wouldn't have wanted to worry you, but as I went up to order, I saw his associate pass by again. He also seemed very focussed in your direction; my thoughts being that an innocent bystander would be more interested in his friend than another customer."

"Ewen agreed?" Matthew waited for Oliver to nod confirmation before he continued, panic rising. "How could they have found us?" It had been so long he'd half thought Morgan Heliodor had stopped looking, but now —

"It's not Morgan," Oliver interrupted, halting his racing thoughts. "These men — they aren't subtle. I was hardly paying attention and I spotted them." He spoke with a quiet confidence as he began to pour some tea into his cup. "Besides, they just don't give off that professional vibe."

"When are you ever 'hardly paying attention'..." Matthew muttered, but his heartbeat no longer sounded as loud. "If they aren't Morgan's, then who are they?"

"I was hoping you might know." Oliver narrowed his eyes. "What have you been doing recently?"

Matthew shifted in his seat, rolling the can between his hands so that the soft metal bent under his fingers. "Nothing notable, just work." He looked away, unable to meet Oliver's fixed stare. Even with only two years between them, the Tactician could make him feel like a child. "...There's one thing I can think of, but that was over two weeks ago."

"What thing?" Oliver's tone had turned icy, and Matthew had the uncomfortable feeling that it wasn't only his friend judging him.

"It was nothing. Really!" Matthew ran a hand through his hair. "Look, I took it on as a quick side job. Something interesting for a change. You know, last week they had me charging lights? Just that. Every day for a week. Because it's still cheaper than getting electricity that far out from the city."

"I don't need to know why you did it, just tell me what you did."

"It was just a lock. Off the books. Nothing special." Matthew shrugged. "Honestly, I didn't even think anything of it until now. Some guy moving here from Vailberg wanted to make sure no one could get into one of his rooms. I whacked on a lock and that was it!"

"You're working for Velbians now?" Oliver seemed surprised, but didn't press further. "What was in the room?"

"It was empty, I don't know. I don't ask questions. It's not as though I'd accept anything dodgy."

"Evidently, that's not the case," Oliver murmured,

sipping at his drink. "Do you at least remember their name?"

Matthew frowned as he tried to remember. "...Marek? Felix Marek, I think his name was."

Oliver choked on his tea. "Felix Marek?" He wheezed.

"What?" The reaction brought back his anxiety from earlier, and Matthew glanced over at the man near the door. To his relief, he was still engrossed in his newspaper.

"You do know he was Aiden Heliodor's business partner?" Oliver's voice had recovered from the tea, but clearly not from the shock. "He just sold off his share and retired. Don't you watch the news?"

"...No," Matthew replied. "I try not to." *Especially at this time of year.* He wasn't pleased to see Oliver's expression morph into one of pity. "Don't look at me like that."

Aiden Heliodor was Morgan Heliodor's nephew, son of the Arch Canlaw, Kaylee of Vailberg. Matthew felt like a lead weight had settled into his stomach.

For a moment, Oliver didn't say anything more. He drummed his fingers lightly against the wood of the table and Matthew focussed on the movement, the world seeming to have narrowed down to a point.

"I still don't believe they know who you really are." Oliver continued eventually. "You say he wanted this lock unregistered? That makes me wonder if it's not thieves he's worried about."

"You're thinking he's hiding something from Aiden? Or Morgan?"

"Could easily be both. Though I doubt it matters either way. My best theory is that this is a silencing operation and they don't know who they're dealing with."

Fear subsiding, Matthew found it replaced by frustration. Couldn't he even have a simple drink without something happening? It was worse that he'd worried Oliver. "I guess we'd better come up with a plan then."

"We have a plan."

Of course we do. Matthew waited for his Tactician to elaborate.

"There's a back entrance to the tea room, along a short corridor past the bathroom. It opens out into the alleyway that runs between this building and the wall of the market. You likely walked past it on your way here."

The market would be a good place to lose a pursuer in the crowd. "What if they have people waiting in the alley? You said there could be more than one person following us."

"You're right. It is likely the back door is being watched, but I don't intend for us to fight our way out." Oliver ran a finger in a line across the table. "If this is the alleyway, and here is where the exit comes out," he pointed towards the centre of the line. "Slightly to the left, in the wall opposite, you will find an entrance to the market. It was boarded up for years, but when I found it I decided it could be useful to incorporate it, and this tea room, into one of our meeting spots."

"You magic locked it?" Matthew wasn't surprised that there had been more to this place than just the pleasant atmosphere and fancy tea.

"Yes, to my signature. It's not ideal but, if we aim to get through quickly, they won't be able to follow. By the time they get round to the main market entrance, we should be out and on our way to the safe house at Wych Cross."

"Fair enough," Matthew leaned back in his seat, attempting to stretch some looseness back into his limbs. "So if I get up first, as if I am going to the toilet, then you follow sometime after and we meet up at the exit?"

Oliver's rejected his suggestion without a pause. "No need. We'll go together."

"Won't that seem suspicious?"

"Only to someone following us," Oliver replied, matter-of-factly. "And if they are, they aren't going to be far behind. We'll save time and be safer together."

Not convinced that Oliver just didn't want to let him out of his sight, Matthew didn't bother to argue.

"Ready then?" Oliver set aside his empty tea cup, and Matthew felt the slight tingle in the air as Oliver's shields went up. Taking the cue, Matthew drew on his own magic, projecting a shield close around his body. He reached back to grab his coat, tucking it over the bag containing Alex's present before using the handle to pick up both.

"Nothing strange about two friends going to the bathroom together..." Matthew mumbled as he stood up to follow Oliver to the door.

It was quiet in the small corridor. Matthew squeezed past Oliver, who placed his hand over the door handle as he cast a basic lock spell.

"Apologies to anyone who needs the toilet," he said, tilting his head to indicate they should proceed along the hall. At the far end was the door that led out to the alleyway, the sign and panic bar displaying its purpose as a fire exit.

"Do you think it will be alarmed?" Matthew queried. Touching his hand to the door, he scanned it for magic energy and picked up nothing. Any lock or alarm would be manual.

"No, I checked that before we arrived."

Accepting Oliver's confirmation, Matthew cast his magic sense out beyond the door. Physical barriers made it harder to pick up the radiating energy of spells or mages, but if anyone was directly outside, he should be strong enough to feel them.

"Anyone out there?" Oliver said, who was no doubt checking himself.

Matthew closed his eyes to focus. There was a strange presence towards their left. A mage, maybe. Or some kind of passive spell? "There could be something to the left, I can't tell for certain."

"You can't tell?" Oliver hummed as he paused to think. "Well, we'll have to deal with it as it comes," he continued after a moment. "It's likely our tearoom friend has sent a message, so let's assume they are expecting us."

Matthew moved aside as Oliver grasped the bar of the fire door, then with a nod he pushed down on the handle and darted into the alley. With a tight grip on the bag in his hand, Matthew followed.

The cobbled path was slippery from the afternoon rain. Magic focused into his shield, Matthew kept his eyes on Oliver rather than looking for the door himself. Now they were outside, the confusing magic presence was far more obvious, almost nauseating, unlike any spell he'd ever felt.

They hadn't made it more than two paces before he heard a shout, followed by a fizzing crack that Matthew felt more than heard. A wave of energy collided with his shield, sending him reeling off balance. He landed clumsily on his knees, pain shooting through his hand as it slammed into the ground. The shield, which should have repelled any attack, warped as it absorbed the energy, and shattered.

Senses returning, Matthew heard Oliver shouting from somewhere above his head. The scene in the alley rushed back into focus and his eyes met those of the man who had attacked him. Smaller and younger than the one who had been watching them in the tea room, he stood frozen, a look of surprise on his face.

Whatever the man held in his hand was still pointed at Matthew, and he scrambled back to his feet. As he did so, his assailant seemed to snap from his daze. He charged forward, blocking their passage to the market door, but a blast of magic from Oliver blew him back. Then Matthew felt his friend grab his arm, dragging him, bag, coat and all, along the alley towards the street.

"I thought we were going to the market!" Matthew called, hurrying to keep pace with Oliver while trying not to slip on the rain slick stone.

"Change of plan!"

Oliver pulled him around the corner as they reached the main road. When he looked back, the man from the alley had been joined by the one from the shop.

"Don't attack. Too many people." Oliver instructed through panting breaths. Another flare of magic, and this time the pavement behind them sparkled as Oliver's spell drained the heat from the water pooled there. The two of them pushed through the crowd, inciting gasps, swiftly followed by the cries of multiple shoppers slipping on the ice spelled ground.

"What the hell did they attack us with?" Matthew shouted as he ran.

"I don't know," Oliver replied. "But it could knock you down, then it's too risky to take chances."

"We need to find somewhere open."

"Park. Across the road ahead. If we can't lose them first."

As if in response, the air fizzed with another bolt of energy. This time, it was followed by screams and a sickening crunch of metal.

Matthew spun on the spot, no longer running. A bus was horizontal across the busy road, the front crushed inwards above the left wheel, leaving it sagging drunkenly. Another car had crashed into it, causing both rows of traffic to come to a standstill.

From here it was impossible to tell whether the passengers were okay. Matthew had begun to force his way back against the flow of terrified people now rushing in their direction, before Oliver caught his arm.

"Look," Oliver pointed. Following his gaze, Matthew saw the crowds had parted around the damaged bus. The man from the tea shop stood there, gesturing angrily at his companion as he grabbed at whatever the smaller man was holding. "Looks to me like they weren't supposed to be creating a scene either."

Sirens began to howl in the distance, their sound causing Matthew's heart to leap in his chest. Even so, he didn't move.

"Healers are on their way," Oliver spoke gently. "Let's get out while we can."

"...Okay." Swallowing his guilt, Matthew followed Oliver as they allowed the crowd to sweep them away.

CHAPTER 4

An official she didn't recognise gave Tamara a polite nod as she passed into the rich corridor of the main palace. She inclined her head in return, letting a mass of dark ringlets fall across her tawny brown face. These rooms were notably different from those in the west wing where her new office was based; all gilt and white and shining. Until now, she could have imagined herself back at the university in Vailberg's capital, rather than in Aedemeer's grand palace.

It was difficult to keep a normal pace. Adrenaline made her want to hurry, whilst apprehension kept her back. The stiff material of her office-wear didn't help. It restricted her movement and only the thin magic shield she kept between the rough fabric and her skin stopped the feeling being unbearable.

Tamara clenched her fists and took a deep breath. Nerves only made her sensory issues worse.

During her induction a fortnight before, Morgan had told her that she shouldn't hesitate to let him know if she encountered any problems or queries; but now that it came to it, Tamara wondered if it was true. People often said things they didn't mean. Regardless, the talk in the breakfast room this morning hadn't been small enough to ignore. There had been an attack in the city.

Not that the news report contained any useful details. Theories seemed to range all the way from gang activity to a rebellion among the mages of Ardveld; neither had any evidence to back up their assumptions. Whatever the reason, the palace staff seemed to believe there was magic involved and that meant, as Head of Magic Affairs, the incident fell under her jurisdiction.

Tamara hadn't arranged a meeting with Morgan, but surely this was exactly the kind of situation that would warrant one. Still, she slowed as she reached the wide staircase she'd been told led to his office.

Despite his reputation, Morgan had been perfectly polite during their brief conversation on her first day. That could just be a public front, but the staff also seemed to speak fondly of him. If he was likely to unleash his wrath on an interrupter, she would hopefully have been warned by the person who'd given her directions.

The upper floor was lined with heavy doors of a carved, dark wood. Tamara wondered what they would have been used for when the royal family lived here, quickly forcing the question of whether the rooms were haunted from her mind.

She was tense enough already without focussing on the silent, empty halls.

Ahead, her magic sense picked up the feeling of a passive spell. It emanated from a door to her left, beside which stood a stone pedestal holding a vase of white roses. They were fresh and blooming, and Tamara let the scent soothe her as she read the golden plaque beside the door: 'High Minister Morgan Heliodor'. She was here.

Tamara straightened her posture and forced her hands to her sides, making a mental note to keep them there during the meeting. Then she gave a light knock on the door, followed quickly by a second one that might actually be heard.

A man's voice answered. "Yes?"

She pushed the door wide enough to poke her head into the room. Morgan's office was spacious, with large arched windows running down the wall opposite, flanked by heavy gold curtains. Sunlight, muted by the thick glass, illuminated an expansive desk to her left, stacked with books and papers.

Behind the desk, bleached by the harsh light of an electric desk lamp, sat Morgan. His formal black suit brought little warmth to his skin, and his tie lay severely aligned despite the warm weather. He looked up at her, placing the piece of paper he held squarely on the desk in front of him.

"Tamara."

There was surprise in his voice and Tamara had the sinking feeling she'd been right; he hadn't meant 'any time'. Deciding it was too late to flee, she pushed the door wider and strode into the room.

"Hi!" she said, giving a slight wave before catching herself and remembering to keep her hands still in front of her.

"How can I help you?"

His voice wasn't amiable, but it didn't contain the hint of scolding she'd feared. With renewed confidence, she looked up, resting her gaze at the point above Morgan's nose rather than meet his eyes.

He seemed younger than she remembered, particularly for someone without magic, and Tamara realised that this was the first time she'd looked at him properly. Though there were obvious lines around his eyes, Morgan's neatly styled hair was still a rich chestnut, glinting dark red where it caught the light.

"I'm sorry to disturb you," Tamara began. "But I'm here about the magical attack that happened yesterday."

"What about it?" Morgan replied.

It was not the response she had been expecting, and Tamara scrambled to find the words to explain why she'd felt the need to come.

"It's just, it seems like a large scale incident involving magic, but I haven't yet received any report or instruction." It didn't make sense that she hadn't at least received a report, and it was, quite frankly, rude that she should have had to find out via gossip and the general news, anyway.

Morgan nodded in response, then gestured at two plush leather chairs positioned in front of his desk. "Please, take a seat."

Tamara scuttled forward and perched on the nearest chair, trying to keep her posture upright and dignified.

"Thank you for coming," Morgan continued, "I apologise that you didn't receive a report as you expected. In this case, I decided that the situation wasn't worth further investigation by our magic department and, for now, we are leaving it to the police force. As I'm sure you are aware, reports of magic use are unconfirmed and so far no arrests have been made. It is likely that the incident was little more than a traffic accident, however I can, of course, arrange for a report to be issued to you for your own notes." He finished matter-of-factly, as though there was nothing further to discuss.

"But," Tamara began, catching the flicker of annoyance that crossed Morgan's face. Striving forward anyway, she continued, "Mages are saying they felt the blast. The front of a bus was crushed! The news is suggesting this is the largest unregistered magic incident in years. With the anniversary celebrations coming up next week, surely it is worth taking seriously in case it is some kind of precursor to an attack?" Tamara clenched her hands into the material of her skirt as she recited the arguments she'd prepared earlier to support her cause. "I don't mean any offence to the police services when I say they might be ill equipped to deal with a mage of that ability, or to investigate what kind of spell caused the damage in the first place."

The frown on Morgan's face had deepened, but she still didn't sense any animosity; more that he seemed to be wondering how best to reply. After a moment, he picked up the paper he'd placed on the table. "Tamara," he spoke again, and she once more found it hard to reconcile the calm man before her with the stories of the takeover. "You're from Avel-Kifaeros, correct?"

"I..." She'd never hidden the fact that she came from the little province that lay between Ardveld's mountain border and the rest of Vailberg. But being Kifaerish came with certain associations. At least from the uneducated. "Yes." She answered, this time truly meeting his eyes.

Morgan did not appear to notice the emotion his question had induced. "In that case," he continued calmly. "Why do you feel they appointed you to the role of Ardveld's Head of Magic Affairs?"

Stunned by the question, it took a moment for Tamara to think of a response. Could he really be questioning her competence? She eyed him warily, but couldn't detect any veiled insult. Perhaps the question was genuine after all.

"Well," she decided to answer sincerely. "I am one of the strongest and most experienced mages in Vailberg. Before this, I held a position as deputy head researcher at Beiriant City University, publishing five manuals on magic efficiency and spell crafting during my five years in that role, whilst also training new graduates, mostly from Ardveld." Morgan nodded as she spoke, studying her face carefully. "It seemed logical that I would have been offered this role, given my experience teaching Ardveldian mages, and as the head university researcher is already occupied in an advising position to the Arch Canlaw..." Tamara trailed off, uncertain under Morgan's scrutiny.

"All very true," Morgan replied, and she experienced a wash of relief as he confirmed her words. "However, that is not why you are in the position you now find yourself."

Tamara noticed she had been running her hands together as she spoke. Now they prickled with sweat in response to Morgan's words. As though sensing her confusion, he sighed and gestured at the paper in his hand.

"I have here a letter from my Head of Defence, or should I say former Head of Defence, considering it outlines the details of his retirement."

Tamara nodded attentively, wondering how this related to her own appointment.

"Tell me," Morgan continued. "Have you met any senior members of staff since your appointment two weeks ago?"

He paused until she shook her head. "And I imagine you did not find it strange that your predecessor was not present to offer you an induction into your new role?"

Thinking back, it did seem unusual that all they had given her was a binder of notes and unfinished projects. It could easily have been normal procedure though; Tamara had no frame of reference for how things usually worked in government.

There was a moment of silence and she wondered if this was a cue for her to ask why there were so few senior staff. Morgan, however, was looking past her into the distance, and she was struck by a strange desire to avoid interrupting his thoughts.

"It is unlikely you would be aware, considering the great lengths taken to keep the matter out of the public eye," Morgan's voice seemed softer now. "But Arch Canlaw Kaylee has been unwell for some time."

Tamara tried to stop her face showing her shock. For him to mention it, the situation must be serious. Serious enough that it was causing his advisers to retire, if she had interpreted his implication correctly. Then, she remembered his personal connection to the situation; Arch Canlaw Kaylee was Morgan's sister.

"I'm sorry. Are— are you okay?"

Morgan's eyebrows rose, and for the first time she saw a slight smile form in response to her question. "I am well enough. Thank you, Tamara. Please do keep this information between us. I simply mentioned it to give a wider context to your situation."

"Ah." Tamara hoped she'd filled in the correct blanks.

Morgan gave a nod of acknowledgement. "Yes, I have had rather an influx of retirement letters as my advisers have become aware." He added the paper he was holding to a stack of others on his left. "Should Kaylee pass away, leadership of Vailberg will naturally fall to her son, Aiden, however with my..." He trailed off as though searching for the right word. "Well, it seems no one with any sense wants to be in Ardveld in the event of any political instability. Unfortunately for you, and your colleagues taking over positions here, you have likely received a poisoned chalice."

The news did not improve Tamara's unease, though in some way, it wasn't as much of a surprise as it should have been. None of her positions had been gained due to interpersonal skills, and while she had made some connections over the years, she hadn't been reluctant to leave the university. It seemed the feeling was mutual.

Even so, she kept her response firm. "That may well be the case. But whatever the reasons for my appointment, I intend to give this role the respect and commitment it deserves." This was going to be a new start, and there was no guarantee that disaster awaited. She always trusted her instincts with people, and after speaking with Morgan, it was hard to believe he would jeopardise his sister's succession. Besides, having no expectations placed on her just made it easier to exceed them.

With that thought, she remembered Morgan had never answered her original question.

"I'm still not entirely sure how this relates to the magic attack in the city?" Tamara said.

"I suppose it doesn't," Morgan's response was infuriatingly vague. "I would just ask that you trust me when I say that this incident should not be looked into further." His gaze was pointed, and Tamara wasn't sure if she should have been able to infer some alternate meaning. "Regardless of how you acquired this role, it comes with the same powers and responsibilities as always. I am grateful for your dedication, but would advise you to learn when best to exercise it."

Tamara gave a stiff nod, conceding the issue for now. She still didn't fully understand what the Arch Canlaw's illness had to do with the investigation, but she doubted any answers would be forthcoming. For now, she was pleased that Morgan had entrusted her with some clearly sensitive information and did not seem to disrespect her or her position.

A sharp rap on the door splintered the quiet mood of the room and Tamara turned her head as it opened.

The man who entered seemed familiar, even in the dim light. Behind her, she heard Morgan get up, and she hurried to her feet herself.

Young and tall, the man's slim figure was accentuated by the tailored suit that hugged his body. His swept back hair was a dark red and she realised why he looked familiar; he had the same intense blue eyes as Morgan. "Who is this?" His voice was a rich velvet.

"Tamara Elden," Morgan spoke before Tamara realised the question had been about her. "My new Head of Magic Affairs. She was just leaving." He finished bluntly, any trace of warmth gone from his voice.

The man's eyes, however, lit up as he turned towards her. "Elden! You're here from Beiriant, correct? I found your work on efficiencies in spell casting fascinating." He thrust out a hand, so excitedly that Tamara flinched back before hesitantly accepting the firm handshake. "Prince Aiden Heliodor. You might have heard of me."

She had, but the teasing smile that lit up his face indicated it had been a joke, anyway. No wonder he looked so much like Morgan. Tamara's mind whirled as she tried to think of an appropriate response.

"As I said, Tamara was just leaving." Morgan's voice came from close behind her, and for a moment she felt trapped between the two men as Aiden looked over her head at his uncle.

"Of course," Aiden replied, and Tamara snatched her hand back as he released her. "Don't let me keep you." He smiled down at her warmly as she darted around him towards the door.

"Thank you," Tamara smiled back though her body seemed oddly unsteady. "It was nice to meet you." The response sounded childish, and Tamara hoped the heat in her face wouldn't be obvious to an outside observer.

Aiden laughed. "I look forward to having a proper conversation before the celebration." The amusement in his voice was a stark contrast to the stern expression on Morgan's face behind him.

Words stuck in her throat and it was a welcome relief when Aiden turned away. Morgan himself no longer seemed interested in her presence, so, deciding there was no requirement for a goodbye, she reached for the door handle and slipped out of the room.

The sight of a man standing to the left of the door dampened Tamara's relief at leaving the office. His magic aura indicated he was a mage, but the black uniform wasn't that of the palace, and she concluded he must be Aiden's personal guard. He didn't turn his head as she passed, and feeling suddenly nauseous, she hurried back towards the stairs. Her hands quivered on the banister as she descended, only calming when she was back at her own rooms.

CHAPTER 5

Matthew paused at the gate. Someone was cutting grass in the distance, the lawnmower humming a reassuring accompaniment to the birdsong from the hedgerow. Ahead of him, a neatly kept path led up to the green door of the cottage, flanked by potted plants, already dry from the morning's sun. His little flat in Larimar might be the address on his driving licence, but this was home.

He'd just have to hope anyone pursuing him was as misinformed as the licensing agency.

Chips of paint flecked onto his palm as he creaked the gate open and a faint chime sounded in the house when he pressed the doorbell. He didn't have to wait long until the door was flung open. Dorothea stood there, her dark brown hair pinned back in a messy bun that didn't hide her curls; the same curls she'd passed on to Alex.

The friendly greeting Matthew had prepared became a hesitant noise, quickly forgotten as Dorothea threw herself into his arms. He pulled her close and let the tension of the past few days leave his body.

"I've missed you," she spoke the words into his chest, leaving a pang of guilt where they landed.

"I... It's good to see you," Matthew replied. She released him from the hug, and for a moment he found himself lost in the deep brown of her eyes. Dorothea smiled and looked as though she was about to say something else, before the sound of approaching footsteps interrupted.

Alex bounded down the stairs to the living room, his face lit up in a wide grin. He looked older, though it had only been a month. Taller too; catching up with Matthew's own height, despite the magic that was beginning to slow his son's aging.

"Dad!" Alex called as he ran up to join them. Dorothea took the opportunity to usher Matthew into the room properly, shutting the door behind him.

"Happy Birthday!" Matthew's smile matched Alex's as he pulled him into a hug. "Sorry I couldn't make it down sooner."

"No worries!" Alex replied. His dark eyes were a mirror of Matthew's own and, not for the first time, he thought how much his son looked like a curlier version of his younger self.

"You're still staying tonight, aren't you?" Matthew heard Dorothea's voice from behind him.

He paused before replying, fighting the urge to instantly agree. Oliver had assured him it would be fine; they'd always tried to keep this place as separate from his other life as they could, but the memory of the past day kept flashing into his head. If his attackers had somehow tracked him here...

There was pain in Dorothea's eyes at his hesitation, and Matthew felt his wall break.

"Of course. I'd love to stay." It was weak of him. His very existence put his loved ones at risk, but he needed this. All he could do was rely on Oliver's promise to dig up some answers while he was gone.

"That's great!" Alex couldn't hide his excitement; as easy to read as his mother. "We can do breakfast tomorrow as well then."

Matthew laughed. "You haven't even told me what we're doing today!" It wasn't like his son to not have a plan, but Alex shook his head.

"I'll tell you in the car."

"You're both off out then?" Dorothea snuggled warm against his body. "Did you at least want a drink first?"

"Can't mum! We need to go." Alex pushed past to grab his shoes and Matthew gave Dorothea an apologetic look.

"I guess I'll see you a bit later."

She looked up at him, shaking her head with a smile. "Don't worry about it. Have a great time wherever you end up. Alex, Don't run your dad too ragged. He doesn't look it, but he's getting old!"

"Hey! No need to call me out."

Alex gave his mum a brief wave of acknowledgement before disappearing out the front door and Dorothea ushered Matthew out after him.

The air in the car was stifling, even after only a few minutes in the midday sun. Matthew reached for his magic and formed a spell to pull the heat away, noting Alex's close observation as he did so.

"Don't sit on the presents," Matthew warned, as Alex climbed in beside him. "Sorry about the scuffed one. That's Oliver's." He received a quizzical look. "Best not to ask."

"Shall I open them now?"

"Maybe tell me where we are off to first, and then open them on the way," Matthew replied. It wasn't much of a guess to say it was something magic related, especially since he'd not mentioned it in front of his mother.

When Alex had been born, he'd almost hoped he would inherit the same lack of magic as Dorothea. There was little stigma left towards non-mages in Ardveld nowadays, and it would have served as an extra precaution against those who might notice the family resemblance. But Alex took after him in more than just his looks. The signs were showing from the moment he'd hit his teens, and though he knew Dorothea was pleased, magic was still something they shared that she could never take part in.

Alex seemed to hesitate before responding. "Do you remember Golebach Court?"

"The old house?" He'd been a few times before and even taken Alex when he was much younger. It was a beautiful preserved site, situated on the mountainous coastline about forty-five minutes north of Couden Cross. Certainly a pleasant place, but unusual for an eighteen-year-old to request for a birthday trip. "Is that where we're going?" He tried not to show his surprise.

"There's a talk there today!" Alex's eyes were full of the excitement from earlier. "On the history of the building and the Champions."

This time Matthew couldn't mask his bewilderment and he could tell Alex had caught sight of his expression. "That sounds great!" he said, trying to cover. "I was just surprised you didn't want to go for your first drink or something. Though, it would be a bit early in the day." He laughed and Alex rolled his eyes.

"Sure dad. First drink."

"Shall I pretend I didn't hear that?" Matthew replied, turning on the car's engine. "We'd better get going then. What time does this talk start?"

"They started touring and talks at ten, but I think it's something like one an hour and they're doing them all day," Alex said. He continued after a pause. "I thought it would be fun for us to do together. Like when I was a kid, you know? I always liked when we'd go out and you'd talk about magic or history or whatever." He gave a dismissive shrug that didn't do much to hide the fact that he was obviously seeking assurance.

Affection flooded Matthew's heart as he realised why his son had chosen this place. He'd never expected him to notice his love of Ardveld's history, his only way of discussing the heritage they shared. The fact that Alex was interested at all meant the world to him.

"It's a really good idea," Matthew said, and he meant it. "Hey, and maybe we can find a decent pub there afterwards."

"Sounds great!"

The rolling fields gave way to a dramatic, wind-swept coastline as they neared their destination. Mountains rose on the horizon, indicating Ardveld's northern border. They hugged the country from the coast all the way to where it flanked Vailberg in the east. The town they were headed for sat at the base of the mountain range, with Golebach Court on a rise overlooking the sea.

Alex opened his presents during the journey. Oliver's

parcel contained a rather boring looking book on electricity that he seemed overjoyed to receive, and once again Matthew was left to wonder if he was missing some important understanding of his son.

The gift from Matthew himself made Alex exclaim in delight. "I was pretty sure you didn't have one already," he explained. "I know they're becoming more common out here, though you might find the signal a bit poor."

The mobile phone was smooth, grey plastic; the newest model on the market. Such technology was a familiar sight in the city and, of course, had been around in Vailberg for years. Now, the infrastructure had been extended far enough into Ardveld that it should be usable, even out here.

"I've already gone and put mine and Oliver's numbers on there, as well as home," Matthew continued. "I can give you a quick rundown on using it if you like, but knowing you, you'll be an expert in half a day." Alex's love of technology outstripped even his love of magic.

When they pulled into the car park at the bottom of the hill, the sun was shining brightly in a cloudless sky. Conversation flowed easily, ranging from friends and work to Dorothea's business; the fresh tang of salty air a welcome balm as they wandered up the steep path to the stately home.

The manor was no longer lived in, and was open to the public for a small fee, but the grounds that surrounded it were accessible to everyone. Matthew saw families already setting up blankets for picnics; children running under the ancient ornamental trees that punctuated the rolling lawn. A little sign by the entrance confirmed what Alex had said earlier; the next talk would be on the hour.

Golebach Court shone above them; three storeys of

sandy coloured stone under an emerald tiled roof. A large entrance hall jutted from the front, encompassing a double door with a haughty, owl-like statue standing on either side. The heraldic shield of the Tactician was displayed above the doorway; a castle tower that Matthew knew would be counterchanged green and silver were it not carved in stone.

Promptly on time, the historian leading the talk arrived. He was a slender old man with glasses and a tidy moustache, and the small group of people who had been milling around the courtyard converged around him as he announced the start of the tour.

Once inside, it took a moment for Matthew's eyes to adjust to the dim light, though the heavy curtains over each window had done wonders to keep out the heat of the day. He had a vague memory that this house had once belonged to a distant ancestor of Oliver's, donated to the people when the cost of upkeep had outweighed the need for yet another home.

Little more than remnants of the kingdom's noble families remained. They had been those with the highest magic levels; an elite ruling class from which the royal family drew their advisers before the takeover. The survivors quickly adapted. Those that didn't had left Ardveld's historic buildings to fall into ruin, or to be bought up by the wealthy of Vailberg.

As they wandered through the rooms, Matthew realised he had been too lost in his thoughts to pay attention to the guide's talk of construction and decor. Alex, however, was listening attentively, and he felt a touch of embarrassment at his distraction. They appeared to be in a dining room now, extravagantly ornamented and dominated by a polished table, laid out for a dinner that would never come.

"...what remains fact, is that many members of the

family did go on to become Royal Champions," The guide continued as Matthew tuned back into the talk. "A role determined by their ability rather than inheritance. The four Champions were said to be chosen by ancient magic; a system that formed the cornerstone of Ardveldian leadership and served as a powerful agent against corruption."

Matthew snorted, earning himself a reproachful glare from their guide.

"As I was saying..." The man's voice drifted off as he led the party through to the next room, beginning some explanation of how disabling life would have once been for a non-mage in Ardveld, and gesturing at the magelights near the ceiling. Only Alex was left lagging behind, and Matthew stopped to wait.

"You don't believe the Champions were chosen by magic?" Alex asked as soon as they were alone. The question didn't surprise him; Matthew knew he hadn't been subtle in his response to the guide's words.

"It's not that," Matthew chose his words carefully. "There's plenty of evidence for the passing of magic from one Champion to the next, as I'm sure you know."

"Yeah, though I can totally see why there would be sceptics. It's hard to believe anyone could change their natural magic level, especially when the stories say some weren't even mages to begin with. Plus, no one knows how the spell worked in the first place. It's kind of a shame." He shrugged, and Matthew gave a hum in response.

"Why did you laugh then?" Alex continued, apparently not ready to let the subject go.

Matthew chewed his lip and thought for a moment about how to answer, "I suppose... I suppose I think it's important to keep a critical mind when hearing these old legends about the magic making the system fair. Like each Champion was some kind of predestined choice."

Alex was regarding him attentively and Matthew realised the rest of the group was now far out of earshot. He continued as they moved to catch up. "It's a good story of course; makes people feel that any of them could have been a Champion, but do you really think the royal family would have left something like that to chance?"

Alex nodded thoughtfully. "I suppose there must be more to it. I always thought it was just because stronger mages would make better Champions, anyway. Since magic's genetic, it makes sense the Champions would have come from high magic families."

"There is often a genetic link, true," Matthew replied, "Though it's not a guarantee. Besides, what makes you think it made them the best for the job?" His mind returned to Dorothea and how much she had achieved.

They caught up with the tour outside, exiting the back of the property onto a patio that led to a short, formal garden. A path ran through the flowerbeds, leading down to a stone structure set into the lawn beyond. Four grey arches surrounded a platform embedded into the ground, cracked and sprinkled with tufts of grass.

A wave of nostalgia hit Matthew as he got closer to the formation; a comforting sensation that he struggled to place until he realised it was coming from the ground itself. Magical energy radiated from the area below the stones, like a slow-moving river running under his feet.

He'd felt magic like this before. It was present at many historic magical sites in the kingdom, but it had been particularly strong at the palace. Back home. Not the one he'd chosen as an adult, but the home of his childhood. Leaving it behind had been like switching off a background sound he hadn't noticed. The silence without it had been deafening.

Basking in the sensation, Matthew stood with Alex behind the others, the sun on his back contrasting with the cooling flow of the ground magic. According to the guide, the original purpose of the stone structure had been lost to time, but some people believed they marked ancient sites of magical significance. A fair enough conclusion given the latent power present.

"Given this reputation, it makes sense why high magic families would have settled close by, and indeed the majority of sites such as this one have a castle or manor nearby." The man drawled on, and Matthew found his thoughts returning to Alex.

He must have heard from the university. Their conversations had skirted the issue so deliberately that Matthew was now sure Alex was avoiding the topic as well. Perhaps he'd been rejected. The idea didn't please him, even with the relief it promised.

Talk over, the group dispersed, again leaving the two of them alone. In no rush to move on, Matthew watched in silence as Alex moved closer to the old structure and ran his hand across the stone.

Matthew walked up beside him. "It feels nice here,"

"Yeah..." Alex appeared to be lost in thought.

"So... did you hear—" Matthew began, just as Alex spoke.

"I heard back—"

They both stopped and Matthew laughed, leaning back against the rough surface of one of the pillars. "Go on," he encouraged, hoping he'd succeeded in keeping the agitation from his voice.

He was met with a nervous smile. "I got in! To Aedemeer!"

"You did?" His throat seemed tight. "That's great!"

"I know, right! Mum was so excited she cried. We're going to start getting some bits for me to take; kitchen stuff, you know."

"You're planning on accepting the place then?" Visions of the two men at the tea house prodded at his mind, accompanied by some other, much older memories that he'd rather forget. "What have you planned for travel? You know if you were closer, you could commute in. It would save on costs, and your mother—"

"Dad! It's Aedemeer!" Alex exclaimed. "It's the most prestigious university in the country! I'm not going to turn them down because the bus is cheaper."

Matthew's shoulders slumped as Alex continued, words tumbling out as his bewilderment turned to exasperation.

"You know I took my prototype generator to the interview? They loved it! They can see how big this could be. It could bring electricity anywhere in Ardveld. Places not connected to the grid."

"You fixed the efficiency issues?" Matthew had seen an early version of the generator months before. Back then, it had struggled to power a lightbulb for ten minutes.

"I did!" Alex met his eyes defiantly. "It powered a concert, no problem. For almost four hours."

"Four hours?" That was impressive, and Matthew felt a swelling of pride. It made sense Aedemeer would want him; Alex was every bit as exceptional as he'd always believed. "How much magic did it take for that?"

"...Not much," Alex became very interested in the stone behind him.

"How much is not much?"

"Like, only a day's worth." He shrugged.

"A day!" That was more than Matthew had suspected, even with Alex's reluctance to answer. He wouldn't put it past his son to go making himself ill, either.

"What? I charged it in the morning and I was back to normal the day after," Alex shrugged. "It's not like it's a problem."

"It's a problem if you exhaust yourself. You said you're planning on using this in rural areas? How much magic do you think people out here have, if it took you a day's worth?" Matthew ran a hand through his hair, trying not to wonder how many people had noticed his son was strong enough to generate that kind of power. "Not everyone's got the magic level you do."

"Then we just get it charged by a stronger mage before sending it out. It will be more efficient by then and—"

"No mage is going to use their entire days' worth of magic on one passive spell," Matthew could usually charge more than thirty spells in one shift, and those wouldn't need a top-up for a month or more. His own day rate would make just four hours of electricity completely unaffordable. "I just don't think it's viable."

Alex didn't respond. Instead, he was looking at the ground, crushing defeat written over his face. *Shit.* This wasn't how he'd planned this conversation to go.

"But, it's only a prototype, right?" Matthew smiled weakly, trying to repair some of the damage. "The potential is great! I can see why the uni loved it."

"Okay Dad." Alex's tone was flat and he didn't look up.

"Hey, I mean it." He reached out a hand, but Alex ducked away before he could make contact. Letting his arm drop,

Matthew buried his hurt. "Why don't we go get some food?"

A change of scene would help. Neither of them had eaten since before they had left the house and hunger, undoubtedly, wasn't improving the situation.

"Sure." Alex was already walking away.

CHAPTER 6

The cruel screech of a car horn ripped Roy into consciousness. He groaned and pulled a pillow over his head. From the glimpse of light he'd seen breaking through the curtains, it could be anywhere between eight in the morning or past noon. Any time before double digits was too early.

A memory of standing on a table downing a cocktail pitcher floated unbidden to the top of his mind, and Roy cringed. With any luck, none of his colleagues would remember last night's events in great detail either.

It was stuffy under the pillow, doing nothing to improve his dry mouth. Sleep didn't seem like it would return anytime soon and, struck by a sudden urge to use the bathroom, Roy dragged himself out of bed.

He stumbled over to the window, slamming it shut to block out the sound of the street below. A faint glow caught his eye as he turned back to his room, emanating from underneath the crumpled T-shirt he'd thrown at his dresser the night before.

That damned wand.

Whatever it was, being shot at hadn't sat well with him, and Roy had no desire to start dealing with unknown magic on top of his hangover. Instead, he headed towards the door. The wand had been lying there for a day now, it could wait another.

His bedroom door was blocked by a chair wedged under the handle. Roy tugged at it, foggy brain struggling to process how to unhook it. Time and alcohol had done much to settle his frazzled nerves from his trip to Felix Marek's, but apparently not enough to stop him barricading himself in.

After some swearing, it finally came loose and Roy wrenched the door open. Immediately, flashing magelights lit up the bedroom sending stabs of pain through his head. He flung an arm over his eyes until, after a few seconds, the spell burnt out.

Being half blinded by his shoddy trap spell was almost as bad as realising drunk Roy was a better caster than he was.

His bedroom led straight into a small, open plan living and kitchen area, and the woman from the flat opposite waved cheerily to him through the front door he'd left half open when he'd staggered in yesterday.

By the time he collapsed onto his worn sofa with a mug of black coffee, his head had mercifully started to clear. It was earlier than he expected, only around half twelve, and he switched on the television, intending to take the day easy.

Weekend television always left something to be desired. He flicked aimlessly through the channels, ignoring murder mysteries and overpaid TV chefs. At this rate, it would be more interesting to watch his betta, Mr Shiny-Sides, swimming round the planted fish tank that made up the only décor in the room. Eventually, he landed on the news. A reporter seemed to be wrapping up their major story, and Roy half listened as he sipped at his drink.

"...reopened after yesterday's accident in the capital, in which a bus collided with oncoming traffic. A spokesman for the palace has confirmed that arrangements for the annual celebration are going ahead as planned."

Ugh, the celebration. That time of year again. Roy's thoughts drifted back to the wand and he gripped his coffee mug tight, the pain of the heat cutting through the remaining fog in his mind.

He'd gone to Marek's for answers. Answers that were potentially sitting on a dresser in his bedroom.

It wasn't like he had anything better to do.

An hour later, showered, dressed, and fish fed, Roy found himself at the entrance of his local magic shop.

The place was almost unnoticeable, slouching between a hairdressers and mini supermarket. A dingy glass door covered in hand written cards blocked any view to the interior; advertisements from registered mages for recharging and home repairs, for those with little magical skill or ability themselves. Roy pushed the door open and heard a pleasant chime echoed throughout the shop, announcing his arrival.

A dusty smell permeated the shop. Many of the items were clearly second hand, and nothing was particularly impressive. A curtain hung behind the unattended counter, hiding the door to the back room.

Despite living only a road away, Roy had never needed to come in before, having enough magical ability himself to solve most of his needs. Even so, the sensation of magic emanating from the trinkets that lined the shelves was rather pleasant, and he amused himself by analysing the passive spells contained within them while he waited.

He supposed he could have got registered. Plenty of weaker mages still managed to earn some money on the side, especially nowadays with so many Velbians in the city boosting the non-magic population. It would supplement the delivery job, but Roy was damned if he was ever going to be on one of Morgan's lists. And, despite his dabbles in breaking and entering, Roy wasn't interested in breaking the law to work unregistered.

A less than polite cough from the counter interrupted him as he spun the blades on what seemed to be a desk fan. A middle aged woman with frizzy brown hair stood there now, peering suspiciously at Roy through her small square glasses. He snatched his hand away, prompting a barking laugh from the shopkeeper.

"Touch if you want," she said dismissively. "Don't think you could break anything."

Not sure if this was a dig at the quality of the wares or at his own magic ability, Roy made his way across to where the woman was thumbing through a stack of papers.

"Can I help you?" she spoke without looking up. "If you need a mage, there's numbers on the door. Unless it's for something more... specific?"

Roy blinked in confusion. "Er... I hope so. That you can help, I mean. I don't need a mage."

The woman took her glasses off, closing them with an audible snap, and looked up at him. There was an awkward pause before he realised she was waiting for him to continue.

"Right, yes. I have something and I don't know what it is," Roy said.

"You have something... and you don't know what it is," she repeated his words slowly, and Roy shifted his feet.

"Yeah, well... Look. I'll show it to you." He dug around in his pocket and pulled out the wad of wrapped tee-shirt that contained the stick. Trying to avoid touching the wood, he unfurled it, using the material as a makeshift handle. Somehow, the wand... stick... whatever it was, had regained the magic it had discharged through him at Felix Marek's house. He'd learnt that one the hard way.

Carved symbols glowed as he revealed them; a visual display of the unsettling magic the wand gave off. "I need to know what it's for."

"Don't point it at me!" The woman exclaimed, and Roy thought he caught a glimpse of fear in her eyes.

"It doesn't do anything if you don't touch it," he explained, lowering the wand. "It's got some sort of magic in it, but I can't work out what it's supposed to do or how it's been charged." He tried to keep vague on the details. After seeing her reaction, he wasn't sure if he was doing the right thing.

"It's rude to point." Any fear he might have seen had gone, and the woman held out an expectant hand. Instinctively, Roy snatched the wand back against his chest and received an exasperated sigh in response. "Do you want me to help you or not?"

Turning the tee-shirt handle towards her, he reluctantly passed the wand into the shopkeeper's waiting hand. With the other, she replaced her glasses and began to inspect it, face so close to the inscribed marks that Roy feared her nose would touch the wood. Then, with a shake of her head, she held it back out. "Sorry, can't help you."

Shit. So this entire experience has been a total waste of my—

"But I can tell you some people who might," The woman continued, interrupting his thoughts.

Roy snapped his head back up. "That would be great," he said, re-wrapping the wand and slipping it into the deep pocket of his jacket.

"Don't look too excited." The shopkeeper's eyes narrowed, and she again held out her hand expectantly. "It'll cost you."

Money wasn't exactly Roy's strong suit. He had some cash on him, but wasn't sure he wanted to piss it away on nothing. Still, this was the only lead he had.

"Take it or leave it." It seemed the woman had as much patience as he had money.

"Look," Roy reached into another of his many pockets and fished out a crumpled note. "I've got a twenty on me, but that's a—."

"Twenty will be fine, thank you."

He barely felt the note leave his fingers as it was whisked away. "Hang on a second! What exactly am I getting for this?"

"Names." The woman replied. "Addresses and numbers. These people don't like me giving their details out to just anyone." She tucked the money into her pocket before ducking down to fish out a piece of paper from somewhere under the counter. As she began to scribble something down, Roy resigned himself to hoping for the best.

* * *

It was early, even for him, when Roy rolled into his local and slumped down in front of the bar. The few regulars dotted about the place didn't look up, but the bartender inclined his head in greeting and headed over.

"Long day?" Will had been working here since before Roy had been old enough to drink. A stocky, round faced man who didn't need a fake smile to put his patrons at ease.

Roy gave a groan in response. His legs ached from traipsing over the city; all likely for nothing, though that last one was still up in the air. Choosing to ignore the stickiness, he rested his arms on the counter.

The first two numbers on the list had gone to voicemail, but the address noted down for one had been a half-hour trip across town. He had arrived at an expensive looking jewellers, where a snooty staff member had coldly informed him that the person he was asking for was on annual leave.

"The usual then?" Will prompted when Roy didn't reply.

"Thanks." Lifting his head, Roy watched as he filled a pint glass from the beer tap.

The second address had found him drinking tea on the floral patterned sofa of an elderly lady who had smiled and nodded as he explained about the wand. He wasn't positive she had quite understood what he needed, and so took her promise to call him if she found any information with a healthy dose of scepticism, but at least she had good taste in biscuits.

Will placed the pint in front of him, and Roy nodded his thanks before taking a gulp of beer.

After finally making it away, he'd decided to give the last number a try. This one had sounded the most promising; the man who answered asked him to come immediately to his office, giving his address and hanging up before Roy could protest.

After a bus trip back across the city, during which he began to question how sensible it was to search out strangers alone, he had entered what appeared to be a tiny museum. The man on the phone turned out to be a short, bespectacled gentleman wearing an old tweed suit that looked as though it had been stitched before Morgan's takeover. He had ushered Roy up the narrow staircase at the back of the building, at the top of which was indeed a small office lined with bookshelves and smelling of dust and stale coffee. The man had inspected the wand closely, making many illustrations of the shapes inscribed upon it, before proudly declaring that the one at the end was obviously the mark of the Royal family.

It was at this point that Roy gave up. He left his address with the man — apparently he disapproved of such modern contraptions as phones — and headed back towards home, or rather to the pub, at which he spent an equal amount of time.

"Was surprised not to see you last night." Will remarked when Roy had made it half way down the glass.

"Nah, it was Friday. I was out with the guys from work."

Will nodded. "Yeah of course. Completely forgot. Was worried you'd gotten yourself caught up in all that trouble down the road." He gestured vaguely towards the door.

"Trouble?" Roy started to ask, but their conversation was interrupted by the arrival of a professional looking man in a suit who sat himself on the rickety bar stool beside him.

Will made an apologetic face as he went to serve the new

patron. "What can I get you?"

Something unintelligible was requested in a posh accent, and Roy assessed the man out of the corner of his eye. At first glance he didn't appear to be much older than Roy, but on paying closer attention he could detect the magic the man exuded. He was a mage. Strong too, making his actual age hard to place.

Roy didn't recognise him, but then again this wasn't one of *those* local pubs. His soft features were handsome enough to hold his attention, even marred by signs of stress and lack of sleep, and the well-fitting suit and waistcoat made him appear expensive. Perhaps he'd just been fired.

The drink Will placed down ended up being a suspiciously ordinary glass of red wine. As the man picked it up, he turned and met Roy's stare with sharp, golden brown eyes.

Averting his gaze, Roy waved the bartender back over, trying to pretend he hadn't noticed the suited man at all.

"What did you mean, trouble yesterday?" Roy asked. He hadn't noticed anything off when coming home, though the majority of last night still seemed to be eluding him. Another mouthful of beer helped chase away the unwelcome return of the table dancing memory.

Will gave him a questioning look, "Didn't you see that the roads were all closed down the market way? Only reopened this morning."

There was something like that on the news. "You mean the traffic accident?" Roy hadn't realised it had happened so close to home.

"Yeah. Traffic accident," Will scoffed. "Is that what the news is saying? I had a load of them in here last night; people who saw it, I mean, and they say it was a magic attack." He leaned across the counter. "I guess they don't want people worrying, with the big party coming up and all."

Roy breathed out a whistle. "You think it's a rogue mage?" Anyone stupid enough to draw that much attention had better make sure they weren't registered. He could imagine the police would be paying a visit to all the high powered magic users on the record books.

Will shrugged, "Doubt we'll ever know. I don't envy whoever it is if Morgan is coming after them."

Roy pursed his lips into a thin line and nodded, then jumped as the man beside him spoke.

"I heard they used a weapon."

Eyes still fixed ahead, he saw Will nod in response to the comment. "That's what some of the guys were saying yesterday too. Never heard of a magic weapon though. What would a mage need one of those for?"

A shattering of glass at a table across the pub caused the bartender to wince. "Be back in a sec gents. Sounds like Steve's destroying the place again." He walked off, leaving Roy and the stranger alone.

Uncomfortable silence fell. Roy could have sworn he'd felt a tingle of magic just before the glass smashed, but there had been no reaction from the man. In fact, he made no movement at all, other than to drum his fingers lightly against the side of his wine glass.

Roy had just decided to finish off his pint when the man spoke again. "Apparently, the attackers were seen with what looked to be a wooden stick that shot out magic."

The glass slipped from Roy's grip, hitting the table with a clunk. "Stick?" His voice came out as an embarrassing squeak that the man didn't seem to notice.

"Indeed. Carved with markings." The man's eyes met

Roy's. "I wouldn't want to be the one in possession of it now. A lot of people are going to be looking for them."

Roy coughed, still recovering from trying to breathe beer, and looked away. "I can imagine."

He needed to get out of here fast. How long would it take for someone to figure out he'd been asking around all day about the wand? That damn woman probably set him up. Her stupid list of stupid numbers. Felix Marek's lot were already after him; now it would be police, gangs, likely Morgan himself. If he'd realised the bloody stick could've been a weapon—

"Are you all right?" The man's question interrupted Roy's thoughts.

"Fine. Yes. Sorry, I think I'm just hung over from last night." Across the bar, Will was chatting with the group who had broken the glass. He could just leave the money, or duck out without paying the tab. Will would know he was good for it; that's if he lived through the night...

"I'd be happy to get that drink for you, if you need to hurry home." The offer should have sounded friendly, but the man's piercing analysis of his thoughts left Roy with a creeping suspicion it had been calculated rather than kind.

"It's fine mate, thanks." Hopping down from the stool, Roy pushed a note across the counter. "See he picks that up when he comes over, will you?" The suited man's eyes seemed to bore into his back as he hurried out.

***

Roy's front door was within sight when he felt the magic take hold. It gripped his limbs, restraining his movement and he mentally thrashed in panic, kicking himself for having not run some kind of shield. The spell was too strong to overpower and the active focus of the caster meant it would take time or distraction to unravel.

A voice rung out from behind him, "Wait, please, I just want to talk."

Well, that's nice. Perhaps he wasn't at the point of imminent death. Footsteps approached from behind, and Roy wished he could turn his head. After a moment, his attacker came into view and he found himself face to face with the smartly dressed man from the pub.

"You!" he spluttered, realising that he was still able to speak.

"Yes. Apologies for this; I had to ensure I had the correct person." Though apparently sorry, the stranger made no move to release him.

Roy wasn't sure how to reply, so decided not to. Instead, he focussed on breaking the spell binding him. It was an active spell; too complex for him to read, but presumably some kind of modified healing since it was affecting his body. Still, every spell had a weak point. All it needed was a nudge in the right place.

The man frowned, presumably in response to Roy's silence. "I know you have the magical weapon we discussed earlier. I would like to make an arrangement."

His smooth accent was infuriating; far too fancy to be one of Marek's lot. Besides, they'd have just killed him rather than chat in the street.

"I don't have it on me," Roy replied, hoping that the man wouldn't check.

"Of course. I hardly expected you would bring it to a pub with you."

Ouch. At this point, he'd rather the guy was trying to kill

him. "Who do you work for then?" Roy didn't expect a response, but at least it would change the topic. "Morgan?"

The corners of the man's mouth twitched upward, but his faint smile wasn't sinister.

"I'm afraid Morgan and I don't see eye to eye," he replied. "Luckily for you. Nor am I from any criminal organisation, though I was being honest when I said both are likely looking for you."

Roy felt the suited man's focus waver. Immediately, he sent a jolt of his own magic against the point in the spell where the intent began. With a mental click, it unravelled, leaving his captor blinking in surprise.

Movement returned to his limbs and Roy backed away, wanting to bolt but having no desire to turn his back on what was a clearly powerful mage. If it came to it, he'd rather go down with a fight.

"I'm impressed," The man remained calm. "Though are you quite sure you want to risk someone more dangerous finding you?"

"I'll take my chances," though he stopped moving.

"Listen," The man said. "All we want is to discover what that weapon is and how it works. From the visits you have made today, I got the impression that you want the same."

She did set me up then. "I'd actually rather live to be honest." He sneered. Maybe he could just give it away and be done.

As if hearing his thoughts, the man replied. "Giving it to me is likely too little too late. Anyone who finds out you were asking will come to interrogate you, whether you have the weapon or not."

"So what? You'll offer to keep me safe in exchange for the wand and information? How do I know you won't just off me later when you've got it?"

"Better than being 'offed' now, surely?" There was that amused expression again. Though the spell no longer bound him, Roy felt well and truly caught.

The suited man held a hand out towards him. "Do we have an agreement? Safety for information?"

After a brief hesitation, Roy took it. "Sure. Whatever."

"Excellent!" This time he smiled warmly, as though he hadn't just attacked an innocent in the street. "And what should I call you?"

Roy let go of the man's hand. "A fucking idiot maybe," he mumbled. "It's Roy."

"Pleased to meet you, Roy." The suited man replied. "My name is Oliver."

Chapter 7

It had taken the biggest rucksack Alex could find to fit his generator. The inbuilt handle would have been easier, but he didn't want his father asking questions. A brief explanation to his parents that he would sleep at Eira's had been enough, and though evening was fast approaching, at least it meant the grounds of Golebach Court would be empty.

"I still can't believe I'm letting you drag me all the way to Golebach on a Sunday night," Eira exclaimed. It would take an extra half hour to get there by bus than it had done in the car, but she'd been easily bribed with promises of Alex buying dinner when they got there.

"At least you can feel your legs," he replied, shifting

around so he was half stretched into the isle. They'd wedged the rucksack into the footwell at his insistence, not trusting the narrow luggage rack above, but now Alex was scrunched sideways with a foot on the chair to make room. "I thought you liked the beach?"

"Yeah, but we're not going to the beach are we," Eira rolled her eyes at him "I'm going to sit next to some old ruin for an hour while you tinker with a machine. As usual."

"Oh, come on. Give me one example of another time I've made you sit around next to a ruin- Ow!" He winced as Eira poked his undefended ribcage.

"You know what I meant!" she laughed, "You always promise these trips are going to be oh so cool, and they are always so, so boring for me." Eira turned away from him to look out of the window. "You never did tell me why we're going now. Weren't you only there yesterday?"

"I felt something there," Alex replied. "There's some sort of magic in the ground by the stones. I'm hoping I can tap it to charge the machine."

"In Golebach?" Eira raised an eyebrow. "What are you charging it for, anyway? We did the concert. Did the uni ask you?"

Alex shook his head, then rested his chin on his knee. "It's something dad said. He says the generator takes too much magic to charge." The bus had left the country roads now, and a thin strip of ocean was visible in the distance, shimmering pink along the horizon.

From the corner of his eye, Alex saw Eira scanning his face. "That's it?" She looked like she was about to laugh, but caught herself upon reading his expression. "I mean, it's unlike you to come hang out when your dad's around, I thought something big must have happened."

"It is big!" Alex exclaimed louder than he had intended. "If it's not viable, then the whole project has been a waste." The bitterness he'd felt the previous day came back in a rush and he realised he was scowling.

"It got you into Aedemeer!" Eira replied, but he barely heard her. Aedemeer would eventually point out the same issue that his dad had found, and he wasn't prepared to just let the project fail.

"It doesn't matter," Alex's scowl had turned to determination. "If I can get this ground magic to work, then it solves the problem, doesn't it?"

"And this couldn't have waited a few days because...?" Eira coaxed and Alex didn't meet her eyes. "Yeah I thought so," she sighed. "You're dragging me to Golebach just to prove your Dad wrong before he goes."

"That's not what this is." Even his own protest sounded feeble.

"Sure it's not. You keep telling yourself that." Eira gave him a smile. "It's fine Alex".

The magelights in the streetlamps were beginning to glow when they arrived at their stop. Between them, they dragged the rucksack out from where it was wedged, thanking the disinterested driver as they lugged it down onto the pavement.

A cool sea breeze whipped at Alex's hair and he took a deep breath, relieved to stretch his legs after the long ride. Their stop was on the high street, which meant they would have to climb the path up to the manor on foot, but the view they would get of the sunset made the prospect inviting. Eira fell into step beside him as they headed off, leaving the warm lights of the pubs and shops behind in favour of the relative quiet of the stoney climb.

"How long's your dad down for anyway?" Eira asked as they walked.

"Not long. Another day maybe." Alex hoisted the heavy rucksack higher on his shoulders. He'd spent the majority of the day in his room after breakfast and now felt a tinge of regret. His dad hadn't pressed him on the reason, and Alex reassured himself that he would make it up to him tomorrow.

"So your mum," Eira began after a moment.

Alex made a questioning sound in response. "What about her?"

"She gets on well with your dad still? You know, with him not really being around as much?" Eira seemed unusually hesitant.

"Yeah?" Without a heavy pack to slow her down, Eira was a few steps ahead and Alex couldn't see her face. "They're friends. Why would they not get on?"

"Just friends?" Eira turned back as she waited for him to catch up. "I've always kinda wanted to ask, because you give the impression like your parents aren't together anymore, but then your dad sleeps over your house and everything."

"I dunno, I've never really thought about it," Alex frowned. "I don't think they've ever been together, as such. Even when he lived here. Dad needs his own place anyway, because he travels for work. When he comes he just crashes on the sofa, you know." He'd rather not closely analyse why the sofa was always empty in the mornings, even when he was the first one awake.

"He lives in Larimar now, right? You think he knows anywhere we could do a gig? The band's been trying to find a bigger venue, but it's hard arranging it from out here."

"I can ask," Alex spoke in between heavy breaths, the

generator weighing him down as the path grew steeper. "I've never been over there."

Eira grew quiet and Alex remembered how she'd still not told him about her own university place. She seemed happy enough, but if she was planning gigs rather than getting ready to leave...

"So," It was his turn to sound hesitant. "The healing college in Beiriant...?" He trailed off, hoping Eira would get his meaning. Beiriant was Vailberg's capital and, with the precision required to learn healing magic, the barrier to entry for its colleges rivalled that of Aedemeer.

"Oh, yeah, they want me to go. I guess I'll be heading off the week after you do."

"You got in?" Alex jogged up beside her, ignoring the burning in his thighs. "That's great!" Healing was hard and its effectiveness entirely dependent on the strict focus of the mage casting it. Sure, simple wounds were easy enough to fix on yourself; much easier to guide a spell when you can feel what's hurting, but doing it on someone else was a different matter. And that was for injuries that were visible.

Part of the trouble was that healing was active. It wasn't as though an expert mage could create a passive healing spell for others to study and use. Each case had to be dealt with individually and the spells formed anew, making it as difficult to teach as it was to learn.

"Yeah. It's really great." Eira smiled, but it didn't seem to reach her eyes. Before Alex could probe further, she darted ahead again. "Look, we made it!"

They had. As they reached the crest of the hill, the glittering ocean stretched out before them; orange and blue fragmented by the rippling waves. A few wispy clouds shone brightly where they caught the dying sunlight, contrasting with the darkening sky above and reminding Alex of the time. He'd rather not have to work on his machine in the dark, even with a magelight.

The manor rose ahead of them, but this time Alex took the right fork when the road split, away from the sweeping driveway and towards the lawn and gardens. They passed a couple sitting together on one of the benches, but as they turned the corner, Alex was pleased to note that the area around the stone monument was empty.

He was looking out for the magic this time, and as he approached he felt it flowing in the earth beneath his feet. It reminded him of the energy given off by a passive spelled item, but fainter and with no detectable purpose, no matter how he tried to analyse it. By the time they arrived at the ring of stone arches, the power hummed against his senses like the gentle purr of a contented cat.

It was a few minutes before Alex realised he had been stood in silence, running his hand over the stone, still warm from the day's heat. Eira was watching him.

"Don't let me interrupt you," she called, as he turned to face her. "I can see you are having an intimate moment with a piece of rock."

"Can't you feel it?" he called back, gesturing to the ground as he walked towards her. "The energy here?"

"I feel hungry!" Eira laughed and tilted her head to the side. "No magic though. Sorry." Alex's disappointment must have shown on his face because she quickly continued. "But look, if you say there's something here then I believe you."

Alex nodded, though a frown still creased his brow. He didn't consider himself a stronger mage than Eira, and it surprised him that she couldn't sense what seemed so obvious to him. Then again, he hadn't immediately noticed it when he arrived yesterday; perhaps it took some time to attune to? The proof would be in if he could tap the power.

Eira settled down cross legged on a rock half embedded in the dirt and fished a little note book out of her pocket.

"I thought you were complaining on the bus that you wouldn't have anything to do?" Alex commented, as he saw his friend begin to sketch something out.

"Yeah, I just wanted to make you feel bad," Eira didn't look up.

Alex smiled and shrugged off his rucksack, settling it gently on the ground. It took some effort to extract the generator, but he was relieved to see it was unscathed from the bus journey. He'd reconstructed the passive spell that morning; just the one that rotated the motor. Layering in anything more complex seemed redundant at this stage. If the ground magic didn't work, he'd spend more time focusing on refining the efficiency instead.

Now that it came to it, Alex wasn't sure how he was going to draw on the magic, anyway. He settled down on the grass and placed a hand on the ground, the other resting on the casing of his machine. The passive spell inside the generator tingled against his mind, ready for whatever magic would be channelled to it.

In contrast, the magic in the ground seemed no closer, even with the focus point of his touch. He reached out with his own energy, like when reading a passive spell, but the power below him seemed to leap away, as though repelled.

Alex stopped and thought. As far as he knew, it wasn't possible to take magic from existing passive spells or from other mages. It was why magic sickness was impossible to heal; all a mage could do was wait until their own body replenished their reserves. Then again, this magic wasn't like any he had encountered before. The way it retreated when he reached for it… Perhaps if he pulled his energy away?

With a slow breath, Alex turned his attention inward. Even the physical barrier of his skin didn't stop some of his magic radiating out – it was how mages sensed each other after all. But with focus Alex found he could start to draw his energy back. Using the hand touching the ground as his focal point, Alex withdrew his own power and, to his delight, found the ground magic flowing closer to the surface in response.

His nerves made it hard to keep the focus, and Alex paused to steady himself before attempting to draw the ground magic into his body. It followed willingly this time, cool and strangely distinct from his own.

Now it was just a matter of channelling it into his generator. He could feel the metal under his other hand, passive spell ready and waiting. With a small exertion of will, Alex directed the new magic inside.

It flowed slowly at first, trickling through the passage granted by his body. To his relief, the passive spell accepted the power easily and with apparently no depletion of his own magic. Confidence boosted, Alex pulled harder, trying to increase the flow.

The trickle picked up speed. For a second, Alex felt like it was still under his control. Then magic flooded his body, crashing through him as though a dam had broken.

White light burned in his mind. Blinding energy blocked out any sense until he was nothing other than a connection between the two points of magic.

"Get to the King! We're under attack!" A deep voice, edged with panic, shouted from somewhere, but Alex didn't recognise it. He couldn't see. He fought for control of his body,

fear rising until, with a violent lurch, the ground seemed to drop away under him.

He was thrown off balance, hands pulled away from both machine and earth as his back hit the dirt. It was enough to break the connection, and the white light faded from his mind, replaced with the twilight of evening.

"Alex!" Eira's scream cut through the fog of his daze. He tried to move, but he ached all over. Black specks raced across his vision as he lifted his head.

In front of him, the generator was whirring. Not its usual low vibration, but a high screech that shook the metal casing around it. Adrenaline defeated exhaustion, and Alex clawed at the grass, dragging himself away from the machine towards Eira's voice.

She must have run to meet him, pulling at his arms to drag him to his feet.

"Alex, what's going on? The earthquake!" Eira's voice shook, but Alex knew there wasn't time. The screech from the generator was wrong. He still had magic though; despite the exhaustion in his limbs, he'd been correct in his assessment that the spell had taken none of his own power.

Without offering a reply, Alex flung a shield around them both. Then, with an ear-splitting boom, the generator exploded.

He felt the shrapnel first. Shards of his machine battered off of the shield and his head pounded as he reinforced it with everything he had.

A wave of raw magic followed, undefined and crackling. Like static, it sparked along his shield, dispersing it as it went. He grappled desperately with his mind to hold the spell together, but the wild power was grounding through his body, taking both his shield and his awareness with it.

Thoughts slipped away and darkness took their place.

CHAPTER 8

Tamara pinched the bridge of her nose and tried to stifle a yawn. Pale threads of dawn had barely begun to weave across the sky when Morgan's messenger had woken her, bringing news that a vehicle would be ready within the hour. She estimated that she'd managed maybe five hours sleep and the soothing motion of the government car wasn't helping her stay alert.

The incident report lay on her lap and she again ran a finger over the note stuck to the front: *'One for you to look into'*. Morgan's handwriting was neat and understated, but his signature below the message was unmistakable. She didn't know whether to be grateful that the document held scant few details; it had made quick reading despite her frazzled mental state, but she still wasn't sure what to expect upon arriving in Golebach.

Gravel crunched as they pulled into the car park of a bleak, grey building that Tamara assumed must be the local police station. She coughed to clear her throat, aware that she hadn't spoken for the entire journey, and attempted to form her face into an expression of engaged interest. After a moment, her driver opened the door and Tamara thanked him with a smile she hoped hid her exhaustion. Report clutched tight to her chest, she straightened her jacket and stepped into the fresh morning air.

There was no one waiting outside and she eyed the door to the building, wondering if she should just walk in. It opened before she had to decide, and she was greeted by a tall policewoman in a crumpled uniform, who looked as though she may have had even less sleep than herself.

"Hi, I'm here from the palace." Tamara stepped forward as she spoke, rotating her folder so the ID card she'd slipped into the front was visible. The woman glanced down at it and back to her face, before holding out a hand.

"It's good to meet you. I'm Head Officer Helen James." Tamara took the outstretched hand as two other people emerged from the building. "This is Officer Barrie. He was first on the scene," Helen indicated to a shorter, plump man who had walked up to her right. "Senior Officer Robinson assisted in securing the site and transporting the suspects involved." The younger, clean shaven man to Helen's left stepped forward and shook Tamara's hand.

"I'm Tamara Elden. It's nice to meet you," she said, releasing the handshake before Robinson could feel the clamminess of her palm. "I read the report on the way down, but it was a little light on detail. Has any more happened since?"

"Apologies for that," Helen's alert manner belied her appearance, and a radiating magic energy revealed her to be a mage. "We alerted the palace as soon as we determined there could be magic involved, however I am aware that meant the report was rushed." The other two officers were looking down at her with wary fascination, and Tamara was glad she had the report to occupy her nervous hands. "Would you like to come inside and I'll give you a run-down of the events?"

A short corridor opened into a small office area dominated by scattered paperwork and a strong scent of coffee. Helen gave a brief wave to the one or two people that looked up as they passed. "Can I get you a drink?" she asked, looking back at Tamara over her shoulder.

The smell and her own tiredness made coffee sound more appealing than it usually would. "That would be great, thanks," she replied. People seemed kinder when you accepted their offers. "Milk and one sugar, please."

"Jason, can you grab some coffees for us?" Helen called to a young man who was attempting to scuttle by with a stack of folders. He dashed off after taking the remaining orders, leaving Helen to lead Tamara and the other officers into what was presumably an interview room.

Chairs screeched on the vinyl floor as they sat and Tamara laid her folder out on the empty white table in front of them.

"In fact, very little has changed since the report," Helen continued from where she had left off outside. "As you will have read, we started getting calls about an earthquake at approximately twenty past eight yesterday evening. One or two of the higher magic locals said they felt magical energy around the same time, but mostly it was just people scared."

"I can imagine," Tamara replied, "Ardveld isn't known for its tectonic activity; there shouldn't be any earthquakes here."

"Exactly." Helen nodded. "So when the call came in about the explosion, things began to make more sense."

A large enough shock wave might well explain the supposed earthquake. Barrie had taken a seat next to Tamara and now cleared his throat with a dry cough. "So I was about to head down to the village when we got the report of a loud explosion from Golebach Court—"

"It's a local historical site that's open to the public," Helen interjected. Tamara opened the file and leafed through to the picture of the manor house, rotating it so the others could see.

"That's the one," Barrie said. "I drove over there, and at this point we're still thinking it's some kind of equipment malfunction or something, but when I arrive— there should be some photos." Barrie waved towards the folder and Tamara pretended not to notice the sharp look Helen gave to her officer. Instead, she turned the page to an image of a stone structure, surrounded by blackened grass and spattered dirt.

"This is where the report says the explosion happened," Tamara said. "Is this near the manor then?"

"The actual bomb site is an ancient ruin, about a hundred meters from the manor," Helen explained. "It's in the grounds but accessible at all hours."

The door clicked open as the junior from earlier brought in their drinks. Tamara took her coffee, cupping the plain mug in her hands to warm her fingers.

"So I get there," Barrie continued when the junior

departed. "And I see the damage, which is basically as the picture shows, however there are two casualties at site. That's about when I decided I'd better call this one in." He took a mouthful of coffee and looked towards Tamara. "I contact the station for medical and backup and basically make sure they aren't dead."

Tamara nodded, eyes not leaving the photo. "Where are they now? The report said they were uninjured, though the male had magic sickness. Is that correct?"

This time it was Robinson who replied. "Yes. After medical checked them over and we had secured the site, we brought them back here to await interview. There were no serious injuries apart from the case of magic sickness."

That was a relief, at least.

"Could it have been an accident?" If she remembered the report correctly, the explosion had supposedly been caused by a device that two teenagers had brought to the site. She pulled the folder back towards her and flipped to the page showing the transcribed text.

"Sure. If you want to call getting caught up in the blast from their own bomb, an 'accident'." Barrie rolled his eyes, and earnt another stern look from Helen.

"They actually admitted they made a bomb then?" Tamara questioned. "Was that from when you interviewed the woman? I can't imagine you would have got much information from the magic sickness case."

Opposite her, Robinson glanced at Helen, and Tamara had the uncomfortable feeling that she had said the wrong thing.

"The transcript in the report is what the female suspect told us as we were bringing them in." Helen explained. "Despite my colleague's assumptions, the suspects haven't confirmed the purpose of the device they brought to site. We obviously haven't conducted any interviews, as the reports of magic place this case under palace jurisdiction. As per protocol, we have waited for you to conduct the interviews when you take over the case."

"Ah."

Take over the case? The room felt even colder than it had before.

It made sense why they might think that. After all, she had come from the palace and so technically was the most senior person here. Tamara sipped at her coffee, burning her tongue. As Head of Magic Affairs she had expected to evaluate the source and mechanism of a magical incident, but Morgan had given her no formal instruction for involvement with suspects. Surely that should fall under defence?

"I believe that I am just here to assist and advise on the magical elements of this case," Tamara placed the mug back down with a clunk, and gave what she hoped was a reassuring smile.

"My apologies, but we are a small operation here," Helen rubbed at her eyes, seeming to have lost some of her professional composure. "Protocol says that we must refer upwards, any case where there are signs of magic involvement, and this... bombing is far beyond what we are equipped to deal with. I was informed that an advisor had been sent from the palace. Isn't that you?"

Three pairs of eyes were scrutinising her now, and Tamara looked down at her report, scrambling to find an answer. Her burnt tongue hurt and she pulled on her magic to soothe it. Maybe it was supposed to be her? The memory of her last conversation with Morgan flashed into her mind;

the dim office where he'd shown her a letter of resignation from the former Head of Defence.

"I— Please don't worry. I'll contact the palace and find out who else is coming to actually take over the case. In the meantime, I will see if I can determine exactly what magic was involved." Tamara finished, hoping her voice contained the authority she wished she felt. Helen, at least, appeared reassured.

"Thank you," Helen said. "Until then, we will assist you in whatever you require. Where would you like to start?"

"Well," Tamara chewed at her lip. "I think it's best that I go visit the site."

* * *

The drive to the manor was short, but the police car had to stop outside a cordoned off area around the manor house and grounds. Helen informed her that, though the ruin was obviously a crime scene, they were also concerned about the structural stability of the manor, given the movement of the ground.

As they approached the ruins themselves, Tamara could see for herself what the picture had implied — a shallow crater surrounded by mud and scorched grass. The two officers stationed there let them pass after a brief explanation from Helen, and Tamara ventured ahead to what looked to be the epicentre.

There wasn't much to look at. The ground was hard from the summer heat, which may have gone some way to limit the damage, but whatever blast had occurred didn't seem all that impactful. That at least explained how the two teenagers had made it out unscathed. Presumably the remains of the so-called bomb had already been safely removed.

Apart from some scorch marks, even the ruin appeared undamaged to Tamara's eyes. Helen had said much the same. No magic that she could sense either, not even from the manor behind them that should be teeming with spells.

"Everything okay?" Helen said as she approached, and Tamara hummed an acknowledgement without turning to look.

A moment later, her brain caught up. "Oh, yes. Sorry. I was just thinking."

"It's no problem."

Tamara flicked her fingers a few times, then stopped as she saw Helen looking. But the Head Officer had been kind and respectful so far, and she felt it was worth an explanation. "I'm from Avel Kifaeros," she said, with what she hoped was a non-threatening smile. "So if I seem a little, well, odd..."

"Ah," Helen nodded. "Don't worry; my nephew's like that. He's Ardveldian, but you know what I mean. Take all the time you need."

It was a good enough response. Though they were the majority in Avel Kiaferos, it wasn't unusual for people in other parts of the world to be born with the typical mix of traits associated with the Kifaerish. If it helped Helen understand, then it was useful, as long as she afforded her the same respect as before she knew.

"There doesn't seem to be any magic around the building." Tamara gestured towards the manor.

"Yes, I've just heard that myself." To her relief, Helen seemed happy to let the conversation return to work. "It seems like whatever happened here wiped the passive spells nearest the manor. Staff aren't happy – they'll need to bring someone in to recast the more complex ones."

A light wind whipped up the dust at Tamara's feet, and she looked back towards the stones. "I don't see how a bomb could have done that. Not without physical damage to the building." Being a mage herself, Helen should know that. Tamara looked up at her face. "And why would anyone want to set off a bomb here anyway?"

Helen folded her arms with a frown. "Pure selfishness? Don't think I'll ever understand what these kids get out of vandalising places that others enjoy."

Blackened dirt came away when Tamara brushed a hand over the closest scorch mark, but the stone underneath remained intact. "There doesn't seem to be much damage to the ruin," she said, dusting her fingers on her skirt. "You said you originally got calls about an earthquake? Before the report of the explosion?"

Helen nodded and Tamara continued, her mind chasing an idea. "Was there any damage in town?"

"Yes," Helen replied. "Not a great deal, but there was some minor structural damage to a few buildings."

This was it. The part that didn't make sense. "Were they just out of range of hearing the explosion then? Or is it possible that the damage in town did genuinely happen first?"

Helen seemed to hesitate before replying. "I'm not quite sure what you mean. You're suggesting we could be dealing with two separate events?" Her expression remained polite, but Tamara wondered if she had just said something incredibly stupid. "With all due respect, it's not something I had considered. Don't you think that would be too much of a coincidence?"

Tamara bobbed her head as she attempted to arrange her thoughts into a reasonable explanation. "I don't necessarily think the events are unlinked," she began carefully. "But I was called here because there was likely magic involved. The damage from this explosion is nowhere near enough to have reached the town. I mean, it barely reaches ten meters and didn't harm the ruin at all. It makes me wonder if there is something magic based going on that caused both the town damage first, and then the explosion."

Helen breathed a sigh, raising a hand to shield her eyes from the sun as she looked up at the manor. "An explosion alone wouldn't have got rid of those spells. You're right about that." With an incline of her head she started walking back towards the perimeter. Tamara took the hint and followed. "But you honestly think two eighteen-year-olds could have enough magic to cause an earthquake?" Helen lowered her voice as she spoke.

"I've never heard of any mage strong enough to cause an earthquake," Tamara replied. "But the boy does have magic sickness. There could be more to it than just having shielded them both. I think I need to talk to them."

"I thought you didn't want to take over the case?" Helen said, opening the passenger door for Tamara as they reached the waiting car.

"I don't, and I still plan on calling the palace for you, but I need to ask more questions before I can give my report to whoever I hand this over to," Tamara replied, settling into the seat. "Will that be okay?"

"Of course." Helen sounded surprised, and again Tamara was reminded of her seniority. "Whatever you need."

* * *

Heavy doors sealed the two holding cells off from a bare grey corridor back at the station. Tamara had to rise up on her toes to see through the open hatch of the first. Inside, a young woman lay on a narrow bed, apparently asleep.

"Don't wake her if we don't need to," Tamara said, putting out a hand to stop Helen from opening the door. "Perhaps the other one is awake?"

"I'm happy to check, but I don't know how much you'll get out of him, even if he is," Helen replied. "Unless, is there anything you could do to speed up his recovery?"

"Unfortunately not," Tamara was unable to help a smile at Helen's suggestion. "Even I can't transfer magic into someone else. The only thing we can do is keep them rested and cared for until they recover their energy naturally."

"Well, he doesn't seem to be asleep anymore." Helen was looking through the hatch into the next room, and Tamara craned herself up beside her to see. The room was a mirror of the previous cell; a small single bed running down the left side of a white brick wall. Sat on the bed, staring down at the floor, was the young man they had been discussing. He didn't seem to have noticed their arrival, despite their conversation outside the door.

"Do you mind if I go inside to talk to him?" Tamara asked. "It's nothing formal, so it seems unfair to move him."

"Go ahead," Helen placed a hand on the door and whatever spell powered the lock clicked open as it registered her identity. "Do you want me to come in with you?"

"I'm sure I'll be fine." Tamara doubted a magic drained teenager would be much of a threat, even if he wanted to be. "He may need water if he has been asleep since the incident." It had been a long time since Tamara had experienced magic sickness, but she certainly didn't envy him. "I'll let you know if he says anything."

Helen gave a nod, "Fair enough. I'll be just down the corridor. Call if there's anything you need." With a push, the door swung open and Tamara stepped inside. It closed with a metallic clang behind her, but the teenager didn't look up.

Tamara slid the report folder from where she had been carrying it under her arm. Thankfully, the woman had given their names on the ride to the station and they were listed in the transcription; Eira Tegwen and Alexander Watkin-Ashe. Closing the folder softly, she walked towards the figure on the bed.

"Hello? Alexander? How are you feeling?" Dark brown curls partially obscured his face, but he stirred at the mention of his name. That was better than nothing. With no other seats in the room, she perched herself further down the bed. "It's okay. I just want to talk. Can you hear me?"

This time, he lifted his head. Tamara saw him squeeze his eyes shut and then slowly open them, as if trying to focus on the room. Despite the tan of his skin, there was an ashen sheen over his face that made her want to reach out and comfort him, just as her mother had done when she was sick as a child.

He made a sound of acknowledgement and Tamara decided to wait to see if he needed some time to process. It was a few seconds before her patience was rewarded. "It's Alex. Sorry. I'm... I'm really tired. Sorry..."

"No, it's okay. I'm sorry, I know you're tired." Maintaining the conversation was important now he was responding. "I just need to ask you some questions. Is that okay?"

The reply came quicker this time. "Yeah... sure. I don't — I don't think..." She watched as he moved his fingers, clenching and unclenching his hands, and remembered the weakness and nausea that came when she overused her own magic.

"You don't think?" Tamara probed, hoping he would pick back up the train of thought.

"Sorry," Alex turned his head, and she found herself looking into unfocussed dark eyes. "I don't think I'm very well."

Tamara's heart twinged with sympathy. "Yes, that's true. You overused your magic. Can you tell me what happened?" She may as well just try asking.

Alex squinted. "We were... we were at the site. The place... with the magic." He waved his hand in a dismissive gesture and gave a small shake of his head. "I can't really think. The name... you know? Sorry."

"Do you mean the ruin near Golebach Court?" Tamara had a vague memory that you shouldn't ask leading questions in an interview, but this wasn't really an interview so it should be okay.

"Yes!"

Tamara was surprised to see him give a weak smile, before he seemed to drift back into his own thoughts. "Okay, so you were at the ruin, remember? Can you tell me why you were there?" she continued.

"Hmmm... We were there, yes." He didn't seem to be able to keep focus for long enough to give her any information. Perhaps this was a lost cause. Tamara ran her fingers over the plastic cover of the folder, remembering the note from Morgan that she had slipped away inside. *'One for you to look into.'*

"I brought the generator. To try... to try the ground magic," Alex spoke again and his eyes seemed to gain focus as they widened. "Eira! She was with me. Is she okay?"

"She's fine. Nobody was hurt." Tamara kept her voice gentle and Alex appeared to relax. His words, though, had set her mind racing. "What do you mean by 'ground magic'?" Could he have caused the earthquake after all?

"Ground magic... you know? It's there. In the ground," He leant forward and buried his head in his hands with a groan. "I'm sorry. I can't think,"

Ground magic in the ground. Not very helpful.

He knew something though. Some kind of magic that hadn't been there when Tamara had gone to the site. That must be the answer. Unfortunately, it didn't seem like she would get much more out of Alex right now. She would have to wait until his head cleared and hope he was still forthcoming with information.

Of course, by that point, he would be interviewed by whoever else the palace sent to take over the case. Tamara had no idea what kind of person they would be.

"I'm going to let you rest now." She stood up from the bed. "I'll arrange for someone to bring you water. Please lie down and don't worry."

It was hard to tell what sort of person she was dealing with while they were in this state, but Tamara just couldn't seem to picture the teenager as a hardened criminal. She walked over to the hatch in the door and called down the corridor for Helen, leaving Alex slumped at the edge of the bed.

* * *

"So how did it go? Did you learn anything from him?" Helen asked once they were seated back in the interview room.

"More questions than answers, unfortunately." Tamara sighed. "I think I'll have to do further research back at the palace."

"Do you know when we'll hear who's taking over the case?" Helen's question reminded her she should probably call Morgan, rather than arranging a meeting when she got back. That's if he even had time to take a call.

They had only given her this role to fill a gap; Morgan had said as much at their last meeting, but she was still the Head of Magic Affairs. Hadn't she told him she intended to do the best job she could? A wrong choice had to be better than no choice after all, especially if she was expected to fail, anyway.

Forcing herself to meet Helen's eyes, Tamara gripped the folder until the edge dug into her palm. She would have to take the teenagers back to the palace with her; it was clear now that the little police station wasn't equipped to cope. "You won't need to wait. I've decided I'm going to take the case over myself."

CHAPTER 9

Oliver had forbidden the use of the closest car park to the safe house. Instead, Matthew was supposed to choose from one of three designated parking spots, to be used on a rotating basis. Normally, what Oliver didn't know wouldn't hurt him, but Matthew felt he owed some repentance for his recent actions and so resigned himself to the walk.

It was about ten in the morning when he'd received Oliver's call. Alex still hadn't come home from spending the night at Eira's, and Matthew regretted losing the chance to smooth things over before he left. His son's curt farewell the day before wasn't lost on him, and even Dorothea's assurance that this was normal teenage behaviour couldn't ease his mind.

The streets were quieter now he had left the main road and Matthew kept a brisk pace. This safe house was one of two he knew of in the city, situated two roads up from a row of shops and food outlets. It was an unassuming terraced building, not run down enough for anyone to capitalise on its emptiness, and not fancy enough to draw attention for the same reason.

Matthew was grateful to be approaching from the opposite direction this time. They had come here after the tearoom, but it was too soon for him to feel comfortable going near the market again. With that thought, he reached out to scan the area with his magic, but there was no answering energy. Either he was alone or his pursuers had no magic. Hopefully no strange weapons either; he shivered despite the sunshine.

Worn steps led up to a smart green door, magic locked with a more advanced spell of the type he'd cast for Felix Marek. The building was split into two flats, of which Oliver owned the upper floor, and the door opened onto a narrow stairwell that led up to the living area. Movement from the top of the stairs answered his arrival, and Matthew looked up to see Oliver, the apprehension on his face replaced by recognition.

"You made it," Oliver said.

The door clicked shut behind him and Matthew made his way up the stairs. "Is he here then?" The question was brusquer than he intended, but his friend appeared unfazed by his tone.

"He is." Oliver stepped aside to let him pass, and Matthew saw he was wearing his usual suit and tie, even though there was no way he had been in the office today.

Little had changed since his recent visit. Lightly furnished, the room comprised a small seating area to his left, with an old, but immaculately kept, dining table against the far wall. Lounging across the grey sofa in the centre of the room was a lanky redhead who Matthew assumed must be Roy.

"This is Roy," The man scrambled upright at Oliver's introduction. "He's been very helpful."

"Hey," Roy gave a half-hearted wave and propped a foot up on the glass coffee table. From the corner of his eye, Matthew saw Oliver wince.

"How did you get it?" This time, Matthew made no effort to soften his words.

The curiosity on Roy's face faded. "Pleased to meet you too." The sarcasm was dripping.

"Perhaps I should make us a drink and we can sit down and discuss this properly," Oliver interjected before Matthew could respond. He left towards the kitchen, leaving Matthew and Roy in uncomfortable silence.

Begrudgingly, Matthew took a seat in the matching single chair and assessed the alleged thief. From the baggy tee shirt and dirt scuffed jeans, he hardly looked competent. Perhaps an opportunist? But you don't get hold of something that powerful by accident, and Oliver said the man claimed to have broken into Felix Marek's house.

"You done?" Roy said, gesturing at himself in a way that made Matthew uncomfortable. "You'd better be buying me dinner after eyeing me up like that."

"You never answered my question." Matthew shot Roy a glare.

"I'm pretty sure I heard your friend tell you the story over the phone," Roy leaned back in his chair and another foot joined the first on the coffee table. "When you walked in, I thought I'd like you more than Mr Fancy Pants, but you could use a few tips from him on how to treat someone helping you out."

"I want to hear it from you." Matthew's nails were digging into his palm, but he tried to keep his voice level.

"Fine," Roy replied, "I broke into Marek's place, got blasted by that stick thing, whatever it is, grabbed it and got out," he flung a hand out dramatically. "Not forgetting I got shot at in the process! Your friend picked me up when I started asking questions and said I'd be safe here in exchange for info."

"You say you got it from Felix Marek's place? Where in the house?"

"He had like this hidden room. Obviously didn't want anyone finding out he had that," Roy jerked a thumb over his shoulder towards the dining table behind. Craning his head, Matthew saw something lying on the polished wood, wrapped in a green cloth. "Believe me, if I knew it was some kind of weapon, I'd have dropped it."

"You couldn't have got into a hidden room. It would have been locked." If Roy's story was true, it essentially confirmed their theory that Felix Marek sent the tea room attackers. But Matthew refused to believe the guy in front of him had undone one of his spells.

Roy gave him a quizzical look. "Er... yeah, it was. I picked it. What did you expect?"

"You can't have done. What was the locking spell like?" It was possible the spell was somehow changed after he left, but why?

Roy paused and an unreadable expression crossed his face. "Why do you even care? It was a magic lock, I picked it, let's leave it at that."

"I'm not going to just 'leave it'!" Matthew snarled. "They came after us. Because of you!" He'd spent the last few days envisioning Felix's people coming for his family and finding Roy lounging in the safe house wasn't easing his anger.

A clatter alerted them to Oliver's return with a tray full of drinks, but Roy didn't look around.

"Way to shift the blame mate," his casual manner had been replaced by a scowl to match Matthew's. "Maybe you should have thought a bit harder before working for Marek. How do you even know how to do a palace lock anyway?"

Shock stunned Matthew into silence. Beside him, Oliver froze half way through placing a can on the table.

"Oh, come on. Why else would you be so freaked out about how I got in the room? I suppose you made the wand as well, and this is just some kind of setup?" He pulled his legs back as though about to stand, but Oliver held out a hand to stop him.

"I can assure you we have nothing to do with the wand, and we are certainly no friends to Felix Marek. I would have thought that should be obvious." Oliver picked up the teapot and began to pour for Roy, who grimaced but seemed to relax back down. "I am curious though; you called the lock you saw a 'palace lock'. Are you implying you have broken into the palace?"

Roy shifted, rubbing a hand over his arm. "That's none of your business. I just know what they look like, alright. How about you tell me why you can do one, and I might tell you how I know."

"That's not up for discussion," Matthew said, not trying to hide the ice in his voice. Roy returned his glare.

"I promised information about the wand. Nothing else,"

Roy turned to Oliver. "That was the deal."

"It was," Oliver nodded and stood up. "In that case, I think it's time we took a look at it."

They headed towards the table in tense silence. As Roy had indicated, the weapon lay there, covered in what looked like an emerald silk handkerchief. Innocent enough, but as Oliver revealed the wood underneath, Matthew was hit once again with the unsettling energy he had felt outside the tea room.

Swallowing his nausea, Matthew fought the instinct to back away. The glowing symbols on the weapon cast an eerie light over Oliver's hand, and Matthew noticed he had made a handle from the cloth, rather than touch the wood.

"We can't hold it directly," Oliver explained. "Whatever magic it contains seems to react badly to our own."

"Learnt that one the hard way," Roy said. "Almost threw up the first time it zapped me."

Matthew chose not to question why there had been more than a first time. "What about non-mages? Those people who attacked us didn't seem to have a problem holding it?"

"I can't say for certain without testing it," Oliver replied. "But I imagine holding it would have no effect on a non-mage." He tilted the wand and Matthew tensed. "The energy inside has no purpose and is therefore unstable. My theory is that, without a passive spell to contain the magic, the wand's power is attracted to a mage's own energy. The two magic types don't mix and so the power runs through the mage and disperses, effectively grounding itself through them and pulling their own magic with it. If the wand has more magic than they do, theoretically it could kill them."

"Undirected magic isn't something I have any experience with," Matthew's head was starting to hurt from being so close to the wand and he had half a mind to ask Oliver if he really needed to see the weapon while explaining. "I wouldn't have thought it was possible."

"We've never heard of it either." Oliver met his eyes, and Matthew knew he was talking about Ewen. If the old Tactician had no knowledge of the wand's magic, then they must be dealing with something new, but he'd need to wait until he was alone with Oliver to confirm it.

"Yeah, no one I asked knew anything," Roy piped up from beside Matthew, as though pleased to be included. "That's the royal symbol there though," he pointed towards the stick and Matthew looked closer at the glowing shapes carved into the wood. "Reckon they made it?"

It was the royal symbol. Oliver had warned him it would be there, and Matthew wondered if seeing it would ever stop hurting.

"I highly doubt it." Matthew heard Oliver reply. If the Royal family had made it, Ewen would know. Then another thought occurred to him.

"Hang on," Matthew exclaimed. "If you stole this last week, then the weapon used to attack us wasn't the same one." He turned to Oliver. "How many of these are out there?"

The severity on Oliver's face showed he had already realised the same thing. "I don't know."

There was too much they didn't know. Matthew leant against the back of the sofa and sighed. "So if the magic grounded through Roy when he touched the wand, how can it still have power now?" Dwelling on the weapons in circulation wouldn't help, but they could at least focus on understanding how they worked.

"It charges itself," Matthew was surprised to hear Roy

reply. "After I first got zapped, I could touch it for a bit. The glow faded too, but the next day it was back like this again."

"I tested it myself last night," Oliver spoke casually, not even having the decency to appear embarrassed. "Roy is correct. By this morning the wand was radiating energy and the glow has increased in intensity, even since then."

"Are you insane, mate?" Roy gaped at Oliver in disbelief. "I already told you what happened."

"And now I've verified it."

"Oliver—" Matthew's scolding was interrupted by a buzzing from his jacket pocket.

When he fished out his phone, it was Dorothea's name that lit up the grey screen. Matthew nodded to Oliver, who inclined his head in understanding, then headed to the kitchen, shutting the door behind him.

"Hey, Dory. Whats up?"

"Matthew!" He was shocked at the distress in Dorothea's voice. "It's Alex!"

Still nauseous from the wand's energy, Matthew felt his stomach twist. "What do you mean? What's happened? Is he okay?" Visions of Felix Marek's men flashed unwelcomely through his mind.

"They say he's been arrested!" Dorothea's words tumbled out in a rush. "Where are you? Are you still with Oliver?"

"Wait! Who says he's been arrested? Where is he?" At least Alex sounded uninjured.

"I just had a call. They said he did something in Golebach. They wouldn't tell me what happened." Dorothea took a shuddering breath, and he wondered if she had been crying. "I need to see you. Are you at Oliver's?"

"I am with Oliver, yes." He couldn't exactly tell her the

truth. "It doesn't make sense though. Why would Alex be in Golebach? He was at his friend's right? Have you called them?" Matthew realised he had been pacing the floor of the little kitchen and stopped to breathe.

"I haven't. I phoned you straight away. Matthew, They had their full names, both of them. I couldn't speak to Alex— I tried, so it might not... I'll call Eira's mum, but I think it's true."

"Okay, you phone Eira's mother and see if he's there. I can make it back in three hours, and if it's true, we'll go down to Golebach and sort this out together. It's going to be okay." Relief at Alex's safety outweighed any other feelings, at least for now.

"No— listen. I'm going to come down to you," rustling sounded in the background, as though Dorothea was shoving clothing into a bag.

"But why would you come here?" It would make more sense for her to go to Golebach immediately without him. "I'll get down there as soon as possible and we'll go get Alex. Just sit tight." She must not be thinking straight.

"Matthew, he isn't in Golebach anymore! The police said someone came from the palace! They've taken them to Aedemeer!"

The palace. It was as though he had been doused in ice water. Matthew gripped the countertop, eyes passing over the sink opposite, again and again.

"Matthew?" He heard Dorothea's voice drift through the phone. "Are you still there? Matthew?"

"...Yes," he said weakly, sinking to the floor. "...Sorry. Are — are you sure?"

"It's just what I was told," she sounded quiet now. "I couldn't get much more, I'm sorry."

Thoughts wouldn't form, and all that came out was a sound of acknowledgement.

"I'm going to call Eira's house. I'll let you know what they say, but it's likely I'll be driving straight to you."

"Okay," Matthew coughed, his throat dry. "I'll meet you at Oliver's then."

The cabinet behind him was rough and uncomfortable, but Matthew closed his eyes. If the palace had Alex... It was a worse scenario than anything he had imagined. Looking back down at his phone, Matthew scrolled through the contacts until he found his son's number.

When he dialled it, it rang twice before clicking through to an automated answer phone. Off then. He tried twice more before returning the phone to his pocket and hoisting himself up from the floor.

The two men had gone back to to their drinks by the time Matthew returned.

"Matthew, what's wrong?" Concern creased Oliver's face, and he shot to his feet, but Matthew shook his head.

"We need to go. I'll tell you on the way."

Oliver gave a quick nod and turned to Roy. "We won't prevent you from leaving, but I would strongly suggest that you stay here until I return. For your own safety."

"Hey! What? You're going? Just like that?" Roy knelt up on the sofa, hanging over the back to get Oliver's attention. "What am I supposed to do?"

"I apologise, but an urgent matter has come up." Oliver grabbed a coat from where it hung by the door, slipping it over his suit jacket. "As I said, we will return as soon as possible, and I advise you stay in the safe house while we are away." He walked across to the table and Matthew noted the wand was once again wrapped in its cloth covering. "I'm ready when you are," Oliver said, slipping the weapon into an inner pocket of his coat.

"Ugh fine." Roy flopped back down onto the sofa, and Matthew saw him reach for the television remote as they walked out the door.

"And please treat my belongings with the care they deserve!" Oliver called back before shutting it behind them.

* * *

"Tell me what's happened." Oliver began as they left the house, hurrying to keep up with Matthew's pace.

"The palace has taken Alex. He's been arrested." Matthew kept his reply short, pounding his emotion into the pavement as he stormed down the road.

"What!" Oliver panted. "No! Why? How could they possibly—"

"We don't know," Matthew said. "We're meeting Dory at your place. Hopefully we can figure out what's going on," he sped up to a jog. "Maybe if I hadn't parked the damn car so far away, we could be there by now." Eyes pricking with heat, Matthew blinked to clear his vision, pushing away the thoughts of what could be happening to Alex.

"Matthew, slow down." The Tactician shrugged off his coat and swung it over his shoulder as he ran to catch up. "It's too hot for this," A flow of magic emanated from Oliver and the surrounding temperature dropped to a more comfortable level. "I know you're worried— I am too! But a few minutes is not going to make a difference. We need to get as much information as we can and think about this carefully."

Carefully... he'd been anything but careful recently.

"I've been so stupid!" Matthew ran a shaking hand through his hair, gripping it as he went. "How could I let myself believe... Why did I think things would be okay?" Tears blurred his sight, but he forced them away, swearing loudly.

Oliver placed a hand on his arm, "Everything could still be okay. I just need some more information and we'll make a plan to fix this. We've made it through everything we faced before."

Matthew wanted to lean in to the comfort his friend offered, but instead turned away, eyes fixed on the grey concrete under his feet. "I've put other people— My son is in danger because of me."

"You've not done anything wrong," Oliver's voice was firm and rang with a hint of anger that Matthew knew wasn't directed at him. "You never did anything wrong. Now, let's get to the car and come up with a plan."

CHAPTER 10

Sensation dripped through the dark of Alex's consciousness. His limbs were too heavy to move, so he didn't. Instead he lay still, eyes shut, adjusting to his continued existence. The surface he was lying on was soft. A bed? Memories half rose to the surface, slipping back into that inky void as he reached for them. If he'd made his way home, he had no recollection of how. Alex frowned as he tried to remember and, with that movement, realised he had the strength to open his eyes.

An unfamiliar ceiling swam into focus; high, with ornate patterns etched into its surface that cast small shadows in the natural light. He clenched his fingers and felt his limbs returning to his control. His head spun as he sat up, and he drew his knees to his chest, catching the scent of grass and dirt from his jeans. They were scratched and muddied... From where he had been knocked to the ground. A fragment of memory broke loose. He'd been at Golebach Court with Eira. Eira!

Alex lifted his head and scanned the sparsely furnished room. An empty desk sat between his narrow bed and a second bed, on which he could see Eira's motionless form. Legs not wanting to carry him, he stumbled across the room and collapsed beside her. She was lying on her back above the sheets, like she had been placed there, and Alex had the creeping realisation that he must have been placed on the other bed in much the same way. At least she was breathing and appeared uninjured, but she didn't stir when he called her name, or even when he shook her.

The explosion. Alex remembered it now. He had tried to shield them both, but from there his memories fractured. A grey room. Cold. Someone speaking to him, but the face or the words wouldn't come.

They must have been taken to a hospital, but it was the strangest one he'd ever seen. Through an open door next to Eira's bed, he glimpsed a small bathroom. The other door, opposite the bed he woke up in, must therefore lead to the rest of the building.

Alex eased his way over and tried the handle. It didn't budge when he pushed it and reaching for his magic only caused another wave of dizziness. Why were they locked in? It didn't make sense. He jiggled the handle again and considered calling for help, but something held him back.

Daylight streamed through large windows that rose almost as high as the extravagant ceiling. How long had it been? The view beyond showed further windows like his own and, moving closer, Alex saw that the building curved around an elaborate patio, descending down to a manicured lawn. Pressing his face against the cool glass expanded his view to where the lawn became gardens, lined with styled hedgerows and scattered fountains. From the height of his room compared to the windows opposite, Alex estimated he must be around three floors up.

"Alex?" The voice made him startle. He turned to see Eira sitting up in the bed and hurried to her side. "Alex! You're awake." She hugged him tight. "I was so worried."

"What do you mean?" Alex said. "What happened? Where are we?" Eira released him, but didn't respond to his questions. "I remember an explosion, but… are you okay?"

"You don't remember anything?"

Alex shook his head. "Nothing. Just pieces."

She pulled away, shrugging off the hand Alex placed on her arm.

"What is it?" he asked. "Are you okay?"

"Fine," Eira replied, though her voice seemed to catch. After a pause, she continued. "I thought… After the generator exploded, you wouldn't wake up. I was calling and shaking you and the ground was all burnt, and the healing I tried wouldn't take." She was speaking so fast, Alex found it hard to follow. "When they found us, they asked me what happened. And what was I supposed to say?" When she raised her head, her eyes were rimmed red; irises their true, un-illusioned hazel.

"I didn't know anything," Eira continued. "I couldn't explain why we were there, or what happened. I thought — I thought you were…." Guilt settled in Alex's chest as he pictured it. "The police told me later it was magic sickness. From where you had shielded the explosion."

"I'm really sorry," Alex said. "I didn't think—"

"Of course you didn't think! You never think. What about your future?"

His future? Alex looked at the room again, gaze drifting to the locked door. Someone could have been hurt. Eira could have been hurt in that blast. And if he had killed someone? They were supposed to be heading to university, but now...

"I dragged you into this," Alex leaned towards her. "I'll tell them. It was me who caused the explosion; it had nothing to do with you. Your university will understand. I'll make sure they do."

"Alex, you're such an idiot," Eira spat and Alex recoiled. "You never pay attention to anything outside your own head!" A tear escaped onto her cheek, and she furiously rubbed it away. "I don't want to go to Beiriant. I don't want to be a healer."

"What? But you've always talked—" Alex cut himself off. In their countless conversations about university, had she ever said she wanted to heal? "But you're so talented." He ended weakly.

"Yeah," Eira's gaze fell to her hands. "How can I turn around and say I don't want to do it? What kind of person doesn't want to help people?" She turned away as though not wanting him to see her face. "It would be a waste if I don't go. There are few enough healers already. It's prestigious." They were all reasons Alex had heard before; one's he'd even said himself. "Even in Golebach, at least I knew something. I could try to help you. It's just..."

Alex placed a hesitant hand on her shoulder and patted. Eira crying was as surreal as waking up in a locked room.

Eira gave a choked laugh. "Nice attempt there." Alex was relieved to hear her tone had softened.

"You shouldn't have to go if you don't want to," Alex

said. "People probably don't care as much as you think, anyway." He went to move his hand away, but Eira placed hers on top, accepting the comfort despite her words. "I should have realised something was wrong."

She squeezed his fingers then released him. "Don't worry about it, I should know you well enough by now," her eyes were still red but at least she was smiling.

"Do you know where we are?" Alex stretched his arms, a twinge of pain flaring through his wrist. "I'm wondering if I should be more concerned about waking up in a strange place with no memory, but this seems kinda unthreatening," he gestured vaguely at the room. "Door's locked though. Manually, at least. I haven't got the strength to check for magic."

Eira got up and placed her hand on the dark wood of the door. "Yeah, some type of magic lock. Not quite so pleasant when you're a prisoner." Alex had to agree.

"It's huge though, isn't it. Too fancy for a hospital, surely?" He walked back over to the window, Eira joining him. "You can't see much from here, but it doesn't look like we are anywhere near Golebach."

"We're not," Eria replied. "Alex, this is the palace."

"What?" Alex spun around. "It can't be. Why would anyone want to take us there? Aren't we basically criminals?"

"That's just it. When we were at the police station, there was a woman there. She said she was Head of Magic or something." Eira's eyes narrowed in thought. "I remember she was there when we were taken to a car, but..." She trailed off, lost in thought.

"Wait. This woman told you she was taking us to the palace? Did she say why?" For the first time since he'd awoken, Alex truly considered his situation. Far from home, without any idea if his parents knew what had happened. The locked room suddenly seemed preferable to facing their reaction.

"That cow! She sleep spelled me!" Eira's sudden outburst made him jump. "I wouldn't have just fallen asleep in a car and not noticed being moved. I can't even— That's so illegal!" She left the window and began to pace the room, fuming.

"Err... if she works for the palace, then she's probably above the law," Alex replied. Shrinking away from the glare Eira shot his way.

"That's not the point! I can't believe I didn't even notice it happen."

"Well yeah, that's why it's not allowed. No one notices until it's too late, your brain just thinks it's tired."

Sleep spells were useless in a fight; easy to resist when full of adrenaline and anticipating an attack. But sitting comfortably? Unsuspecting? Noticing the spell isn't enough once the target's thoughts are too fuzzy to defend themselves.

"I'm going to the bathroom." Eira stalked to the door by her bed, slamming it shut behind her. Pipes groaned as a tap turned on and Alex licked his lips, trying to recall the last time he had drunk anything.

A sharp rap on the door startled Alex from his thoughts. Before he could react, it opened, and a woman entered, followed by a tall man dressed in, what he assumed to be, the uniform of a palace guard. Eyeing them warily, he got to his feet.

The woman stood a whole head shorter than him, with wide, brown eyes that gave her a youthful appearance, despite her formal office attire. Black ringlets hung in disarray to her shoulders and the memory of the grey room nudged again at his mind.

Food smells wafted from the tray the guard carried, and Alex's stomach growled as it was set on the table between the beds. After a bow of his head to the woman, the guard departed, closing the door behind him. Whoever she was, she seemed unconcerned about being left alone.

"Hi, how are you feeling?" Her smile was disarmingly warm, though Alex noticed she wouldn't meet his eyes. Instead, she walked over to the tray and began unloading the items. "It's good to see you awake. I thought you must both be hungry, so I arranged for some food," she glanced back in his direction. "Is your friend okay?"

"She's— she's fine. Yeah. Just in the bathroom." Alex inclined his head towards the bathroom door. Now she was closer, the magic aura of a strong mage radiated from the woman's presence. "I'm sorry, but who are you?"

"Sorry. I'm Tamara," she lifted her hand in a small wave, before returning to the tray. "We did meet in Golebach, but I suppose you don't remember. Here, would you like a drink?"

Alex gratefully accepted the glass of water and settled back onto the bed. If she meant to harm him, he reasoned, there had already been ample opportunity.

"Please, help yourself to anything here," Tamara continued. She pulled out the desk chair and sat down, though Alex noted she left a sizeable distance between them. He didn't remember her, but he didn't remember much of anything right now.

"Are you the one who brought us here?" Alex ventured the question just as the bathroom door opened.

No trace of tears remained on Eira's face as she entered the room. Her hair was back to a powder blue with eyes illusioned to match, and Tamara's smile froze as Eira turned on her.

"It's you!" Her expression was as frosty as her eyes. "You realise it's illegal to sleep spell someone? I don't care if you do work for the government."

"I can assure you that I read all the guidelines to my role before taking it," Tamara's seemed calm, though she was rubbing her fingers together in her lap. "I don't believe I am prohibited from using a sleep spell, in light of the circumstances, though I apologise that it caused you distress."

The shift to formal speech seemed almost rehearsed, and Alex wondered if Tamara had been anticipating a backlash. It was more surprising that she cared at all. His father had always expressed scathing views of the government.

Eira didn't appear to know how to respond. Arms folded across her chest, a brief silence fell over the three of them before she continued. "You could at least tell us why we're here."

"Yes, I should explain," Tamara nodded. "Do you want a drink?"

"I'm fine." Eira's reply was short, though she consented to sit beside Alex on the bed.

Tamara looked between them. "I was called to investigate the incident at Golebach, because the police suspected there was magic involved. I'm Head of Magical Affairs now, so it falls under my jurisdiction."

She said her title like it was nothing, and Alex wasn't convinced he had heard correctly until he made eye contact with Eira, who mouthed, "I told you," at him.

"I wasn't going to get involved in the case more than to advise, but when I spoke with you, Alex, you mentioned something about magic that made no sense to me. I was unable to get you to clarify what you meant, and didn't want to risk losing you in the system, so I decided to bring you here. You aren't under arrest, by the way. I just need to keep you until I figure out what's going on." Tamara smiled, but Alex didn't relax.

"It doesn't exactly seem like we're allowed to leave," Eira said pointedly.

"I believe there is a technical definition of 'under arrest'," Tamara replied. As if the explanation was at all helpful. "We're on government property. You must see that you could be a risk. I can't exactly let you go wandering around unsupervised."

"You can't just keep us here!"

Tamara flinched at Eira's words, and her expression changed to one of annoyance. "I think I can actually," she appeared to be running out of patience and Alex didn't consider it wise to forget that they were speaking with a government official. "If you weren't here, it's still unlikely you would be free to go. You were both involved in a magical attack on public property and I'm trying to do my best with the situation."

"What is it I said that made no sense?" Alex interjected. Maybe if he could clear up the confusion now, then they would be able to go home and no one would ever have to know about this.

It had the desired effect. When she replied, the frustration was gone from Tamara's voice. "You talked about magic in the ground. That was apparently the reason you were there?"

It wasn't the question Alex had expected. "Yeah," he nodded enthusiastically, hoping this would at least absolve them of malicious intent. "It wasn't a bomb or anything, it's a generator. I made it to turn magic to electricity. I hoped I could tap into the magical energy at Golebach Court to power the machine, but I guess it overloaded," Alex grimaced; the loss of his machine still stung. "I honestly had no idea that would happen."

Tamara's brow furrowed as he finished recounting the events. "You say you felt magic at the site? Do you mean some kind of spell?"

"No," Alex blinked in confusion. "Nothing like that. More like it was just there. It didn't have anything it was supposed to do," now that he thought about it, he had never encountered magic energy without a readable purpose before. "Didn't you go there?"

"I did, yes," Tamara confirmed, "But I didn't notice magic there at all." She turned to Eira. "Did you feel it too?"

Alex caught his breath, hoping for confirmation, but Eira only gave him an apologetic look. "I'm sorry, I didn't sense magic there either."

Was he going mad? Dismissing the experience would be easy, but then he remembered the explosion and the rush of magic that had overwhelmed him. "There had to be something, though! Otherwise, how would my machine have drawn on it?"

Tamara made a sound of agreement. "Yes. I'd have dismissed what you told me in Golebach if there wasn't such firm evidence for it. The earthquake and damage in the town can't possibly have been caused by two teenagers acting under their own power," she rubbed a thumb over her other hand as she spoke. "I know there must be some explanation, but so far you're the only one who has experienced anything."

Eira was looking at him as though she wanted him to provide the answers, but he was at a loss.

"Do you think you could explain more what this magic felt like?" Tamara's question was gentle and Alex's fears calmed.

"Yeah..." He closed his eyes and breathed, trying to recapture the sensation he had experienced in Golebach. Instinctively, he reached out his magic sense and to his surprise, found a rush of response. Cool energy flowed against his own power, exactly as he had felt at the ruins. Heavy and comforting, Alex realised it had been there since he woke up, he'd just been too exhausted to notice.

"It's here," Alex snapped his eyes open. "I can feel it here, just the same. You just need to reach out and you'll notice it."

Concern met his eager declaration. "You feel the magic here too?" Tamara's tone was neutral, but Alex knew she was sceptical.

"It is here," Alex looked back to his friend. "Eira, you can feel it, right?"

"I can't Alex, I'm trying, but I don't feel anything."

"Could this be something that you can sense everywhere, Alex?" Tamara's question made him pause, but he shook his head.

"I don't think so. I'd never felt it before Golebach, and its not been anywhere else apart from now," There'd been no trace of the magic when he had gone home after visiting Golebach Court with his father, so it wasn't some recent change to his perception. "I don't know why I can feel it, I just know it's there."

Tamara was looking out the window, and Alex wasn't sure she had even been listening, but then she got up, sliding her chair back under the desk. "I'm going to see if I can find any information on what you are experiencing. Unfortunately, that means you'll both have to stay here a little longer." His disappointment must have shown, as she stepped towards him, eyes finally meeting his with surprising warmth. "Please, don't worry. I'm sure it won't take long. Can I trust you if I leave the tray of food here?"

Alex didn't know what risk he would pose with a tray, but he also didn't care. Seemingly unphased by his lack of reply, Tamara nodded. "I'm going to figure this out. It's going to be okay." As she left the room, he caught a glimpse of the guard still stationed outside.

"I don't trust her," Eira stated once they were alone.

The bed creaked as he flopped backwards, flinging an arm over his eyes. "I don't know. I kind of do." He reached out with his magic again, sensing the strange energy flow to meet him. It seemed so real, but he wasn't sure he could trust his own mind. "Maybe I'm just going crazy."

Even if he was, there was nothing to do now but wait.

Chapter 11

"It's like you don't even live here." Matthew sat at the edge of the beige sofa, not risking harm to the soft material. Being on his feet had soothed his nerves until, apparently tired of the relentless pacing, Oliver had ordered him to stop wearing through the carpet.

"At least sit properly," his exasperated Tactician entered from the kitchen. "How many times have you been here? You ought to know by now the purpose of a sofa." He pressed a glass of water into Matthew's hand. "I'm going to go upstairs and make some calls. Will you be fine down here alone?"

"Yeah. I'll give you a shout when Dory arrives."

Once his friend was out of sight, Matthew set the drink

on the glass coffee table and fished his phone from his pocket. Still no answer from Alex; the only call he'd received since the news was from Dorothea confirming she was on her way. He hovered a thumb over the call button, wondering if he should try again, or maybe check with Dory to see how far away she was. Instead, he clicked the button on the side, sending the screen black, and placed the phone down beside the glass.

An almost unnaturally well-behaved child, Alex had never been the type to get himself in trouble. As for something criminal... Matthew couldn't think of any reason why his son would be involved, other than by mistake. Of course, searching for a valid reason was just a futile effort to drive away his actual concern.

The sound of an engine alerted him to a car pulling into the driveway, and Matthew threw himself to his feet, knocking his shin painfully against the table on his way to the door. Dorothea's little car was parked next to his own, and her face flooded with relief as she ran to meet him. He hugged her tight, her presence soothing the nerves that had been building since their phone call.

"Did you have things to bring in?" Matthew asked without letting go.

"Later," Dorothea replied. "It's not important right now."

He led her to the living room, but stopped at the door. "I'm going to tell Oliver you made it." He gave her hand a reassuring squeeze and headed to the stairs.

Previous visits had left him with an intimate knowledge of the house. Even so, Matthew never felt comfortable going into his friend's office. The door was shut, faint conversation audible through the wood, and he hesitated before giving a light knock. There was a brief shuffling before it opened, and Oliver poked his head through the gap, barely hiding the rows of stacked bookcases that lined every wall.

"Dory's here," Matthew stated. "Just wanted to let you know."

Oliver nodded. "Just give me a few moments; I'll come right down."

Returning to the living room, Matthew couldn't help a small smile when he saw Dorothea sat on the edge of the sofa. At the sight of him she stood, but he waved her back down.

"Ollie never changes," Dorothea scooted across so he could sit beside her. "I never feel presentable enough, no matter how many times I come here."

"I told him the same thing," Matthew replied. "Though, to be fair, it's actually quite comfy once you get past the beige." They both fell quiet, small talk not hiding the tension.

"Did you hear any more?" Matthew said, finally breaking the heavy silence.

"Nothing more than what I said on the phone," she shook her head. "I just can't understand it. Alex would never get in trouble with the law. Let alone something serious enough that the palace would be involved! Besides, he had Eira with him."

Footsteps on the stairs announced Oliver's approach, and Dorothea got up, sweeping him into a hug as he entered the room. "Ollie. It's good to see you."

Oliver appeared to stiffen at the unexpected touch, but his smile was warm. "Apologies for not greeting you when you first arrived. The calls proved fruitful, however; I found some more information as to what happened in Golebach."

"What did you find?" Matthew got up, unable to hide his impatience. "Is he okay?"

"I believe so. At least, no major injuries were reported." Oliver's expression was serious, but held none of the agitation Matthew felt. "The phone call Dorothea received was accurate, though. Alex and Eira have been taken into custody at the palace. By the Head of Magical Affairs." Fear jolted through Matthew's body, but Oliver continued before he could speak. "It's being claimed they performed a magic attack on Golebach Court."

"A magic attack?" Dorothea repeated the words as Matthew processed them. Confusing emotions muddled his thoughts; relief mixed with shock and doubt.

"Indeed." Oliver nodded. "I was able to confirm reports of an explosion at the manor, with minor damage around the village itself. The local police seem to believe they had some kind of bomb."

"No, that's ridiculous!" Dorothea exclaimed. "Why would he want to attack a building? Wasn't he only there with you the day before?" She turned to Matthew, whose blood ran cold. Alex's distance since their conversation at the ruins – he should have paid closer attention.

"This supposed bomb, Oliver," he turned to his friend, words spilling out in a rush. "Did they say any more about it? What it looked like?"

A frown flashed across Oliver's face. "No, it seems like it was destroyed in the explosion."

Beside him, he saw Dorothea's eyes widen as she caught up with his own thoughts. "You're not thinking it was that machine he's been working on?" Her face was frozen in horror, and Matthew imagined he looked much the same. "I don't know if he took it — I never thought to check!"

"His generator?" Oliver's skin had blanched and Matthew remembered he would have seen it during Alex's visit; when he'd stayed here before his interview at the university. The scolding he'd given Oliver about it in the tea shop seemed a lifetime away. "I should have considered— But why would he have taken it to Golebach?"

Matthew sank back down onto the sofa and Dorothea followed his lead, settling beside him, her warmth a welcome comfort against his body. Oliver took the seat opposite.

"I- I think it could be because of me," he began, as the weight of the room's attention turn to him. "When we were there, at Golebach Court, Alex spoke to me about the generator. He said the university had loved it; that he'd recently used it to power a concert, but I..." He clenched his hands, the fear he'd felt that day a cruel irony. "I told him it needed more work. That it used too much of his magic for it to be worthwhile."

He hadn't thought much of it at the time. Too caught up in his own feelings and Alex's disappointment to notice his son showing the same fascination with the ruin as he felt himself. The fact they were right there when Alex mentioned his invention.

"Of course he would have thought to use the natural magic there to try and boost the power."

Dorothea put an arm around his shoulders, leaning close. "You couldn't know he would try that, It's not your fault." Despite her own lack of magic, he always appreciated how hard she worked to be supportive of Alex's interest. The words would have helped, but the shocked expression on Oliver's face was giving him pause.

"I'm afraid I don't follow, Matthew," Oliver hesitated, as though afraid he would offend. "You said 'natural magic' as though I should understand, but there isn't— I've never heard of such a thing."

Matthew's brow furrowed in confusion. "You do know. It's at most of the historic sites, remember? The heavy energy in the ground?" His words were met with a blank stare, and Matthew's frustration built. "We've talked about this, I know we have! It's the feeling like back— back home." Even after all this time, he had never encountered a stronger source of the magic than at the palace.

"I always assumed that your passion for history was due to... nostalgia," Oliver was clearly being careful of his words, mindful of Dorothea's presence in the room. "I didn't consider that the feeling was literal."

Matthew started to reply, but noticed the subtle change in Oliver's expression indicating a mental conversation. With luck, Ewen would offer them an explanation. Instead, he turned to Dorothea, who shrugged. "You know this kind of thing is lost on me."

Matthew rested his head against her shoulder, apprehension beginning to turn his stomach.

"Matthew," There was a quaver in Oliver's voice when he spoke again. "We might have a problem."

The nausea he had been trying to suppress rose stronger, and he dug his nails into his palm to ground himself. "What? Tell me?"

Oliver's eyes flickered over to Dorothea, but he spoke anyway. "I just remembered a conversation I had with Ewen on the phone," The alternative truth flowed with practiced ease. "People... Ordinary people don't sense natural magic in the ground. It's not something that should exist."

Heat rushed to Matthew's face, "I'm not crazy, Oliver."

"I wasn't implying that you were," he was drumming his fingers against his knee. "It shouldn't exist, however, it's not completely unheard of. How much Ardveldian mythology do you remember?"

Matthew blinked. "Enough," it wasn't likely he could have grown up in the palace without being made aware of it, but he trusted Oliver had a good reason for asking. "The original Royal Champions, right? Where they apparently came from?"

The history of Ardveld's Royal family was more myth than truth; the mechanics of the spell that bound Oliver and himself, lost to time. Its function, however, was common knowledge. Even those born since Morgan's takeover knew about the Royal Champions. Guardian, Tactician, Spy, Friend; at least, as they were commonly known. After the monarch, the awoken Champions had been the strongest mages in the country; a power that once passed on after their death to the next chosen. It was the only known instance of a mage's innate power level increasing and, if the legends could be believed, of non-mages gaining magic.

"No," Oliver's reply shocked Matthew from his thoughts. "This is earlier than that. It wouldn't surprise me if you don't remember. I'd forgotten it myself." Again, he hesitated, as if seeking permission to continue.

"It's fine, Oliver. Go on." Despite the protest in his heart, Matthew didn't want to send Dorothea away. They'd find some way to explain it if she asked.

"Before the Champions, back to the first King, writers of the time claimed his right to rule came from a connection with the land. At least, the mythology states that Ardveld was formed from magic itself, and that the ancestors of the Royal line literally shaped the country into what we see today." He waved a hand as if to gesture at the world around them. "Of course, it's a tidy explanation for Ardveld's natural defences. Bordered by sea or mountains on all sides; a concentration of magic users not seen anywhere else in the world. You can see why early Ardveldians might have claimed their country was created with magic."

Dorothea shifted beside him. "Please Oliver, I know you wouldn't waste time, but what has this got to do with Alex?" She sounded pained and Matthew experienced a stab of guilt. "Are you saying Ardveld really is made of magic? That's what Alex and Matthew are feeling?"

Oliver opened his mouth, closing it again wordlessly, as Dorothea's words began to process through Matthew's mind.

"People in Golebach claim there was an earthquake, Matthew." Oliver began after a moment. "Caused by magic. I didn't consider it overly important, but when you mentioned the energy you felt... There's only one reason I can think of that only the two of you feel it."

"Ardveld doesn't have earthquakes," Matthew's voice cracked, and he sunk his head into his hands. It was rubbish. It had to be. Just a made-up story to explain Ardveld's convenient geography. But the ground had moved. Moved enough that the palace had taken an interest.

He'd never thought about the natural magic until he'd left the palace; never noticed it until he felt its absence, and he had more than enough of his own power to ever consider trying to use it. If anyone else in his family could sense it, Matthew had never asked. Not that his father had been the type to answer questions.

"If you could figure that out, what's stopping someone else?" Matthew's words were muffled by his palms. "Alex has no reason to hide why he was there. They're going to find out!" He raised his head to lock eyes with Oliver, speaking much louder than he'd intended.

"That's exactly my concern," Oliver's tapping had stopped, and his fingers were pale where they gripped his knee.

Dorothea's voice cut through Matthew's panic. "Will you please tell me what's going on. Alex is my son!"

Matthew froze. From the corner of his eye he saw Oliver lean forward to begin an explanation, but the words died as Matthew held up a hand. "There... there's something I need to tell you, Dory."

Oliver's eyes widened, but then he stood. "Think I'd better make another cup of tea." He gave Matthew a nod before leaving the room.

Silence stretched out between them that Matthew searched for the courage to break. Dory beat him to it.

"I've never asked," she began. "I knew you would tell me if you ever felt you could; but I'm not stupid Matthew. Did you two really think you didn't stick out when you first came to Couden? It was like you'd never been around real people before. Your clothes, the way you spoke, It was lucky I was there to jump in before Oliver had the whole pub staring at him!"

Matthew uncurled, Dorothea's hand gentle on his back. "I guessed you were both probably from one of the old magic families," she continued. "I can't imagine you were the only ones hiding out, what with the deaths and disappearances. I know you're scared, but... it's me. I knew what I was getting in to."

"It's not— It wasn't," Matthew stumbled over the words. "It wasn't just an old magic family." His breathing felt shallow. "I— Oliver and I. We came from the palace."

"From the palace?" Dorothea leant forward, gaze burning into the side of his face. "You worked for the Royal family?"

"No. Not exactly. Sort of." This conversation was not

going the way he had planned it in his head. "Oliver did. I—My parents," he choked over the word, it sounding alien in his mouth. "My father was King Samuel."

The silence that followed was not quite the reaction he had expected. Dorothea hadn't moved and Matthew looked up in concern, worried that she hadn't heard.

"That doesn't make sense, Matthew." She moved her hand from his back, leaving a cold imprint in its absence. "Everyone there died."

Her words splintered through his heart. "Oliver got us out." An image from that night flashed through his mind, but Matthew forced it away. "We were the only ones."

"No, stop," Dorothea had pulled away completely now, regarding him with an almost horrified disbelief. "You can't be. If the King was your father that would... but that would make you—"

"I'm sorry. I should have told you." He wished it wasn't true; that he could take it back and stop her looking at him the way she was.

"I don't believe it. You can't seriously expect me to believe you are the Prince of Ardveld." She shook her head slowly, as if trying to convince herself the conversation wasn't happening.

"You said yourself that we obviously didn't belong when we met," Matthew wasn't sure how he could convince her. He hadn't anticipated he would need to.

"What does that make Oliver then? Your servant?!"

"Oliver Venlare. High Lord of Operational Strategy," Matthew smiled grimly as he realised he'd now known Oliver longer by his chosen surname of Griffin than by his birth name. "That would be his official title. He's my Tactician. The last of the Royal Champions."

Dorothea threw herself to her feet, backing away from him. "No. No, that's not... Oh no! Alex!" She put a hand to her mouth and Matthew saw the same realisation dawn on her face that he had experienced earlier. "He's in the palace!"

"I know! I'm going to fix this, I promise. I'm going to get him back," he got up, holding out his hands, speaking all the assurances he had wanted to hear himself. "It's going to be okay—"

"None of this is okay, Matthew," she snarled, panic turning to anger in an instant. "I can't believe you! You never thought I had a right to know? He's my child!" The back of Matthew's legs hit the coffee table as he retreated. "When were you going to tell me? Never?"

"I was! It's just— It was never the right time."

"When exactly is the right time? Were you going to do a nice candlelit dinner?" Matthew flinched. "Oh, how about when your son gets arrested and taken to the fucking palace! He could be killed, Matthew!"

"You think I don't know that!" Matthew's volume rose to meet hers. "You don't think that's why I never told you? Why I never told anyone?" He clenched his teeth until it hurt. "I just wanted you both safe."

"I'm sorry. I need a moment." Dorothea swept past him towards the kitchen, leaving Matthew standing alone. He sank down to the ground, head against his knees. Then he slammed his fist into the floor hard.

* * *

The light was fading when Matthew found himself alone in Oliver's kitchen. The windows of the houses opposite reflected a vivid sunset that stained the tidy lawn red. A mug of tea sat cold and untouched on the work surface beside him, but he didn't move until soft footsteps approached from the hall.

"Hey."

Matthew turned when he heard Dorothea's voice, apprehension tempering the relief he felt at her presence. She was leaning against the doorframe watching him, a fluffy dressing gown hugged close to her body, over her day clothes.

"Oliver's sorted the bedrooms for us." Dory continued. Then she walked over to look out of the window beside him. "This isn't exactly how it goes in the fairy tales." He gave a choked laugh in response and, at the sound, she wrapped her arms around him, resting against his back as they watched the setting sun. "I'm sorry. I'm sorry about what happened. It must have been so hard."

"...Yeah." Matthew's heart had begun to pound. Blood clouding the water. Oliver dragging him away. Each image threatened to obscure his view of the present and suck him back into that moment; Dorothea's weight against him his only tether to reality. He took a steadying breath. After twenty-three years he had hoped the memories would fade, but they were always there, lurking under the surface.

"Do... Do you know how Morgan did it?" Dorothea voiced the question that Matthew, Oliver and countless others had wondered since that day. The strongest magic users in the country, all slain by their Velbian guests with hardly a mage among them. It shouldn't have been possible.

"No. I wasn't there. Inside, I mean." A shudder dispersed the last of the memories. "No one knows." He turned around to face Dorothea, who hung her head.

"I'm sorry, I shouldn't have asked."

"It's okay." Matthew brushed over the hair that framed her face, resting his fingers on her cheek. "It doesn't bother me anymore."

"They were your family," Dorothea replied, and Matthew tilted her chin up until she met his eyes. "I should have understood why you were scared."

"No," Matthew dismissed her apology. "I should have told you. Should have been there more for you both. I was just... I've been so stupid." Dorothea reached up to his hand, lacing her fingers between his own. "You're my family, Dory. You and Alex, and Oliver. That's all I need." He brought his head down until their foreheads touched and he could feel the rise and fall of her breathing. "I'll bring him back safe. I promise." Matthew closed his eyes. "I lo—" he began, but was cut off by Dorothea's lips pressing softly against his own. Forgetting words, he wrapped his arms around her and held her close.

Chapter 12

The words in the heavy textbook blurred as Tamara's body gave in to fatigue. Her mage light flickered from where it floated above the wide, heavy table, and she sent another burst of focussed energy to steady it. Even the shield that she always ran against her skin had become too much effort to maintain. Long empty, the cosy isolation of her favourite corner of the palace library had kept her far longer than intended, but getting up to leave seemed more exhausting that simply curling up in the chair.

With a yawn, Tamara closed the book and added it to the growing pile of discarded tomes. Her first assignment in this role and she was getting nowhere. Worse, she had promised

Alex she would find answers. After speaking with him properly, Tamara was confident her instincts in Golebach were correct; the explosion was an accident, and they deserved to go home. That, however, required proof.

An echoing creak jolted her alert. Tamara snapped her head up to look, but a row of bookcases blocked the view of the library's tall double doors. After a moment, the bright glare of an electric bulb flared into life near the entrance, causing her to squint as the shelves turned to silhouette.

Pins and needles shot down her legs as she unfurled them. Ignoring the discomfort, Tamara let the mage light die and headed back towards the entrance, mindful of the sound of her steps on the hardwood floor. She hadn't expected anyone to arrive at this time of night, and curiosity outweighed her desire to avoid an interaction.

The entrance to the library was an open foyer, with a wide sweeping staircase that led to further rows of shelves. A man came into view as she approached, standing in front of the framed map that showed the layout and literature sections of the two floors. Tall and slim, there was a sheen of red to his slick brown hair, and for a second Tamara thought it was Morgan. Then he turned towards her and she realised why.

"Who's there?" Aiden Heliodor's smooth voice sounded exceptionally confident for someone surprised in the dark. Tamara stepped into the open, deciding that that any chance of escaping notice had long passed. Though she had only met him briefly, Aiden had seemed friendly enough in Morgan's office and she wondered if he would remember her.

"Tamara?" A smile broke across his handsome features. "Apologies if I startled you; I didn't anticipate company this evening." His words seemed unnaturally loud in the towering space, the bright light from the chandelier above the entrance spotlighting them as the rows of bookcases faded into shadow.

"Please, don't worry." She returned the smile, suddenly conscious of her crumpled clothes and obvious exhaustion. "I really should have left hours ago." For his part Aiden showed no sign of weariness, crisp shirt and grey blazer as fresh as his face. At least he didn't seem offended by her approach.

"Again then, your timing has proved lucky for me," Aiden crossed the space towards her. There was an amused spark in his eyes, and Tamara looked away in embarrassment as she remembered her unwelcome intrusion to Morgan's office. "I'm thrilled we finally have a chance to speak properly."

"Oh," wariness tinged her voice before she could hide it. People weren't usually pleased to see her and she wondered what motive Aiden had for his flattering words. "It's nice to talk to you again as well." She pulled her jacket tight against her chest, wishing she had changed into something more comfortable than office-wear. It seemed colder here, away from the warmth she had cultivated in her corner, and she briefly considered casting a spell for heat.

"It's a shame we didn't meet sooner. If you were still in Vailberg I would never miss the opportunity to add such a prominent magical researcher to my team. I admit though, my loss is clearly Ardveld's gain."

Relief flooded through her at the mention of work and Tamara latched onto the subject, choosing to pretend her mind hadn't considered some other reasons for his interest. Physically, Aiden posed no threat, but even she wasn't naïve enough to discount his position.

"Are you here regarding your own research?" Her

hurried question saved her from dwelling further on the praise. "The librarians all left for the evening, but I might be able to help you find what you are looking for. I've spent a lot of time in here since coming to Ardveld."

"Perhaps you can," Aiden studied her, his amusement replaced by a passing displeasure that vanished as swiftly as she noticed it. "It has been some time since my last visit and there is only so much I am able to source remotely. I'm looking for unusual symbols; very old and uniquely Ardveldian."

Back at the university, Tamara had rarely paid attention to anything outside her own field of magical efficiency. Still, she should have remembered Aiden's own prowess as a researcher. Studying magic without any power of his own, the academic achievements of Vailberg's prince were exceptional, even if he hadn't been Arch Canlaw Kaylee's son. His business, Sunstone Enterprises, was successful enough to have financed the projects of many of her contemporaries at its private research centre.

"Could you tell me what they look like?" Now that she thought about it, she could have seen something during her frantic searching for information on the ground magic. Half the Ardveldian history section must be stacked at her desk.

"I can do one better," White teeth flashed as his smile returned, and Tamara caught the perfumed scent of his clothes as he moved closer. "Though you will have to forgive me for boring you with a work discussion." Aiden reached into the inner pocket of his blazer and pulled out a small, leather-bound notebook, marked throughout by coloured flaps of paper.

"I don't mind at all," Tamara shook her head, using the movement as an excuse to regain some distance. "It sounds fascinating."

"It certainly is. Though I am sure any researcher would feel the same about their own subject of interest."

Aiden flipped the little book open and Tamara could see each page held a hand drawn symbol, precisely inscribed, with notes below that seemed to explain a meaning or purpose. Each followed a similar pattern, fine lines that ended with circles, and Tamara was sure she had seen something similar before.

"They relate to the original magic of Ardveld," Aiden explained. "Perhaps used side by side with what we know today as passive spells. Or even used in their place." He traced a finger over the symbol on the page. "I am yet to determine their full capabilities, but I can assure you, nothing anyone is working on right now could come close to the importance of what I am about to discover."

Tamara caught her breath as Aiden looked down at her, the blue of his eyes almost black in the shadowed light. Arrogant perhaps, but there was a passion to his words that made her believe them.

"I think I might have seen one, yes." She remembered now. "I have the book out already. Just over at my table."

There was a dull snap as Aiden closed the notebook and slid it back into his inner pocket. With it went the intensity of the moment, and the air seemed to lighten as Tamara's breathing returned to normal. Turning away, she jumped at the touch of a hand on her back.

"Please, lead on." Aiden's voice was uncomfortably close, and she darted forward, inciting a chuckle in response.

Without the magelight to illuminate it, the table in the corner was dark. Tamara conjured a new one, catching Aiden watching her as she focused her will on the growing light.

"I think there was something in here. Typical it would be

at the bottom." Tamara began to disassemble her book tower, feeling some more of the tension ease now she had something to occupy her hands.

"Ardveldian history. Not something I would have expected anyone else to be reading at three in the morning," Aiden gave a conspiratorial wink as she handed the book across. "Don't make me regret not recruiting you even more."

"Three! I hadn't realised it was so late." Tamara exclaimed. No wonder she had been flagging.

"Time gets away from us all when we're having fun, will I be seeing you at the dinner tomorrow evening? Or rather, this evening, considering the time."

"Oh, yes." She had been so occupied with Alex and Eira that she had forgotten the formal celebrations were so close. That must be why Aiden was in Ardveld after all. The private dinner, and a public garden party the day after; every Ardveldian official would be at the anniversary events, along with quite a few Velbian representatives of various degrees of importance. It wasn't something she was particularly looking forward to, though having a friendly face to talk with would help. "I should definitely be there." Hopefully Morgan wouldn't find the time to ask about her progress on the case.

"Excellent!" Aiden tucked her book under his arm. "In that case, I look forward to some intriguing discussions."

He turned to walk away just as an idea sparked in Tamara's mind.

"I— Sorry, I should have asked before," she scrambled to re-stack her book pile and chased the few steps after him. "Speaking of old Ardveldian magic. I don't suppose you know of any kind of natural magic? Some way magic could exist on its own, without a purpose?"

Aiden stopped walking and turned back towards her. "Why do you ask?" There was no charm in his expression, but Tamara could tell she had caught his attention.

"It doesn't make much sense, I know. Magic is tied to a mage's life force, I've never heard of any other source. It's just, I'm working on a case and something's not adding up." Tamara was regretting mentioning it already. Saying it out loud made the discussion with Alex seem even more ridiculous.

"Tell me." The command made her palms prick with sweat.

"There was a magic... incident. In Golebach," she hurried to explain, Aiden's frown making her feel as though she was being interrogated. "An ancient site was damaged. I spoke to some... some witnesses when I was there, and one said that they had felt a kind of magic from the ground." Willingly bringing suspected criminals into the security of the palace seemed far less sensible now she was talking to a superior. "I wouldn't have given it much thought, but what I saw there couldn't be explained by a mage acting alone. It removed every passive spell in the vicinity! Residents are also saying there was an earthquake, but Ardveld doesn't have—"

"Doesn't have any tectonic activity." Aiden finished the sentence for her.

"I can't find anything about magical earthquakes or ground magic anywhere," Tamara sighed, looking back at the books. "I'm starting to think I was a fool for looking." She was supposed to be a respected magical researcher, not some conspiracy theorist chasing after the ridiculous notion of an eighteen-year-old.

"This is—" Aiden stopped and Tamara looked back at him, expecting to see disappointment. Instead, his eyes were wide, staring past her. "I didn't bring it... I'll have someone fetch it from Vailberg immediately." He muttered the words as though to himself, his fist clenched against his chest.

Unsure how to respond to the sudden shift, Tamara watched Aiden's agitation in silence. Then, before she could react, he had clasped one of her hands between his own. "If you find any information about this, I want to be the first to know."

Without her shield, Tamara flinched at the contact. Still, she didn't pull away. Aiden's eyes bore into her own until, to her relief, he released her. Then, turning on his heel, he swept out of the library without another word, leaving Tamara once again alone in the echoing silence.

Chapter 13

The novelty of being left to his own devices in the safe house had worn off surprisingly quickly. Roy flicked through the television channels, but apparently nothing had changed in the last ten minutes. He supposed he should be grateful there even was a television; the place seemed barely used, and Oliver didn't seem the type to lounge around watching a drama. The lack of a games console hadn't shocked him in the slightest.

Roy grabbed a slice of last night's pizza from the box on the table, jolting it with a heating spell before taking a bite. He didn't remember seeing a microwave in the kitchen when hunting for coffee that morning (he'd finally found a pot of instant, a month out of date, behind around eight varieties of loose leaf tea) and anyway, he didn't feel like getting up off the couch.

Switching off the television, Roy picked up the book he'd retrieved from the second bedroom; the only one he'd been able to find that wasn't a damn textbook. Before he could get much beyond the first paragraph, there came the sound of a slamming door and footsteps in the stairwell.

He was no longer alone.

With a burst of vigour he didn't know he possessed, he chucked the book onto the coffee table and flung himself down behind the sofa.

"What the hell happened here?"

The voice was familiar, and Roy poked his head out. As he thought, it was the man from before; Matthew, if he had overhead correctly. Dark eyes matched the straight black hair that fell around his sharp features, and though Matthew's build was slim, Roy easily sensed the powerful magic he exuded. To his relief, Oliver also stood in the doorway behind him.

"Hey, you actually came back," Roy said, standing up. Matthew caught sight of him immediately, but Oliver was scanning the apartment, having gone rather pale.

"W—what," Oliver stammered weakly. Under other circumstances, Roy would have enjoyed being the one to shake that cool composure, but Matthew's glare was ruining the moment. "What are you wearing?!" Oliver finally turned to him and Roy remembered the grey dressing gown he was still sporting over his clothes.

"Ah, hope you don't mind. I found this in the bedroom," Roy jerked a thumb towards the door beside the kitchen. "Ended up just crashing on the couch again." As on the first night, he had avoided using his designated bedroom, even after Oliver's insistence. Somehow, it made the experience easier.

"I can see..." Oliver hadn't moved, still seemingly transfixed by the room.

"I couldn't get the wine out, sorry," Roy rubbed guiltily at a red splatter blemishing the fluffy material. "I'd have thought you'd spell it stain proof, though. Everything else in your wardrobe was."

"You spilled wine on my— What do you mean 'everything else in my wardrobe'?" Oliver did not look happy. "You... What else did you open?"

"What was I supposed to do?" Roy shrugged off the dressing gown, missing its warmth as soon as he did so. Oliver took it from him wordlessly. "You didn't exactly tell me when you'd be back. I got bored. Nathaniel's a hilarious name for a fake ID, by the way; nothing suspicious there." Roy snorted. "Unless that's your actual name," he clarified quickly. "In which case, cool name, mate."

Making fun of the people protecting him from Marek might not be the best idea, and, given the quality of the paperwork he had found in that spell locked draw, Oliver and Matthew were clearly professional in their illegal activities.

"...How?" Oliver shook his head slowly. "That was magic locked. How did you—"

"Oh, don't worry! I wasn't actually looking for documents and I put them all back. I was looking for money," The explanation didn't seem to be helping his case. "Since, you know, I'm only here because I'm helping you guys out, and I don't have any cash on me. I found some, by the way. In the third drawer. That's how I got the pizza."

"Wait, you got pizza delivered? To a safe house?" Matthew had been silent until now, listening to Roy's explanation with an expression of vague disbelief.

Not liking the implication, Roy rolled his eyes. "You told me not to leave! Anyway, I paid in cash, I'm not an idiot."

"Could have fooled me..." Matthew mumbled, seating himself in the single chair furthest from where Roy stood. "How did you even know the address?"

"I saw it on the way in." Roy shrugged. The street name and number on the door had been easy enough to remember. He wasn't sure if knowing the phone number of the takeaway by heart was something to be proud or ashamed of.

"...It feels nicer without the protective spells." Oliver muttered to himself, running a hand over his dressing gown dejectedly.

Roy hopped back onto the couch and reached for his coffee mug, realised he'd grabbed the one full of wine dregs, and put it back down.

"Maybe we should talk about what we're actually here for." Matthew directed his words at Oliver, who seemed to shake himself out of his daze.

"Yes... apologies. You're right." Folding the garment, Oliver hung it on the back of a dining chair and settled at the far end of the sofa. They weren't just here to check on him then.

Matthew leaned forward in the armchair, clasping his hands in front of him. "Roy, isn't it? We need to know if you can get into the palace."

"Hey look, I'm not getting involved in anything there. I've got enough people after me as it is!" Felix Marek was bad enough; if these guys were planning some sort of palace heist they'd have Morgan after them, and Roy doubted Oliver's promise of protection would hold up under those circumstances, no matter how competent the guy seemed. He folded his arms across his chest. "I can't help you, anyway. Marek is one thing, but what makes you think I could break into the palace?"

"You recognised the lock installed at Felix Marek's home and called it a palace lock," Oliver explained from beside him. "We might be wrong, but we concluded that you would only know the palace used that type of spell if you had encountered it there."

Yeah, he could see how they had figured that; damn his stupid mouth. What were the chances the palace even used those locks anymore? "I can't help you. Sorry mate."

"Please, this is important," Matthew interjected. He was running his hands together, leaning so close Roy thought he might fall from the chair. "If you know a way in, you need to tell me."

"Makes a change, hearing 'please' from you." Roy shot back. He hadn't so quickly forgotten the interrogation he had been subjected to at their last encounter.

"Listen, I'm sorry. I need your help." The desperation in Matthew's voice made Roy blink in surprise. "It's— The palace has my son. I need to get him and his friend out. Please." He tilted his head down into his open palms, as though the words were too much to face.

It made sense now why Matthew had changed his tune, though picturing him as a father was jarring. "What'd he do?" It must be bad. Roy tried to suppress a pang of sympathy. This likely wasn't some little kid; despite his own feelings about Morgan, he hadn't heard of the palace kidnapping people.

"It's a misunderstanding," Oliver took over. "He isn't a criminal, he's only eighteen—"

"Eighteen's old enough to be a criminal, trust me."

"He's not." Oliver's voice was firm. "I can't go into detail, but he's in terrible danger there, through no fault of his own. I understand I've asked a lot of you already, but all we need is knowledge. Is there a way in?"

"Look, I feel for you, I really do." Roy was no stranger to the palace being dangerous, and this discussion was shaking him more than he wanted to admit. "I don't know how to get into the palace. Genuinely. I haven't been there in years."

"The lock, though? How did you know?" Matthew said, raising his head.

Roy pinched the bridge of his nose and took a heavy breath. Light was seeping through the thin blinds over the window. Another bright summer morning, just like the day he'd heard the news.

"My mum. She taught me."

He wasn't sure why he said it. They didn't have a right to the story, but Roy found himself continuing anyway, words stiff after a lifetime of being unsaid. "Look, she... she worked in the palace, alright. When she'd come home, she'd set little locks for me. It was a game we'd play." The memory was still raw, choking him as it came out. She had been so proud when he cracked one. The mischievous smile they'd shared, like co-conspirators. Perhaps that's why he'd always had a taste for being in places he shouldn't.

"Where did she work?" Oliver asked gently.

"I dunno. For the royal family, she was there when... well you know."

"She died in the attack," Oliver said. It wasn't a question, but Roy nodded.

"I'm sorry," Matthew looked like he genuinely meant it, and Roy was unexpectedly touched.

"Eh, nothing to do with you." He shrugged again, but Matthew seemed to flinch as he said the words.

Oliver gave a deep sigh. "Unfortunately, that means we need an alternative plan."

Traffic hummed past outside, muffled by the closed window. He had been truthful when he said he didn't want to get tied up in any more criminal activity than he already was. The palace though. To be where she was. There wasn't anywhere else Roy could think of that was so out of his reach, and yet so close to his heart.

"You know," Roy said, breaking the silence. "There's that garden party tomorrow." From his experience, forcing your way into a building was the least efficient method. He'd done it at Marek's out of necessity, but he always preferred being let in through the front door. "If it was me, I'd try and get hold of a ticket. Well, if it was really me, I'd swap shifts with a mate and get on the delivery crew, but that ain't really an option for you." He'd wanted nothing to do with that damn party when they were assigning the jobs, but now... he was starting to see things in a different light.

"The anniversary." Matthew muttered, looking towards Oliver. "I can't believe it, but I'd forgotten it was tomorrow." He unfolded himself from the chair and crossed over to the dining table. Roy craned his head back as far as he could without having to move from the couch, but Matthew was just pacing the length of the room silently.

Oliver didn't react to Matthew's actions. Sat straight, he was drumming his fingers, slowing against his leg. "Finding a ticket is no simple task," he stated finally. "Even if you were able to procure one, I'm sure there is a specific guest list." He turned to Matthew, "I'll locate a list of the attendees. Perhaps seeing it will offer up a viable option."

Roy couldn't suppress the smirk that formed as Oliver spoke. "You don't need a list, mate. I know exactly who's got one, though you're not gonna like it." Behind him, he heard Matthew stop moving. "Don't you guys know Marek goes every year?"

"Felix Marek," Matthew spoke the name flatly. "What is your obsession with him, anyway? Why do you know that?"

"I'm not obsessed!" Roy whirled around, kneeling up over the back of the sofa to challenge the accusation. "The bastard made a ton of money, alright. After the takeover. You worked for him; didn't you have any idea how he got so rich? Or did you just not care?" Roy scowled at Matthew, who didn't look away.

"Tell me," Matthew growled and Roy sank back down.

"They say he got a big payout for his 'contributions'." Roy made air quotes with his fingers. "He used to work in weapon design back in Vailberg, up until he got into business with Aiden Heliodor. He knows how they did it. I fucking know it. Why'd you think I broke in there? I was looking for answers."

For a moment, Matthew didn't move, an unreadable expression flashing across his face. When he spoke again his tone was softer. "So say we get the ticket from Felix Marek. What's to stop him just telling the palace?"

"I dunno." Roy flopped back down next to Oliver, who jerked away from the touch.

"Matthew," Oliver said thoughtfully. "The lock you were asked to install at Felix Marek's property. Presumably this was in preparation to hold the wands."

"Go on," Matthew walked back around to listen to Oliver

speak.

"I don't believe it is thieves that are his primary concern," Oliver said and Roy didn't miss the glance that was sent his way when he mentioned thieves. "The people who attacked us didn't seem like they were supposed to draw attention. I don't think Felix Marek wants the weapon traced back to him."

"So what? You're suggesting we threaten to turn him in if he doesn't get us into the party?"

"I'm just saying it could be leverage. We have a wand. Felix doesn't know about our relationship to Morgan Heliodor; he has no reason to believe we wouldn't take him down with us, so to speak, should he try to hand us in." Matthew ran a hand through his hair and Roy felt Oliver shift in the seat beside him. "I don't like it either, it's dangerous. I'm just suggesting the option."

"You're not seriously going to go to the man trying to kill us all and ask him to take you to a party?" Roy couldn't believe what he was hearing.

Oliver steepled his fingers. "Felix Marek doesn't know me. I should be able to arrange a meeting—"

"No," Matthew sharply interrupted Oliver's rationalisation. "Marek and I have business to settle. I don't appreciate being attacked in the street, especially when they drag my friend into it. When I'm done with him, we aren't going to need leverage."

"Er... can I just say if attacking Marek directly was always an option, why the hell have we been hiding from him?" As ridiculous as it sounded, Roy got the impression Matthew intended to face down Felix Marek and all his guards alone. It seemed a bit unfair that he'd been stuck hiding in a safe house, if they could have just threatened

Marek to back off the whole time.

"Things have changed." Matthew didn't seem like he was going to provide further explanation, and from the expression on his face, Roy decided he wouldn't want to be Marek right now.

Oliver seemed to have accepted Matthew overriding his plan, though Roy could see he had reassumed his tapping, expression sombre. "If you convince him to get you in, you'll be alone."

"I know," Matthew replied.

A conversation he wasn't privy to seemed like it was taking place beyond Matthew's simple reply, and Roy shuddered. Matthew planned to break into the palace alone, right under Morgan's nose, with only his enemy for company, at the most important official event of the year. Roy didn't feel like he was the stupid one this time.

"You promised you'd get Marek off my back right?" The two men looked up at Roy as he spoke, but he continued before they could comment. "Hey, I'm not saying I'm going to risk my neck for you, but Oliver sounds like he's got it right to me. You'd be an idiot going in there alone." He hoped he wasn't going to regret this. "I'll swap a shift; there's always someone who won't want to work those hours. Just make sure I never have to hear from Marek again. Or Morgan for that matter."

Roy half expected them to just tell him he would be in the way, and to be honest, they would probably be right. Instead, Matthew extended a hand. "I'll make sure of it."

Roy clasped it in his own, Matthew's fingers cold to the touch.

CHAPTER 14

Empty plates clinked as dinner drew to a close, the sound joining the cacophony of conversation that filled the lavish banquet hall. Tamara found her smile beginning to falter. Bodies pressed into the space around her chair; guests milling between the tables as they searched for more engaging company than could be found in their assigned seats. She had scarcely spoken during the meal, instead nodding along to a conversation that she couldn't quite discern. It was impossible to distinguish the words from the background noise of a hundred other guests talking nearby.

Though hot, she was grateful for the ball gown she wore. The wine red satin firmly corseted around her waist gave a reassuring pressure and, though it impeded her movement, the heavy skirt reminded her of being snuggled in a weighted blanket. Only her bare shoulders left Tamara feeling exposed; the neckline cut wide above laced sleeves that thankfully weren't hurting her skin.

"—don't you think?" A statement, directed at her from the woman to her right, intruded on her thoughts.

"Oh, I'm sorry," Tamara reinforced her smile. "I was thinking about work." She hoped that the explanation would seem endearing to the grey haired Velbian minister beside her. The woman's lined face crinkled in confusion, and Tamara realised the engaged expression she had been performing must have worked too well.

"We were discussing Morgan's closure of the academy," The woman explained politely, though Tamara perceived the change in her demeanour to frosty suspicion. "It must have had an impact on your role?"

As far as Tamara knew, the academy wasn't technically closed. A handful of mages still resided in the rooms that made up the west wing of the palace, but although being Head of Magical Affairs also put her in charge of the academy, she had never had to deal with them. The only notable benefit had been using an old student room to house Alex and Eira.

"I'm still very new to the role, so I don't think I can comment on how things have changed," Tamara replied. She watched the woman's mouth carefully, not wanting to miss a response due to background noise.

"In any case, I imagine he was right not to waste any more resources on it," The comment came from a large man sat opposite, whose cheeks shone with a rosiness that must be from the empty wine glass in front of him. "Vailberg's universities are full to bursting with Ardveldians nowadays, without the need to send any more."

"Indeed. I half feel we are overrun," the older woman sighed. "At least it's better than the ones from Avel Kifaeros, though you're probably too young to recall that catastrophe," she swirled her own wine glass then looked at Tamara with a thin smile.

Tamara wasn't too young to know the story. Like Ardveld, almost everyone born in Avel Kifaeros had magic ability. The tiny territory was situated directly between Ardveld's mountainous border and the once fractured states that united to form Vailberg under the first Arch Canlaw, Kaylee and Morgan's father. Many Velbians considered Avel Kifaeros to be part of Vailberg itself, making it the obvious choice when the newly formed country looked to bolster their mages. It had been a disaster on both sides.

"I'm very familiar with the history, I'm Kifaerish myself." Tamara didn't hesitate, though saying the words made her body tense. "I left to study in Vailberg when I was eleven."

"You? Really? You don't look it."

Tamara wasn't sure what exactly she was supposed to look like. The woman raised an eyebrow and took a sip of her wine. "I guess you must be one of the lucky ones. Though are you sure you can cope with your role here?"

The material of her skirt was scrunched tight in her hand before Tamara realised she was gripping it. "Yes, I think I will be fine."

The man leant across the table and, for the first time that evening, she wished his voice had been too difficult to hear. "If you're here at all, then you must be different. Most people in Avel Kifaeros can barely communicate, let alone want to leave the place."

It was a painful generalisation, and Tamara reached up to run a soothing thumb over the smooth garnet in her necklace. Her sister had sent it. Her sister, who never spoke in words and communicated perfectly well through the visual imagery of her illusion spells. Even if she didn't, who were these people to declare what she was capable of?

"That's not—" Tamara was cut off as the conversation continued.

"Oh that's not true. I've met some that are quite normal; even exceptionally skilled, as long as whatever you need them to do catches their interest. Difficult to work with though," The woman paused her analysis and turned to Tamara, as though remembering she was there. "You don't seem that way though, dear. I doubt anyone would be able to tell." She patted Tamara's arm with a wrinkled hand, clearly meaning the words as a compliment.

"Thank you." Tamara unclenched her jaw and forced a smile, despite the anger bubbling in her chest. This reaction was hardly new, and it wasn't worth it. Even so, a pressure was building in her head, the room becoming a blur of colour and noise. "I'm sorry, I need to leave." She didn't wait for their reaction as she fled the table.

Gold curtains partially concealed a pair of tall glass doors, beyond which a stone balcony ran the length of the dining hall. Tamara barely remembered how she got there, her muted focus only widening when a cool breeze brushed the heat from her skin. A way out. She slipped through into the fresh air, ears ringing in the sudden quiet.

From three floors up, the terrace had a sweeping view of the palace gardens. To her right, the west wing blocked the sun from view, though a red glow in the clouds suggested it must be a beautiful sunset. There was a sweet scent to the air and Tamara felt her tension unwind until she looked left and realised she wasn't alone.

Morgan stood at the far end of the balcony. Even from this far away, the shimmering gold and white of his court attire was instantly recognisable, and in stark contrast to the grey of his face. As she got closer, she saw he was leaning heavily against the stone railing. The buttons of his high collar were undone, his breath coming in rapid gasps, and Tamara increased her pace.

He heard her approach. Panicked eyes flicked between her and the balcony door and Morgan pulled his posture straight, though the hand gripping the stone hard enough to blanch his fingers gave away his distress.

"Would you like me to call for a healer?" Tamara spoke softly, keeping her distance. Morgan shook his head in reply. No. "Then, is it okay if I stay?"

His rejection of the healer wasn't a shock. She had seen this before, and it wasn't something medicine or magic could cure. Another gasping breath turned into many as Morgan lost what little composure he'd forced at her arrival; but he nodded, and Tamara settled beside him.

"It's okay. We're safe here," she tried to ignore the pounding of her own heart as she spoke, uttering the words in a soothing monotone. "It looks like the roses are in bloom. If you take a deep breath, you can smell them. I've always loved the smell of roses." She imagined it sounded like she was rambling about nothing, but Morgan seemed to be listening. "It's nice how the stone holds the heat, isn't it? It feels so rough..."

Somewhere in the city a bell tolled the hour, chiming through the birdsong that rose from the hedgerows below, and Tamara kept describing; speaking aloud the sensations of the evening as they came into her head until Morgan's breathing had slowed and the colour returned to his skin.

"Something from Avel Kifaeros?" Morgan's voice cracked as he spoke, but it wasn't weak.

"...Not exactly," Tamara realised her own body was shaking, and she reached up again to her necklace for comfort. "It's a type of grounding. For anxiety. It doesn't really help me when I— Well, I thought it would work better for you than a darkened room." This refuge was the closest either of them would get.

Daring a look up, Tamara was surprised to see a soft smile on Morgan's face. "It was appreciated. Thank you." He pulled a gold embroidered handkerchief from his pocket and wiped at the sweat that had formed around his neck. Together they stood unspeaking, listening to the faint sounds of chatter from the diners, overlaid by the evening chorus.

"...Is it like this every year?" Tamara hesitated before breaking the silence.

"I'd say the canapes have got worse."

"That's not what I meant."

Morgan sighed, and she hoped she hadn't overstepped a boundary.

"Yes. Every year." Silence fell again as she struggled to think of how to reply, but this time Morgan broke it. "How much do you know about the takeover?"

"I, um... just what we are taught," Tamara stammered at the unexpected question, fully aware of who was asking. "It was... twenty-three years ago. Vailberg sent a team to remove the old royal family and took over governing of Ardveld." The succinct summary was as emotionless as she could manage.

"Very tactful," if a laugh could carry despair, Tamara had just heard it. "Twenty-three years ago tomorrow, to be precise." She saw Morgan again grip the stone rail, but this time his breathing remained steady. "It was here that it happened. This weather. This room. It's the same, every year."

His words made the hair prick on the back of her neck. This room. It should have been obvious, it hadn't even crossed Tamara's mind that she was standing in the place they had died. Visions of the blood soaked hall from the stories flashed into her mind, the red of the sunset seeming far more sinister than it had moments before.

"It didn't look like this," Morgan continued as though reading her thoughts. "I had it stripped out. The furnishings, wallpaper... I am aware that hardly helped the rumours." He met her eyes and Tamara found herself unable to look away. "You can leave now, if you wish."

Her breath caught, but she didn't want to leave. She wasn't sure if it should appal her that she didn't. The Morgan from the stories jarred awkwardly in her mind against her impression of the man in front of her, even after hearing it from his own mouth. "I'd rather stay." She broke the eye contact, letting her gaze fall to his gilded coat, collar still hanging loose.

Morgan turned away from her, his expression hidden as he looked back out over the gardens. "That makes one of us then." The response was barely audible; a whisper that seemed more for himself than for her. She wondered if he regretted the events that happened here; opened her mouth to ask, then swallowed the words. What answer could he give?

"I will always do my duty for Vailberg." Morgan's response to her unspoken question told her she was correct not to probe.

A chill breeze picked up from the lengthening shadows and Tamara tried unsuccessfully to hide a shiver, not wanting Morgan to think it was due to him.

"Are you cold? We should go in." He pocketed the handkerchief and refastened his collar, before holding out an arm.

Tamara lifted a hand but paused, not convinced she understood what was expected. Before she could decide, Morgan lowered his arm and stepped away.

"I'm sorry. It's not you! I—" Tamara stumbled a response, realising what her hesitation might imply.

"I take no offense," Morgan said, and when she looked at his face, he didn't seem to. Rather than the hurt she had been expecting to see, there was a warmth in his eyes that did nothing to help her quickened heart. "You aren't comfortable with physical touch?"

"There you are!" A voice splintered the moment. Aiden Heliodor stood blocking the door to the hall. He must have been searching for Morgan, but it didn't look as though he had attended the dinner at all. Though smart, his attire was nowhere near the embellished uniform he should be wearing at such an important occasion, but the fact didn't seem to concern him. A breeze played over mahogany hair, so like his uncles, and a smile broke across his face when Tamara looked at him.

"How can I help you?" The words were polite, but the chill in Morgan's tone made her freeze. Before she could catch sight of his expression, he stepped forward, blocking her view of Aiden completely.

"I have some urgent business to discuss with Tamara."

She peered around Morgan's back at Aiden's reply. *With*

her? There was no smile on his face now.

"I'd apologise for the interruption," Aiden continued. "But shouldn't you be inside? I am sure our guests desire to toast your achievement. Modesty doesn't suit the conqueror of Ardveld."

"We were just about to head in," Morgan's reply betrayed no hint of distress. "Though it is not modesty that will lead me to raise a toast to your mother. It will be many generations before we see another of her greatness."

For a moment Aiden's face twisted in rage, then the expression vanished, as though wiped clean.

"Pay no heed to my uncle; we have exciting things to discuss." He turned to face Tamara and she got the impression this wasn't a request. In any case, if Aiden had found information regarding the ground magic then she was interested. "Come with me." Without looking back, he thrust the curtain away and strode inside. With an apologetic glance at Morgan, Tamara followed.

***

She had to hurry to keep up with Aiden's pace. After brushing off the multitude of people in the banquet hall who tried to capture him in conversation, he was now racing through the palace corridors with unexpected urgency. There had been no conversation on the way; nothing to hint at why she had been summoned, and rather than the library, they seemed to be heading in the direction of the guest rooms.

"Did you not go to the party in the end?" Tamara ventured the question, hoping that he might at least slow down. They had passed no other people in the halls, the occupants of the rooms likely all at the dinner.

To her relief, Aiden allowed her to catch up. "I decided I had more important matters to attend to. I'm sure you agree, parties are too frivolous for intelligent people like us. My uncle could never understand." He withdrew a key from his blazer. "We need somewhere private for this conversation and my rooms are just here."

She stopped walking and Aiden laughed. "Does it scare you to be in my room alone? I promise I shall be nothing but a gentleman." A bolt clicked and there was a faint flare of magic as the locking spell recognised his key. "Please, come in."

Tamara entered first. Though large, the seating area of Aiden's suite seemed impossibly cramped. Stacks of books and computer discs littered every available surface, the only illumination coming from the screen of a laptop sat in the centre of an expansive desk. A rare sight, and one that served as a strong reminder of whose room she was in. Flicking on the light as he passed, Aiden crossed to the desk and pushed the laptop shut.

"Are you going to sit down?" When he turned back to her, he held a hearty book in both hands.

"No, don't worry. I'm fine," Tamara wasn't sure why, but she'd rather be on her feet. At least it would imply this wouldn't be a long stay.

"Don't be ridiculous, sit. You shall make me seem like a poor host, standing there." Aiden carried the book to the coffee table and Tamara saw the pages shimmer silver as he set it down. With his hands free, he then began to clear a space on the chair large enough for both of them.

"Now then," Aiden continued once Tamara had settled beside him. "Yesterday, when you mentioned magic moving the earth, I knew I had read something similar before." The thick pages crackled as he peeled the book open. "It's lucky I was able to have it retrieved from Vailberg so quickly. Read this."

A paragraph of text took up the centre of the first page:

'The esteemed Royal lineage and Champions of Ardveld; country of magic. As their power once raised the mountains and carved the rivers, may it continue to shape Ardveld's future. Blood and land forever entwined.'

"Fascinating that I should end up returning a book I had already removed from the palace library." Aiden mused to himself as Tamara read. "Do you see?"

"What does it mean though?" Tamara replied. "That Ardveld itself was made through magic? I might not have explained properly, but I couldn't sense any magic in Golebach, and neither did any other mage I have spoken to." It was possible that, having no magical ability himself, Aiden had misunderstood.

"No!" Tamara flinched at Aiden's raised voice. "Don't you see? The king shaped the lands. The royal family! Of course you wouldn't be able to feel it, or any other mage."

"But, there aren't any royal family left," After speaking with Morgan this evening, Tamara was certain of it. "And even if there was, I'm not confident they would be causing earthquakes in Golebach." She smiled. It was easy to forget how young Aiden was. Despite how close they looked in age he would have only been around two during the takeover; too young to remember more than stories of Ardveld's royalty. "It's a nice thought, but that seems a lot to draw from such a vague piece of writing."

"You said you spoke to witnesses," Aiden hissed and Tamara's smile fled. "Do you remember what they looked like?" He hefted the book onto his lap and flicked through to the far end, slamming it back onto the table in front of her. "These were the last living members of the royal line."

The pages she had seen Aiden flick through had been full of pictures, from copies of painted portraits through to posed photographs as, she presumed, the people in the images were born closer to the present day. These last photos showed the former king, a dark haired man with a styled moustache, the queen, and finally... Her eyes came to rest on the last photo and a cold sweat pricked over her body.

Aiden was watching her face intently; she could see it from the corner of her eye, and Tamara attempted to mask her expression into one of confusion.

"If any of them live," Aiden said. "Then the royal Champions would still exist." His gaze was starting to burn, but Tamara didn't take her eyes off the book. "A spell that could turn anyone into the strongest mage in Ardveld. In the world! Losing that knowledge was a tragedy."

"I— I don't think even they knew how it worked," Tamara stammered but forced herself to lift her head. "Otherwise there would be records—"

"We could find out! Experiment!" Aiden exclaimed. "Imagine what we would achieve! If any of them lived—"

"I'm sorry," Tamara's heart was pounding, words tumbling out too fast. "I don't recognise anyone in these pictures. I can get back in touch with the police at Golebach though, to see if they could ask the witnesses if they saw anyone…"

"That would be helpful. Yes." Aiden didn't seem like he was going to press further, yet when she met his eyes they were narrow and cold.

"May I borrow your book?" Tamara said hurriedly,

placing a hand over the image on the page. "I'm sorry but... it would be good to copy the pictures. So I can send them across to the police station."

Aiden inclined his head in confirmation. "Go ahead."

The tome was heavy and Tamara hugged it against her body. "Thank you. I'll let you know as soon as I hear anything. This has been incredibly helpful." She scooted around the table, not turning her back on Aiden but, as she got to the exit, he stood up from the sofa.

"Let me get that," before she could make it to the door, he had caught up, blocking her exit as he reached for the handle. "If you do know anything, Tamara, you will tell me." He was close enough that she could feel the warmth of his breath on her skin. "I promise that no harm will come to you if you do." The assurance was not comforting.

"Of course, you'll be the first to know." Tamara pulled the tome tighter to her chest, releasing a sigh of relief as Aiden nodded and opened the door.

"Thank you so much for your help." A lightness returned to his tone when she stepped into the corridor, and he gave a friendly wave as she turned to walk away. Suppressing the desire to break into a run, Tamara proceeded down the empty hall, certain she could sense his eyes on her until the end.

CHAPTER 15

The crumpled paper landed in the suspended bin with a shower of sparks.

"Nice!" Alex punched the air. It was a tricky shot to curve the projectile from the bathroom door to the target above his bed, but Eira's wind spell directed it true on the fifth attempt. Her celebratory light show was a nice touch; a rather complex passive spell that combined regular magelights with her usual artistic flare. It had taken the better part of half an hour to craft, but it wasn't as though there was anything better to do.

"Want to try from the other door now?" Eira said. The rectangular bedroom didn't lend itself to challenging throwing positions. "Maybe you should turn around and throw it backwards?"

"Yeah, let me just grab a drink."

If he was going to be stuck somewhere, at least it was with his best friend.

Alex walked over to the latest tray the guard had brought, checking for any food they might have missed. Over a day had passed since Tamara's visit. She'd assured him that she would figure out the ground magic, but Alex doubted it would take priority over her official engagements.

It was dark outside. The curtains still hung open, but all the glass revealed now was his own reflection; the people they had watched arranging marquees in the grounds for tomorrow's garden party, long gone. He had felt stronger that morning; enough at least to use simple magic again. Even so, Eira had picked up much of the slack, cooling the air in the room that would otherwise have been stifling in the summer heat.

They'd talked casually about escape plans, Eira rightly commenting that being locked in a room was, at the very least, a fire hazard. Between them, they could probably brute force the spell on the window — definitely if Alex was at full strength, but decided it wasn't worth endangering their delicate 'non-criminal' status. Even then, they were still three floors up.

"You know, I'm thinking I'll just head to bed," Eira yawned. "Guess we'll just have to look forward to more waiting tomorrow. Doubt she's going to come talk to us with that party on."

"Yeah, you're probably right," Alex pulled the curtains shut and flopped down onto his bed. He wasn't looking forward to another night sleeping in jeans, but at least he'd managed to wash a majority of the filth off his clothes in the shower. Thankfully, he'd regained enough magic to dry them; even after growing up together, being undressed in the same room as his friend felt wrong.

Rolling onto his stomach, Alex cast his eyes towards the heavy door. The guard was still outside. He could sense them.

Since his conversation with Tamara, Alex had done some experimenting of his own. At first, purely to reassure himself it was there, he'd close his eyes and let the ground magic fill his awareness. Soon he found he was able to feel movement in the energy, like ripples in a pool of still water. The disruptions in the ground magic were detectable from far further than his regular magic sense had ever reached, but at a distance the anomalies seemed to merge together. Alex hadn't realised it was mages he was picking up until the latest guard brought their dinner.

"Someone's coming." Alex turned to Eira, who sat up in bed. Though he'd struggled to explain what he felt during his ground magic tests, she had believed him without question. Now, as he focussed, he sensed the telltale disturbance in the natural energy, caused by a mage's magical aura as they moved closer.

When the door opened, he was surprised to see Tamara stood there. Her elegant ball gown swished against the floor as she entered, but the makeup around her eyes looked worn and smudged. She must have just come from a formal event, though the heavy book she clutched to her chest seemed conspicuously out of place.

"Alex, I need you to come with me," Tamara said, her voice commanding and far less like the friendly manner in which she had approached him before. He didn't move from the bed, still shocked by the sudden intrusion.

"Just Alex?" Eira replied, and he was grateful that she saved him the need. "Where are you taking him?"

Tamara glanced in Eira's direction, hugging the book tighter. "We're going to my office. I need to talk to him about something important. I'm sorry, but you will need to stay here."

After Tamara's last visit, they'd joked about mysteriously 'disappearing'; suddenly the idea seemed much closer to reality.

"Talk about what?" Alex found his voice as he got up from the bed and slipped on his shoes. He was hesitant to leave Eira alone; she had been present for everything up to now. Still, he'd prefer not to be dragged out of the room if it came to it.

"Alex, you can't just go!"

"Don't worry about it. This shouldn't take long, right? I'll tell you all about it when I get back." He looked to Tamara hoping she would confirm his assumption, but she had turned to open the door.

"It shouldn't take long," Tamara finally spoke, as though just catching up to his words. "Thank you."

She seemed relieved that he had got up to follow, and Alex felt he sensed some of her previous warmth in her words. A glance back into the room showed Eira stood, as though she was debating whether to follow him anyway. Then the door swung shut, and she disappeared from view.

Standing in the corridor, Alex was interested to note it wasn't as grand as he had imagined. A strip of worn carpet, that looked like it had once been a vivid sapphire blue, ran down the centre of the dark wooden floor panels. On either side of the narrow corridor, doors matching his own blocked off further rooms, though the smell of dust and lack of movement confirmed what the ground magic had indicated; no one else inhabited this floor. The guard outside his own door nodded as they passed, but didn't leave his post.

"It doesn't look that much like a palace. From the corridor, you know," Alex said as he caught up. He had been a tourist in enough historical buildings to know only certain areas were designed to impress, but making conversation was worth looking ignorant.

"This is the academy. It was for students." Tamara's curt reply dashed his hopes of a friendly chat. At least it explained the room they were being kept in. He followed her the rest of the way in silence, down an enclosed spiral staircase to a wider corridor, where they stopped outside an ornate carved door. A gold plaque to its left stated 'Head of Magical Affairs' in embossed text.

A trickle of magic eminated from the door when Tamara placed her hand on it, as the locking spell recognised her permission to enter. Mage lights burst to life as it opened, casting a warm glow over the cosy office. There were no visible walls; every space lined with cabinets and bookcases, with the exception of a window and a narrow staircase in the far left corner that must lead up to her living quarters.

"Sit down, please." She indicated to one of two low, leather couches to Alex's right, with a coffee table in between. Leather creaked as he sunk into the well-worn cushions and he leant forward, the seat being too wide to sit up straight. Neither the seating area nor the large, claw foot desk in front of the window looked the style he would expect from Tamara, but then Alex remembered she was new in the role and likely hadn't had time to change anything.

Tamara took a place on the couch opposite, laying the heavy book across her lap. For a moment the only sound was water, trickling over a small, stone fountain sitting at the edge of her desk. Alex eyed it curiously until Tamara spoke.

"Could you tell me again, why you were at Golebach Court when your device exploded?"

Alex frowned. "I was there because of the ground magic, remember? Isn't that what you said you were going to look into?" He was dismayed to have put faith in someone who couldn't even keep track of their conversations.

"I have been looking into it. That is why I need to clarify some things with you. Can you explain again how you first realised you sensed magic there?"

He wasn't certain he had ever clarified that in the first place, but decided not to comment. "I'd gone there with my dad the day before. That was the first time I felt it — at least the first time I remember. I hadn't been there for years."

"You went with your father?" Tamara's gaze seemed to sharpen as she asked. "Could you tell me more about your family? Who do you live with?"

"Um... my mum. Dad comes down to visit when he can. He lives away. Because of work." Alex shuffled his feet. This felt much more like an interrogation than their previous conversation.

"I see. And you parents? Are they both from Ardveld?"

"Yeah, I think so. Well, my mum's dad I think is Velbian? They actually live in Vailberg, so I don't ever see them." He did have quite a small family, though it had never seemed strange to him before, especially as Eira didn't have much of one herself. "Dad's quite a good mage, so pretty sure his family's all Ardveldian."

"Do you not have grandparents on your father's side?" Tamara tilted her head, and he noticed she was running her palm over the cover of the book.

"I think they died before I was born," Alex shrugged. "I

never really thought to ask, sorry. It just doesn't come up."

"And you have no aunts, uncles... cousins that you know of?"

He got the impression that she was reaching now, as if avoiding the real reason they were here. "No— Well, there's Uncle Oliver, but we aren't technically related so..." An idea popped into his head as he said it. "I could ask my dad if you like! If he can feel the magic too? Is that what you are trying to find out? Whether there's a genetic link?" That would explain all the family questions. Perhaps the reason for questioning him alone was in case there had been anything sensitive.

A thin smile broke through Tamara's stern expression, and Alex saw her reach up to fiddle with her necklace, before dropping her hand back down to the book on her lap. "I think I would very much like to speak to your father, yes. Though I'm not sure he would want to speak to me," she paused. "Alex, can I ask your father's name?"

"Um, sure. It's Matthew. Matthew Ashe."

The name seemed to have an effect. Tamara bit her lip and laid the book closed on the table between them. Now that it was closer, Alex was able to read the upside down gilded text. 'Royal Lineage and Champions of Ardveld'.

The Royal Family? Alex struggled to suppress a smile. Clearly Tamara had never been to Couden Cross; it wasn't exactly the kind of place you'd go to dig up lost royal relations.

"This is going to seem like an odd question," Tamara said, opening the book towards the back and shifting to the last few pages. "But I need you to look at some pictures and tell me if they look like anyone you know." Stopping on a page of formal photos, she rotated it to face him.

Alex's eyes jumped immediately to the first picture; an imposing man dressed in lavish blue and silver robes. Text beside the image declared him the last King of Ardveld, though Alex had never seen a photo of him before. His gaze flicked over the other images and text before landing on a picture of a teenage boy. Dark eyes looked back at him, instantly familiar, and Alex sucked in a breath. The boy in the photo could easily be a younger version of his father. Jumping to the writing beside it, he rapidly scanned the contents.

'Crown Prince Matthew of Ardveld.'

His mind went blank. He read the text again, and then a third time, as though not sure he had taken the words in. It didn't make any sense. Alex tried to think back to what he knew about the old royal family; not much apart from they all died twenty something years ago.

"I— er..." He looked up to see Tamara watching him intently. This was it then. What she had been leading to with all those questions. Fingers digging into his palm, Alex sat straight and narrowed his eyes. "That's a cruel trick." She must have researched him to create it. No way Tamara didn't get information about his family after he'd been arrested. "What were you trying to get from this? That you could accuse me of treason?"

Tamara pulled back, confusion written across her features. "No. I didn't—"

"Is this because I know something about magic that you don't?" Alex spat. "You couldn't work it out so you need a reason to get rid of me?" He'd thought Tamara was going to help him, that he could trust her. Now he didn't know what to think.

He got to his feet, wanting to run from the room; run

back to Eira. Back to his prison, he thought bitterly.

"Alex, please! Sit down and listen," Tamara had stood as well, but she didn't make any move towards him. "I don't want to fight you, and you won't be able to get out the room anyway. It's locked."

"I don't want to listen to you," Alex mumbled. He was an adult; he should be able to figure out what to do. Instead, he just felt vulnerable.

"You have to." Tamara's reply was firm, but gentle. "I don't mean you any harm. I'm sorry. I'm really sorry that you think I would make this up. That I would try to trick you," she looked down and Alex followed her gaze to where the book still lay open on the table. "I didn't know what to believe myself, when I saw it. That's why I wanted to show you." Tamara met his eyes and Alex realised how intense her stare was when she did make eye contact. "Honestly, I thought you knew and had been lying to me."

"I don't know anything because there isn't anything to know," Alex flung a hand towards the book. "It doesn't work out anyway, the dates would be all wrong. The name... My dad would have told me."

"Okay," Tamara nodded as he spoke. "Perhaps that's fair, I don't know your father's age, after all. I actually saw the picture and thought it looked so much like you."

Like him? Now that he looked at again, he could see the similarity in his own features. Perhaps that was how they had made the image; Alex doubted even the government would be able to dig up childhood photos of his father. He'd never seen any around the house.

"Do... do you know your dad's age?" Tamara hesitated, as though afraid he would shout again.

"I dunno, forty? Forty I think," Alex shook his head, not

sure why he was still answering her questions. "He looks younger, because of the magic." The takeover had been, what? Five years or so before he was born? If the teenager in the picture really was his father that would have to make him—

"Seventeen then. He'd have been about seventeen when the takeover happened." Tamara finished the thought for him. "I know you don't believe any of this, but the ages match up; the name. Isn't it worth looking into?" She crouched back down and began to turn the book's pages. "I didn't even tell you about the writing in the front—"

"—I don't want to see it."

Tamara looked crestfallen, but Alex didn't care.

"It just... I think it would explain why you can feel the ground magic. If your father really is Prince Matthew..."

"I don't want to hear anymore alright." Alex shook his head again, backing up a step towards the door. "I just want to go back to bed." He still didn't believe it. Did he? All Alex knew was that he had been hit with a wave of tiredness and a desperate need to be anywhere but here in this stuffy office.

"I'll take you back," Tamara shut the book on the desk with more force than necessary. "Please don't try anything on the way—"

"I'm not going to. I just want to go to bed." He turned away and waited as Tamara unlocked the door.

"Thank you for speaking with me."

Alex didn't reply.

CHAPTER 16

The steps up to the palace entrance were as smooth as Matthew remembered; the grey stone worn by the passing of generations of feet. Behind him, another car pulled up in the gravel courtyard. Its occupants, dressed as finely as their expensive vehicle would suggest, joined the crowd queuing towards the guard check at the door.

He'd ridden in such a car himself, moments before. Not that Felix Marek had been happy about picking Matthew up from their agreed meeting spot, a road down from the palace. They now stood together in the cold shadow of the building, surrounded by the chatter of the other waiting guests.

The suit that Oliver had provided fit perfectly and

Matthew had no worries about anyone suspecting he wasn't among his peers. Even Marek seemed begrudgingly impressed. Still, his breathing was restricted and shallow, as though each step he took was forbidden. At least he was now too close to see the building in its entirety. He'd hardly been able to take his eyes off of the palace the whole drive; the journey mirroring every memory of the experience as a child. Now, Matthew found himself scanning the carved entrance way, the familiar steps, the gilded doors, as if seeing them for the first time.

The presence of the natural magic pushed stronger against his mind as he got closer. Matthew resented its intrusion; Oliver's explanation tainting what once brought him comfort. It was just another thing marking him out as different. A remnant of something that no longer existed, like the building in front of him.

An impatient cough told Matthew he had been holding up the queue. He rushed the next few steps two at a time, earning a disgusted sneer from Marek and a smattering of murmurs and suppressed laughter from those behind. This wasn't home anymore. He would have to be more careful.

Familiar smells of wood polish and musty fabric crashed him through a wave of emotion as they entered the wide entrance hall. Morgan had changed the floor. The tiled image of the royal crest was gone, replaced with a block pattern of gold and white that extended through to the opposite doorway. Roped off on either side ascended two curving staircases that Matthew knew lead to the state rooms above.

His magic sense told him there were mages amongst the guards, likely sensing for spelled weaponry as well as being there for general defence. Matthew tensed as they looked him over, but none tried to stop him. Instead, they nodded a greeting as he and Marek walked across the glossy ceramic towards the far doors.

Though overcast, the light streaming in from the gardens made Matthew squint as they passed outside. Groups of guests were scattered across the patio terrace and a gust of wind snapped at a marquee set up to his left, causing the sides to billow out.

"I don't care what you want here, just make sure you keep away from me," Marek broke their tense silence to hiss under his breath. "I agreed to get you in, not be your babysitter."

The shorter man's wispy hair caught the breeze, flicking up in a display that made a mockery of his attempted menace. Felix Marek had been compliant so far, though perhaps it shouldn't be a surprise. It wasn't often that Matthew flexed his full power, and having the mage you tried to kill storm into your home should be enough to make anyone think twice. As per the discussion with Oliver, Matthew had found Marek quite approachable once he mentioned the wands and his direct implication in the attack on the city.

Opening his mouth to firmly remind Marek of his position, Matthew was interrupted by the approach of a large nosed man in a cream summer suit.

"Felix Marek! Good to see you lured out from that country retreat." The man pulled Marek into an enthusiastic handshake and looked Matthew up and down before offering him too, a hand in greeting. "David Hayes," he paused, expectantly awaiting an introduction in return, but Matthew's memory went blank. What was the name Oliver had given him to use? He'd never been great with names, but before he could give up and stutter something out, he was saved.

"Don't mind him," Marek waved Matthew away and leaned close to the man's ear. "An old friend called in a favour; his cousin is starting a business and needs to do some networking." Marek raised his voice again so Matthew could hear. "In fact, he was about to head off and do just that."

"Oh, I was looking forward to meeting the beautiful lady that would accompany you this year," David winked and Matthew realised his presence might be more conspicuous that he hoped. "But in that case you must tell me some more about this business venture."

The exasperation Matthew saw cross Felix Marek's face likely mirrored his own.

"It's not—" Marek began before Matthew interrupted him.

"It's power generation," The answer came in a flash of inspiration. "Converting magic into electricity. We hope it will be an efficient way to bring power to areas that are not currently on the grid." He hoped it sounded boring enough that David would drop the subject, though Matthew gave a mental apology to his son for the thought.

"Well, that sounds fascinating," unfortunately, David looked like he meant it. "Especially for Ardveld, of course. Perhaps pass me your business card? I'm on the board of a few companies that might be interested in such a thing."

"Uh, oh dear. I'm sorry; I must have left them in my other jacket." Matthew patted his pockets unconvincingly as David gave him a confused look, and Marek silently fumed. "I'm just going to..." He indicated vaguely towards the drinks table then ducked past an approaching waiter into a group of other attendees. A glance back revealed Marek visibly glowering before he was lost in the crowd.

The conversation had shaken him more than expected.

Without thinking, Matthew found his legs carrying him away from the other guests, down the patio steps to the gravelled garden path below. It wasn't much quieter here, but the smell of summer flowers began to calm his nerves. Roses. Matthew's sigh of relief caught in his throat.

He was inside. He just needed to hold it together until he got to Alex.

Music carried from a roped off area to his right; a second marquee rising in the background. That close to the palace's east wing... Matthew staggered back as he realised the restricted area must be for Ardveld's leaders and officials. Blood rushed in his ears as he scanned the distant attendees for Morgan, but if he was among them, he wasn't visible.

It was open here. Too open for him to be shielded from view, no matter how many flowerbeds he tried to put between himself and that marquee. Before he realised it, he'd left the patio behind completely, music and voices fading back, replaced by birdsong and the inescapable trickling of a fountain.

A cold chill dripped through Matthew's body. He didn't want to turn to look at where his instinct had pulled him. In the nightmares, he could never look away. Now, even in the glaring light of day, he was certain the scene behind him would be just as he'd left it, all those years ago.

It was evening then. Mage lights glowing in the grounds. The smell of flowers mixing with the food scents that wafted tantalisingly from the palace kitchens.

Xander had snuck them a fresh loaf and so many cheeses that Matthew had been sure the servers would notice the absence. But enough wine would have flowed by that course that the Velbian diplomats wouldn't care.

He'd skipped enough formal dinners to know his father

would give him a strong scolding that evening. Apparently it was as insult for the crown prince to not deem their guests worthy of his attendance, though Matthew could never see why. It wasn't as if any of them had ever spoken more than a few platitudes to him.

No. He'd much rather be watching Xander throw bread to the fish in the pond, than pretending he cared about his royal duty.

Of course, he should have predicted Oliver would be sent to bring them in. Despite only being a potential, the nineteen-year-old shadow of his father's Tactician was more of a stickler for the rules than any of the actual Royal Champions. In contrast, Xander, for all his good breeding, spent enough time in the kitchens that you could be forgiven for assuming he was a baker's boy, rather than a potential Champion himself. Something they both enjoyed using to torment Oliver's delicate principles.

The initial shots from the palace were a foreign enough sound that Matthew first thought of fireworks. It wasn't until Oliver collapsed, barely missing the pond, that they thought anything could be wrong.

He'd been cradling Oliver in his arms when he watched the same happen to Xander. He'd never seen an awakening before. Had no idea then what it meant. If he'd have realised...

The man in the Velbian uniform who emerged around the boxed hedgerow seemed at first as though he was there to help them. Oliver's shouted warning came too late. Unconscious, with no magic to protect him, the bullet faced no resistance. Matthew could only sit, frozen, as Xander's blood clouded the crystal water of the pond, ears ringing from the crack of the gun.

It was only thanks to Oliver that he hadn't faced the

same fate. The older boy's shield, strengthened with the magic of a fully awakened Champion, encircled them both and the shot meant for Matthew ricocheted uselessly into the bushes.

He'd known he had to move, could hear Oliver begging him to get up, but he couldn't tear his eyes from his fallen friend.

When he asked later what had happened to the guard, Oliver had been evasive. For his part, Matthew only remembered the flare of magic from beside him; the blast that fired the Velbian back beyond the hedge. Oliver hadn't wanted to speculate on the man's survival. When he'd finally dragged Matthew to his feet, they hadn't looked back.

"Hey!"

Matthew looked up with a start. A server was coming towards him and for a second he had the urge to flee before he recognised Roy's red hair.

"What are you doing all the way out here? Took me ages to find you." Looking closer, he saw that Roy appeared to have simply shrugged on a waiter's jacket, and the rest of his outfit didn't quite match.

"...Sorry." Matthew shook his head rapidly to rid himself of the memories. Out of the corner of his eye, he was relieved to see clear water, disturbed only by the ripples of the fountain. "Sorry. You're right. Let's go."

Roy didn't press for an explanation. Instead, he held a hand out to stop Matthew from walking back up the path. "About that. We might have a problem."

His stomach flipped again at the words. "What do you mean, 'a problem'?"

"It's Marek. I saw him slip a note to one of the guards. I can't guarantee it, but I'm gonna bet it's about you. Let's get this done quick and get out while we can."

Matthew swore viciously. His first thought was to confront Felix Marek, but if Roy was correct, then it wouldn't do much good now. "Okay, fine. Oliver's plan was we go in through the secondary kitchen. I don't see why that should change." Without waiting on a response, Matthew began to lead the way back up towards the palace.

Due to the party, the smaller kitchen in the west wing would be in full use; a fact Roy had confirmed once he swapped onto the delivery shift. The west wing once contained the rooms of the Champion potentials, but had become an academy for mages under Morgan's rule, at least until recent years. Regardless, as Head of Magical Affairs, that was where the woman's office would be, and with it, their best chance of finding Alex.

"If we stick close, it'll just look like I'm helping a guest," Roy jogged up beside him. "You'll have to slow down a bit though, mate, or people are going to think something's up. Walk like you belong, remember?"

Matthew inhaled deeply and slowed his pace. Roy was right; he'd be no use to Alex if he got caught. As they drew closer to the entrance, glamorous guests were replaced by a stream of servers filling in and out. None of them looked their way as Roy and Matthew slipped amongst a group entering the kitchen.

Inside was a storm of noise and organised chaos. Even sticking to the edge of the room, Matthew scarcely escaped a plate of canapes being tipped over him; the rushing server sending a sharp word his way without looking back. Before he had time to register a response, they were at the rear door and through to a mercifully empty cloakroom.

Roy audibly exhaled a breath of relief beside him and

Matthew watched bewildered as he popped a canape into his mouth. "Well, that went well at least."

The room was half as wide as the kitchen, though still large enough for a dozen people. Bags and clothes were piled in every available space, blocking sight of the hooks and cupboards they hung on. Only the doors remained clear; two of them, other than the door they had entered through. Though closed, Matthew knew the one opposite led to the main corridor of the west wing, with the door on his right opening onto the staff entrance hall.

He crossed the room and extended his magic sense to the area beyond the right hand doors. As expected, he couldn't reach far through the walls, but it was enough to detect the energy of at least one mage.

"A guard that way. At least one." Matthew moved to the other door.

"They were checking IDs when I came in," Roy replied. "You can feel them through a wall?"

The disbelief in Roy's voice was obvious, but Matthew ignored it, occupied instead with the locking spell on the door to the main hall. "You think you can get this open?" It was solidly complex, though not the kind he remembered from his childhood and had installed at Felix Marek's.

"Yeah, easy." Roy walked up beside him and put a hand on the door. "Just give me a sec."

A tingle of magic emanated from Roy as he worked. Matthew stood in silence, shifting from foot to foot and listening out with both his hearing and magic sense for any change behind either door. Roy had sounded confident enough, and he didn't want to draw attention by blasting away a spell he didn't have to.

After what seemed like far more than a 'sec', Matthew

felt the rush of dispursed magic and Roy stepped away from the door, grinning. "Told you!"

"Not bad." Matthew had to admit he was impressed.

The corridor they walked into hadn't changed since his childhood. Chipped panelling and faded blue carpet showed a lack of upkeep in stark contrast to the main entrance hall; the stale scent so familiar that he half expected to hear voices he knew, echoing from the empty rooms on either side.

He remembered some of the layout. The first door to his left had once led to a dining room, with reception areas further down and a little library that paled in comparison to the grand one in the east wing. Now though...

As they walked further Matthew felt a strong passive spell emanating from a room ahead. The plaque beside the door answered his question: 'Head of Magic Affairs'. It was locked.

"Do we go in?"

Roy voiced Matthew's own thoughts. He couldn't detect anyone in the room, but his regular magic sense could be clouded by the radiating energy of the door spell. Closing his eyes, he instinctively reached for the natural magic from the ground instead, just as he had done when he was young. Immediately he was met with the distortion caused by several bodies of energy; some from the floor above, but two approaching rapidly from the stairwell ahead.

"Someone's coming." Before he could process how he had felt them, Matthew grabbed Roy and dragged him through the nearest unspelled door.

They found themselves in what must be a disused classroom. Chairs sat upturned on desks, and heavy curtains blocked the light that would have streamed from the palace courtyard. To his credit, Roy stayed silent beside him. Soon, footsteps confirmed what his senses had told him; two mages heading down the corridor towards the room they were hiding in.

They stopped too close, and Matthew cursed his luck.

"Door looks secure." A voice said on the other side. They must be checking the office.

"Doubt he would have bothered with it anyway." Came the reply. "If he came through the kitchen, he'll have likely headed straight to palace proper. Nothing to steal around here."

Matthew heard Roy swear under his breath, but was too distracted by the spell he was forming to acknowledge it. Hopefully the guards wouldn't be able to sense them through the door, but if they did, he would be ready to fight.

"I'll head over and make sure the guys at the entrance know no one's allowed through. You tell the kitchen to keep an eye out. I'm sure they'll be well pleased."

The footsteps started up again and Matthew exhaled, letting his spell disperse. "Shit," he hissed. "Looks like we aren't walking out the front door then."

"Look, we knew Marek had said something," Roy folded his arms. "At least now we have some idea what's going on. It's not ideal, but they're looking for one person inside the main palace. That means we can just pick up your kid and his friend, and hang out 'til we can leave."

Matthew shook his head. "I felt some people on the floor above. It could be them, but if they're under guard, then we won't be able to wait around. Someone's going to realise and come hunting, plus Felix Marek will have given my description," he tugged a hand through his hair. "I'll fight my way out the staff entrance if I have to, but with Alex…" Matthew trailed off. The thought of his son in a battle turned his stomach.

"Sounds like its plan B then?" Roy's reply caused Matthew to snap his head up in surprise, but the man just shrugged. "I heard you and Oliver talking. What is it, and why is it so dangerous?"

Plan B. He'd had the same thought himself, around the time he'd realised why he could feel the guards and the people upstairs; his old life forcing itself into his present. Just being here was enough that he'd automatically reached into the ground magic to extend his range. As a child, he'd never even separated it from his own magic sense.

"Plan B means going deeper into the palace," Matthew heaved a breath. "There's another way out. Through the throne room. But getting there now won't be easy." He turned towards the door. "Let's find Alex first. We'll decide what to do after that."

Roy got there before Matthew could pull the handle. Palm against the door, he held it shut. "They're only looking for one person. How about I give them someone to find?"

Matthew's grip on the door handle softened. "You're going to cause a distraction?"

"I don't intend to get myself caught. Once they see me, I'm bailing. But if they're after me, it should give you guys a clear run to your exit." He moved away from the door and extended a hand to Matthew. "Keep calm. Act like any other guest and with luck, we won't have to deal with each other again. Just hope you don't need any more doors unlocking on your way."

"You can't get out the way we do. Not alone."

"I'll take my chances. This is what I do."

Matthew narrowed his eyes. "Didn't you get shot at last time?"

"Out of practice," Roy didn't lower his hand. "Won't happen again. Besides, it's much easier to hide out alone until this blows over."

Matthew hesitated, then grasped Roy's hand in his own. "Okay, but listen." He paused for a moment, not sure how much he should say, but dismissed the concern. "If you're looking to create a disturbance, head through the far door and up a floor. You'll end up in the state rooms; any of those doors should be alarmed. After that, if you need to get out quick, get to the library. The upper floor has a small window at the back on the left side. It's a short drop out to the main kitchen roof, then from there you can get down to the gardens. It's still in the grounds, but you'll at least be out of the building."

"That is... both incredibly vague and very specific," Roy raised an eyebrow. "Do I ever get to know how you know this?"

Matthew inclined his head. "As you said. Hopefully we won't have to see each other again."

CHAPTER 17

The air cooling spells inside the marquee had dropped the temperature unpleasantly low, but the cold did little to ease the churning in Tamara's stomach. A champagne flute clutched close to her chest, she paced back along the table that ran down the side of the tent, pretending to be fascinated by the floral tributes and other gifts displayed there.

A band was playing outside and Tamara swayed as she walked; the rhythmic motion soothing and easily explained away. Through the open doors of the marquee, she could almost glimpse the window where Alex was being kept and, once again, she debated whether to head outside, braving the noise and conversation, and look for Morgan. But the people milling at the entrance meant she would have to push through or interact.

Even if she found him, what would she say? After last night, bringing up theories of Prince Matthew's survival, no matter the evidence, would be seen as making light of their conversation. Additionally, as much as she felt a growing sense of familiarity towards Morgan, Tamara had to admit that she barely knew him. What she did know wasn't enough to predict his response. He was still the leader of Ardveld, and though she didn't want to think about it, the risk he posed to Alex's safety was large.

A passing server held out a tray of decorative pastries, but moved on when Tamara shook her head. Maybe she should force an exit through the back? It would be almost unnoticeable, especially with so few people in the room. She could get away from the party, let Alex and Eira go, and forget all about this. She'd come up with something to tell Aiden—

"I thought I might find you in here."

Champagne splashed up in the glass as Tamara spun around. Morgan stopped a pace away from her, resplendent in his official outfit; a high collared white jacket with shimmering gold detailing the buttons and shoulders. There was no trace of last night's vulnerability, and Tamara hoped her reaction hadn't made her look too guilty.

"I apologise. I didn't intend to startle you." Something akin to sorrow crossed Morgan's face, and she felt a sudden need to assure him the approach wasn't unwelcome.

"Sorry! Don't worry, I was just thinking. How are you feeling today?"

"Ah. Yes, of course. I am very well. Thank you." Morgan's

awkward reply belied his composed demeanour, and immediately Tamara regretted her words. It should have been obvious he wouldn't want her to mention their last conversation. "In fact, that is actually what I came to discuss. I wanted to express my regret at bringing personal matters into our professional working relationship. I hope that you will see fit to resume where we left off before... Well, you understand."

Tamara forced herself to look up at him, directing her gaze at the point between his eyes to relieve the intensity. "Oh. Of course. That's perfectly fine." She spoke lightly, but her smile felt painfully stiff. It hurt. The sense of closeness shattered as she was pushed away. At least she hadn't been fool enough to tell him about Alex.

Behind Morgan, a colourful display of people streamed into the marquee and Tamara thought she heard him groan as the group approached. For her, it was the opportunity to slip away unnoticed. Ducking towards the tent entrance, Tamara skirted past the crowd.

Her momentary glimpse of freedom didn't last. Before she had taken more than two steps, the doorway was once again blocked. Entering the tent, with two of his personal guards, was Aiden. Tamara froze and, for a brief moment, hoped he might not see her; but she had left the crowd behind with Morgan and there was nothing to block his line of sight.

Aiden strode towards her, face lit up with that smile. He too was dressed in the Heliodor colours, though his outfit was in a civilian style rather than the militaresque look of Morgan's; a white morning suit with gold detailing. It had been less than a day since she'd taken his book. Nowhere near enough time for her to get in touch with the Golebach police. With the party today, the excuse was almost true.

Tamara raised her hand in a wave of greeting. Perhaps it would best to confide the truth to him after all? Aiden was a researcher, not a killer. His excitement at the prospect of a royal family member being alive was surely proof that he meant them no harm. She dismissed the idea as soon as it came. Even she wasn't oblivious enough to admit to having lied directly to the Prince of Vailberg.

"How are you finding the party?" she said when he was close enough to hear.

"Better now." Aiden sidled closer, almost brushing against Tamara's habitual shield. "I am excited to hear if you have thought any more about our little chat last night."

His words should have triggered her nerves, but Tamara was finding it hard to focus. Aiden's guards stood beside him, close enough now that she recognised the logo of Sunstone Enterprises on their dark suits. Aiden's company. From their energy, she could tell they were both mages. One shook their head at an approaching partygoer; not unexpected from a guard instructed to keep people at a distance from their charge, but still intimidating. Perhaps that explained why she was so dizzy. As she struggled to form a response, Aiden followed her gaze and Tamara realised she had been staring.

"Go and wait outside." Aiden directed his command at the mages, and her brewing nausea settled as they left. "They're distracting," he said, turning back to her, "But when you're me, protocol insists. No need for them now though; I doubt even my mother could find me a better guard than Ardveld's Head of Magical Affairs."

"Oh," Tamara wasn't sure what expression to make as she processed his comment. "Ah, well, I suppose I am strong enough…" She trailed off as she saw Aiden's grin fade. He'd been making a joke. A sip from her champagne flute might have hid her embarassment, but her startle with Morgan had left it almost empty. Instead she stepped backwards, stumbling straight into the person behind her.

"I do hope I'm not making a habit of sneaking up on you." Morgan's voice came from above her head, and Tamara understood why Aiden's expression had changed. She sprung away, turning enough to bring them both into view.

"Excuse the interruption," Morgan said, "However, I'm sure you won't object to me inviting my advisor to a dance." He extended an arm, the request apparently directed at her.

Aiden leant back, smoothing down his coat. "My good nature clearly precedes me." There was an edge to his voice, but his face remained expressionless. "Go ahead. We'll speak later." Without looking her way, he spun on his heel and strode out of the tent.

Morgan and Tamara were left in silence. She hadn't taken the outstretched arm and now wasn't sure that she should.

"I'm not going to insist—" Morgan stopped as Tamara placed her hand on the fabric of his coat. "Thank you." His voice had regained the ease of the previous night. "It would have been most embarassing for the leader to Ardveld to have their first dance request rejected."

Her surprise must have been written on her face because Morgan laughed. Then he took the empty glass from her hand and set it on the tray of a passing staff member, before escorting her outside.

The music grew louder once they left the tent, and Tamara clung tighter to the stiff material of Morgan's sleeve as the crowd parted to let them through. Apart from brushing off any party attendees that approached, he had said nothing since she accepted his request. Now though, she saw heads turning towards them.

"I was honest when I said I don't ask people to dance." Morgan broke the silence as they reached the temporary flooring that had been installed outside the marquee. "I hope an audience doesn't bother you."

It certainly did, and Tamara had a sudden, horrible awareness. "I don't— I mean, this probably isn't a good idea, actually!" She released Morgan's arm and pulled away, but he caught her hand gently, stopping her flight.

"Just follow my lead." Morgan gave a small tug and Tamara reluctantly stepped closer. There were enough other people on the dance floor that she might not be obvious, though she noticed with dismay that the other couples were spreading out to make room.

The hand Morgan placed on her waist made her jump in surprise, his touch warm over her thin summer dress, even through the shield she kept against her skin. She stumbled after him, grateful that the music was slow enough for his movements to guide her, despite her lack of rhythm.

"See, you could be worse," Morgan said. When Tamara looked up, he was smiling.

"You seem completely fine!" She blurted out just as comprehension caught up with her. "You liar." Despite her inexperience, she couldn't fail to notice the confidence in his movements.

"We both know it wasn't technically a lie." His smile now held the hint of a tease. "I'm afraid the choice of learning wasn't mine to make."

Morgan must think her completely naïve. Still, her embarrassment was tempered by a flutter in her stomach as he leant his head down towards her.

"Tamara," his breath against her ear sent a tingle through her spine and she instinctively moved to strengthen her shield before realising she didn't really want to. "I don't know what business my nephew has with you, but you must trust me when I tell you to keep your distance from him."

She jerked her head back, but Morgan cut her off before she could question. "I can't tell you why, just allow me to impress upon you the importance of this. Please." His blue eyes were imploring, but Tamara would never make a promise without knowing she could keep it. Mind distracted, she missed her footing, only caught by Morgan's hold.

As he steadied her, she saw a palace guard approaching. The woman looked flustered, though she didn't hurry; instead, weaving politely through the guests towards them.

"Excuse me, High Minister, for the interruption." The guard gave a short bow and Tamara felt the chill of Morgan's absence as he released her.

He held up a hand. "Not here."

Guests stepped aside to let them pass, and Tamara followed him and the guard, only wondering if she should have stayed behind when they were far enough to not be overheard.

"Please, continue," Morgan said. To her relief, he made no move to dismiss her.

The guard glanced at Tamara, but didn't pause. "We have received a report of an intruder in the palace. We immediately dispatched guards to search the building and have placed restrictions on anyone entering or leaving."

Morgan's expression was severe. "Where did the report come from? Does it suggest there is a threat to the guests?"

"It was a guest who informed us, High Minister." The guard continued. "The report was of a potential thief in the vicinity of the academy. We do not believe there is any threat at this time, but will continue to monitor the situation, unless you have further orders."

The academy. Sweat pricked on her palms. It was her first palace event; perhaps this kind of thing was a common occurrence? The reassurance did nothing to sooth her rising panic.

"Very well," Tamara heard Morgan speaking over her pounding heart. "Continue as you were and let me know if there are any developments."

From the corner of her eye, she saw the guard bow to Morgan before departing. He turned back to face her, but she was already stuttering an apology. Before he could respond, Tamara had left, pushing her way through the crowd of guests towards the palace.

CHAPTER 18

Thick carpet muffled the sound of Roy's steps as he crept through the empty state rooms. Even the air smelt more expensive up here. Arched windows to his left provided a sweeping view of the party that continued in the gardens below, but there was little time to admire the scenery; he needed to find something alarmed.

He stopped under a painting that would have spanned the length and height of his own bedroom, and noticed the red dot of a security camera blinking from the corner of the ceiling. Taking it out might well cause the disturbance he wanted, but as he was preparing the spell, he paused.

What were the chances they'd notice one camera?

Destroying more would just spread the guards looking for him over a wider area and limit his escape options, not to mention reducing the effectiveness of the distraction. Better to draw them to a single location and give Matthew the space he needed. He was still wearing the jacket he'd taken from the staff room; with any luck, it would keep the surveillance team off him until he wanted it.

Roy pressed on, casting out with his magic sense for something more dramatic. A multitude of passive spells answered his exploratory sensing, but none of them were alarms as Matthew had promised. Perhaps he wasn't supposed to have gone up as far as the top floor?

As if in answer, the room exited onto a long, wood panelled corridor. A wide staircase descended to his left, curving down to a landing and on out of sight. Doors lined the hall ahead, along with a vibrant magic signal that could only mean an advanced lock. Roy hurried forward, ignoring the distant sounds of movement and talking from the floors below.

The source of the magic was a door of carved, dark wood. Beside it, a pillar held a vase of freshly cut flowers and Roy plucked a white petal, rubbing it between his finger and thumb, as he assessed the passive spell. As expected, it was a strong lock, though not the type he'd practiced with his mother. Trying to enter without authorisation would cause the distraction he needed, though he couldn't tell whether that would be an audible alarm from the door itself, or somewhere else in the palace.

Eyes seeing only the magic, it took Roy a moment to notice the golden plaque beside the door: 'High Minister Morgan Heliodor'

He crushed the petal between his fingers; fear and rage fighting for dominance over his pounding heart. This was

Morgan's office. Years of questioning. The very reason he had broken into Felix Marek's house in the first place. All that might stand between him and the answer to his mother's death was a piece of wood. He was going in.

Decision made, Roy focussed his mind to task. With his hand on the door, he searched for the subtle energy shift that would indicate the caster's starting point; the place where they had most strongly focussed their intention. He bit his lip as he found more than what he was searching for.

A subtle, second spell lay under the first; a backup alarm that would alert if the main lock was deactivated. It would be easy enough for him to remove now he'd noticed it…

But Matthew needed a distraction.

Roy looked back at the door. There'd be another alarm further along. He just needed a bit of time to poke around, then he'd set off the next one.

Even as he thought it, he knew he was kidding himself. Matthew didn't have time, and Roy doubted any of the information he was looking for would just be left in the open. Besides, it had taken him long enough to find this one. This room was exactly what he'd been looking for; his chance.

Both the alarm and lock spell shone bright in his mind. Then, with a momentary lament for his reputation, he sent a spur of energy directly into the lock's weak point. There was always next year.

The moment he did, his vision went black. He barely felt himself falling as a wave of dizziness and nausea rushed through his body.

As fast as it had come, the darkness receded. Roy sat up and rubbed the side of his head where it had struck the wall. *What the hell was that?* There had been no sign that the secondary alarm contained a defence mechanism, and it hadn't been an effective attack anyway, unless you counted the bump. Even so, he'd hoped causing a distraction would be less painful.

As the sore spot eased, he stood and opened the now unlocked door. Light from the corridor illuminated a large desk to the left, but his eyes hadn't adjusted enough to make out more. From here, it looked just like an ordinary office. He lifted a foot to cross the threshold.

"Stop right there!"

The shout came from behind him and he froze. Part of him had still hoped he'd have time.

"Freeze! Don't move!" The voice came again as Roy backed away from the door, and he thought he detected a squeak.

A few paces towards the stairs, partially obscured by the pillar, stood a young guard. He held some sort of gun, the barrel of which was quivering but pointing straight at him. Great. Roy rolled his eyes and held his hands out the way he had seen in those Velbian movies.

"I'm not moving, see," Roy said, working on generating a shield as he spoke. At least there was only one of them and, given the fact he couldn't sense him, this guard wasn't a mage. That likely made him as young as he looked. "I'd appreciate it if you didn't, you know, point that at me," he wiggled a finger in an attempt to indicate the weapon. "Apparently I really don't deal well with being shot at, and I'd rather not go through it again."

"Quiet! I have backup on the way."

Roy didn't like the way the guard jerked the gun as he talked. He could deflect a few bullets, sure, but this was a long corridor with a direct line of sight and he believed him about the backup.

A line of sight... There was no way back past the guard, and beyond Morgan's office the corridor ran straight until it reached a corner. Roy had no idea what was around there, but it looked like the only option.

"I said, don't move!" The guard shouted again, more forcefully. Seemed like time was up. He had been getting bored anyway. Drawing on his magic, Roy wove the familiar spell for a magelight. With his intention focussed, he squeezed his eyes shut and directed the brightest glow he could muster directly in front of the young man's face.

The resulting flash lit Roy's closed eyes up red. A cry from the guard made him tense, but to his relief there was no accompanying gunshot. Still, it wouldn't stall him for long. Dismissing the light, Roy blinked his scalded vision back. Then, with a gust of magic directed air, he hurled the vase of flowers towards the guard's stomach with all his strength.

He'd only meant to wind the guy, but the vase shot across the room, taking the guard with it and slamming him hard against the wall. The plinth it had been standing on followed, and Roy scrambled to redirect its fall; sending it crashing down on top of the gun rather than onto the man's prone body. For what felt like a lifetime, he didn't move.

"...Mate, you okay?"

Then he heard the guard groan. They would have a healer in the palace, Roy assured himself, as he turned to bolt down the corridor.

Matthew said he should look for the library, right? Pity he hadn't stopped to specify where he would find it. As he turned the corner, the hall opened out into a landing, with another set of stairs descending on his right and more closed doors ahead. He paused, relieved to ease the stitch forming in his side, then chose the stairs.

Half way down, he almost collided with someone heading up the other way. Roy had seen Aiden Heliodor's picture before, but it took a moment for his brain to equate the sneering glare of the person he had just bumped into with the smiling man from the papers. He clattered to a stop and tried to breathe like he hadn't been running.

The expression on Aiden's face implied the encounter was mutually unwelcome. No guards accompanied him, which probably meant he wasn't here to face down an intruder. With luck, he didn't know there was an intruder at all.

"Your Majesty," Roy swooped into as deep a bow as was possible on stairs. "It is an honour to be in your presence." From the corner of his eye he saw Aiden leaning away from him, arms folded across his chest. "I'm afraid I can't let you go this way; there's trouble up ahead."

"You can't let me," Aiden repeated the words slowly, as though savouring the taste. "What kind of trouble?" The edge of his mouth twitched up as he said the words, and Roy got the distinct impression his time in this conversation was limited.

"An intruder. A dangerous one." Roy rushed a reply. Aiden was shorter in person than he'd expected, but his presence made the space feel tiny. "I would advise you get to safety and avoid this area. The library, too. We've heard that could be a target." There was no sound of anyone chasing him, but it took effort to keep his eyes fixed ahead

"That is most interesting, considering I was just there."

"Well, it's lucky you aren't there anymore then! I'm sure guards will be here to deal with the issue soon. If you would let me escort—"

"No. I think not." Aiden narrowed his eyes and Roy saw

him reach a hand towards the inside of his jacket.

"They're a powerful mage!" Roy blurted the words out, not wanting to face down another gun. "They've broken into Morgan's office. I really must insist—"

"Morgan's office?" The ice in Aiden's tone thawed to surprise, and he lowered his arm a fraction.

"Yes, but as I said, guards will be here soon and—"

"In that case, I must thank you for your concern for my welfare." Aiden's face took on a charming television smile, and Roy let out a breath as the arm reaching for a weapon fell back to his side. "I will, of course, head directly to safety. But in the meantime, may I suggest you check the library? It is a potential target after all."

Roy wasn't quite sure why, but it seemed that Aiden was going to let him go. Not a moment too soon either; he could hear voices growing louder from the corridor above him.

"Do hurry along. We wouldn't want any guests left unwarned, would we?" Aiden kept his eyes on Roy as he moved around him. "Down the stairs. Double doors, on your left."

Unsteady with nerves, Roy stumbled the rest of the way down. Then, walking as fast as he dared, he followed Aiden's directions. *I cannot believe that worked.*

The library was much cooler than the corridor. Dimly lit, the hardwood floor made his footsteps echo as the smell of books assailed his senses. Tall windows on the far side reached as high as the second floor, which circled the room like a balcony. Shelves lined every other available space.

Roy darted to the staircase on his left, grateful to put some distance between himself and the door. The windows were stained glass and his approach confirmed his initial fears; none of them looked like they would open.

How would Matthew have even known? Oliver seemed more the type to have a floor plan, though it had never come up in conversation and Roy doubted it would be detailed enough to show a window. After coming this far... He ran his hands around the bottom edge of the glass and even sensed for a spell, but there would be no exit that didn't involve smashing.

Footsteps from the floor below reminded Roy that he was still in full view of the library doors. He slipped behind the nearest bookshelf, craning his neck to see who was there, but no one came into view. Great. Now he was stuck here. He might even have to resort to reading something while he waited.

As he slouched back against the bookcase, Roy realised that the narrow space seemed lighter than it had any right to be. He looked to his right and was met with the sight of a small, square window. Small, but passable. Didn't Matthew mention the library being at the corner of the building?

The window didn't look like anyone had opened it for years; the glass too fogged with dirt to see through. Even unlatched, it didn't budge when Roy tried to shift it, though whether this was due to age or human intervention he couldn't tell. He cast a shield to dull the sound and pushed again with more force. This time, with a splintering of wood and paint, it cracked open, and Roy caught sight of the palace grounds beyond.

He was two floors up, at least. But just as Matthew had claimed, there was a flat roof sticking out from the side of the palace below him. It would be a drop of just over his own height; nothing he hadn't done before, and at least this time he wasn't falling down some scaffolding while deflecting bullets.

Glad he hadn't gone for the double pizza order more often, Roy sucked in a breath and squeezed through the gap. Once through, he turned around and lowered himself down, dropping the last bit to the roof below. With a nudge of wind magic, the window swung shut behind him. It would be one to remember if he ever felt like snooping around the palace again.

The breeze was cold on his face, grey sky threatening a summer storm. From here, Roy was hidden from both the garden party and the expansive drive at the palace front, though he didn't feel ready to try an escape in either direction. He dusted his hands on his trousers. At least he was no longer inside. Perhaps he'd just —

"*Not bad.*" A voice interrupted. "*I always wondered how he got out.*"

CHAPTER 19

Alex poked a twirl of cold pasta around with his fork.

"You're thinking about your dad again, aren't you?" Eira's voice from the other bed told him she had been watching, and he dumped the still full bowl onto the desk with a clatter.

"I'm not!" He glared out the window, not wanting her to see the lie on his face. "I'm just not going to eat food given to me by liars. They must be stupid to think anyone would believe it anyway."

With a sigh, Eira set her empty bowl beside his. "Alex, we've been through this."

"I don't know how you're still eating!" His scowl

deepened. "They're probably going to come up with some wacko conspiracy about you too."

"That's why I'm still eating. I don't want to be too weak if I have to fight for my life." Eira rolled onto her feet and joined him beside the window. "Party still going on then?" Alex just snorted. "I wish you would take this more seriously."

"Exactly how am I not taking this seriously?" His jaw ached from where he'd been gritting his teeth. Even knowing he was being unfair to Eira, he couldn't help the rage that had been brewing since his meeting with Tamara. "She's trying to frame me as some kind of... I don't even know! They can't get away with this."

"I thought you told me the palace could do whatever they want." Eira was smiling, but Alex saw she was hugging her arms close to her body.

Concern calmed his anger. "Are you doing okay?" She was caught up in this because of him. There was a chance they wouldn't need more than one scapegoat, but she must be worried about what was going to happen to her.

"Not really." Eira's reply was more honest than he'd anticipated. "Every time I hear the door, I expect someone to come for you again. Next time, you might not come back."

Alex shook his head. "No-one's going to come for me. The moment anyone looks into this, it'll be obvious it's not true. Mum and dad will tell them — They'll go to the papers. If the palace try anything they'll look really bad."

"What makes you think they care about how they look? If that woman made this up to cover her mistake, then we'll just disappear. She obviously wanted you to confess." Eira pulled away from him, expression severe.

"Well, I'm not going to confess to anything." His words

came out less confident that he'd hoped. "...I can't believe I trusted her." Outside the white marquees shook in the growing wind. Last night, Tamara had been dressed like she'd just come from a party. Was it all just an act? "I told her everything. I really thought she was going to help us."

"What else could you do?" Eira came to sit beside him, resting her head against his shoulder. "I'm pretty sure lying would have made things worse."

Alex's stomach growled, and he thought back to what Eira had said about needing enough energy to fight. He was a pretty strong mage, for Couden Cross anyway, but turning his magic against someone? He wasn't sure he could.

A light thud against the door made both of them jump. Alex whirled to his feet, though his legs were unsteady. Beside him, Eira's magic flared as she cast a shield and he reached into his own power to do the same, scolding himself for not paying attention to the ground magic and the warning it would have provided. He sensed it now though; the ripples caused by an approaching mage's energy.

"...That was nothing, right?" Eira broke the silence just as a blast of power forced the door open.

It took Alex a second to recognise the man stood there. "Wha— Dad?"

It was his father. At least it looked like him, though Alex couldn't remember ever seeing him like this. There were heavy bags under his eyes, and the dark suit he wore did nothing to help the pallor of his skin. When he caught sight of Alex, his face flooded with relief and, before he had time to react, his dad had scooped him into a hug.

"You're okay." Matthew croaked, and Alex had the uneasy impression that his dad might be crying.

"Y— yeah, I'm fine," Alex stiffened, fighting the urge to

lean into the comfort of the hug; the smell of home assuring him that this really was his father who had somehow appeared. Instead he pulled back, trying to meet his gaze. "What are you doing here?"

"It doesn't matter. We need to go, now." It was a command and as Alex looked up, he was reminded that he hadn't yet caught up with his father's height. Matthew reached out, as if to grasp his hand, but Alex snatched it back.

"No." He could feel Eira's eyes on him. They should leave; at least for her sake. But a creeping suspicion was forcing its way to the front of his mind. "I need to know what's going on."

"I'll tell you later, I promise." Matthew held out a hand again, eyes flicking to the door as though he wanted to bolt. "Now Alex! Come on, we don't have time for this." There was a hint of anger in his raised voice, but Alex didn't care.

"There is time!" Maybe his parents had just found out he was being framed, or a palace official had called them to come and get him; any reason would do.

"Yeah, people who say they'll tell you later normally never do." Eira chimed up from beside him, and Alex had a rush of gratitude at her support.

Matthew sighed, running a hand through his dark hair in a familiar gesture of exasperation. "Please, Alex. Not here. I want to explain properly—"

"I know, Dad." Alex cut off his father's words. "I saw the picture. The one of you." Curled pages and aging photographs shone clearly in his memory. "It's actually true, isn't it."

His father looked away. "I don't know what you mean." But Alex could see by the expression on his face, he was right.

"They told me you're the prince, Dad! I thought they were lying, but... you're here," he hesitated. "Why?"

Pain twisted Matthew's face. "I didn't think... You know why I'm here then. If they know, then you're in danger. We all are." He reached out again, but Alex just stared at him.

"I should have heard it from you."

A silence followed his words, the party outside murmuring in the distance.

"You're right." Matthew finally nodded. "I'm sorry. I was trying to keep you safe."

"Well, that didn't exactly work out, did it?" Alex shrugged and gestured at the room. "Let's go then."

Their guard was slumped against the wall next to the door. "Is he...?" Eira wavered in the doorway.

"Just asleep," Matthew confirmed. He reached his arms under those of the sleeping guard and hoisted him past her into the now empty bedroom.

"But that's— that's so illegal." Eira's protest was weak, as if she'd caught up with her own words in the middle of saying them.

Alex watched in silence as Matthew returned and began to cast a lock to replace the one he had destroyed. With the door closed, the walls seemed close and cramped, but they hadn't stood there long before his father headed off down the corridor. It was the same direction Alex had gone the day before with Tamara, and he hurried after, Eira close at his side.

"I can't believe he actually didn't change his name," she whispered as they walked.

"I was never very good with names," Matthew's unexpected reply came clearly from ahead of them. "I finally got Oliver to stop nagging me about it when I told him only an idiot wouldn't change their name, therefore no one would be looking for me under it." He made an amused hum and Alex caught a brief smile on his Dad's face as he rushed to catch up.

"Wait, Uncle Oliver knows too?" It hadn't crossed Alex's mind that his father had told anyone about his past. Somehow, the idea stung.

"I should hope he does." Matthew shrugged off the question but stopped as he saw Alex's face. "Oliver's my Tactician, Alex. A Royal Champion. My only Champion. He's been there since the beginning."

An image of Oliver rose in Alex's mind. The staid accountant he'd never seen out of a suit. The books he'd given for every birthday. None of it reconciled with the stories from history. Perhaps it made sense though; Oliver was the only person he had ever seen his Dad close to. Well, except...

"And mum?"

"She knows... As of two days ago." The last part was barely audible, but Alex heard.

"You didn't tell mum!"

"I wanted to leave it behind! I didn't think it would ever matter." There was hurt in his dad's voice. "I was wrong."

The staircase that led to Tamara's office was empty and Matthew hurried on, seemingly confident in the way. Alex reached out into the ground magic as they descended, not wanting to be caught unawares a second time, and was met with a signal from below just as he stumbled into his father's back.

Eira caught him before he could tumble forward. Matthew had stopped a few steps up from the ground floor, his magic flaring and causing the air to shimmer with the shield he cast. Whoever Alex had felt, his father must have sensed them too.

"Stay behind me," Matthew began in a hushed voice. "Eira, hold on to him for me, will you."

"Oh come on—" Alex shook himself free of Eira's grasp, his anticipated protest over before it could begin. But his indignation at her betrayal was interrupted by a quiet voice from the bottom of the stairs.

"Hello?"

A familiar face peered up at him, and as their eyes met, Tamara stepped into full view.

The summer dress she wore told Alex she must have come from the party outside, but she didn't look surprised to see him. She made no attempt to move closer, instead eyeing Matthew with a wariness Alex hadn't seen from her before.

"Don't," Tamara said. "You know I'm a mage. That won't work." Alex realised his father had been crafting a spell, and a jolt of panic shot through his heart.

"You don't want to fight me." Matthew's words came out as a growl.

"You're right. I don't," Tamara replied. "I know why you're here," her eyes flicked to Alex before his father's back obscured his view.

"Let me talk to her!" Alex stepped forward, eliciting a cry of protest from Eira. "Dad!" He tried to push his way down the stairs, but Matthew threw his arm out.

"It's okay, Alex—" Tamara's words were cut off by his father's interruption.

"Don't speak to him!"

She fell silent, her brow creased.

"You're the one who told him," Matthew stated.

"I thought he already knew."

In front of his father, Tamara looked tiny, but there was

no fear in her stance. She had told him the truth last night, and Alex felt a surprising regret that he had reacted with anger. Even so, she worked directly for Morgan. Even if she let them go...

"No one else knows," Tamara said. "I can help you get out, if you come with me." She took a step backwards, inviting them to descend, but Matthew didn't move.

"I can't believe that," he said. "You're Velbian. I know who you work for. Why would you let us go?"

"I'm not Velbian," Tamara shot back. "And I don't want Alex and Eira to come to harm any more than you do. I didn't realise when I brought them here."

"Look, I don't care what you are, or what your intentions were. If you really want to help, you'll stay out of our way." Matthew's shield still shimmered across the stairwell, but Tamara tilted her head.

"The palace is in lockdown. How are you planning on getting out without me?"

A dread settled in Alex's stomach at her words. He believed her. She hadn't lied to him up to now, and if people really were looking for them, having help from the Head of Magical Affairs might be their only way out.

"That's none of your concern. Just be grateful I'm going to let you live." Matthew lowered his shield and descended the remaining stairs. "Now, get inside your office. That is your office, I presume?" He gestured towards the door that Alex remembered as being Tamara's.

"No," Tamara stood her ground. "I promised I would return them home safely. If that means protecting them from your own stupidity—"

"Move. Now!"

At Matthew's shout, Alex leapt the last two stairs and

thrust himself between them. "Dad, leave her alone."

Shock seemed to halt his father's reply; his mouth hanging open as he stared at Alex. Then he moved as if to grasp him. "I told you to stay back."

Pulling on his magic, Alex's own shield flared and Matthew's attempt to drag him aside touched nothing but the invisible barrier between them. "I don't know you anymore. Is this who you really are?" There was a tremble in Alex's limbs as he faced down his father.

But the fury he feared to see on his father's face didn't manifest. "I..." Matthew stalled.

The sound of a door opening sent a jolt through the stalemate and the four of them froze as a pair of guards entered the corridor from the main palace.

"Minister!" The older of the two called out, and Alex realised how their current situation must appear. "Do you require assistance?"

Eira rushed to his side as Matthew stepped in front of them again, but Tamara was faster.

"I'm perfectly fine," she smiled and Alex sensed her magical defences fade. Only one of the guards was a mage, but she clearly wanted to put them at ease. "Can I help you? Is everything well at the party?"

The taller guard, a young mage with honey coloured hair poking out from under a white peaked hat, glanced nervously at his companion. "We have had a report of a suspicious individual inside the palace." He was looking past Tamara now, straight towards Matthew. "I'm afraid I will need to request some identification, Sir."

None of them moved, but Alex felt his father tense. Then, Tamara spoke. "These are my personal guests. I don't appreciate being them harassed outside my own office." She stood straight, with an authority Alex hadn't witnessed during any of their previous conversations.

"Even so, we cannot make exceptions." The second guard's face was emotionless, showing none of his colleague's fear. He took a step forward, but Tamara moved to block his path.

"You can't be intending to interrogate every guest at this party! As Head of Magical Affairs, I can assure you, these people have every right to be here." She tossed her head, sending a cascade of dark curls over her shoulder. "If my authorisation is not enough, then I suggest you take the issue to High Minister Morgan."

"My apologies but—"

"I can't imagine he would want to cause further distress to the guests, particularly when they have been prohibited from leaving the building," The older guard hesitated at Tamara's interruption, though Alex could see the mage was still staring in his direction with skittish suspicion. There was no way he or Eira looked like guests. "I expect the complaints have already started coming in."

"Your concerns are understandable." Eventually, the guard nodded, retreating as he inclined his head to Tamara and Matthew in turn. "I apologise, Minister, for the disturbance. Please be assured, we consider the safety of the guests our highest priority. For now, once you are finished here, I would suggest you all return outside until further notice."

"Of course." Alex was shocked to hear his father reply, but then the guards were gone, heading past them towards the opposite end of the corridor.

As soon as the door closed behind them, Alex let out a sigh of relief. "Thank you."

"I don't know if I can get you out of the palace," Tamara began, and Alex saw her hands were shaking as she rubbed her fingers together. "That worked for now, but they will be stricter if you try to leave. Maybe if you all sit in my office and I—"

"We won't be leaving via a usual exit," Matthew's reply was cool, but there was no anger left in his voice. "I need to get to the throne room, if it's even called that anymore."

"I'm not sure. I assume it wouldn't be…" Tamara hesitated, looking as confused as Alex felt.

"I know the way," Matthew's assurance was a crushing reminder of why they were here. "Can you get us through?"

As though feeling Alex's gaze, Tamara looked towards him. For a moment, she met his eyes and the uncertainty on her face was swept away, replaced by the same confidence she'd shown to the guards.

"Yes, I will."

CHAPTER 20

The throne room was on the ground floor of the east wing. They'd toyed with it as an option, Oliver never being the type to have only one plan, but Matthew hadn't seriously thought he'd have to use it. A single line of text via the burner phone they'd set up was all the notice his Tactician would get – *Plan B*.

His father had shown him the passageway as soon as he was old enough to take the knowledge with the severity it deserved. A way out, should they ever find themselves in danger or under siege. As far as Matthew knew, it had been there since the palace was built, never having the chance to serve its purpose. With luck, that was now going to change.

Obstructing their path was the main palace entrance; the same tiled foyer Matthew had passed through to reach the garden party. There was no avoiding it without heading outside or to a higher floor and, as Matthew feared, the area was swarming with guards rushing up and down the twin staircases.

Reliant on Tamara's authority to get them through, it was a pleasant surprise when barely anyone turned their way. Someone had attacked a guard and set off an alarm near the staterooms upstairs, and the man who stopped them buckled immediately at Tamara's insistence they pass; apparently too busy to concern himself with errant guests. Matthew sent silent thanks to Roy as they left the investigation behind.

The halls were quiet after that. Every step they took brought with it memories from his childhood, and he was somehow grateful for the tense silence in which they were making the trip. Alex was burning with unasked questions, Matthew knew him well enough to know that, and he was sure he would feel the same were the roles reversed. But answers would have to wait.

He reached out to his son as they walked, the hand he grasped matching the size of his own rather than that of the boy he had once been. Alex allowed the squeeze, but pulled away quickly. Still upset with him then. A small smile broke out on Matthew's face; he hadn't dared to hope to find him as well as he was.

As for Eira, he still wasn't sure what they were going to do with her once they got out; Oliver's plan to send her home scuppered by the knowledge she now held.

A pair of familiar double doors blocked the end of the wide corridor. "This is it." Matthew slowed his pace as they approached, reaching out with both his own magic sense and his attunement to the natural magic that flowed from the ground beneath his feet. The room beyond seemed empty.

Ahead of him, Tamara placed a hand on the door. It clicked open and Matthew realised she must have been given high level access to all areas of the palace.

"That's a relief," Tamara turned back to them with a smile. "I've never been here before, so wasn't sure I'd be able to get in."

He wasn't confident he trusted her, but Alex seemed to, and she'd got them this far.

"Look," Matthew shifted his feet. "I shouldn't have threatened you—"

"Don't worry about it," Tamara brushed off his attempted apology with a shake of her head. "I've heard worse. Besides, I understand why you did." The genuine warmth in her words only enhanced his shame.

"So, is anyone going to finally explain why we're here?" The question came from Eira, and they all turned to Matthew for a response.

"Come on and I'll show you." He walked to the unlocked door and nudged it open just enough for him to see inside. It was as vacant as he had hoped. With a sigh of relief, he usherd Alex and Eira through. "You may as well come too," he said, seeing Tamara's hesitation.

She smiled and ducked around him into the room. "Thank you."

"Well..." Matthew trailed off as he let the door swing shut, then shrugged and turned to scan what was once the throne room.

The carpet that originally ran the length of the long room was now gone, as was the throne that had sat on the raised dais in front of them. Regardless of their absence, the room was impressive. Six pillars of white stone ran down each side, polished to a shine that matched that of the blue and silver tiled floor. Dark wood lined each wall, interspersed with smaller doors and fabric hangings that gave off a faint stale smell he couldn't believe he had forgotten.

Crowning it all was a giant mural painted on the wall behind the dais. Silver stars, depicted by dots and circles shone against a navy backdrop, like constellations in the night sky, none of which he recognised.

He watched the others looking around, taking in the rare sight with wide-eyed fascination, and Matthew felt a touch of disappointment that he couldn't show Alex how this hall had once looked, with the paintings of his ancestors that had hung here.

Their footsteps echoed in the cavernous space as Matthew led the group to the far wall. Picking out the largest star, just as his own father had shown him, he mentally drew a line down.

"Alex, come over here," Matthew looked back to where his son was watching him and beckoned him up onto the dais. "Touch the wall there." He guided Alex's hand until his palm was pressing flat against the painted surface.

His father had only shown him this once, and Matthew held his breath as he waited. Then, with a soft glow, symbols lit up in an arch above Alex's fingers. As they did, Alex snatched his hand away, retreating as a panel of wall the size of a door swung silently out into the room, as though on an invisible hinge.

"Well, that proves it, doesn't it." Matthew chuckled as Alex stared between him and his own hand.

"Wha— How?" A draft from the doorway ruffled his hair, and Matthew gestured to the cold passageway that lay beyond.

"It's an escape route," he explained. "I don't know who made it — I don't think anyone does, but the doorway only responds to a member of the royal family."

"Where does it go?" Eira had scooted closer to peer around Alex into the passageway. "It's not dark."

She was right. A soft glow lit the tunnel, coming from small magelights in the roof and floor. Only, they weren't magelights. As Matthew looked closer, he saw they were small symbols, just like the ones he had seen light up on the door.

"You don't have to say where it goes in front of me," Tamara spoke up from behind him, obviously interpreting his silence as reluctance to answer Eira's question. "I should probably say goodbye."

Turning away from the passage, Matthew followed Tamara down from the platform, leaving Alex and Eira in front of the tunnel entrance.

"Thank you—"

A creak caused them both to jerk around to the double doors of the room.

"Tamara?" The man who entered was a dazzling image of gold and white uniform, mahogany hair framing a face Matthew wished he could forget. Cold eyes met his own and his body turned to ice. The rest of the room dulled to grey as he stood, transfixed by the dawning recognition on Morgan Heliodor's face.

"Alex! Go! Now!" Matthew's voice cracked as he shouted. White noise rushed in his ears and he backed against the dais, unable to tear his eyes away to see if Alex was obeying. He had to move, conjure a shield, anything, but his brain couldn't grasp the thought long enough to enact it.

Morgan's surprise morphed into a scowl as he stopped to assess the scene, but it took a second before Matthew realised his nightmare was no longer looking at him.

"I see." The simple statement was as frosty as Morgan's gaze, and from the corner of his eye, Matthew saw Tamara flinch.

"Wait! Please! This isn't— He's not—" She began to stumble an explanation, but Matthew stopped listening as he heard his son's voice from behind him.

"Dad..."

The word brought the world back in a rush of colour. Matthew wrenched on his magic, throwing it into a shield wide enough to cover them all. Alex and Eira were huddled, wide eyed, by the tunnel entrance. "Alex! Take Eira and go! Oliver will meet you." He hoped his friend had made it to where the tunnel came out.

Tamara backed into him. Her silence told him she had given up on any explanation. Morgan now held a handgun, though it was thankfully pointed down at his side.

"I'm not going without you!" Alex's voice came again, but this time Matthew didn't turn to look, eyes focussed instead on the weapon and the man who held it.

"Tamara, I need you to get them out." Matthew kept his voice low, though he knew Morgan was close enough that it wouldn't matter.

"No! I can't—"

"They're here because of you. You told me you wanted to protect them, if you actually meant that, you'll do this." he was counting on her guilt, but there was no time to soften his words.

Leaving Morgan alive would mean an active pursuit, but he couldn't trust Tamara to fight for him. Alex's best chance was with her.

To his relief, he saw her nod. With a swish of her dress, Tamara left his side and Matthew heard the clatter as she rushed towards the passageway. A cry of protest from Alex answered her movement, but Morgan's attention was once more fixed on him.

"I've wondered every day when you would come for revenge," The High Minister's voice sounded calm. Then, he swung the gun up and Matthew swallowed as it pointed at his chest. "Get on with it then. Let's see what time has made of you."

"I didn't." The words spilled from his mouth before he realised he had spoken. It made sense that Morgan assumed he was here to kill him. Perhaps it would have been better to let him continue to believe it.

Behind him, magic flared, followed by shouts of objection. "I am not going. Get out of my way! Dad—" The passageway closed, cutting off his son's cry, and Matthew found a strange calm descend upon him. Alex was out. He was safe.

The fine lines on Morgan's brow furrowed in confusion. He'd aged. It should have been obvious; Matthew had seen him enough times in pictures, but the living, breathing figure confirmed it. Morgan was just a man. Not even a mage. A man with a gun that would provide no defence from what Matthew could do. A man who faced him, knowing he was facing his own death.

"You knew I was alive?" He finally processed the words. If he'd known, why hadn't he sent people after him?

"Why did you come here?" Morgan's gaze flicked past Matthew towards the sealed passage. "Those two? They're yours?"

Matthew didn't answer. Alex had called out for him enough within Morgan's earshot that the man must have worked it out. "We just want to be left alone." He lowered his hands from where he realised he held them, half raised, as though the physical defence would somehow reinforce the magic of his shield.

Morgan tilted his head. "...And Tamara?" He seemed to hesitate as he asked.

"I just met her an hour ago."

The words seemed to have an effect, as Morgan's expression soothed. Slowly, he lowered his arm and Matthew followed the movement, fixated on the weapon that no longer threatened him. "...What now?" The question echoed around the hall.

"Can you leave through there?" Morgan nodded towards the hidden passageway.

"I can." Matthew's heartbeat had calmed, but his hands were still shaking. He clenched his fists to hide the movement.

In a smooth motion, Morgan returned the gun to the folds of his coat. "Go then."

Matthew didn't move. The words sounded surreal in his mind. Go... Could he really do that? It would be easy for Morgan to send people after him if he left him alive. This could all be a bluff to do just that. But then, in all these years, he never had. The man had slaughtered his family, taken his birthright. To walk away and leave him unchallenged... To hope for a normal life. He would be turning his back on his entire heritage. But hadn't he already? He knew now that he didn't want revenge.

A bolt of energy splintered his thoughts. Magic, wild and nauseating, collided with his shield from somewhere out of sight. For a second, it held. Then it shattered.

"No!"

Morgan's cry came from above him and Matthew realised he'd sunk to his knees, weakened by the wave of exhaustion that accompanied the attack. He'd felt this before. In the alleyway outside the tea shop. But this time there was no one to pull him up.

"So, I follow a trail of intruders and this is what I find." A silky voice Matthew didn't recognise came from his right, and he forced his head up, begging his eyes to focus. A man was leaning against the pillar in front of him; slickly handsome with dark red hair and familiar features that Matthew struggled to place until Morgan spoke.

"Aiden. Leave. This does not concern you." Morgan sounded like he was speaking through clenched teeth.

Aiden. The Arch Canlaw's son. With a heaving breath, Matthew felt some of his strength return, and he pushed himself unsteadily to his feet. He could see it now; the glowing wand in Aiden's hand, though it seemed brighter than either of the two he had encountered before. *Stronger.*

"I think you'll find it does concern me, uncle. Unless you would prefer my mother hear about this? To think you must have known, all this time." Aiden turned towards him, the delight not hidden on his face. "It is an honour, Prince Matthew."

"He is not yours to take!" Anger gave Morgan's voice a threatening edge. He stepped between them as Matthew stumbled backwards. "I will not allow —"

"I will not allow you to take this from me!" Aiden screeched in return. Familiar nauseating energy emanated from the wand as he pointed it at Morgan. "This might not kill him, but you – I would hate to be forced to find out what it would do."

Instinct pulled Matthew towards the passageway, but he knew he couldn't lead Aiden there. He must have entered the throne room through one of the side doors, and Matthew's only hope was that he hadn't seen Alex and the others leave. Whatever this man wanted from him, it wasn't good.

"I knew it!" Aiden's eyes were sparkling as he pushed past Morgan. "I knew from the moment I heard about the land moving, someone had lived." Raw magic bled from the wand and Matthew knew that it would be useless to cast another shield. "I've always dreamed of working with you. It's pleasing to see you're already familiar with my invention."

Matthew's stomach turned, though this time it wasn't from the weapon. "You? You made them?"

"Of course I did. Quite genius." Aiden flicked the tip of the wand upwards and Matthew flinched as it pointed towards him. "They're still in development, though I have a fair idea who has been leaking my prototypes into circulation." He hummed at the thought, tilting his head and fixing him with a predatory stare. "I do hope you will forgive the mistreatment."

Matthew threw himself to the side as a blast of energy shot from the wand. Pain jolted through his wrist as he landed, but he ignored it, rolling back to his feet as he looked for something to put between himself and Aiden. His eyes landed on the stone pillars and he sprinted. A second blast sent a wave of nausea and dizziness as it grazed him. Shards of chipped stone pelted his unshielded skin, drawing blood. But the pillar he darted behind held strong. He sunk against the cool surface, heart racing.

"Don't make this harder than it needs to be." Aiden's

voice drawled from across the room. "Believe me when I say it breaks my heart to have to do this to a peer."

"Aiden, stop this!" Morgan's shout received no response and Matthew could hear Aiden's footsteps echoing as he approached.

"You really think hiding will help?" Aiden laughed. "I suppose running away has always worked for you up to now."

There was no way to fight the wand, not directly. Perhaps if he got it out of his hands? Destroyed it? Aiden had no magic of his own.

Matthew hissed a curse and bolted down the line of pillars, trying to maintain his distance from the weapon. It was impossible to think with that energy assaulting his senses, not that he'd been the best at plans, anyway. Oliver would have an idea. The thought came to Matthew, bringing with it a pang of regret until he thought of Alex. No, Oliver was where he needed to be right now.

Lungs burning with every heaving breath, Matthew forced his will into the shape of a spell. Heat. Fire. If that wand was like the one Roy had found, then it was made of wood. Confident in his crafting, Matthew closed his eyes to steady himself. Then he stepped into the open.

The hunger that crossed Aiden's face at the sight of him made Matthew want to shrink back in disgust. He fought the urge, instead eyeing the raised wand as he used his line of sight to direct the spell he had prepared.

He released it just as Aiden's attack landed.

Acid seared the back of Matthew's throat as the undirected magic grounded through his body. He collapsed, striking the ground hard enough that he would have felt the pain had he any strength left to care.

But his own spell had also struck true.

Through blurry eyes he saw Aiden's expression falter as the wand in his hand began to smoke. He dropped it with a cry, clutching his hand to his chest, handsome features warped in rage.

Matthew followed the wand's path. It bounced towards him. Once, twice; shedding burning fragments with every collision. Then, with a blinding white glow, it cracked.

The energy held in the fragile form burst out as the wand disintegrated. A wave of wild magic crashed through his senses, dragging his consciousness with it as he was lost to darkness.

CHAPTER 21

Alex's inexperience had given Tamara her opportunity. She drew on her magic, weaving it into a spell to reduce the friction on the floor around the tunnel entrance. A flare of energy told her Alex had thrown up a defence, but that shouldn't be a problem; instinct meant most mages generated shields to block physical attacks, but not air movement, unless the caster intended to suffocate themselves.

It took only a moment to force a gust of wind. The slick floor did the rest.

Eira cried out as Alex tumbled backwards into the passageway. "Go! Get in!" Tamara barked the order at the girl, mind distracted by the spells she was commanding. She nodded shakily and darted after Alex, slipping a little on the spelled floor, and Tamara dismissed the magic before following.

Inside, Alex was scrambling to his feet, his face a picture of rage as Tamara blocked the entranceway.

"I am not going. Get out of my way! Dad!"

Tamara ignored him, instead turning to scan the door for a way to close it. A stone handle was carved into the back, and she grabbed it, catching a final glimpse of Matthew and Morgan before tugging the door closed.

In a second, Alex was beside her. "Let me through!" He shoved against her in an attempt to reach the handle, the unexpected touch screaming through her senses and eating into the tenuous reserve of control she had left.

"Get away from the door!" Tamara shoved him back, far harder than she had intended. To her relief Alex didn't fall, but he stumbled away, a new apprehension in his eyes. "Sorry! I'm sorry. I shouldn't have done that," Tamara leant against the cold stone and took a heavy breath. "I told him I would get you both to safety—"

"—But that's Morgan in there!" Eira shouted. "He'll kill him!"

"He won't!" Tamara hoped it was true. "Matthew's too strong for that, and Morgan—"

"Morgan did it before! They were all mages!" Eira interrupted her assurance, but Tamara saw behind her that Alex's face had fallen.

"I know what happened... in the past." The how was still a mystery, but Tamara didn't think speculating on the fate of Alex's ancestors would be helpful at this point. "I know you're worried, but you must see that the only thing your dad cares about right now is that you're safe. If it helps, I'll stay with you part of the way and then come back for him. I can't do that though unless we go now." Alex looked down at her and Tamara forced herself to keep the eye contact until she saw him nod. "Go on. I'll follow." *Just in case someone comes after us.* Tamara found her thoughts finishing the sentence.

The passageway was surprisingly dry, even as it sloped further into the ground, and Tamara noticed that what she had thought were magelights were actually symbols, glowing with the same soft light as those that had appeared above Alex's hand at the entrance. Old Ardveldian symbols... She chewed her lip as she thought back to her encounter with Aiden in the library. These must be what he was searching for.

"When are you going back?" Alex broke the silence, filled only with their muffled footsteps.

It must have been long enough. "Can I trust that you'll go on?" If they followed her, it would negate everything Matthew had asked of her.

Alex halted and Tamara almost tripped into Eira's back, not anticipating the sudden stop. "We'll wait at the end."

"Okay." She would have to accept his words as a promise. Hadn't Matthew said someone would be waiting for them? Perhaps it was for the best that she didn't accompany them all the way. "If I don't see you again—"

"Stop. Just— just go and get Dad, okay?" Alex interrupted, clearly trying to suppress the quaver in his voice.

"I'll make sure he goes," Eira said and Tamara nodded.

"Thank you."

The journey back up the passage felt shorter than the first time. Though the air smelt dry with dust, the chill of the stone walls had crept in and Tamara shivered, her dress designed for the warmth of a summer day. It was clear now that the tunnel must curve, as the door wasn't visible until she was close enough to make out the handle.

The handle. Hopefully it wouldn't be locked. She didn't relish the thought of being trapped in the passageway. As she arrived at the door, Tamara pressed her head against the stone, attempting to reach out with both her hearing and magic to the room beyond. Nothing. Either the door was too thick to feel through, or the magic imbued in it was blocking her senses.

She grasped the handle and gave a gentle push, hoping that it would swing out as silently as when Alex had opened it. It didn't budge until she added more force, easing it open until a sliver of electric light shone into the passage. With her face pressed to the gap, Tamara peered through.

The acrid scent of charred rock hit her first. A chunk of stone was missing from one of the pillars; chips of white debris scattered across the tiles. Nudging the door further, she saw Morgan, gun in hand. But lying at his feet—

Tamara's breath caught in her throat.

A laugh echoed from out of sight, and Morgan lifted his weapon, his stance wide and wary over Matthew's motionless body.

When she'd left she had been more afraid for Morgan than Matthew, but the memory of her conversation with him on the balcony couldn't be ignored. He had killed mages before; the strongest in the country, and she had no idea how. There had been regret in his tone, kindness in his treatment of her, but now...

"You really think to threaten me?" A chill ran down Tamara's spine as Aiden stepped into view. "Everyone's expecting it. My blood thirsty uncle making a bid for power while my poor mother is on her death bed. You'll be responsible for war."

"I know what you've done, Aiden." Morgan didn't flinch.

Aiden shrugged, seemingly unfazed by the weapon pointed at him. "If you know, then you should understand all I have achieved. With the Prince of Ardveld—"

"He's not a tool. You're talking about people! If you weren't Kaylee's son—"

"But I am." Aiden replied flatly. "The mages volunteered to work with me. They were proud to participate in Vailberg's progress."

"They didn't volunteer to die," Morgan's words were quiet and Tamara had to strain to hear. "How many lives?"

"How many lives?" Aiden spat. "How many did you take in the name of duty, uncle? Don't think to lecture me on death." He lifted his hand in a flourish just as a door creaked open from the side of the room. Morgan, glanced back, face pale.

"This isn't duty."

Tamara heard Morgan's reply through a wave of nausea. Magic, strange and dizzying, flowed from the five uniformed guards that entered the room; overwhelming even from her hiding place. The sunburst logo on their outfits was immediately familiar; Sunstone enterprises. Aiden's mage guard.

"Your Highness." The closest guard to Aiden inclined his head.

"You will take Prince Matthew to my rooms for now, while I arrange transport." Aiden called to the guards, and Tamara breathed a sigh of relief. Matthew was still alive. "I can assure you that there will be consequences for your actions today, Morgan."

Tamara knew she had to move. Those guards... She didn't know what kind of magic they were using, but Morgan couldn't protect Matthew alone. Swallowing her discomfort, she pushed against the weight of the door. Her limited vision showed Morgan lowering his weapon.

Then the crack of a gunshot split the air.

CHAPTER 22

A story about researching a book, along with all the cash on him, was enough to convince the bar manager to let Oliver down to the wine cellar. This had to be one of the oldest pubs in the city, and though he didn't consider himself particularly tall, he still needed to duck low as he made his way to the stairs. Centuries of spilt alcohol had permeated the wooden beams, mingling with the sweat of the packed tourists seeking relief from the heat outside. With any luck, the crowds brought by the anniversary holiday would keep the staff too busy to come and check up on him.

"*This is the right place, Oliver,*" his mentor, Ewen, must have picked up on his anxiety. As he bade farewell to the staff member who had escorted him to the dimly lit cellar, an image of the same room flashed briefly into his mind. One of Ewen's memories. *"I'm relieved to see no substantial change. You really should have made a point to keep track of this place."*

"You know that's not what's bothering me," Oliver replied, ignoring the thinly veiled criticism. *"Something's happened. This plan was tenuous at best but—"*

"Panicking isn't going to help," Ewen's thoughts were a calm contrast to Oliver's racing heart. *"Your job is to advise. We must now hope that the safety nets we put in place work as they are supposed to."*

"I should be there with him." Oliver knew he had broadcast the thought, but it was really only for himself. He should have insisted on finding a way into the palace with Matthew, and the disapprovingly loud silence from his mentor showed he agreed. *"Where does the passage come out?"*

The reply came as swift as his thoughts in the form of another projected image from Ewen; a glowing open door on the far side of the cellar, between two racks of barrels. The image seemed fuzzy in his mind, and the racks were no longer there. *"Not one of yours?"*

He felt Ewen's confirmation more than heard it. *"A predecessor's memory of this place."*

With a deep breath, Oliver flexed the stiffness from his fingers. Ewan was right; all he could do now was hope. It was too risky to contact Matthew via the burner phone. The only information he had about what was going on inside the palace had been the simple text: Plan B. He settled himself down onto a sturdy looking wooden crate and waited.

After almost an hour, movement from the wall opposite drew Oliver's attention. A tweak to an illusion spell had done enough to dim the electric lights in the room, ensuring he would avoid unwanted attention from upstairs. That the darkness might give him an edge if he needed to fight hadn't been unintended either. With a faint grinding of stone on stone, a rectangular door eased open, letting in a light that caused Oliver's gloom accustomed eyes to squint.

The entrance to the passageway was just as it had looked in the memory from Ewen. At any other time, Oliver would have relished the opportunity to observe it. Now, though, he barely gave it a cursory examination as he hurried towards the figures in the doorway.

"Alex?" Oliver found his own voice unnaturally loud after the silence. It was definitely Alex, and Eira too, illuminated in the glowing light of the passageway. They both looked exhausted. "Where's your Dad?" He peered into the tunnel, breath catching in his throat as he noticed Matthew's absence.

Alex didn't reply. He was scanning the room and blinking, eyes unadjusted to the darkness of the wine cellar.

"It's okay, it's just me. You're safe." Oliver stepped into the light. Recognition dawned, and Alex rushed into his arms.

"I didn't want to leave, but we had to!" Alex's words spilled out faster than Oliver was able to follow. "Tamara — the Head of Magic, she's gone back, but they need help —"

Oliver pulled back, holding up a hand to slow Alex's explanation as his anxiety twisted. The Head of Magic? Something had gone terribly wrong.

Movement behind Alex stopped Oliver before he could clarify further. The door to the passageway swung shut as Eira joined them in the room, closing off the magelights from the tunnel and plunging them back into darkness. Alex flung himself towards it with a cry. "No! We have to go back!"

He removed the dimming spells he'd set on the electric lights, and saw Alex palming at the wall in a frenzy. "You can't open it?" Oliver stepped forward, running his own hand over the stone. But where the door had been, was now flush with the rest of the surface. Did Alex even know how? After all, it must have been Matthew who opened the passageway at the palace end.

"*It makes sense,*" came Ewen's detached drawl in his mind. "*Any entrance to the palace, even one only royal blood could open, is a risk to defence. A disgruntled cousin or sibling looking to stage a—*"

"*That is not helpful right now!*" Oliver shut down his mentor's explanation, just as Eira spoke.

"Oliver, he's with Morgan."

Cold panic flooded his body like ice. He suppressed it, focusing on keeping his voice level as he addressed them both. "You need to tell me what happened." A secondary wave of emotion from Ewen told him his mentor's fear matched his own. "*Matthew's powerful enough.*" Oliver tried to reassure himself. "*If he kills Morgan, then that's another problem, but we can deal with it.*"

"*Morgan has killed powerful mages before.*" The regret in Ewen's voice reminded him that the old Tactician knew far too well the threat that Morgan posed.

"They stopped us going out the main entrance," Alex began, unware of the conversation happening in Oliver's mind. "We went to the throne room instead. That's where the passage was."

Oliver listened as Alex explained. It was in line with what he had agreed with Matthew, though notably, Alex made no mention of Roy. "We were about to go through, but then Morgan— He found us. I'm not sure how—"

"He saw you?" Oliver interrupted. If Morgan recognised

Matthew, it wouldn't take much to make the connection. It was worse than anything they had anticipated.

"Yeah..." Alex glanced across to Eira as though seeking her confirmation, but then his expression morphed into one of concern. "Eira?"

She was slouched against the wall, eyes glazed and unseeing. Without thinking, Oliver caught her as she slid limply towards the ground.

"Eira!" Oliver heard Alex call again as he crouched down beside him, but there was no response from the girl cradled in his arms. "Uncle Oliver, what's going on?"

"I'm not certain." She was breathing and Oliver could sense her energy, far stronger than he had ever realised before. Fainted perhaps? There was no sign of physical injury, but he was competent enough at healing to help should she need it. "*Ewen, ideas?*" He shot the thought just as Eira began to stir.

"What happened?" Alex leaned over his shoulder as she pushed herself up. Her eyes were open now, but still held the dazed look they had possessed before she fell.

"Matthew? No, he's not..." There was confusion in her voice and a growing sense of dread nagged at Oliver's mind as he watched her. With a moan, Eira sunk forward, covering her ears with her hands. "No. I don't know. Go away!"

"Eira, what's wrong?" Alex reached out towards her, but Oliver had gone numb.

"He won't stop talking! He keeps asking about your Dad, and Oliver. I don't understand."

She looked at him, wide eyed and afraid, but Oliver couldn't find any words of comfort. Instead, he dragged himself to his feet, slamming a fist against the closed passage hard enough that stinging pain shot down his arm.

"Alex! You have to open it! I need to get through!" Not waiting for a reply, he hit the wall again, this time with a jolt of magic behind it. *It can't be...* He clawed at the stone, pouring out his energy into half-formed spells that did nothing to the unyielding surface.

"That won't work, Oliver." Sorrow tinged Ewen's thoughts, but he couldn't stop. *"Exhausting yourself will achieve nothing. Alex needs you."*

"Matthew needs me!"

"He doesn't anymore." The blunt reply was a blade through his heart. With an agonised wail, Oliver sunk against the wall, letting the magic he was weaving fade away. At the edge of his awareness, he heard Alex trying to speak to him, but he ignored it.

"I won't believe it. Perhaps it's not what we think— It could have happened another way!"

"The girl is Alex's Friend. You know an awakening when you see one." Images flashed through Oliver's mind from Ewen; all the memories he held of previous Champions awakening. Oliver simply remembered his own. The dizziness. The momentary blackness before he had returned to consciousness in Matthew's arms, Ewen's warnings screaming through his mind. *"You need to get them away from here."*

"I can't." Oliver sucked in a shuddering breath.

"Uncle Oliver..." Alex had backed away, fear in his eyes. Beside him, Eira was watching with a new level of awareness.

"We need to go," Oliver's voice cracked. "Come on. Dory — your mum's waiting for us." She would never forgive him, and he deserved it. He got to his feet and started towards the stairs that led back up to the pub, but neither followed.

"What? You're not going to wait for Dad? Aren't you supposed to be his Tactician or something? You can't just leave!" Anger had replaced the fear in Alex's voice and Oliver stopped, unable to look back. "Talk to me! I know who you are. Who Dad is. Maybe if someone had thought to actually tell me, we wouldn't be here!"

"Alex," it was Eira who spoke his name so carefully. "Let's not do this now. We should go."

"No!" Alex shouted. Oliver turned around to see Alex swat away her touch. "Eira, you were there! Tamara said she was going back for him. They're going to come."

"I don't think..." she trailed off painfully, and Oliver winced as she met his eyes. *She knows.*

He interjected before she said any more. "If you know who you are, then you must see that I couldn't be the one to tell you." He'd understood Matthew's hesitation, even as he had advised against it, but it was his friend's choice to make.

"But you can tell me what's going on now." Alex's glare hardly hid his need for reassurance.

"...I will," Oliver walked forward and placed a hand on Alex's shoulder. "Just not here. Please." He couldn't tell him here. He didn't think he'd be able to say the words even if he wanted to. Without Matthew, they were in more danger than he had planned for. The priority had to be getting Alex and Eira to the safe house where Dorothea was waiting. When they got there... He didn't know what he was going to do anymore.

"You promise Dad will know where to find us?"

Oliver swallowed the lump in his throat and nodded.

Chapter 23

Tamara lurched in shock. A high whine rang in her ears as the gunshot echoed through the hall. Then magic jolted through her body and her remaining senses dissolved to nothing.

Screaming. The sound pierced her consciousness, and with it came awareness. Her vision swam, and she saw she was on the ground; the cold of the passageway seeping into her limbs, leaving them stiff and aching. Focusing on the voice, she began to make out words, echoing through her mind as though they came from within.

"Do you hear me? We're under attack! You must get up! Get to the dining—"

Tamara slammed the voice away, forcing it from her mind with her will, just as she would when defending against a magical intrusion. The words mercifully silenced, but she realised the screaming hadn't stopped. An inhuman rage screeched from the throne room, beyond the sliver of an opening she had left from the passage. With a shake of her head, she leaned forward and peered through.

Morgan was still standing, unmoved from where she had last seen him. Around him, Aiden's mage guard had frozen in place, glancing nervously between him and their liege.

"You! You traitor!" Aiden's face was flushed a deep red. "You'll die for this, Morgan! I'll have you—"

"You will do nothing," Morgan's voice cut through Aiden's tirade. "I follow your Mother's orders." He took a step forward. "The intruder is dead. The Ardveldian royal line ended. If you wish to inform the Arch Canlaw of something, you can tell her that."

Tamara felt sick. Matthew still lay where he had been moments before, but she was too afraid to look closer. Closing her eyes, she rested against the side of the tunnel, deep breaths doing nothing to quell the nausea. She wouldn't believe it, not yet.

"You're going to wish you had thought through you loyalties more carefully," Aiden's snarled reply reached her even in the dim passageway, but it was met with silence.

She didn't know how much time passed before she noticed there had been no further action from beyond the door. Reluctantly, she opened her eyes, surprised at how bright the tunnel seemed from the glowing symbols.

With shaking hands, she scrambled to her feet. As she did so, the magical presence she'd repelled before nudged again at her mind. Instinct caused her to push back and once more it retreated, leaving behind a pricking fear. If a mage was trying a mental attack, why didn't she sense them nearby? The thought of one of Aiden's mages knowing she was here made her shudder, but she couldn't hide forever.

Legs quivering in protest at the movement, Tamara braced against the wall and pushed the passage door wide. It opened and she fell forward, catching her balance clumsily before stumbling down the dais.

At the noise, Morgan jerked and spun towards her. He was alone, face ashen, the gun held limply in his hand. His shadow flickered across the floor, drawing her vision down to the dark puddle spreading from the body at his feet. Bitter acid rose at the back of her throat, and once again her legs threatened to stop holding her weight.

Without seeing him move, Morgan was suddenly in front of her. He grasped her arms, keeping her steady. "Tamara. Look at me." His body interrupted her view of the bloody floor, but she found herself still unable to turn away. "Look at me." He cupped her face with his palm, tilting it until she met his eyes.

"Why?" The question became a sob, and she buried her face against Morgan's chest.

"You need to leave." His tone betrayed no emotion, and Tamara didn't raise her head. Layers of clothing hid his heartbeat, the white jacket providing no warmth to her chilled skin.

"He can't be..." Tamara heard the words as if she wasn't saying them, her voice raw and alien. "You can't have..."

Morgan's stiffened. Then he released her and stepped back.

"Go to your rooms. Get your things." He spoke softly.

"Go home."

"What?" The dismissal compounded the crushing weight of her failure. How could she leave after everything she had done? She needed answers, but the words she wanted to say wouldn't come.

"Make your own way back to Avel-Kifaeros. Don't let anyone know you're leaving. You no longer work here."

Tamara's vision blurred as her eyes burnt with tears. It was too much. Gritting her teeth to stop their flow, she fled the room.

CHAPTER 24

Roy whirled around, but the library window remained shut, just as he had left it moments before. Flattening himself against the palace wall, he crouched low and edged to the side of the roof. A clamour of voices emanated from what must be the kitchen under his feet, words muffled and inaudible, but none called out an alert. Maybe the stress was getting to him.

He let out a breath, taking in the smell of cooking that drifted up from the open windows, and reached out with his magic sense. Immediately, he picked up the energy of mages in the room below; far stronger than expected, given the distance and brickwork between them. Perhaps this roof was thinner than it looked? Roy eased his way back to the corner of the building. No one appeared to have noticed his presence, but falling through the ceiling wouldn't help.

"You done?"

He jumped at the sound of the voice. It was close, as though having come from right beside him, but there was nobody. "Don't mess me about!" Threats he could handle. Mostly. But if someone was playing with him, he'd rather not give them the satisfaction. "If you want a fight, then damn well come out and do it."

"I'm afraid I can't 'come out' as you so put it, and I would get no benefit from fighting you," The reply came in a masculine drawl. *"Besides, I couldn't kill you even if I wanted to. And trust me, I'm getting the unfortunate impression that I might want to."*

"What's that supposed to mean?" Roy glanced back up to the closed window, the brickwork at his back doing little to reassure him of his safety. At least being attacked would prove he wasn't losing his mind.

"Nothing." The voice responded. *"You aren't losing your mind, by the way. But I would advise you stop talking out loud, unless you want someone else to come along and do the job for me?"*

The guy could read his thoughts? Roy squeezed his eyes shut, the cold of the stone seeping through his stolen server's jacket. For a moment there was nothing other than the shifting patterns of his eyelids and the sound of his own breathing.

"Oh no. Darkness. My one weakness." The voice spoke with a biting sarcasm, and Roy yelped in surprise.

"Okay, you need to tell me what the fuck is going on," He growled, heat flushing his face.

"Thoughts only, please. I can hear them just fine. And, yes, you should be embarrassed. What are you? A child?"

A breeze broke the muggy air, brushing chill against Roy's sweat damp hair and swirling the dirt on the little rooftop where he crouched. He might not feel thirty-one, but he'd been through enough in his life to deserve some respect.

Roy felt more than heard the self-pitying laugh. *"Thirties? Please tell me I won't have to spend another hundred years like this."*

"Look, I don't know why you've decided to telepathically pick on me, but if you aren't going to kill me then can you please just sod off?" He thought the words, trying to project them with the same glare he was wearing. *"You might not have noticed, but I'm a bit of a difficult situation here."*

"You're going to look pretty stupid if you make that face every time we talk." The voice replied, and he wondered if punching himself would hurt them too. *"You really have no idea what's going on, do you?"*

"You think?"

"Okay," somehow the voice gave an exasperated sigh, despite the fact Roy hadn't heard it breathe. *"I suppose some congratulations are in order. Apparently — and don't ask me how — you've been chosen as a Royal Champion. Unfortunately, that also means I'm dead."*

Roy blinked. *"Wait... You're— you're a ghost?"*

"I'm not a ghost."

"You literally just said you're dead!" His skin prickled; he didn't like that this had delved into the paranormal. It was pretty shady up here, but even so. *"I thought ghosts didn't come out in the day?"*

There was a silence.

"...Why— why would you even think that?" The reply brought with it a flash of memory; a plush, emerald couch, legs draped over the armrest, thumbing through a dog-eared copy of 'Hauntings of Ardveld'. A memory that definitely

wasn't Roy's. *"Anyway, that's not the point of this conver—"*

"Wait! What was that?"

"What was what?"

"That," Roy gestured vaguely into the air before realising he couldn't point at a mental image. *"With the book and the chair and everything."*

"Oh..." The voice sounded embarrassed and for the first time, Roy sensed he had the upper hand. *"I didn't mean for you to see that. I haven't quite worked things out from this side, and it's been a long day."*

"That was you, wasn't it? Like, before you were a ghost?" Somehow having settled into the rhythm of this bizarre conversation, Roy stretched out his legs and leaned back to look up at the grey sky. A rumble in the distance told him the heat of the past few days was about to break.

"...Ghosts don't exist. But yes, that was me."

Sorrow twinged Roy's heart, and he realised it came from the presence in his mind. *"Hey. I'm really sorry you're dead."* He'd seen enough television to be wary of the supernatural, but apart from a bad attitude, the ghost hadn't caused any harm. *"I guess you need me to help you move on or something?"* As if getting out of here wasn't causing him enough issues already...

Roy chewed at his lip, running over his options, when a thought suddenly occurred to him. *"Wait— you didn't die back in the takeover did you?"* Another silence followed his question. *"You still there, mate?"* He probed, wondering if his newfound psychic powers had departed as quickly as they had arrived.

"...What do you mean by 'the takeover'?" An emotion hung behind the question that Roy couldn't place.

How to even explain it? A shock wave had run through the country when the news broke; adjustment to Ardveld's new leadership happening like a surreal dream, one that had become mundane faster than he'd ever imagined. Today's celebration was proof enough of that.

"How long has it been?" The question reminded him that the voice was able to follow his thoughts.

"Twenty years or something. Look, I'm sorry, I should have broken that more gently."

"I had the impression some time had passed but... It's fine." The voice finished brusquely. *"That goes some way to explaining you, at least."* Roy wasn't sure how this related to him at all. *"Listen quietly,"* The voice continued before he could interrupt. *"I worked for the King; one of the four Champions. I was in charge of Ardveldian intelligence."*

"Intelligence?" This time Roy couldn't help himself. *"You were a spy? Like, the Spy, spy?"* What limited information he had about Ardveld's Royal Champions was common knowledge; Friend, Tactician, Guardian, Spy. After the King, they had been the four most powerful mages in the country. Roy must have been the last generation to learn any Royal history in school and even back then he had wanted as little to do with them as possible.

"Spy is such a vulgar term, but if you wish to refer to yourself that way, I suppose I can't stop you." The Spy obviously sensed Roy wasn't following, as he gave another sigh. *"I already told you. When one of us dies, the power is passed on to the next... suitable candidate. Apparently, you were the best it could find."*

"What!" Roy exclaimed out loud, just as the first drop of rain spat onto his nose. He wiped it off, forming a shield above his head to block the shower. *"No! Why would you choose me? You've definitely messed something up there."*

"I'm afraid I have no control over who the power goes to. Not that we didn't try, of course. There are certain conditions that we know

influence it."

"You can shove your conditions! There isn't even a Royal Family anymore. No Champions. Everyone who was there died that day. Everyone..." He grit his teeth. The injustice still burned. It wasn't like his mother had ever been a threat to Vailberg.

"That's your mother?" Curiosity emanated from the Spy and Roy forced the image away.

"Get the fuck out of my memories."

"...I apologise," he didn't sound particularly sorry. *"What's your name, kiddo?"*

"Roy. And I'm not anyone's kiddo."

"You can call me Julian. We may as well be on a first name basis, since it appears we are going to be working closely together for some time."

"Yeah, about that," There was no way Roy was getting involved with anything to do with Ardveld's Royal Family, no matter how much this Julian was talking like he had no choice. "I quit. Find someone else."

He felt sorry for the guy, he was dead and all, but Roy had been promised no further involvement in anything palace related after helping Matthew on this insane break-in. Once he was out of here, he was going to go home, have a drink, and get back to his actual job.

For a second, he seemed to have stunned Julian into silence. *"...You can't quit."*

"Watch me."

"No, I mean you can't quit. That's not possible. I'm not quite sure why you would want to. From what I saw, you weren't exactly a competent mage before."

"Fuck you too." Roy snorted and flexed his numb legs. The patch of roof he was sitting on remained dry under his shield, but his limbs were growing stiff with cold and he still had the problem of getting out of the palace grounds. *"How long have you been watching me?"*

"Only since you broke into that office," Julian replied as Roy got to his feet. *"The guards did not seem particularly welcoming. Foolish of you to set off such an obvious trap. I am confident that second one intended to kill you."*

"The second one? You do realise that was Aiden Heliodor, right? And I knew about the alarm. I thought you could see my thoughts?" Of all the people to run into, the only one worse would have been Morgan himself.

"Heliodor..."

Julian's presence faded back as Roy crossed the roof. The edge was slick from the wet, but the drop wasn't far if he lowered himself down first. After that, he would have to rely on the rain for cover if he wanted to slip out. Hopefully Matthew would have an easier route. He'd overheard something about a tunnel when Oliver thought he was out of earshot, but it was clear they hadn't wanted him involved in the specifics of the plan.

"I can't see anything from before the awakening, unless you show me the memory." Julian's voice came again, any bitterness banished from his tone. *"And the one I just saw is particularly intriguing. Who was that, may I ask?"*

"Urgh, that's why I'm here. I owed him a favour to get someone else off my back." Roy pushed the thoughts of Matthew from his mind. He didn't want to admit it, but he'd started to develop a fondness for the guy. Must be something to do with the shared mortal peril. *"He's not important. I'm not gonna see him again once I'm out of here."*

"You may want to revisit that line of thought," Julian replied. *"He's grown."*

Another memory flashed into Roy's mind, but this time

it didn't fade instantly like the one of the chair; a teenage boy, black hair falling across his sharp cheeks. His dark eyes held a rebellious glint that, Roy now recognised, time had not fully erased. Despite the fancy clothes in place of rough jeans and a worn T-shirt, he was unmistakable.

"What the hell?" That was Matthew. Much younger, but obviously him.

"Young Prince Matthew certainly had the right idea about formal gatherings," Julian continued. *"He was conspicuously absent on the evening we were entertaining our Velbian guests. Presumably it worked out in his favour."*

"Wait..." This was moving too fast. "You're not actually trying to tell me that Matthew is the Prince of Ardveld?" He couldn't think of anyone less princely. Well, maybe that was a bit harsh, but he'd met people who were more princely. Oliver, in his damned suit, sprang immediately to mind.

"Oliver's with him? Good. At least Ewen should have a handle on things."

"You know Oliver too?"

"He's a Champion, Roy. Keep up. Matthew's Tactician."

Why was he still surprised? He was starting to doubt they ever worked for Felix Marek at all.

"I should imagine that was a ruse." Somehow, Roy got the impression that if he could see Julian's face, he would be rolling his eyes. *"We need to go after them. This rain will make a good cover."*

"No way. I told you, I quit. I don't care if he is a prince, or a king, or if he was the damn Arch Canlaw herself. I'm not getting involved." It wasn't like Roy knew where Matthew was, anyway. Now that he thought about it, no wonder he'd seemed so freaked out about his son being in the palace.

"Matthew has a son?"

"Will you stop that!" This was becoming a serious breach of privacy, even if he had been moved by the unexpected warmth flowing from Julian at the news. He flexed his fingers, peering over the edge to make sure there was no window directly below him, before relaxing his rain shield and lowering himself down.

"How I wish I could but, from now on, I see everything you see." The mocking tone was back, all trace of sentimentality leaving as soon as it had come.

"Everything?" Hanging from his fingertips, Roy released his grip, dropping the remaining distance and landing in a low crouch with a wet splat. *"For how long?"*

"Oh, only until you die."

"Until I die!" The idea of being stuck like this for the rest of his life was in no way appealing. *"And you're seriously telling me I can't switch you off? Ever? Even when—"*

"Even then." Roy felt Julian's amusement at his horror. *"Awful, isn't it? And don't worry, when you die, you get to do the same as I am now, for the next in line,"* Julian hummed, as though musing on the prospect. *"You know, I'm starting to think you were right about quitting."*

Damn right he was right about quitting. Roy wiped his hands on the back of his trousers, replacing his shield as he did so and resentfully noting that it barely drained his magic. It seemed Julian had been honest at least about the power transfer. A musty smell had permeated his clothes from the rain, and, making the most of his newfound energy, Roy pushed heat into the water that saturated them, releasing a small puff of steam that dispersed through his shield into the humid air.

To his left were the gardens, but if he turned right, he could bypass the palace entrance and head straight to the main gates. That's if he could figure out how to make it across the courtyard without being seen.

"You know, this can't be much fun for you either, right? You really want to be stuck in my head doing deliveries?" Roy returned to the conversation rather than deal with trying to figure out a plan. *"Come on, I'm obviously not Spy material."* Perhaps if he could convince Julian that he was no good for the job, the Spy would let him know how to back out.

"I'm certain you can feel my distaste at the prospect." Julian wasn't wrong, and Roy tried his hardest not to be offended. *"However, I have no choice in the matter. The only one who might have a chance of releasing us could be the King himself..."*

Roy sighed and started towards the courtyard, feeling ahead for mages as he went. *"I thought I told you, I don't know where he is now."*

"I wouldn't expect you to," Julian replied. *"But he has his Tactician. Now, I may not know Oliver that well, but I worked closely with his mentor, and Ewen practically raised the boy. They'll be meeting at one of my safe houses."*

"One of them?" Roy muttered out loud. The palace wall was the bigger concern right now. It jutted out artistically in enough places that he was forced to dart into the open, risking detection by the guards on the distant gates, before slinking back to the safety of the shadowed alcoves. He counted the large windows as he ducked under them, getting to seven before Julian made a comment.

"Keeping track of the distance? Perhaps you're more cut out for this than you thought."

"Huh?" Roy gave his head a shake, frustrated by the break in his concentration. *"Tell you what, I'll make you a deal."*

"Hmmm?"

"You wanna see Matthew, right? I'll agree to go to this safe

house of yours, if you make sure he lets me quit. He can find some other host to put up with you."

"*I fail to see a downside to this deal.*" Julian seemed sceptical at Roy's sudden compliance.

"*Yeah, but after that, I'm done, okay?*" Even if Matthew couldn't get him out of this ridiculous Champion business, he was still going back to his old life. Julian would have to just learn to sit back and shut up.

An aura of magic ahead alerted Roy to the patrol guard heading their way. Shit. The illusion spell he'd used at Marek's might be enough to blend him into the shadows, especially given the rain, but it was a long shot. He supposed he should be grateful that this was the first guard he'd seen; the rest likely still caught up in the commotion he'd caused inside.

Cursing himself for not thinking of it earlier, Roy drew on his magic.

"No need. I can help you kill this one."

The comment was so dismissive that Roy thought he must have misheard. *"You did not just say you want me to kill someone."*

"They're an enemy, Roy, and this will be much more efficient." Cold pleasure seeped from Julian's presence; enough that Roy guessed this wasn't just about being efficient.

"I'm not becoming a murderer just so you can take out your revenge on some innocent guard."

"...Fine," Julian said begrudgingly. *"But you're rapidly running out of time. Focus back. Let's see what we're up against."*

As he re-focused, Roy felt the approaching guard bright in his mind. They were further than he'd first assumed; likely a consequence of the Champion's extra strength amplifying his senses, and he was heavily aware of Julian's consciousness observing alongside him.

"Just a rain shield. Easy."

It was just as Julian said. The only active spell running was a weak shield above the guard's head, a mirror of Roy's own, that wouldn't even stop a sideways draft, let alone an attack. Any other magic was small and passive; spells Roy would never have noticed without Julian directing his attention. Waterproofing, anti-fraying in the uniform, a defensive charm from an item held close to their chest.

"*That's a kind of shield.*" Roy pointed out. It would stop a bullet, at least.

"*It's not going to stop us.*" Julian sent an image... no, it was more of an intent into Roy's mind. The framework of a spell, complex and sharply focussed, designed to shape air movement around a space, with a layer of monitoring—

"We don't have time for you to analyse it," Julian scolded as Roy paused. *"Just hold the intent and form the spell. I'll teach you properly some other time."*

"*This isn't going to kill—*"

"*Just do it.*"

Roy stepped out from the wall, giving himself a clear line of sight. Then he pushed his magic into Julian's spell and fired it at the startled guard.

The man stared at him and opened his mouth, but no sound came out. His eyes went wide and Roy watched in horror as he clawed at his throat, falling to his knees in the wet gravel. The seconds dragged until the guard finally collapsed and Roy rushed to their side.

"Bring him across, carefully. We don't want the uniform getting filthy," Julian said.

"*What did you do?*" Roy heaved the guard across his shoulder, dragging him to the shelter of the building's side.

"I took a lesson from my mistakes." There was a dark anger beneath Julian's words. *"He's not dead. The spell released as soon as he passed out, but you won't have long."*

Movement of the guard's chest confirmed the assurance and Roy relaxed as he bent his head down to hear the breathing for himself.

"Luckily for us," came Julian's thought. *"He seems about your size."*

CHAPTER 25

Rain splashed against Alex's shield as Oliver rushed them through the crowded high street, kicked up water soaking his jeans and causing them to cling uncomfortably to his legs. Umbrellas and mage shields bustled against each other as their owners fled the sudden downpour, and he couldn't tell if the rest of his clothes were damp with rain or sweat.

Abruptly, Oliver veered down a street to their left. Alex and Eira followed. The rumble of car engines from the packed road was left behind almost instantaneously, leaving only the beating rain. No one had spoken since exiting the pub, but now Oliver had slowed his pace enough for Alex to fall into step beside him.

"Where are we going?" Alex asked, but his uncle didn't respond.

The street they were on was little more than an alley; narrow and lined with disused doorways, their crumbled paint flaking, and fire escapes leading from the backs of the high street shops. Cars passed on a road at the far end, but before they made it much closer, Oliver halted.

They stopped in front of a set of stone steps that led up to a dishevelled green door hanging askew in its frame. There was no sign of any handle or lock, but Alex felt the small burst of magic as Oliver placed a hand on it. It swung open onto a dim hallway, bare except for a neat door mat that fit perfectly across the entranceway, and another closed door at the opposite end.

"Come on in." Oliver held the door open and Alex didn't wait to be told twice. He followed Eira inside the narrow space, dropping his shield as he got out of the rain. "Don't worry about shoes," said Oliver as Alex kicked off his wet trainers. "Go through. Your mother's inside."

Alex looked towards Eira, but she didn't meet his eyes. He'd had no time to press her for the reason she collapsed at the pub, but she knew something. Oliver knew something. And neither of them seemed like they were going to tell him. His panic since the events in the palace had settled into a heavy dread, and part of him wasn't sure he wanted the truth. He was cold, numb and damp.

A cosily furnished sitting room greeted Alex as he pushed open the second door. Magelights hovered near the exposed beams of the low ceiling, giving the space a homely glow that in no way matched his expectations from the alley outside.

Next to a drooping, olive sofa stood his mother. The

tension in her face washed away as she caught sight of him, but though Alex wanted to rush to meet her, his body suddenly felt weak. Too stiff to move properly, he sagged against the door frame, falling down into her arms as his mother pulled him into a tight embrace.

"Alex!" She reached up to run a hand through his hair, unravelling the remaining threads of strength that had held him together over the past few days. He hid his face in her shoulder, afraid that if he spoke he wouldn't be able to return to this moment.

It was Dorothea who broke the silence. "Eira," his mother reached out an arm to pull his friend into the hug. "Thank you for taking care of him."

Alex opened his eyes as Eira stiffened beside him and pushed herself out of the embrace. For a moment it seemed she was about to speak, but then she looked past him to where Oliver now stood, leaning heavily against the wall as though he would collapse without its support.

"Oliver..." His mother released him from the hug enough for him to turn around, the three of them now looking at his uncle. The dread was back; this time bringing with it a painful pounding in his heart. Alex felt his mother grasp his hand. "Where's Matthew?"

"I..." Oliver clenched his fists, voice so quiet that Alex had to strain to make out the words. "I—I'm sorry. He..." The blood seemed to have drained from his face and his mum's grip tightened.

"No— Dad's coming. He's going to meet us here..." Alex looked between Eira and Oliver, desperate for one of them to confirm it. His uncle had told him Dad would find them. He'd promised. But Oliver was shaking his head.

"I'm sorry. I couldn't..." He took a ragged breath and

fixed Alex with red-rimmed eyes. "He— he didn't make it out, Alex. I'm so sorry."

"What?" The floor felt unsteady under his feet. "But you can't— How could you know that? You weren't there! He's going to come."

"Alex," Oliver spoke his name feebly.

"No! You told me! You told me it was going to be okay!"

Oliver closed his eyes, head falling forward as Alex shouted. Beside him, his mother sank backwards onto the arm of the couch with a wail. "Mum! It's not— It can't be..." His voice was raw and strange, like it belonged to someone else.

"Alex," This time it was Eira who spoke. "He knows. He knows because of me."

She was stood by the door where she had retreated, watching him with eyes full of pity. Somewhere out of sight, a clock ticked away the seconds. "What do you mean?"

"What happened down in the cellar. There's someone—" Eira paused and looked at Oliver, who remained unmoving. "I can hear a voice, in my mind. They say they were a Champion — a Royal Champion."

A Royal Champion... Because his father was the prince, right? But why Eira? "That doesn't make sense." Alex couldn't follow what she was trying to say.

"The king is meant to have four Champions," Oliver's voice cracked as he spoke. He had lifted his head, but his gaze was distant, as though looking at something beyond Alex's sight. "When we were attacked, everyone died. All of Matthew's potentials, as well as the awoken."

"What about you?" Alex remembered now that his father had called Oliver his tactitian. A headache was building up the back of his neck, pressure spreading across his scalp that he couldn't release.

"Your father and I were the only ones that made it out. I awoke that day. When my mentor passed, I inherited the power," Alex watched as Oliver shifted his view to focus on Eira. "But there was no one else. Matthew never—" Oliver stopped and Alex saw him squeeze his eyes shut again as if in pain. "...There are conditions." His murmured words were almost inaudible. "I'm sorry. I can't." With a shake of his head, Oliver pushed himself away, crossing the room towards a door on his right. As it opened, Alex saw that it led to a small bedroom, the bed stacked with bags, before his uncle closed it behind him.

An empty silence filled the space he had left. Alex's mother pressed a warm hand to his back, but he couldn't bring himself to turn to face her.

"Alex, not just anyone could become a Champion." Eira's words gently brought him back to the room. "They used to..." She paused as though listening. "They set up potentials; people who were raised close to the royal family, who the power would pass to when the previous Champion died."

"That doesn't explain anything though!" Alex didn't want to raise his voice, but no one seemed prepared to give him a straight answer. "So what! What does it matter that dad never had any Champions?" That didn't mean he was... That didn't mean he wasn't coming.

"Your dad only had Oliver because all the other potentials died. They must have thought the line ended, that there wouldn't be any more." Eira glanced towards the closed door through which Oliver had left. "But now there's me." She slowly flexed her fingers, looking down at them as though in wonder. "Alex, I'm a Champion."

The pressure that had been building in Alex's head

pushed forward to prick at his eyes, but he forced the stinging tears back. "But how can you be his Champion? You hardly knew Dad!"

"Because I know you, Alex. My whole life." Eira reached out and placed a hand on his arm. "I'm your friend. And you're the king."

CHAPTER 26

Tamara barely saw the stares as she fled to her rooms. A guard called out to her as she once again pushed past the palace entrance, but she ignored them. They didn't follow; perhaps recognising her or not seeing her as a threat. Either way, she didn't care.

Her vision had narrowed to a point when she finally slammed the door of her office shut, the memory of how she got there already fuzzy. Magic sparked from her body, flickering into the air before dispersing. It frazzled against her senses, like white noise screaming in her ears, and Tamara felt herself losing control; pain, stress and lack of sleep culminating into a storm that was too far gone to stop.

Everything was wrong. Everything she had done. Leaning against the closed door, Tamara slammed her head back. The shock of pain brought brief clarity, before the turmoil resumed. She turned towards the offending surface, striking at it again and again with her fists, fury building at the lack of response from the thick wood.

The presence she had been blocking from her mind flowed against her consciousness; free, now that Tamara had no will left to hold it at bay. Its voice joined the turmoil, screaming words she knew she should recognise, but couldn't follow.

"Go away!" She clamped her hands over her ears, squeezing her eyes shut, but the voice didn't stop. "Shut up! Get away from me! I swear I'll hurt you. I'll kill you if you don't get away!" She pulled her turbulent magic into a bolt of energy ready to slam against her attacker, no longer caring if it was one of Aiden's mages. There was nothing left to feel.

"You can't hurt me."

With a snarl, Tamara opened her eyes, but her office remained insultingly empty. Pressure pounded in her skull, compounding the pain of muscles wound tight with adrenaline, but the presence still pushed against her mind. As it drew close, its essence seemed to dull from heightened panic to a forced stillness that projected over her own frazzled emotions.

"Think of the music and calm down." The voice came with a backdrop of notes, more akin to recollection than listening. Piano notes, though it was no song she recognised.

"No! I told you. I told you— I told you to leave me alone!" Tamara screamed, blasting her pent up magic into the floor of the office. There was a loud crack, and she watched in horror as the wood split; a long fracture running from her feet to where it disappeared under the central rug of the room.

She sunk to the ground, curled her legs to her chest, and sobbed.

"I'm sorry. I thought the music would help."

"You can't help me! Just leave!" A throbbing in her wrist showed her attack on the door had done some damage, but she had no focus to heal it.

"I can't." Another emotion flowed from the presence; this time grief sharp enough that Tamara gasped in pain. *"My name is Nathaniel. The King's Commander. I need—"*

"I don't care who you are."

"Please! The awakening has chosen you. I need answers!"

Tamara made no attempt to reply. Cold seeped into her limbs from the floor, bringing with it a mix of returning sensations. The trickling of the little fountain on the table by her desk. A light pattering of rain on the study window. She realised the shield she kept over her skin had dropped, the short sleeves of her dress now cutting into her arms.

"That man... Tell me that wasn't the prince. How has so much time passed?"

Hot tears pricked at her eyes without anger left to keep them at bay. "Matthew's dead. I should have... I promised Alex... I..." Her sentence faded into a choked gasp as she remembered their last conversation in the passageway.

"I don't understand! The awakening is supposed to happen immediately. You're not one of my potentials. What has happened?"

"I don't know what you're talking about."

"The awakening! You are the next King's Commander. The Guardian! How can you not know?"

"I'm nothing. I'm going home. Leave me alone." Tamara let her eyes drift closed as she thought the words. Home seemed a lifetime ago. The blaring sounds and blinding lights of the city had become so normal she hardly noticed the effort of masking her distress, but it was too much. Too many people full of goals and agendas she didn't understand, as though a wall of glass separated her from everyone here, no matter how hard she tried to do the right thing. Perhaps this was for the best. She'd stumbled into something far too big for someone like her. *For someone from Avel Kifaeros*, she thought bitterly.

"You're Kifaerish?" The voice who called himself Nathaniel, replied. *"How? Who were you to the prince?"*

"No one. This is all my fault. I brought Alex here." Then she snapped alert. Nothing about her home had been said out loud, and yet the voice had answered.

"I can perceive your thoughts. It's part of the awakening." Nathaniel's words were soft, and now she realised they weren't words as such, more, an impression of words flowing straight into her consciousness. *"Alex is Matthew's son? If he lives, we must find him. He may be in danger."*

"I don't know where he is." She winced as she pushed herself up, accidently putting weight on her injured wrist. Even if she knew, how could she go to him? How could she explain her failure? *"I can't face him."*

"You have to. Please, you need to focus. You're his Champion now."

His Champion? Nathaniel had referred to himself as the Kings Commander. The title had meant nothing to her at first, but her recent research on Ardveld's royalty meant she should have recognised it immediately. *"You're a royal Champion?"*

To her right, the book she had shown to Alex lay closed on the coffee table, the imposing weight of it made heavier by its contents. 'The Royal lineage and Champions of Ardveld'. Aiden's book. If he came looking...

"*No. You are!*" The urgency in Nathaniel's voice pulled her from her rumination.

"*What?*"

"*The spell has appointed you! You are Alex's Guardian now!*" Frustration seemed to take over, Nathaniel's thoughts once again barking through her head. "*You should never have left him!*"

"*I went back for Matthew.*"

"*You shouldn't have left Prince Matthew behind! It's the job of the King's Commander to protect the Royal family, and you have done nothing except throw a tantrum! We don't have time for this.*"

"I did what I thought was right!" Tamara's voice rang jarringly in the silent room, and for a moment Nathaniel didn't respond.

"*Well, your judgement is flawed,*" He stated it with a finality that brooked no argument. "*We're getting nowhere. I'm not sure who you think you are, but you will start acting your status and do what I—*"

The words cut off as she forced Nathaniel's presence from her mind. At least it was still possible, though it seemed the block required some vigilance to maintain.

Everything hurt. She shifted her legs, trying to relieve the discomfort of her position to focus on a healing spell, but before she could, she caught sight of the crack in the floor.

The shame always burnt harder than the pain.

Volatile. Dangerous. Tamara didn't need to hear people say it to know what they thought. To Nathaniel it was a tantrum, as if there was something she would gain. As if it was something she could control! At least she should be grateful it was property damage and not a person she had hurt. Pain was a just consequence.

Forgetting the healing spell, her eyes once again fell on Aiden's book. She crawled to the table and pulled it towards her, flicking through the silver edged pages to the area she had bookmarked. She turned the page without looking, unable to bear the sight of Matthew's image. The section after was the one she was looking for now, anyway; Ardveld's Royal Champions at the time of the takeover.

Nathaniel's name stood out straight away, below a picture of a squared jawed man with dark hair cropped into a regimented side sweep. Narrow, unflinching eyes looked out from the photo, and Tamara sensed the same obstinate energy in his upright posture she had felt from his voice. Other Champions took up the remaining space: Ewen, Julian, Nicholas; none of the names were familiar.

Relaxing her block on Nathaniel, Tamara reached out with her thoughts. *"Why me? Why would I be chosen?"*

"I have no idea," Nathaniel spat. *"The magic is expected to choose someone worthy—"*

"Fine. If you're going to be like that, I'll block you out."

"Don't you dare disrespect me further! I would never have treated my predecessor the way—"

Tamara hissed through her teeth as she closed down the connection, swaying back and forth until her heart rate slowed. The confrontation with Nathaniel wasn't helping her nerves. She shut the book, but a spasm of pain as she struggled to lift it told her there was no point ignoring her injury any longer.

With a deep breath, she reached for her magic and realised that it was hardly depleted. In the past, the energy lost during a meltdown would leave her at least disorientated, but this time she had none of the tell-tale signs of magic sickness. The answer came to her almost as soon as the question; Aiden's words, from the day he had shown her the book. *A spell that made them the strongest mages in Ardveld.* The Champion spell was the only known instance of a person changing their natural power level.

The gunshot echoed in her memory, and Tamara dug her fingers into her palm. Nathaniel's voice must have been the one she had blocked out in the passageway, which meant Matthew's passing had been the trigger.

She pushed away the thoughts that threatened to drag her back into despair, instead focussing on the spell she needed. Despite her extensive experience with magic, healing wasn't an easy skill and she hoped she wasn't dealing with much more than a bruise. With her intent defined, she sent a flow of energy towards the source of the pain, speeding up the natural recovery until the discomfort in her wrist reduced enough that she could flex it.

This time it was only fatigue that impaired her as she stumbled with the book to her desk. The bottom drawer was locked, with the key still in the hole, but the locking spell she'd placed there rendered it superfluous. Inside were the documents she had brought from the police investigation in Golebach, along with the few belongings that Alex and Eira had with them when they were taken into custody. Alone, Aiden's book wasn't incriminating, but any connection to Alex had to be destroyed. It might be the last thing she could do for him.

As she reached out a hand towards the drawer, Tamara suddenly stopped. Then she pulled the book towards her and turned back to the page on Ardveld's Champions.

"Who is Oliver?"

Nathaniel's emotions flooded her mind once more as he

drew close; still prickly, but to her relief he didn't berate her. *"What do you mean?"*

"Matthew said it, when he sent Alex and Eira into the passage. He said Oliver would be waiting at the end for them." She looked down at the book in front of her. *"I wondered if he might have been a Champion, but his name isn't here."* It was stupid, really. Surely it would have been known if a Champion had survived. Then again, Matthew somehow had.

"Oliver is alive?" Nathaniel seemed to have forgotten his anger as Tamara felt his hope surge.

"I don't know, I just heard the name," she replied carefully. *"Who is he?"*

An image flickered into her mind; a young man with straight, sandy brown hair that flopped around golden brown eyes. The emerald frock coat he wore was tailored to a gangly form that hadn't yet filled out enough to catch up with his height. He only looked around Alex's age; not what she'd been expecting at all.

"He was Ewen's apprentice," Nathaniel spoke over the memory. *"Ewen always said that he never had the time to waste on more than one potential, though I did try to convince him that it was risky business."*

"Potential? What's that?"

Nathaniel exuded exasperation. *"Potentials were raised with the Royal family. They came from high magic families; trained, practically from birth, to be the next generation of Champions. Never in my memory, nor that of any of my predecessors, has anyone outside that structure awoken!"*

"They must have all died in the takeover." Tamara mused half to herself. It seemed somehow worse after seeing the image of Oliver. They weren't more than teenagers. *"Could that explain why it's come to me?"*

"I don't know. You haven't given me any answers and I don't have any for you."

The lock spell flared as Tamara opened the draw. She pulled out a clear plastic bag and tipped the meagre contents out onto the table. Coins, the stub of a bus ticket, a tangled mess of headphones attached to a music player; but it was the other device that she was looking for.

"What's that?"

"Alex's phone," Tamara replied as she picked up the mobile. *"It's possible that Oliver's number is in there."*

"Alex's phone?" Nathaniel seemed confused. *"You mean you have a telephone number for his house?"*

"No, I have his phone." She held down the button on the top of the smooth grey case and the monochrome display glowed into life. Not locked. That was a relief. A second later, she almost dropped it as the phone buzzed in her hand. 'Missed Call'. Her stomach twisted as the notifications piled up.

"How many years did you say it had been?"

"Over twenty." Tamara answered as she clicked through to the contacts. There it was, in bold pixel text: 'Uncle Oliver'. Her thumb hovered over the call button, but she couldn't bring herself to press it. What would she even say? The thought of having to break the news about Matthew made her sick.

"Why are you waiting?" Nathaniel didn't hide his impatience, but phonecalls broke her out in a sweat at the best of times. Right now she was exhausted. Tamara pushed the top button on the mobile again, the glowing screen blinking away to black. *"What are you doing?"*

"I can't speak to him," she shook her head. No amount of magic could fix how drained she felt from the past few hours.

Even if Oliver answered, she doubted she could force any words out.

"Don't be ridiculous!"

"I can't!" Tamara interrupted. *"I will. I promise. I just... I just need some time."*

Chapter 27

The few bags they had brought were stacked on the neatly made bed. Essentials only; he'd recommended they travel light. Oliver had the distant thought that he should move them, but his arms didn't respond. Instead, he let himself drift towards the curtain covered window. It seemed so long ago now that he had closed them. For some reason, he had felt it important.

Perhaps that was why it smelled so stale in here. Maybe he should open the windows more. As he reached out, he caught sight of his fingers, crusted over with blood. Strange... He pressed his thumb against the chipped nail, studying the sharp pain that stabbed through the wound as he remembered the cold wine cellar. Alex must have been so frightened watching him.

They'd broken the news, though he didn't know if he could have done it without Eira. The girl was barely an adult, but she put him to shame. Oliver crushed his fingers until they burned. He should have done better. Should have said something useful, something to comfort them. Every time he closed his eyes, he saw the devastation on Alex's face.

He supposed he would have to tell Matthew... The thought stopped almost as soon as it had begun, and Oliver let the bed catch him as he finally gave up on standing.

"*Oliver*," Ewen's voice pushed into his mind, but he didn't respond. "*Oliver, come on now.*" It wouldn't take much effort to shut out his mentor's presence, but he couldn't seem to process the task. It was easier to just let the words wash over him. "*You can't do this. Alex needs you. You need to compose yourself.*"

He sunk his head into his hands, palms pressed over his eyes. After the way Alex had looked at him, he was sure he was the last person he would want to see.

"*You know that's not true.*" Ewen responded. "*Matthew would want—*"

"Don't talk to me about what he would want! Don't you dare. Not now."

Ewen's presence pulled back and Oliver suddenly felt alone. The corner of a bag was digging uncomfortably into his side and he shoved it away. For a moment it teetered at the edge of the bed, then it tumbled over the side, contents spilling across the worn carpet. With a stifled howl, he threw himself down against the sheets and turned his face into the pillow.

"I've been in your place, Oliver, but dwelling on emotion is a luxury we can ill afford." His mentor's words cut through the muffled silence, and Oliver now noticed a quiet sorrow that was not his own.

"He wasn't— Matthew wasn't just... He was my friend." Damp fabric clung to his cheek as he lifted his head. Light pattering told him the storm had passed into a summer drizzle; the fuzzy glow of the afternoon sun still visible through the closed curtains. He wondered what time it was; how long it had been.

"Matthew was your King first," relentless as ever, there was no emotion from Ewen now. *"You have a duty to perform. They're going to come to you soon, looking for answers. Looking for guidance. And you need to provide it."*

"What guidance can I give? If my guidance was worth anything, Matthew would still be alive. Alex would still have a father." Oliver drew a ragged breath, "...I don't want to do this anymore."

"Your feelings are of no consequence. It is the price we pay for being chosen—"

"Chosen? You chose me! I was a child!"

He'd never questioned it. Too young to inherit his parent's estate after their passing, it made sense that he would have been offered to the palace as a potential. It wasn't until he was being shunned by his peers that he realised he was different, and by that point he was too busy with his duties to care. "I never had a choice."

Ewen's silence gave away nothing. What did it matter, anyway? He'd long ago given up on the world he had been born into. "I wouldn't have cared if it ended with us. I just wanted to see him live a good life." Oliver shut his eyes, as if it would stop the memories. "I know... I know you always expected more from me."

"We can never see every outcome." A faint knock interrupted the silent conversation. *"I feel your grief as my own, my friend. With time, it will ease."* Ewen's presence faded, and Oliver became aware of the door to the room being opened. He pushed himself up, hastily rubbing the redness from his eyes.

Dorothea was there, a smudged silhouette leaning hesitantly into the room. "Hey Ollie," she spoke gently. "You've been in here a while. I thought maybe you could use a tea."

He blinked to clear his vision, then remembered that all his usual magic had faded along with his will. Fixing his eyesight had become so natural he barely noticed the spell, but right now, even that seemed pointless. Instead, Oliver tried to muster a weak smile. "Thank you."

"I'm sorry about the mug," Dorothea picked her way through the spilled contents of the bag, passing the drink across before settling on the bed beside him. "I don't think I'm really thinking right now."

He looked down at the cup. 'I hate Mondays' was scrawled along the side, above a cartoon face with X's for eyes. One of the ones he'd picked up from the last office clear-out. A bitter laugh stuck in his throat and became a sob. Eyes hot and stinging, he turned away from Dorothea before she could see.

Her arm around him did nothing to slow the tears. "I'm so sorry Ollie." He leant against her as grief wracked his body. The mug in his hands was scalding, but he gripped it tight, the discomfort a welcome distraction from the weight in his chest. He wanted to say that he was the one who was sorry, that none of this should have happened, but he couldn't get the words out.

They sat together in silence until the wave eased. Eventually Oliver pushed himself straight and Dorothea's arm dropped away as he took a sip of the tea. It was sweet and milky and helped to settle the nausea in his stomach.

"Thank you," he said. "I mean, I'm sorry. This is wrong. You shouldn't be here comforting me."

"We comfort each other," Dory gripped his hand, and Oliver met her eyes. In the dim light he could make out the puffiness in her face, but the tears that had been there no longer showed.

"Is Alex doing okay? And Eira? Are they coping?"

"He's... alright." Dorothea looked away. "Well, as best as you would expect." There was a pause. "It's hard when... When he didn't see it. I know you wouldn't have told us if you didn't know for sure."

"I wish I didn't."

A burst of shouting from outside made him tense until he identified it as revellers from a nearby pub. Dorothea got up and pulled the curtain back to look. "I'd forgotten," she murmured almost to herself. "Of course, it's a holiday. I guess we should expect noise tonight. I was going to open the window, but if you think it's too loud?"

"Please do," Oliver replied. "The air feels close in here, and I would rather be able to listen out."

A breeze caught the curtain as the window opened; cool air bringing the scent of dampened dirt from the sun baked ground. Oliver finished his tea and placed the mug down onto the bedside table.

"Are we in danger, Oliver?" Dorothea didn't turn from the window.

"I don't know."

He didn't know, though he would need to assume the

worst. The plan they had made was in tatters and he had no idea what to do.

As if following his thoughts, Dorothea didn't ask any more. "I'm going to see about making some food," she said, moving to take the mug but Oliver put his hand out to stop her.

"Please, you don't need to take that. The dishes can wait."

"Honestly, I'd rather the distraction."

Without the strength to protest, he just nodded. "I think there's some pasta in the cupboard. Tins, too. I'll come—"

"I'm sure I can figure it out myself," Dorothea interrupted him, not unkindly. "Take as long as you need." Relieved he didn't have to try to stand, Oliver let himself fall back onto the bed. The door closed softly behind her as she left and he found himself once again alone, listening to the rain.

* * *

A cry from the living room jolted him out of a dreamless sleep. It was darker now than he remembered, though he had no reference for how much time had passed.

"Oliver!"

It was Dorothea's voice that called for him, her fear apparent even through the closed door. He flung himself to his feet, vision fading to a rush of black dots that caused him to stagger into the door frame as he groped for the handle. Automatically he reached for his magic to establish his spells, sight returning as he opened the bedroom door.

Dorothea, Alex and Eira were huddled near the entrance to the hallway. Fury clouded Alex's expression, and as he looked closer Oliver saw Dorothea was gripping his arm. A loud knock from the front door interrupted him before he could speak and the four of them snapped around to face the sound.

"Don't move," Oliver spoke as calmly as he could muster. He reached out for Ewen, mentally imparting the events as his mentor swept into his mind. *"No one should know about this place."*

"It's a palace guard," Eira whispered. "I looked through the door hole when I heard a knock."

Tension stiffened Oliver's body. "All of you, get to the kitchen. There's a door there that will lead you out the back." He nodded at Eira.

"Nicholas can watch over them if it comes to it." Ewen voiced Oliver's own thought. Nicholas had been the last Friend; Matthew's father's Champion. If he didn't make it out then at least, through Eira, the others would have some guidance.

"If I die here, then I'm going to take some of them with me."

"No! I'm not running away again!" Alex shook off his mother's arm with a growl, and Oliver sensed the rush of magic from him, unconstrained in his anger.

"Alex—"

"They killed Dad!" His words ripped through Oliver's heart. Alex's anger was understandable, but his safety was more important. He didn't think he could cope with another loss.

Another knock came from the door, this time more urgent. "Matthew? Oliver? You there, mate?" The voice was familiar, and Oliver's mouth fell open. "If you don't answer, I'm just gonna come in, okay?"

Ignoring their stares, he pushed past the others towards the door.

"Oliver! What are you doing?" Dorothea's cried out as he pulled it open.

Roy jumped back at the sight of him. He was dressed as Eira had said, head to toe in a uniform of the palace guard. For a second they stared at each other in silence, then Roy raised his hand into a wave.

"Hey."

CHAPTER 28

"No! You promised me you would be making the call to Oliver. You're being ridiculous."

Tamara held her emotions steady as she pulled the door to her rooms closed. Nathaniel's scolding was expected, but she still didn't want him to see her doubts. *"And what could I tell him if I called him now?"*

"You tell him who you are, and we arrange to meet."

He said it like it was simple, but she didn't need much of an imagination to guess how that would turn out. Alex's phone weighed heavily in her pocket, a constant reminder of how long it had been. She'd only intended to rest for an hour or so, but the sun streaming through the window as she awoke told her it had been much longer. A look at the clock confirmed it. Eleven in the morning; almost a day since the events at the garden party, and she still had no answers for Alex.

At least she'd been able to change clothes. Soft brown leggings and a navy tunic replaced yesterday's summer dress, with flat shoes pulled tight, in case she needed to run.

"You want me to tell him I watched Matthew die and did nothing?" She doubted Oliver would offer a warm welcome to the person who brought Alex to the palace in the first place.

"Regardless of how you came to be a Champion, your place is with the prince. They trust the system. They will accept you."

"They deserve answers. I owe it to him to say why it happened. I owe it to Alex." It was a half-truth, and she knew it. Even as she was unable to wipe the image from her mind, she couldn't bring herself to believe Morgan had wanted to pull that trigger.

"You don't need those answers," Nathaniel dismissed her with a coldness that barely hid his simmering resentment. *"Morgan killed everyone I ever loved. Surely that is enough?"*

"There has to be more to it. I watched Morgan, trying to stop Aiden from taking him. I know he didn't want Matthew dead—"

"—And yet you saw it with your own eyes. When will you face the evidence in front of you? People like him don't change," Nathaniel spat. *"You could be walking us to our death!"*

Something behind his words gave her pause. They had passed into the gilded rooms of the main palace, as though somehow retracing her steps from a week before. Silent and empty, the white and gold halls now seemed clinically sinister.

"Are you afraid?" She ventured the question without judgement. Fear wasn't an emotion she would have expected

from the Guardian, but there was an urgency beside his anger that she couldn't place. It made sense though, she realised; if she died, Nathaniel would be gone for good. The thought of herself awakening in a stranger was too uncomfortable to dwell on.

"Never," Nathaniel replied. *"I would happily give my life for king, country and even revenge. But my duty lies with Alex. To throw our lives away here will amount to nothing when we should be by his side."*

The door to Morgan's office came into view as she rounded the stairs, the gold plaque beside it displaying the title of the High Minister. Something about it looked different, and as she got closer, she noted that the plinth that had been standing beside it was now gone.

Swallowing her nerves, she raised a hand to knock, letting it fall against the wood without a sound. *"Morgan wouldn't try to hurt me."* Her reassurance was as much for herself as for Nathaniel. *"Besides, I'm strong enough to face anyone here, especially as a Champion."*

"We thought the same."

Tamara shook off the tremor that followed his words. *"This might be a hard conversation for you to go through. If it helps, I can shut you out?"*

"Oh no. I want to look the murderer in the eyes."

As she reached back towards the door, Tamara realised the enchantments that should have been there were conspicuously absent. Someone had broken in, she remembered, but surely the lock should have been replaced by now? With no magical ability, Morgan wouldn't be able to tell.

She closed her eyes as she inhaled. There was no point knocking; if he was there, then he would just send her away.

Giving up on slowing her racing heart, she entered the room.

Morgan stood in front of the window, the grey sky providing the only light. Whatever sun had woken her that morning had vanished behind the threat of another summer storm. He turned upon hearing the door, eyes widening as he saw her, and Nathaniel's rage blazed enough that she found herself clenching her fists.

"We need to talk." Tamara suppressed the snarl that accompanied the words, pushing down the anger that wasn't her own.

"We have nothing to discuss. You need to leave."

"No." The door clicked shut behind her and Tamara weaved a simple lock to prevent interruption. "I'm not going until I get an explanation." She stood as tall as her height would let her, glaring into Morgan's eyes until he looked away.

"I could call the guards to have you removed," he said, eyes darting towards the heavy desk to her left.

Tamara folded her arms. "Try it. I'd like to see how well their training holds up." A burst of energy into her shield expanded it wide enough that the surrounding air flickered visibly in the darkened room.

"Against you?" Morgan breathed a soft laugh. "I would rather not risk the structural integrity of my office. The hallway has seen enough destruction already." She didn't quite follow, but at least the tension seemed to have eased. "Why are you here, Tamara?"

For you. The answer she didn't want to admit came unbidden to her mind. She forced it back before Nathaniel made a comment. "You warned me about Aiden. Why?" She moved closer, and this time, Morgan couldn't hide his surprise. "I saw him there. In the throne room."

"That doesn't concern you."

"You have no idea how much it concerns me."

For a moment he didn't answer, then he sighed. "Mages that get close to my nephew have a nasty habit of disappearing. I couldn't let him." Morgan's voice seemed to catch. "Not to you."

Tamara blinked, trying to ignore the emotion that stirred at his admission. She was fixed under his gaze, the blue of his eyes almost hidden by the deep black of pupils blown wide in the dim light.

"Disappearing? What do you mean?"

"I mean exactly that. Research assistants. Mages at his company. Too many are never heard from again."

"But—" She paused, her breathing shallow as though the air had fled the room. "How? How does nobody care? Wouldn't there be an investigation?" It wasn't possible for something like that to not make the news.

"I know very little of the workings of it," Morgan took a step backward and Tamara felt herself breathe again. "Finding a reliable source is difficult at best, and his status has done much to protect him. I have been strongly encouraged to turn a blind eye, even when weapons of his making are unleashed upon our own city."

"The magical attack last week was Aiden?" No wonder he had warned her off of the investigation. But Aiden wasn't a mage. For him to have made a magical weapon... It flew in the face of everything Tamara knew about magic.

"The weapon used was certainly of his creation, though he seemed surprised one had made it into public hands."

"But how can you just— You're suggesting he's killing people!"

"Those who worked with him did so voluntarily," he

said coolly. "Though who could turn down the Arch Canlaw's son."

A distant rumble heralded the arrival of the storm, and Morgan turned his head to gaze out to the sky. Beside him, Tamara watched as the first droplets of rain chased each other down the glass to puddle together at the bottom of the pane.

"Then Matthew..." Tamara trailed off as Morgan's face twisted into a grimace. "What was he going to do to him?"

"Aiden was always fascinated with magic." Morgan murmured. "The Royal family and the Champions. Even as a child he'd ask me about them, every time he came here. The idea of people gaining magic ability– being chosen." He turned back to meet her eyes. "I don't want to imagine what he would do to someone who could provide that information."

The memory of Aiden showing her the book on Ardveld's royal family sprung into her mind. *We could find out! Experiment!* His words took on a much darker meaning as she realised why he had latched so quickly onto any evidence of their survival.

"If he finds out about Alex..." Nathaniel echoed her own fear.

Tamara studied the side of Morgan's face. His lips were pursed into a fine line, and he looked as pale in the pallid light as he had been standing over Matthew's body. After everything he had told her about the takeover. His panic on the balcony outside the dinner party. Making that decision must have been unimaginable.

"Don't do that." Morgan turned to face her, and this time she looked away. "Don't ever pity me for what I've done."

A piercing fury from Nathaniel answered the words, and

Tamara suddenly felt cold, despite the still warmth of the closed office.

"What happened during the takeover?" The question spilled out before she thought to stop it.

"You already know."

"I know the official story. I want to hear it from you." She couldn't tell him how personal the information was now. What he'd done shouldn't have been possible.

"Hmm," Morgan turned from the window and lowered himself into one of the chairs by his desk. "How much time do you have?" Without replying, Tamara took the seat beside him. "I'm sure you know that Vailberg was once a multitude of scattered territories, before uniting under my parents."

She nodded, watching as Morgan ran a thumb over the knuckles of his other hand. Even now, despite technically being incorporated into Vailberg, Avel Kifaeros still held a fierce loyalty to its own identity.

"A predominantly magicless population;" He continued. "Even after unification, Ardveld paid no mind to a self-declared country clawing its way towards civilisation. Their own land relied on inborn status. A magic based hierarchy of which we would have been the lowest. It wasn't until their own citizens began utilising our advancements that Ardveld's leaders seemed to notice what Vailberg had become."

It was difficult to imagine a time where Ardveld had been the dominant power. Tamara had been only eleven when the takeover happened, and by that time Vailberg was well established as a technological powerhouse.

"Their attempts to destabilise what we had built came quickly after that," Morgan continued. "Disputes amongst former territories arose, despite years of holding a united identity. I was twenty one when it escalated into an attempt on my sister's life."

"That's ridiculous!" Nathaniel's words boomed through her mind and she startled at the sensation.

"Ardveld tried to assassinate the Arch Canlaw?" Tamara asked the question for them both. To her relief, Morgan didn't seem to have noticed her reaction to the interruption. His head was low, gazing at his hands.

"If Ardveld wanted her dead, then she would have been. It was a Velbian national, spurred on by a desire for independence. We put it down, but Ardveld's interference had become too much to cope with."

"No. Julian wouldn't have..." Nathaniel spoke, but his voice was quiet and uncertain. *"I would have known."*

Morgan brushed a palm across his knee, then let hands fall to his sides. "I volunteered immediately to lead the mission. We needed someone with enough status to ensure that the entire royal entourage would be present, and by now I had enough for that."

"How, though?" They were the strongest mages in the country. No non-magic weapon should have been able to overpower them.

Morgan looked her up and down. "You use a shield, correct?"

Tamara nodded. She ran one so often it was effortless, scarcely noting the force of will or energy loss.

"You are actually rather skilled," Nathaniel mumbled, and she wondered if he had intended to send the thought.

"A mage shield will block a physical attack. It will block a magic attack if the mage is powerful enough. It's why Velbian weaponry is traditionally ineffective against mages," Morgan listed the facts without emotion. "Tell me, when you use a full shield, how do you breathe?"

Tamara's brow furrowed in confusion. "Breathe? Well, the same as always—" She stopped, feeling Morgan watching her as she thought. Even with a constant shield running close to her body, she had never considered casting it strong enough to block airflow. "...Air just... passes through," She whispered.

"Even the strongest mage is helpless when unconscious," Morgan continued. "Velbian weapons were no threat to them. The canisters we smuggled in raised no alarm."

"What..." A sickness rose at the back of her throat as Nathaniel responded to the words.

"You poisoned the air?" She almost didn't believe it. The secret weapon; the mystery that had struck fear into the hearts of the Ardveldians and brought glory to Morgan in Vailberg was just an exploited weakness.

"It didn't kill them," Morgan's voice was flat, but she noticed his hands were shaking. "That was by design. We knew about the Champion succession; this inheritance of power that the Ardveldian's prized. Our instructions were to remove the prince and potentials first, then there would be nowhere for it to jump to."

"But Matthew?" If they had been told to kill the prince first, how could he have survived.

"The prince never showed. Supposedly he had a habit of it. A flaw in our planning." Morgan gave a thin smile. "I sent someone to search as discretely as I could, but we had no time to wait. Once I..." He faltered. "When the first gunshots went off, it didn't take long to lose order." The stories Tamara was told as a child came unwelcome from her memory. A bloodbath. Not even the servants made it out.

"After it was over, I went to find the man I'd sent. It was

in the gardens that I found him. Dead." Tamara went cold at the word and she worried Morgan would notice, but he was staring off into the middle distance. "He wasn't alone. The boy... He was barely more than a boy." He paused, and Tamara wasn't sure if he was going to continue. Then he clenched his fist and his shaking stopped. "The body was put with the rest. It wasn't the prince; I knew well enough what he looked like. But it's easy to skew the numbers with so many dead. Who could question me?"

"You knew Matthew survived?" Tamara stared at Morgan. "All that time... What if someone had found out?"

"I would have taken the consequences," he shrugged. "The two that were with him, did they make it out?"

"I— I think so," Tamara replied. "Listen, there's something I need to tell—"

"—That Matthew had a child?" Morgan interrupted. "He confirmed as much himself."

"He told you?" The news that Matthew would willingly give up Alex's existence was hard to believe.

"Not in as many words. It was easy enough to deduce from the situation. I assume then, that it was you brought them here?"

"I didn't know." The explanation she had prepared tumbled out. "It was because of the explosion, the one in Golebach. Alex caused it. He didn't mean to, and I couldn't just leave them." Morgan was listening patiently, though Tamara wasn't confident she was making sense. "He told me he sensed magic there, but it's only because he's Matthew's son." She gripped her clothes nervously. "I only found out two days ago, but even then I wasn't sure I should..."

"You thought I would kill him?" It wasn't a question. "Just the boy, then? There were two of them in the throne room."

"Yes. Eira's his friend. She was in Golebach with him." She'd told him the truth without thinking, but she wasn't afraid anymore. No matter Nathaniel's feelings, she was sure now that Morgan wasn't a threat. "There's something else. When Matthew — when he died, I..." Tamara paused, unsure how to explain. "I know this is going to sound like I'm going crazy, but something happened to me. He called it awakening."

Glancing up at Morgan's face, she noticed his eyes had widened. "You hear them speaking? In your mind?"

"I— Yes," Tamara stuttered in surprise, the material of her tunic crumpled in her grip. "I don't know how it happened, and I understand if you don't believe me—"

"I am aware of the effects of the Champion succession," Morgan's expression was grave. "Who is it?"

"His name is Nathaniel."

"The King's Commander," he sighed. "After all these years... This complicates things."

A sharp ringing made them both jump. Heart pounding, Tamara realised it was coming from the telephone on Morgan's desk. He rose and lifted the receiver, leaving her waiting and uncertain.

"Are you okay?" She nudged gently at Nathaniel's presence. He had made no comment on the information she'd given up to Morgan, but he was still close, listening.

"No." The reply was short and numb.

"I'm sorry you had to listen to that. Maybe I shouldn't have—"

"Stop." Nathaniel halted her stumbled apology. *"For you, these events are history. For me, it was yesterday. I knew those people. Their names; their lives. That boy..."* Pain flashed through her heart before Nathaniel pulled the emotion back. *"I have no*

words for this. I'm not okay. I need to think."

Abruptly, Nathaniel's presence faded, taking with it a heavy weight she hadn't known was there. Across the desk, Morgan was nodding, phone held to his ear. It was impossible to tell what was being said on the other end from his brief responses, but his expression was no less severe. By the time he placed the handset down, his mouth was set in a firm line.

"My sister is dead."

For a moment, Tamara wasn't convinced she had heard correctly.

Kaylee. The Arch Canlaw. During her first meeting with Morgan, he had explained that his sister was unwell, but the timing seemed unreal. "I'm sorry." Tamara groped for some words of comfort, but Morgan waved her away.

"I should have suspected..." He leant stiffly against the desk, and Tamara strained to follow the words. This time, when Morgan lifted his head, she saw fear written across his features. "This is my nephew's doing."

Tamara opened her mouth wordlessly. The suggestion that Aiden had just murdered his own parent seemed impossible.

"I imagine he ordered it shortly after leaving me," Morgan said. "There's no doubt that he's had people well placed for months now. It seems my actions yesterday were sufficient to force his hand."

"You think he did this because of Matthew?" Was it just for revenge on Morgan? "He can't know, can he? About Alex? We were gone before he saw us."

"As far as I'm aware, he never saw or heard anything about the boy." Morgan confirmed, but Tamara's mind was racing.

"Unless..." Sweat pricked on her palms as she remembered her last conversation with Aiden. "When I first brought Alex here, I asked Aiden about the case. That's what he wanted to speak to me about, the night of the dinner, and at the party yesterday. He'd somehow figured out that the ground magic meant a royal was involved."

"You told him Alex was in the palace?"

"I didn't." Tamara shook her head urgently. "I said I'd spoken to witnesses in Golebach, and he asked me to get back in touch with the police to find out more about them. I didn't need to, of course, but if he thinks to contact the Golebach police himself, then the case notes would show it was two teenagers involved." She tried to calm her breathing. It was more than likely that Aiden had forgotten. Surely he would put the incident down to Matthew, the only royal who he had seen with his own eyes. But even Matthew couldn't pass for an eighteen-year-old.

"Aiden isn't the type to forget. Not about this." Morgan was looking at her intently. "You said he suspected Ardveldian royalty simply from your description of what happened at Golebach? It's likely they don't have long." He looked even weaker than he had at the window; knuckles blanched as he gripped the edge of the desk.

Alex's phone still rested in her pocket, and Tamara brushed her fingers across the shape of it. "I might be able to find them," she said. "I think Alex has another Champion with him. I'm not sure they'll trust me, but I have Alex's mobile. Maybe we can at least send a warning?"

"A warning isn't going to do them much good. If they have any sense, then they will already be trying to get out of the country." He pressed his fingers against the bridge of his nose and exhaled. "Assuming Aiden is aware of the boy's existence, then he will first aim to lock down the border."

Tamara felt her eye's drawn to the window, as if the boundaries of Ardveld were close enough to see beyond the darkening sky. "How long will that take?"

"In theory, as long as it takes for Aiden to send the message. He's now Arch Canlaw," Morgan replied. "However, for now at least, I still rule Ardveld. Call them. Tell them I'll get them out."

CHAPTER 29

The living room was heavy with the smell of coffee when Alex pushed open the door from the second bedroom. Dark and windowless, he had no way to tell how long it had been since he'd managed to fall asleep, but he wasn't the first up.

The man who had turned up on the doorstep yesterday was slouched on the sofa where he had presumably slept, the guard's jacket he had been wearing slung across the edge of the seat. Oliver had introduced him as Roy, though had remained light on the details of how they had met; skulking off in the direction of the kitchen once he'd satisfied himself that the man knew nothing about Alex's father's death. Eira was perched on a chair opposite, though neither seemed to notice him enter.

"...So when it happened, did you collapse too?" Eira asked, and Alex realised they had been in the middle of a conversation.

"Yeah, I did! I'd forgotten," Roy replied. "I just put it down to some magical attack from the door I busted open. It wasn't for long though, right?"

"I don't think so. I don't remember much apart from hearing the voice. After that..." She trailed off and Alex winced.

Roy sighed. "Sounds like it was pretty rough."

"Yeah. I'm not sure any of us really know what's going on."

It was strange knowing that the change in Eira was because of him. He'd read plenty about the royal Champions in the past, but none of his books had mentioned hearing voices. Without Oliver's confirmation, he would have struggled to believe it. Her energy felt different though; much stronger, and he had to keep reminding himself that there was now someone else looking at him through her eyes. The unsettling realisation struck him that through every interaction with his uncle, there always had been.

"It's awful, isn't it!" Roy exclaimed, and Alex felt a stab of hurt. "The guy just won't shut up! Lurking there, poking his nose into every thought. Have they never heard of privacy?"

"You do realise you can block them out, right?" Eira laughed, and Alex saw Roy's face crease with confusion. A faraway look came to his eyes, and the confusion turned to anger as he presumably communicated with whoever now shared his consciousness.

It helped, listening to them talk. No one seemed to want to when he was around, as though they might make it worse.

At least, for a little while, he was thinking about something else.

The loud buzz of a vibrating phone cut through his thoughts, and Alex groped instinctively at his pockets, before remembering he no longer had his. A second later a jingling ringtone joined the sound, coming from where the coats hung next to the door.

Beside him, the door to the other bedroom opened and Oliver rushed into the room. His usual suit jacket was creased, tie loose and askew. Like Alex, he must have slept in his clothes. Without acknowledging the others, he began to rummage through the hanging coats. Finally, he pulled out a mobile phone, but when he looked at the screen Alex saw him freeze.

"What is it?" His mother poked her head out from the kitchen, the calm in her voice betrayed by the fact she was wringing a damp tea towel tightly in her hands.

"It's nothing. I'll deal with it," Oliver said sharply. He strode back into the bedroom and Alex overheard a hushed 'Hello?' before the door was shut behind him.

Who would be calling Oliver? Work maybe, but his expression said it was something serious. Not that he knew anything about his uncle anymore. Was he even an accountant? He must be, who would make that up?

"He's always like that?"

Alex looked up to see Roy leant over the back of the sofa, gesturing at the bedroom door. "I thought it was only with me."

Towel hung over her arm, Dorothea crossed the room and swept Alex into a tight hug. "Hey honey," she held on a little longer before letting go. "Did you get to sleep?" He nodded wordlessly and his mother gave a sad smile. "Why don't you go sit down. I'll bring you a drink."

He heard Eira reply to Roy as he made his way over to the empty spot on the couch. "Yeah, Oliver's always been a bit... Uptight." She turned to face him. "Are you okay?" Eira mouthed the words, but Alex looked away. It hurt to see the pity in his friend's eyes.

To his left, Roy snorted. "Yeah, you should have seen him when I was at his other place. I thought he was gonna lose it when I spilt wine over his dressing gown."

"You didn't!" Eira gasped in mock horror and Alex couldn't help a weak smile. His uncle always did seem to take things very seriously.

"It wasn't much!" Roy protested, propping a long leg up on the coffee table in front of them. "Though compared to this place, that house was pristine. This doesn't seem like Oliver's style at all." He waved a hand at their surroundings and Alex agreed. The room was cosy and comfortable, but the dim light and dark furnishings were nothing like his Uncle's own home.

Roy cocked his head to the side, the distant look coming back over his eyes. "Oh, Julian says it's because this one's still like it was when he left it. My head guy." He explained further at Alex's confusion. "He used to run these safe houses before Oliver did." For some reason it hadn't occurred to him they would have names. "Oh, and he says we shouldn't 'insult his decor.'" Roy made finger quotes in the air as he spoke. "Wanker."

Extra participants in his conversations seemed like something he would have to get used to, though he hadn't seen Eira communicate with her Champion since they'd arrived. "Is yours listening too?" Alex hesitantly asked the question.

Eira shook her head. "No. It was a bit much for him, I think. For us both." She brushed a lock of dark blonde hair out of her face; the sight of her natural colour as much a sign of their situation as the safe house itself.

"Still can't believe you got one who leaves you alone." Roy grumbled under his breath.

Silence had settled over the room when Alex's mother came back from the kitchen, bringing with her a hot mug of tea and an offer to the others for more drinks. She looked so deflated at their polite refusal that Alex found himself wishing he could request another, despite the warmth of the mug in his hands. He understood not wanting to stop, as though the crushing grief could be outrun by an endless list of tasks. When she sat on the floor beside his seat, Alex wasn't sure if the pain on her face hurt him more than his own.

Everyone looked up expectantly when the bedroom door clicked open, eager for any news to break the monotony.

"That call was from the Head of Magical Affairs." Oliver's tone was sombre, but Alex's heart leapt. "You mentioned her to me before, as the one who helped you?"

"Tamara." His voice shook as he spoke above the rush of questions that answered Oliver's words. "How? Did she say anything about Dad? Does she know what happened?"

"How the fuck does the Head of Magical Affairs have your number?" Roy added to the clamour from beside him.

Oliver held up a hand for silence. "She has your phone, Alex. That was how she was able to contact us. And yes, she knew about your father. I'm sorry."

It was true then. If Tamara knew, then his Dad really was dead. Guilt returned, heavy and suffocating. He'd been angry the last time they had spoken. Now he wanted to throw up, as though he could physically expel the ache inside.

"There was nothing you could have done," Oliver spoke gently. "Morgan wasn't responsible."

"What?" It was Eira who shouted. "Morgan was the only one there when we left. How could it have been anyone else?" She was scowling when Alex looked back, and he wondered if her Champion was there too.

Oliver met Alex's eyes. "It was the Arch Canlaw's son. Aiden Heliodor."

"I bumped into him!" Roy exclaimed, shooting up to his knees on the couch. "In the palace after I set off the alarm. I didn't think he was going to let me go."

"In that case, it seems you should count yourself lucky," Oliver replied. "Aiden is hunting us — Ardveld's royal family and Champions, and she suspects he knows about Alex." He hesitated. "...The High Minister has apparently offered us his help to flee the country."

A cacophony of voices rose in response. Alex let the sound wash over him as he tried to process. Aiden Heliodor had killed his father. He could now be coming for all of them. *All because of me.*

Roy's voice rose above the others. "Have you gone absolutely insane! You can't seriously be telling me you're going to listen to her? How many years have you been hiding and now you're just going to offer yourself right up? I thought you were the smart one. Do you honestly not have a plan that doesn't involve working with a murderous dictator?"

"I had a plan!" Oliver shouted back, and Alex couldn't remember if he'd ever heard his uncle raise his voice before. "I had a plan to get Matthew, Alex and Dory out of Ardveld. I did not plan on having to deal with you! Or with—" Oliver broke off suddenly, and Alex watched his eyes flick from Roy to Eira. "Things have changed." He finished weakly.

Alex's thoughts took a second to catch up. The bags in the rooms made sense now; his parents had been planning on leaving the country. No question what he had wanted, and Eira—

"You were going to... leave me?" Eira's quiet words were clearly audible in the silence.

"Eira. Please," Oliver replied, "You have a home, and it simply wasn't feasible to—"

"What were you gonna do? Just pack me off on the train? No explanation?" She was seething. "You've known me my entire life! You know it's like at home." Eira stopped, jaw clenched. "Xander was right about you."

Oliver blinked. "Wait, Xander?" The emotion on his face was unreadable. "You... don't have Nicholas with you?"

"His name's Xander," Eira confirmed. "He knows you, and he's right. You've never care about anyone else's feelings. I'm sorry we're such an inconvenience to your carefully crafted plan." She finished with a snarling sarcasm.

"Yeah, that was cold, man. Even Julian thinks so." Roy turned away, flopping back down into his seat. "You really need to get over yourself."

Alex saw his mother get up and head to Eria's side. Her soothing words were inaudible, but he could guess well enough what was being said. On the other side of the sofa, Oliver stood frozen.

"How did Morgan want to help us?" Alex asked, breaking the tense silence. Roy opened his mouth as if to protest, but closed it when Alex shot him a glare.

"She says Morgan can help us head for Avel Kifaeros." Oliver sighed. "It's close enough to the original plan and now, with so many of us, I think it's worth considering." He gave Roy another warning glance. "That's not all. Tamara told me they received a call announcing the Arch Canlaw has died. They believe Aiden will use his new authority to close the borders, effectively trapping us in Ardveld."

"Oh, you and Tamara are on a first name basis now are you?" Roy sneered. "Look, if it's that close to your original plan, why not just take Eira and go now? You'll have better luck than trusting some Velbian."

"It's not her I'm trusting!" Oliver flung out a hand in exasperation. "When Matthew died, Tamara awoke as a Champion. Just like you, and just like Eira. I may not trust her, but I trust Nathaniel."

The news struck Alex like a thunderbolt. Tamara was another of his Champions. With her, that was all of them. Four people whose lives had been shattered because of him. What did that even mean for her when she worked for Morgan? It wasn't as though she could come with them if they left Ardveld, and it certainly didn't seem like Roy had any intention of doing so. Would they just be stuck like this their whole lives?

"I still don't believe it," Roy said dismissively. "It's easy enough to make up, especially if she knows about you and Alex."

"That's why you and I are going to speak to her first," Oliver explained. "Ewen chose the location. Somewhere that was close to all of them. She should only know where to meet us if Nathaniel is with her. Alex and Eira will stay here with Dory until we've confirmed the situation."

"What!" Alex blurted out. "No! I am not staying here hiding like a child while you go off without me!" He was the one who knew Tamara. It was his fault she'd awakened. Now he was going to be excluded? Left locked up again while everyone else decided his future for him? Alex felt like he'd gone from one prison to another, like some kind of artefact to be tucked safely away out of sight.

"I like how you just decided I would come with you." Roy joined Alex's complaints. "I told you, I came here to quit. I didn't sign up for this."

"You're a Champion! You don't get to quit!" Oliver looked at Roy with disbelief, before turning to Alex. "If Tamara really has awoken, then she could be in danger herself. I can't just ignore it."

"I don't see why not?" Roy interrupted before Alex could respond. "Just leave her to die if she's dumb enough to get found out. Someone else will just get the power, right?" He shrugged, but looked away, as if avoiding the harshness of his words.

"If she dies, then Nathaniel dies with her." Oliver closed his eyes for a moment and took a deep breath. "The Champions have years of memories, going back from each of their predecessors. He won't have had time to pass that knowledge on. We lose everything if there's a mistake. Just like with Eira and Xander!"

Alex flinched at the word 'mistake' and looked over to see his friend still watching the conversation with narrowed eyes. Roy must have been feeling the same, because a disgusted expression returned to his face.

"Morgan murdered my mother." Roy pushed himself up, kneeling so he was level with Oliver's eyes. "If you wanna just ignore the past, go ahead, but don't forget he wanted you dead too."

"How dare you," Oliver hissed. "I was there! I will never forget." He was shaking as he pinned Roy with icy gold eyes.

"And where were you? Twenty-three years I've been doing this. Where the fuck were the rest of you when I was babysitting our prince? When I was managing your safe houses? When I spent every day trying to protect him from whoever was coming for us next? I did everything. I had to be everything. Alone. For a man who wanted nothing. And I still have to do everything! Do you think I ever got to have a choice?" Alex saw Oliver's eyes flick to him for a split second, but it was enough.

"Go then!" Alex heard his own shout as if it came from someone else. He uncurled from the chair, throwing himself to his feet to face his uncle. "I didn't ask for you to be here! I didn't ask for any of this."

"Alex, I'm sorry. I didn't mean—" The darkness left Oliver's voice as soon as it had come. He reached out, but Alex swatted his hand away.

"Get off of me!" Hot anger burned behind his eyes and he blinked the tears away furiously. "You say you were protecting Dad, but you didn't, did you? You're supposed to be his Champion, but he's still dead. Where was that in your damn plan!"

"Alex, stop!" His mother cried out, but he didn't care.

"No! I'm just a job to him. Some obligation. Well I don't need anyone babysitting me. I'm not Dad!"

Oliver had fallen silent and, as his vision cleared, Alex could see his uncle's face was drawn. Stiffly, he turned his back on them, unhooking his coat from the hanger as he walked towards the front door.

"Ollie, don't. Wait, please." Dorothea stood up, but the door had already slammed shut. A hand over her face, she drooped against the couch and Alex's anger was replaced by the cold trickle of guilt. Weak limbed, he sank down onto the arm rest.

"Hey, kid," Roy looked over at him pityingly. "I'm gonna head to the pub. Want to come get a drink?" Unfolding his limbs in a stretch, he got to his feet. Alex shook his head, unable to reply. "Sure, mate?" He turned to Eira. "You?"

"Not right now," she said softly.

"Suit yourself." Roy nodded to Alex's mother as he headed towards the door, but Dorothea didn't look up. As the door slammed again, Alex let his tears fall.

CHAPTER 30

The growing warmth of the day wasn't enough to dry the puddles formed by the recent shower. Roy danced around one, shivering as a trickle of water from an awning above seeped through the white shirt he'd taken from the guard. Damn it. He didn't have a coat anymore, and it wasn't like he could go back and grab one.

This near to the city centre, there was no shortage of pubs crammed full of people enjoying a lunchtime drink. Now that the rain had stopped, their patrons spilled back out into the street, likely to escape the suffocating humidity of closely pressed bodies inside. Roy scanned his options, weighing up whether it was worth taking out another loan just to get pissed. There was a good reason he rarely came so close to the tourist spots.

"*If I can make a suggestion.*" Julian's voice floated through his mind, but Roy pointedly ignored it. As he continued to wander aimlessly, an older bar caught his eye. Built into the corner of the street, the mahogany building had a curling facade with a black sign running along the top that declared it 'The Bridge'.

Yearning emanated from Julian's presence. "*That one! Oh, come on...*"

"*Sod off.*"

"*Wait a second,*" Julian continued as if Roy hadn't spoken. "*You aren't banned! We can get in!*"

"Like hell I'm going in! I want to forget my worries, not add to them." If anything, this place looked more expensive than the others. "And what are you talking about, banned? You were a royal Champion."

"*Not when I was out drinking, I wasn't. Go on. You look smart enough.*"

"Don't see why I should listen to you." Roy grumbled, but it didn't seem like there were many better options. "If it will get you to shut up, at least I can sit down in peace." With a sigh, he headed towards the double doors of the entrance.

It was busy inside, but less than Roy expected. Probably a consequence of the prices, and maybe because it was barely one in the afternoon. He admitted the last part grudgingly. Most of the patrons were clustered around the bar in the centre and, slipping through the crowd, he managed to order himself a pint of the cheapest beer they had on offer, before settling into an empty booth in the far corner.

Roy ran a thumb along the smooth surface of his glass as he took in the room. The high ceiling was painted red, with a swirling pattern that drew his eye to the hanging groups of lights that illuminated it. Their warm glow was likely intended to mimic the original magelights, but he could tell these had been upgraded to electric.

He'd made it through half his pint before the uncharacteristic silence from Julian grew suspicious. *"You're not going to rip into me about what happened back there?"* He sensed the spy's presence close enough to know he was still watching.

"Oh, I can't possibly comment." Any emotion the man might have been feeling was well hidden, and Roy continued his drink, trying to be grateful for the peace.

"You think Oliver's going to go meet her by himself?" He sent the words after a few more minutes of silence.

"I'm sure that's likely." Julian's reply triggered a pang of regret. *"I'm not concerned. The two of them are certainly capable. Quite frankly, I'm not sure what use you would have been to him."*

"I can shut you off, you know." Roy scowled at the remains of his pint. *"You lied to me."* Julian didn't respond and he downed the rest. He was sure now that there was never any chance of reversing the awakening. His only option was to spend the rest of his life forcing Julian from his mind, and he only found out he could do that because of Eira. If there was anyone he wanted less to do with than Morgan, it was the royal family, and now he was stuck with a permanent reminder. Even the small satisfaction that his incompetence was causing Julian frustration had dried up, especially as the Spy no longer seemed to care.

"How about we get another drink?" Julian commented as Roy placed the empty pint onto the table. *"There's something I need to tell you."*

"Oh yeah? Something else to manipulate me?"

"You can decide that for yourself after you hear it."

With an audible groan, Roy slunk back to the bar. He deposited his pint glass on the countertop and scanned the colourful array of bottles that lined the upper shelves as he waited to be served.

"That one there," Julian drew Roy's eyes to an unassuming amber bottle.

"Uh uh," Roy began to shake his head at the inaudible conversation before catching himself. *"I don't do fancy drinks."*

"Trust me. Ask for a dash of elderflower. On ice."

"I said no." He forced a smile at the approaching bartender, raising a hand in greeting.

"Don't make me beg." Julian whined in his head and Roy suppressed a sigh.

A few minutes later he returned to his booth, tumbler in hand, and feeling unjustly poorer considering the scant amount of liquid he'd received. When he tilted his wrist, the ice cubes clinked satisfyingly against the edge of the glass and he swirled them around before giving the drink a suspicious sniff.

"I hope you're figuring out a way to pay for this." He shot the thought at Julian as he took a sip. A caramel sweetness coated his tongue, chased instantly by a fire that settled comfortably in his stomach. Roy licked his lips.

"I'm confident I have at least one account that Ewen never plundered." If Julian had a face, he was sure he would be smirking. *"I was right then."*

Roy knew he didn't need to respond. Instead he lifted the glass again, this time savouring the honey wood smell that filled his nostrils.

"What's your issue with Ardveld's royalty, then?" Julian's question caught him off guard. *"It appears to me that you dislike*

us almost as much as Morgan himself."

"You know why. You've poked your nose into my mind enough. My mum was killed, just because she worked at the palace. A ton of innocent people were. Your lot always made out you were so special, so much more worthy than the rest of us, but you didn't even see it coming." He realised he was gripping his glass tightly. *"Mum never cared about your politics, but she died anyway. She never came home because of you."*

Roy wondered if he'd hit a nerve. He could sense Julian's emotion had soured, but when the spy's response came, it was calm. *"Celia cared more than you realise."*

"I thought I told you to stay the fuck out of my memories," he snarled at the use of his mother's name.

"It's not your memory, Roy." Julian replied. *"It's mine."*

An image flickered into Roy's mind. A portrait lined room with a high ceiling and silver patterning on the dark blue doors. He knew without needing to ask that it was the palace. Muffled chatter came from the shut off dining room next door, but it was the woman in front of him that caught his attention. Her dark, bobbed hair framed a face tense with concern, and Roy's heart quickened as recognition dawned. She looked so different in this memory; serious, professional. Shorter, he realised, suddenly aware that he was looking at her through Julian's eyes.

"We found these in their belongings." Roy's mother's voice was distant, but brought with it a wave of longing. She was holding some kind of metal canister, but he couldn't work out what it was before an ear-splitting bang made them both jump. The vision whirled towards the doors, just as the memory faded.

"Wait! Bring it back!" Roy tried to grasp for the image, but nothing came.

"*I won't show you any more,*" Julian said. "*She'd been watching them for some time, but wasn't able to pinpoint anything to confirm her suspicions. That day, Celia came to me but... it was too late.*"

A multitude of emotions hit Roy at once. If that memory was from the day of the takeover, then that meant it was moments before Julian's death. Moments before his mother's death. Roy understood now why he had refused to show him the rest.

"*She worked for you.*"

"*Did you really think just anyone can do the kind of spell-breaking she taught you? Of course she worked for me,*" Julian confirmed. "*Perhaps I should have recognised you immediately, but then again, it's hard to see your face from inside your mind.*"

Another image came; this time, a group of people holding drinks and laughing together outside in the sunshine. A pudgy toddler with familiar red-brown hair stumbled his way across the neatly manicured lawn towards them, holding a fistful of grass. Roy saw his mother again, younger this time, but her smile matching his own memories. She bent down and scooped the boy up, resting him on her hip as he fought to get back down.

"*I met you at one or two of our little parties.*" The unusual affection in Julian's voice gave Roy a wash of embarrassment. "*You've grown somewhat.*"

"*I don't remember any of that.*"

She'd looked happy there, with her colleagues. Even moments before the takeover, there had been a determination in his mother's eyes. It surprised him. Roy had never known what she actually did at the palace. He'd always believed it was just a job; an obligation drawing her from her real life until it took her away completely.

"You were very small. She stopped bringing you as you got older, I believe your father didn't approve?"

"Sounds like him." Roy took a mouthful of the sweet drink to purge the bitterness that came at the mention of his father. The man's tirade echoed through his head as if he had just heard it; work keeping her away, how he was left looking after 'the little shit'. *"We haven't spoken in ten years."* It was long enough that Roy could almost pretend he never thought of him.

"I wish I could say I was more surprised."

Roy tilted his head. *"What do you mean?"*

"Celia occasionally spoke about her home life. It wasn't my place, but..." Julian paused, and Roy could tell he wasn't sure how much he should say, but the affirmation had taken him by surprise.

There was no way Julian knew what happened after the takeover. The rages. The drinking. It had never been his father's job to raise him, if you could even call it that. Roy knew he'd just been another burden on top of the grief, but if it wasn't for the royal family, his mother would still be alive.

"I'm sorry. I should have considered the threat with the gravity it deserved. I just never believed—" For the first time, Julian's thoughts were heavy with remorse and Roy felt his own anguish magnified through their connection.

"I walked straight into it, like a fool," Julian spat, and Roy realised he knew how the Velbians had done it. *"The pressurised containers; they must have affected the air—"* He stopped, as though aware of the implications. *"All I remember is becoming light headed and then nothing."* He continued gently. *"There was no pain."*

Roy drew a juddering breath. *"I guess I should thank you for telling me."* There was a satisfying burn as he downed the last of the drink. "*Even though it took you long enough.*"

"*You seemed like a flight risk. It wouldn't do to take any chances.*" Julian sounded like he was back to normal. "*Besides, I'd already died enough times for one day.*"

Roy snorted as he swirled the melting remains of the ice around the now empty glass. He finally had the answer. Something he'd spent so many years wondering about, and yet now it seemed almost insignificant. He'd never signed up for this Champion thing; he was happy being alone. And yet, for a moment there...

Part of him had wanted to see Matthew again when he got to that safe house, but now he was gone. Alex had lost his father, and Oliver... Roy couldn't stop the tug in his heart as he considered the prickly tactician. "*I thought you said you weren't going manipulate me anymore.*"

"*I believe I said that you could decide for yourself.*"

"*Go on then,*" Roy set his glass down and got to his feet. "*Where do I find him?*"

CHAPTER 31

The corridor was dark when Tamara stepped out of Morgan's office; the thick glass windows above the main staircase providing only a filtered half-light from the overcast sky.

"Are you sure you're comfortable going alone?" Morgan followed her to the door, keeping his voice low despite the empty hall.

"I don't believe Oliver will want to fight, especially if Alex is there." She turned to face him and smiled with an assurance she wished she felt. "Besides, it would probably create more problems if you were with me." He wouldn't be much use in a fight anyway, but Tamara kept that thought to herself.

Morgan made a sound of reluctant agreement. "It's not Oliver so much I'm worried about. Verdant Park is public enough, but we have to assume Aiden has people looking for them."

"There's no way he can know where we'll be. If it looks like there's any danger, I'll leave immediately." Tamara couldn't resist a glance over her shoulder, but the corridor was as empty as it had been moments before. "It's so quiet."

"I sent the staff home; as many as we can do without."

It took a moment for her to process the implication. If Aiden made a move against Morgan, he would be completely alone. Apparently he intended it that way.

"Now I'm worried about leaving."

"Don't be. The chances of anything happening here are low, and you have bigger concerns." He seemed confident, but Tamara couldn't tell if it was a lie to make her feel better. "I trust you will be reassured if I stay in my office?"

She nodded. With Nathaniel's help, she had recrafted the lock on the office door. It was now an advanced spell, of a kind she'd never seen, and though she didn't know how well it would hold up to Aiden's mage guard, it would at least provide some protection.

Morgan took a step towards her, and Tamara had the sudden compulsion to pull him into a farewell embrace. She caught herself when she saw the hand he offered instead, accepting the handshake with a flush of embarrassment and hoping he hadn't realised.

"We'll speak soon." Inclining his head in farewell, Morgan released her, leaving Tamara's hand tingling at the absence of his warmth.

"Were you really about to hug the man who murdered me?"

Nathaniel commented scathingly.

"*I wasn't!*" Heat returned to her cheeks despite her protest.

"*I think you'll find I can ascertain exactly your feelings,*" he replied. "*And I want it to be known that I am not in the least pleased about it.*"

Without a good answer, Tamara stayed silent.

"*I don't know how I'll ever get accustomed to this.*" Nathaniel continued to grumble as she started down the stairs, the bleed of his emotions turning her own embarrassment to frustration.

"*If you're just going to complain, I may as well block you out,*" she snapped back. "*You know this is new to me as well.*" Had she met him in person, she might have been intimidated, but being able to sense his feelings gave her a confidence that Tamara rarely experienced with other people.

"*It's not the same. Everything I feel is so much more intense than when I was alive. Smells. Sounds. Fabric! No one ever mentioned this.*"

There was genuine distress behind the bravado, and Tamara smiled, irritation vanishing as she realised what was going on. "*Why do you think I run a shield? This is how I always feel.*"

Being Kifaerish, Tamara was very aware that her sensory experience was different to the majority of Ardveldians. Or rather, to almost everyone not born in her home country. But she'd never considered how that might feed through to her new companion.

"*This is because of you?*" Nathaniel's tone had softened. "*How are you able to tolerate it? I can barely think.*"

"*You get used to it.*"

"*Have you?*"

Tamara paused at the landing. "*Well, yes and no.*" She

stroked a hand over the smooth wood of the bannister. *"I'm working on it."*

Any reassurance she'd received from Morgan about their safety was banished as she turned down towards the ground floor. A man wearing the dark uniform of sunstone enterprises passed the bottom of the stairs, and she shrunk back out of sight. One of Aiden's mages. The double doors of the main palace entrance were just beyond. So close, and yet...

"We could fight our way through." Nathaniel followed her thoughts.

"There's no guarantee they would try to stop me," Tamara replied. *"Even with most of the staff gone, there should still be palace guards around the entrance. Maybe Aiden won't want them to draw attention."* She wasn't convinced. *"Otherwise, we double back. Try and get across to the staff entrance via the upper floor."*

"And walk into an ambush in a more remote location," Nathaniel groaned. *"Where is Ewen when you need him."*

It was worth trying the other route. Tamara eased her way up a step, mindful of any creak that might give her away. After a few more, she whirled around, intending to rush back the way she had come.

"Can I help you, Minister?"

Instead, her heart sank as she locked eyes with a second of Aiden's guards above her.

Tamara straightened, smoothing down the fabric of her jacket and brushed a lock of hair out of her face as she gave them a warm smile. "Oh, no thank you. I was actually just heading out for a walk. Thank you for the offer, though. I'm sure I'll see you again later." She laughed, though there was no humour in it, her own nervous babble sounding ridiculous to her ears. Bannister gripped tight, she backed down the stairs. There was no reason they should be looking for her. None at all. Just walk to the doors and leave.

Her heart rate quickened as the exit came into sight. The first guard was still there, but now there was someone else beside him.

"Where are you going, Tamara?" Aiden's voice now seemed a silky facade after the screaming rage she'd heard in the throne room. "Perhaps I can accompany you?" His sharp eyes looked her up and down as he stepped closer, but Tamara could no longer see his features as handsome.

"Ah, well, I didn't plan to go anywhere in particular. Just a wander, really," Tamara said. "I wouldn't want to bother you. Especially since..." She cut herself off before revealing too much of what she knew. For someone whose mother had just died, Aiden seemed unsettlingly content.

"That's a shame," Aiden's smile vanished. "I thought you might have something to tell me."

Her head began to spin as a third guard came into view. "I'm not... I'm not sure what you mean." She pulled on her own magic, strengthening her shield as Aiden closed in.

"My Uncle was right, I hadn't forgotten about Golebach. But bugging Morgan's office was a far more effective way to get the truth." White teeth glinted as he grinned, and Tamara's blood ran like ice.

"He knows."

In her mind, Nathaniel joined her in assessing the threat. Excluding Aiden, there were three mages, but this close their energy was wild. Too confusing to detect how strong they were, or even what defences they could have.

"What kind of magic is this?" she asked, but Nathaniel seemed as confused as she did.

"I don't know. Regardless, if we stop him here, the threat to Alex

is negated," Nathaniel said. *"Don't falter."*

"I didn't intend to." Placing a foot behind her to steady her stance, Tamara considered her first strike.

"You're going to attack me?" Aiden looked amused at the prospect. "I knew you were a traitor, but I didn't expect you to be so overt. I am now the Arch Canlaw of Vailberg." She froze, and he laughed. "Though of course, you know that already."

"I don't care what you are." She hoped her voice sounded stronger than she seemed.

"A valiant sentiment. But what about what you are?" He lifted his head to look behind her, and with a sinking dread, she turned to follow his gaze. Two more of Aiden's guards appeared, this time, holding Morgan between them.

"Tamara! Go quickly! Just leave—" Morgan's words were cut off as he was struck; the man on his left slamming an elbow against the back of his neck.

Tamara hissed and lunged forward. But the guard on the stairs was ready. A bolt of nauseating energy shot past her body and her focus fumbled. The attack she'd been forming dispersed as she stumbled against the wall.

"It's tragic, really," Aiden continued as though there had been no interruption. "That so soon after my mother's death, I also had to suffer the loss of my beloved uncle. Murdered by his own adviser... I should have seen it coming. After all, is it that surprising that someone from Avel-Kifaeros might take advantage of such uncertain times?" A different kind of sickness settled in Tamara's stomach as she realised what he was implying. "Your people are so easily overwhelmed. I wonder how much support will remain for the territory's independence after your conviction."

Anger burned stronger than any weakness left by the

warning shot. "I could just kill you first."

"Perhaps. Even if you succeed, Morgan will die," Aiden looked down at her. "But he doesn't have to. You have what I want. Must we resort to killing for information you can so freely give me?"

"Ignore him!" Nathaniel screamed through her head. *"Whatever happens to us, Alex's safety is more important!"*

"You must see you weren't meant to be a Champion, Tamara," Aiden hissed. "This is my life's work. Everything I've ever wanted. Think! If you help me, we could bring magic to everyone. To anyone who wants it!"

"To you, you mean."

"You don't deserve it!" He gestured towards the guards behind her and Tamara heard a thump. She spun around to see Morgan forced to the ground. "I'm sick of looking at both of you. Make your choice or he dies now."

Memory replaced carpeted stairs with shining tiles, dripping dark red.

"Tamara," Morgan's voice was tight with pain. "Don't."

"No!" *Not again.* Blocking out Nathaniel's protests, she rushed down the step to grab at Aiden's arm.

Around her, the strange magic of the mages flared, and acid forced its way up the back of her throat as a bolt of energy struck her shield. It was ripped into nothing and she fell against Aiden's body. "Don't—" She gasped a breath. "I don't know how the Champion spell works. None of them do!"

"Then it seems we'll have to find out." Aiden sneered as he pushed her back into the arms of his waiting guard. Blindly, she elbowed them away, their proximity increasing the assault against her already frazzled senses. He gave a tut at her reaction. "Come on now, I don't have time for any more games."

"I'll come with you," Tamara flinched at Aiden's glare. "I just don't want to be touched."

He snorted then lowered his face towards her, breath hot on her unshielded skin. "Fine. I would never want to cause you discomfort. In fact, I have already arranged a comfortable place for you both to wait."

Wait? Tamara's confusion must have showed, because Aiden's smile was back.

"Of course. I regret that we can't begin right away, but it seems I have an important meeting to attend in Verdant Park."

CHAPTER 32

It was only when Oliver saw the sign indicating he had made it halfway to Verdant Park on foot, that he realised he'd instinctively headed towards the arranged meeting spot. He shot the sign a glare as he passed. Even now, he couldn't escape his duty.

The damp seeping into his clothes did nothing to improve his mood, but he was too exhausted to do anything about it. Sleep hadn't come easy, and the busy street warped into a surreal mix of clarity and muted colours as he passed the shop fronts and office workers out on break. He wondered if he would ever return to his own office. As far as they knew, he was just off sick. Well, he felt sick enough now.

"It's been a while since we've been to Verdant Park," Ewen commented delicately. *"Always a pleasure to see how little it has changed, though the surroundings are certainly different from when I was young."*

Oliver grunted a response, not caring if anyone heard. How long had it been since Ewen was there in person, anyway? Not so long that he wouldn't know the iconic office blocks that now graced the skyline.

"What you're really wondering, is how long it's been since I was young." There was a gentleness to Ewen's words that, despite the weight of the day, left Oliver curious.

"Go on then. I know you're trying to distract me." He tried to hide his gratitude under the brusque reply. *"Why Verdant Park?"*

The crowd of shoppers dispersed as they left the high street; storefronts replaced by a wrought-iron fence, interspersed with trees, which bordered the park.

"It's been a good sixty years, though obviously not as long for Nathaniel. We were just potentials then, some of many, but I'd already noted Julian as a trouble maker."

It was strange to hear Ewen speak about the previous Champions. Having been the only one for so long, Oliver had never considered that their relationships had gone beyond the professional. Perhaps that was why neither of them had ever brought it up; it was a topic too raw to touch when they both needed to accept being alone.

"There was a public jubilee celebration in the park. It was Samuel's father's — Matthew's grandfather's of course — and I could have overlooked Julian sneaking out to attend; even then, he had a habit of turning up in places he wasn't supposed to. Not a bad trait in a potential intelligence operative I suppose. But this time he'd convinced Nicholas to go with him."

Sorrow accompanied Nicholas' name, and Oliver thought back to how he'd left Eira and Xander in the safe house. If anyone knew what it was like to awaken so young, he did; but with a scared teenager as a guide instead of an experienced mentor... He owed Eira — no, he owed them both an apology.

"Well, after the incident with the cat, I didn't think it was right to allow Nick to get caught up in any more trouble. Especially with him being a favourite of Samuel's." Ewen continued over his thoughts, despite the fact Oliver knew the strategist would have sensed them. *"And once I informed Nathaniel of their intentions, he insisted on accompanying me. We set out to head them off, but by the time we arrived Julian pointed out that, we too, were out of bounds on the day of a formal event."* Laughter emanated from Ewen and Oliver smiled, caught up for a moment in his mentor's emotion. *"He was quite right too!"*

"You ended up staying?" Oliver turned through the arched gateway that marked Verdant Park's entrance, his footsteps crunching on the gravel path. The flat, grassy space was empty of people except for a dog walker and a lone jogger in the distance; a beneficial side effect of the earlier rainfall. From here, Oliver could see across to the other two entrances, but the one to his far right was closest to the palace and the direction from which Tamara would likely approach.

"Well, given the circumstances, we decided it wouldn't do any harm to have a drink." Ewen sounded sheepish, and Oliver wondered if it had been more than just one. *"And before you ask; no, I am not going to show you any of that night,"* he finished firmly.

"I wasn't going to ask!" Moving towards the middle of the park seemed the best option, given that he would be able to observe the entire area with a safe distance between himself

and anyone entering. A group of trees at the centre might provide some cover too, though the small bandstand next to them would draw the eye. *"All those times you've judged me. You're such a hypocrite."*

"Even with your lifespan, you won't live long enough to make every mistake yourself. Be grateful for what I've saved you from."

Oliver sighed as he reached the circle of trees and leant back against the trunk of what he now saw was a sweet chestnut. The expected entrance was in sight opposite him. *"You agree with this position?"* It was still early for the meeting time he had set, but he preferred it that way.

"I do. Even if she makes it here, we shouldn't let down our guard."

A cool breeze whipped through the summer air, catching the leaves of the trees that lined the park's edge and flicking them into a sparkling display of green. Oliver's eyes followed the movement, landing back on the park's gateway.

He remembered Nathaniel and the others of course. As Ewen's apprentice, he had seen the previous Champions more often than any of the other potentials. Odd to think that, having missed the last twenty-three years, they were now closer to his age than to Ewen's.

Except Xander.

The correction came before he'd finished the first thought. In his mind, Ewen stirred, as though about to comment. Instead he stayed silent, but Oliver didn't need to hear the words to know the meaning. Nicholas was gone. Truly gone. It shouldn't hurt; until yesterday they'd believed the same for all of them.

"It's different this time, isn't it."

Ewen didn't reply.

Damp from the grass was soaking up the bottom of his trousers, and he extended a little energy to dry them as he straightened his tie. Through the distant entrance opposite, a car rolled to a slow stop outside the gateway, and he made out the shape of people exiting. Five of them; four in dark clothes, the last in a cream white jacket. It didn't look like they were there for a leisurely stroll.

"People on lunch break?" Oliver raised the possibility, despite his suspicions. *"She said she would come alone, and it is still early."*

"Unlikely." Ewen barely paused to consider it. *"If they head this way, we should retreat."*

Oliver got up from the tree as though reassuming a casual walk, keeping watch from the corner of his vision. The man that strode to the front of the group wasn't anywhere near as subtle. As they approached, Oliver could tell he was being watched.

"We should leave," Ewen said, but Oliver paused. Now that they were closer, he could make out the familiar sunburst logo on the clothes the strangers wore. Sunstone Enterprises. These weren't simply people sent by the palace.

He moved before thinking to be afraid. The face of the man in the cream blazer came into focus as Oliver sped towards them, confirming what had first seemed like wild suspicion, and fury rose within his heart, channelling into the magic on which he intuitively drew.

"You must be Oliver." The sound of Aiden Heliodor's voice was like oil marring clear water. "I thought I might arrive before you, but I see that I've been outmatched."

Aiden smiled, and Oliver struck; a bolt of energy, sharp and deadly, slicing invisible through the air.

The mages around Aiden would have felt the magic, and he braced for the flash of attack striking shield. Instead, the closest guard to him sidestepped into its path. Air fizzed as it hit, and Oliver's stomach lurched as a burst of magic assaulted his senses. The power was familiar; wild and unformed, just like—

"—*Oliver! What are you doing? Listen to me!*" Ewen's voice, loud and urgent, broke into his awareness. Before him, the only sign of his attack on the guard was faint shapes of glowing light that seeped through the material of the man's uniform. "*We don't know what kind of magic those people possess. You can't just—*"

"It doesn't matter."

Ewen was right; he hadn't known what to expect from his attack, but he did now. Somehow, these mages possessed undirected magic. It was the same as when he'd fought the wand with Matthew. The same as when he'd picked it up and its energy had rushed through him, grounding his own magic and leaving him drained.

Aiden's gaze turned cold. "I had hoped we could have a civil discussion, but apparently not." He waved an arm at his guards, and the three not protecting him dispersed, moving to encircle the area where Oliver stood.

A steady calm descended over him as he watched them. With a deep breath, he dropped every shield he had, keeping only the spell that corrected his vision. He likely wouldn't even need that one much longer.

"*If they land a strike on you, it's over,*" Ewen cautioned, even as Oliver sensed the Tactician following his thoughts. As long as his attacks avoided contacting the mages directly, they shouldn't be absorbed. No shield would protect him, but he only had one target.

"I just want to talk," Aiden spoke again as Oliver shaped the spells in his mind. He was off the grass now, gravel path loose under his feet. "This doesn't need to end in further pain for you."

With a flick of his wrist, Oliver directed his magic towards the ground. A gust of wind swirled around him, whipping up dirt and stones as it went and flinging shrapnel in the faces of the encircling guards. The air crackled sickeningly behind him as a shot from one grazed past his body. Too close.

As the air current continued to gather force, Oliver flung his second spell below the guard protecting Aiden. It pulled the heat from the moisture in the ground just as the wind he had crafted hit them. The guard toppled on the newly formed ice, and for the first time, he saw a glimpse of fear in Aiden's eyes. Gritting his teeth, he shaped the strike that would end this.

Air was forced from Oliver's lungs as the first bolt hit him. He reeled off balance as he loosed his shot, not seeing where his spell fired, only the dirt that rose to meet him as he sunk to his knees. Another strike forced bile up his throat as the undirected magic ripped through his body. Oliver sucked in a breath as the attacks from Aiden's mages tore away his energy, clinging to his consciousness even as he knew he wouldn't survive much more.

"*Oliver! I need to say— I might not get another chance.*" An urgency from Ewen flooded his mind as Oliver's quivering arms failed to keep propping up his weight. "*The last time... I never got to say goodbye.*"

"Don't." Oliver was prepared to die, but losing Ewen... He wasn't ready. He felt like he hadn't been ready for anything in his life.

With no spell to sustain it, his fuzzy vision could only distinguish the shapes of the guards around him. They should have attacked again by now, surely? He tried to look for Aiden, too weak to easily turn his head. There he was. Still standing, but hunched, gripping his shoulder tightly.

"I should have you killed for that," Aiden snarled, leaving Oliver momentarily relieved that he couldn't make out his expression. It looked as though his spell had hit.

Closing his eyes, Oliver spoke. "I yield."

He finally let himself sink down fully to the ground, the gravel sharp and wet against his cheek. *"We need to know what he wants,"* Oliver sent the thought simply. *"Dying here, I won't have any answers for the next."* His breathing was heavy, but Oliver knew he'd won the battle for consciousness with his weakened body. *"I can't risk that happening, like it did to you."*

Rough hands gripped his clothes, lurching him to his feet. He staggered, leaning his weight heavily onto his captors, even as his head spun from their dizzying energy. When he blinked, Aiden's face swam into focus, pale and angry, and Oliver could now see there was blood dripping from a deep tear in his left shoulder.

Blinding pain shot through Oliver's stomach as Aiden's fist landed. He cried out as he collapsed forward, gasping for breath and held upright only by the guard's steel grip on his arms. At the edge of his senses, he heard Aiden breathe deeply. There was a grinding on the gravel as he turned away, then Oliver felt his feet slipping across the stones as the guards dragged him after.

CHAPTER 33

"Don't move!"

Roy froze at Julian's shout. A gust of wind rustled the branches above his head, knocking drops of water onto his hair. On the path ahead, Oliver stood surrounded, but none of the group looked to where Roy squatted, half hidden in the treeline that bordered the park.

"What the hell is he thinking?" Roy chewed his lip. Oliver had attacked. He'd attacked Aiden with a spell strong enough to sense from here. Even with his boosted senses, that level of magic should have done something! But the guard he'd hit was unscathed.

"He isn't thinking," Julian replied.

Another spike of magic flared from Oliver's direction. Dirt swirled through the air, briefly blocking Roy's view of the scene. He scrambled forward, legs cramping from his crouched position.

"*I said don't move!*" Julian's voice bellowed through his mind, but he needn't have bothered. A wave of static energy exploded from the circle of guards as they responded to Oliver's attack and Roy staggered back, each burst sending his head spinning.

As fast as it had begun, the assault stopped. When he looked up, the air had cleared. Oliver was on the ground, his slumped form almost obscured by the guards surrounding him. For a moment Roy couldn't breathe, then he saw them hurl the Tactician limply to his feet. "*They took him out like it was nothing,*" he flattened himself back against the tree. "*What the fuck are they?*"

"*I don't know.*"

"*That bastard!*" Roy growled as he watched Aiden strike Oliver hard in the stomach. He'd like to see how well Aiden would fare without a bunch of goons to hide behind. At least Oliver was alive.

"*Alive is potentially the problem.*"

Roy didn't bother to mask his disgust. "*What is wrong with you? You need to help me get him out of there!*" Aiden was striding back across the park, his guards dragging Oliver along with them. The window for action was running out, and Roy dreaded to think what would happen once he got to wherever they were taking him.

"*Oliver couldn't beat them, what chance do you think you have?*" Julian's emotionless reply only fuelled Roy's anger.

"*I'm not going to sit here and do nothing!*"

"*Oliver's too useful to kill,*" Julian spoke slowly, as though explaining to a child, and his mouth went dry as he processed his meaning. *"If the woman is to be believed, it's not just him he's after."*

"He wouldn't tell them about Alex. No way." Roy wanted it to be true, but after seeing how easily Aiden had overpowered any opposition, he didn't want to bet on what else the man would do.

"He won't want to, but trust me, everyone has their limit," Julian replied and Roy caught a sense of bitterness under the spy's cool demeanour. *"What we can do is mitigate the damage. We get Alex and the others away while we still have the chance."*

"You want me to go back? What am I supposed to say? That I just watched Oliver get taken? Why would they listen to me after that?" Guilt twisted as he heard the door to Aiden's car slam. Maybe he could follow them. If they were headed to the palace—

"If you go running after him, you'll be another liability at best. At worst, you get to find out exactly what Aiden wants from us. Would Oliver be happy that you left the others defenceless?"

Julian was right. As much as it hurt to abandon Oliver to whatever fate awaited, Roy knew it was the only option. With an audible groan, he pulled his eyes away from the departing car. *"Fuck. I'm going to have to tell the kid."*

CHAPTER 34

The house was cooler when Alex opened the bathroom door. A breeze that had drifted through the little windows hit his towel-dried hair with a pleasant chill. It felt better being clean. There had been fresh clothes for him amongst the bags, but despite his relief at finally being able to change, seeing his entire existence reduced to what could be carried was an unpleasant sight. His books, games, projects; all had been left behind.

Eira grabbed an extra glass from the cupboard when she saw him enter the kitchen. She filled it with water and Alex accepted gratefully, remembering the mugs of tea he had let grow cold.

"You okay?" she asked. It seemed that was all anyone was asking nowadays.

"Yeah." Okay would have to be enough. "You can borrow some of my stuff, you know, if you want to get changed?" It wasn't a practical suggestion. He doubted much would fit, but Alex couldn't help but feel bad that nothing had been brought for her. Even though the original decision to send Eira home had been made without him, it was still his fault she was here at all.

"Oh! No. That's not how it works."

Alex looked at Eira in confusion at the strange reply. "Huh?"

With a blink, her eyes refocussed on him. "Sorry! I wasn't talking to you." She gave her head a shake as though to clear it. "You were saying something, weren't you? I'm sorry, it's so—"

"Don't worry about it." Alex cut off her apology with a wave. "It must be weird to get used to, right?" Another thing that was because of him.

"I keep forgetting I don't have to speak out loud." Eira hopped up to sit on the kitchen counter, swinging her legs as her eyes drifted back to the middle distance. "He says he can hear my thoughts, but it's hard to adjust."

"You weren't doing it so much earlier," Alex commented, then wished he hadn't. He didn't want to think about what had happened with Oliver.

"Yeah, he'd sort of... gone, if that makes sense? I think he can go away if he wants, like when I block him out," Eira said, and Alex nodded, though he wasn't sure it was possible for him to understand. "After we first got here, I guess it got a bit much. Then when everyone was arguing... Well..."

Alex took a mouthful of water, hoping the glass would

hide his expression. There wasn't any point getting upset about it, especially not for Eira's pity.

"Want to head back to the couch?" he said, not feeling like standing any longer.

The lounge was still empty, though noises from the bedroom indicated his mother was sorting through the bags and items that had fallen over the floor. It was a comforting imitation of normality; he could almost pretend they were on a holiday rather than in hiding. Alex rested his head on his knees and inhaled deeply as he noticed his fresh clothes smelt of home.

"What's he like then?" he asked, as Eira came to settle beside him.

She rested her chin on her hand and gave him a sideways look. "Posh," she laughed. "And with a lot of outdated ideas that we're having to quickly sort out."

Alex smiled as he imagined the scolding Eira's Champion must be getting. "I'm starting to feel sorry for the guy!" He earnt an elbow in the side in response. At least she didn't seem too bothered by the experience, though whether it was a brave face for his sake, Alex couldn't tell.

"It seems like no time passed for him at all," Eira continued. "I've had to explain everything that happened. Well, as much as I can."

"...Oliver seemed to know who he is." It hurt to say his uncle's name.

"Well, yeah." Eira paused. "They were friends." The glazed look briefly returned, then she rolled her eyes. "Fine. Maybe not Oliver's. But he's your dad's best friend." When she glanced in Alex's direction, he saw the pitying expression was back. "I'm sorry. We don't have to talk about it if you don't want to."

"I do," Alex insisted. "I want to know."

Eira curled her knees up to match him. "He says it's weird seeing you. Xander's still seventeen, so his best friend having an adult kid was a bit of a shock. Seeing Oliver too."

Alex turned away as he remembered his father's picture in the book Tamara had shown him. He and his Dad looked alike; people always said so. It was weird to think he was currently older than his father had been in that photo. Older than Xander was now. An uneasy thought came to his mind. "His name's Xander?"

"Yeah. Well, apparently it's actually Alexander, but—" Eira broke off as realisation crossed her face.

They sat in a deafening silence until Alex spoke again. "...Dad never told me. He never told me anything."

"I'm sure it was just hard for him." Eira's hand came to rest gently on his arm, but Alex ignored her touch, instead smothering his face further into his knees. "He said, didn't he, that he wanted to forget about it all?"

"Yeah, well I must have been great news then." Alex hoped Eira wouldn't notice the way his voice caught in his throat. "Bet he really wanted a kid as a reminder."

He was interrupted before she could reply.

"That's not true." It was his mother's voice.

Alex lifted his head and looked over the back of the sofa to where she stood, arms folded, in the bedroom doorway. How long had she been listening? Unable to speak, he simply watched as she walked around to where he sat.

"Your father wanted you. He loved you more than anything." She placed a hand softly on his head, running her fingers through his dark curls just like she had done when he was small, and Alex squeezed his eyes shut so that she wouldn't see the tears that threatened. "I won't say that he wasn't scared. Matthew never had to talk about his past for me to know something had happened to him. When he asked me about your name, I think that was the closest he ever came to telling me."

Alex pulled away as he looked up at her. "It never bothered you? That he wouldn't tell you?"

"I love him. It only bothered me that he was dealing with it alone." She smiled sadly. "He wasn't alone, though. Not as much as he thought."

"He was there, Alex," Eira spoke up from beside him. "Xander's last memories are with Matthew and Oliver. They must have watched it happen."

Dorothea nodded. "I guessed it was bad. I'm just grateful that he always had your uncle."

Alex barked a hollow laugh. "Didn't you hear Oliver? It was only a job to him." His uncle had made that clear enough. The only reason he'd ever stuck around was obligation.

"Alex," his mother crouched down in front of him. She moved her hand to his cheek, tilting his face until he was forced to meet her eyes. "Oliver is hurting, just like you. We all are. He thinks it's his fault."

The memory of his last words to his uncle made him wince.

"He's not going to hold it against you," Dorothea continued, as though having read his thoughts. "When he comes back, we'll figure this all out. Everything's going to be okay."

"He's not coming back. I told him to go. And I don't want to see him anyway." He scowled, knowing he sounded like a child.

With a sigh, Dorothea got to her feet and Alex watched in

hurt confusion as she headed back to the bedroom. For a moment he wondered if his mother was leaving him too; too ashamed of his behaviour to be in the same room. But then she returned, carrying a small item in her hands.

"Is that...?" Alex realised what she held as she came closer. The little machine had been one of his first prototype generators. He'd first brought it on a trip to his uncle's house, almost two years ago, to show him. Oliver had seemed so interested that Alex let him keep it; he'd already begun working on the improved version for his interview, anyway.

Dorothea placed the device in Alex's hands and he turned it around, examining it with nostalgia. There was a hum of magic there; his passive spell still lingering on the mechanics with a faint charge. With his current knowledge, looking at the generator made him wonder if his uncle had just been humouring him with his praise. It was so basic; the spell he'd crafted so poorly designed, that he couldn't believe it had lasted this long alone.

"Oliver told us the project you were working on got destroyed in Golebach," Dorothea explained. "He hoped having this might help. I know we couldn't bring anything of yours from home." Alex held the machine limply as she spoke. "He loves you."

Eira wrapped an arm around him as Alex's vision blurred. He leant into her comfort, wiping his wet eyes with the back of his hand. The tears kept coming and this time he let them, too late to pretend he was fine.

"You should have seen them both when you were born." Dorothea's voice hitched despite the lightness in her voice, and Alex noticed she was crying too. "Your father insisted on building the cot alone, though I'm quite sure he'd never built anything in his life." She laughed. "He was furious when

Oliver tried to help him. Said that Ollie had already done all the research and now it was his turn to do something. To be honest, the whole thing would have been faster if I had done it myself, but it made them happy." She wiped her eyes and got up from the floor to sit in the chair opposite. "You know, I think it really drove your Dad to keep trying things."

Imagining his father struggling through a simple task was strange. Alex had always known him being so driven and competent; so much further ahead than he could reach. The idea of him stumbling, helpless into the real world after being raised in the palace was something he wouldn't have believed if it wasn't for the past few days. Who would he have been without the takeover? Alex realised that he himself would never have existed at all.

A click from the front door set Alex's senses to high alert. The others had noticed it too; Eira springing up in her chair, while his mother stood. Could it be Oliver? Alex got up as well, setting his device on the coffee table just as a shout came from the hall.

"Guys? Guys, don't attack! It's me!"

"Roy?" Eira's voice echoed Alex's thoughts. What was Roy doing back here?

Roy's face was flushed red when he burst through the inner door to the living room. The white shirt he wore was damp with sweat and clinging to his body like he'd been running.

"You're still— you're still here," his speech was staggered, interrupted by heavy breaths. "Crap, I need to do more cardio. You can't stay here much longer. It's Oliver."

"What's Oliver? What happened?"

Roy pulled out a chair from the dining table beside the kitchen and collapsed down in a heap. "Aiden's taken him."

Alex's heart skipped. "What? How can you know that?" The question came out more aggressively that he'd intended.

"I didn't want to have to tell you. After everything. He went to see that woman. I followed him, but Aiden was there instead, with a bunch of guards. It must have been a trap. I couldn't do anything. I'm sorry."

He felt sick. This couldn't be real. But Roy's face was wracked with guilt.

"He's alive," Roy interjected. "I saw them take him away only..." He looked away, picking at his nails nervously. "If the palace has him, it means Aiden could find out where you are."

The dread in his core worsened as he understood his meaning.

"Did Oliver leave anything you can use? Fake ID or cash?" Roy looked to Dorothea, whose hands were shaking.

"I— I'm not sure. I can go look."

"We can get you and Alex away, if you find the stuff." Roy turned to Eira. "You and I will have to go into hiding until we can meet up with them later. Julian can get hold of money, enough to keep us afloat, if you're okay with it?"

The conversation swirled around Alex, but all he could think of was his uncle. Oliver was alone. Would be hurt, likely killed, while he hid in safety. He watched his mother hurry towards the bedroom.

"No! I'm not going to just leave him."

Roy looked into Alex's eyes. "Listen, I understand what you're feeling. I've been there. But Oliver would want you safe—"

"You don't have a clue what I'm feeling!" Alex shouted. "I don't want anyone else to die for me."

"Mate, you think I wanted to just watch him get taken?

There's nothing you can do. Aiden wasn't alone. He's got people with him — I don't even know if they're people — they took him out, like that—" He snapped his fingers in front of Alex's face. "Magic doesn't work on them. Tamara's betrayed you. We've got nothing. All I can do for Oliver is make sure Aiden doesn't get hold of the rest of you as well."

"She hasn't betrayed us. You said it yourself, she wasn't there." Alex clung to the only point he could refute. "Aiden's after Champions. I can't abandon them."

"I think Roy's right, Alex," Eira said. "There's nothing you can do." She turned to his mother, still standing by the bedroom doorway, as though trying to silently plead with her to convince him.

Alex interrupted before she could respond. "You don't know that. I just need—"

"It's stupid!" Eira whirled round. "Your dad just died to get you out of that place, and you want to go running back? You're just being selfish!"

Her words stung like he'd been slapped. Silence followed, and the anger died on Eira's face. "I'm sorry, Alex. I shouldn't have—"

"No. You're right." He croaked, voice almost a whisper. "It is selfish... I know. And it's worse, because I need your help."

She opened her mouth as though to reply, but no words came.

"I can't save them alone, but maybe we've got a chance together. Please." It wasn't fair to ask, but even if he ran; even if he lived only for the people he'd lost, just so his mother and Eira wouldn't have to hurt anymore, Alex knew he'd never forgive himself.

"None of us are trained to fight," Roy interjected. "And

anyway, those guards don't just absorb magic. They've got this weird energy they give off. Sends your head spinning."

"Then... Then maybe we just avoid them?" Eira finally spoke, the doubt apparent in her voice.

"Yeah, because it's so easy to just waltz right in there without being spotted." Roy got up from his chair and stretched with a groan. "I can't believe I have to break into the palace again. We had an actual Tactician last time, and that didn't exactly go according to plan." He turned to Alex. "Don't suppose we can go back though the same tunnel you got out with?"

Alex just stared. Then he shook his head. "No— Wait, you're agreeing to come?"

"Well, when you think about it, you're technically my boss now, right? I can't exactly force you to run. So if you're going after Oliver, then I've got no choice but to tag along." Roy shrugged, but despite his outward exasperation, Alex saw a victorious glint in his eyes. "As your Champion, you know."

"I'll be coming, too," Eira said. "I can do some healing at least, if we do end up in a fight."

Roy raised an eyebrow. "Impressive, but I don't think getting hit by one of Aiden's guards is something you can heal your way out of."

Alex looked between them. "...Thank you." Even having asked, he hadn't expected the support. Now he wasn't sure he was making the right choice. They were following him into danger, but he had no plan at all. "Maybe we could use a different type of magic." His Dad had used a sleeping spell on the guard outside their room in the palace. "Is it only offensive spells that don't work?"

"If they absorb magic, then don't use it."

The three of them turned at the words and Dorothea exhaled a deep breath. "You're so much like your father. He always looked for a magical solution first." She pressed her fingers into her temples as though rubbing out a headache. "Whatever guards Aiden has, if they're human, they'll have the same vulnerabilities as anyone else."

"Mum…" Alex said. "You're fine with this?"

"Of course I'm not fine with it." Her arms dropping to her sides. "I want you safe, Alex. I want to keep you protected forever. But I can't. I can't help, I know I can't stop you going, and I'm not going to beg. You don't need to be worrying about me as well."

The sorrow on her face made him want to promise that he'd stay. Instead, he turned away, catching sight of where his makeshift generator still lay on the coffee table. "I promise I'll come back safe," he said instead.

"That's nice and all, but we still don't even have a plan for getting inside in the first place." Roy leant back against the table and crossed his arms.

"Yeah… Unless—" Eira hesitated. "Well, I'm actually an illusionist. And I guess I'm stronger now. Maybe enough to sneak us in?" She didn't sound confident, but Roy seemed to perk up.

"What kind of illusions we talking?"

Alex let Eira's explanation drift into the background as his gaze once more returned to his prototype machine, mind grappling with the idea that had just occurred to him. His mum was right; he'd been so focussed on a magical solution that he'd not considered anything else. They had enough time, as long as there was everything he needed.

"Alex?" Eira interrupted his thoughts. "Were you listening?"

"No," Alex smiled apologetically. "You can tell me in a minute. I think I know what to do about Aiden's guards."

CHAPTER 35

The ground floor room had been stripped of anything small enough to fit through the door. Early afternoon light from the uncurtained windows scattered over dust particles dancing in the air, disturbed from years of rest by the recent activity. Even the stool of the grand piano was gone, so Tamara leant against the instrument instead, unwilling to approach the only other item of furniture left in the room; a curving, high-backed sofa where Morgan sat.

He hadn't spoken a word since they had been left here. Only the glare she received after Aiden's guards dumped him on the hardwood floor told her he had acknowledged her presence. She'd held back when he got to his feet, relieved to see any injuries he'd received weren't severe. Now they were alone, she wished she had done more.

He must be furious, Tamara thought. *And now it looks like I don't care at all.* On the opposite wall, a large portrait looked down on her disapprovingly. She'd never been any good approaching emotional people, and it wasn't as though an apology would fix the mess they were in.

"*It continues to astound me,*" Nathaniel replied, "*that you care more about that man's feelings than the fact you are in very real danger.*"

She dragged her eyes from the painting with a sigh and tugged the fabric of her top away from her body. The heat in the room was rising along with the peak of the day, compounding with the dust to leave an uncomfortable stickiness over her skin, and instinctively she reached for her magic to pull the warmth from the air.

Around her, carved symbols along the top of each wall lit up brilliant gold. They flashed bright as the magic she had cast was pulled away and absorbed. Then the light retreated; marks fading down to their original dim glow. Tamara clenched her jaw as she saw them. For a moment she'd forgotten.

Neither she nor Morgan had tried the room's only door, but the sound of a key in the lock had been enough to assume they couldn't just leave. It was likely that Aiden would have left a guard, and the ground-floor windows would still be protected by their magical reinforcements, regardless of whether she could cast a spell. No magic. No way to defend herself, and no way out.

"*The symbols are too high to reach,*" Nathaniel commented as Tamara eyed the piano. He was right. Even with Morgan's extra height, they would be too far to touch, and even then, she doubted they could be removed by hand.

"*I'm sorry.*" Tamara slumped her shoulders. The smooth keys of the piano were cool under her fingers, and pressing them lightly was enough to feel the soothing sensation of give, without a resulting noise.

"Do you play?" Nathaniel's question was surprisingly gentle.

"*I don't. I would like to learn an instrument, though. One day.*" The thought came to a jarring halt as she realised there may not be many days left. "*You don't seem angry?*" He had a right to be. Aiden was going after the others; was likely there with Oliver now. If he was harmed because of her —

"*—There's no point dwelling on it,*" Nathaniel interrupted. "*What's done is done, but while we still live, it's not over. We just need to work with what we have.*"

What they had didn't seem like much. Perhaps she should try the window, just in case. But before she could take a step, she heard Morgan's voice.

"Why did you do it?"

His back was to her, and he didn't move from the sofa. Her mind groped for a response, but no words came, and for an instant she considered pretending she hadn't heard at all. Instead, she walked closer, rounding the couch until he came into view.

Morgan was leaning forward, head buried in his hands.

"Why didn't you just leave?" His voice was emotionless, and Tamara suddenly felt self-conscious of her movements, despite the knowledge that he wasn't watching.

"You must know..." She began as Morgan lifted his head. "He said he would kill you."

"And you should have let him! You had a responsibility to fulfil."

"I couldn't watch someone else die!" Tamara found her voice rising, though she couldn't look at Morgan's face.

"So you put others in danger to delay the inevitable? You no longer have a duty to me, Tamara." He sighed, and she got the impression that he was trying to gently explain something that she should already know.

"That's not..." She hesitated. Did he really think she was so stupid that she would risk people's lives for loyalty to a job? "I care about you."

A blank stare met her words. They were... friends at least, weren't they? After everything they had been through. Everything Morgan had told her. It must have meant something to him? Unless... Perhaps she had misjudged. After all, Morgan was the leader of a country. It should be obvious how different he would see their stations. He was probably just being kind, and now she had said something horribly inappropriate.

"*Friends. Of course that's what you meant.*" Nathaniel didn't mask his disapproval and Tamara recoiled in embarrassment.

"I... am not a good man, Tamara." Morgan's soft words cut through the internal conversation and she finally realised the reason for his hesitation.

"I know what you've done, better than most." She moved a step closer to him. "But it doesn't change how I feel." Nathaniel's grief still burned in her memory, alongside the events she had witnessed herself, but Morgan wasn't trying to hide from it. No matter how hard she looked for evil, all she saw was regret. "Are you going to hate yourself forever?"

"Yes," Morgan snarled. "What I am isn't forgivable, and you're a fool to think any different."

Tamara flinched. "I'm not—"

"We only had a working relationship, Tamara. And now we don't even have that."

Before she could reply, he got up walking stiffly to the window, where he stood staring silently out at the grounds. Their conversation was over.

"You said nothing wrong," Nathaniel spoke as soon as the thought occurred.

"I'm such an idiot. I just thought... I must have misunderstood." She sunk down into the space Morgan had left.

"No." His reply was quiet. *"This isn't about you. What he needs to work though, he has to do alone."*

Tamara wrapped her arms around herself and tried to breathe through the stuffy air. Sweat damp clothes clung uncomfortably to her skin as she rocked her body back and forth, the movement soothing away some of the pain of Morgan's words.

"Why would you comfort me?" she asked.

"Your distress is unpleasant for us both," Nathaniel hummed as he mused. *"And perhaps... Perhaps I'm getting used to your way of thinking. You have a good heart. My anger is not towards you."*

Their conversation faded to silence and Tamara let her eyes drift shut; warmth and stress and lack of sleep dragging her into a light doze from which she could hardly sense the time passing. It wasn't until she heard the turning of a key that she realised someone was outside the room.

She stood, making sure the sofa formed a partial barricade between her and whoever would enter. Then Morgan was at her side, stepping around in front of her so that Tamara had to crane her head to see.

Cool air flowed into the room as the door opened, but the first glimpse of one of Aiden's mage guard found her recoiling back. When she looked again they had pushed inside, accompanied by a second guard who dragged with him a man she didn't recognise; a muddied coat over his dishevelled suit.

The man staggered limply in the guard's grip, to the point where she couldn't tell if he was as much restrained as simply being held upright. His face was drawn with exhaustion, fair hair falling into his eyes, and when the guard shoved him forwards he collapsed onto the carpet as though his legs weren't able to support his weight.

"Don't bother getting up."

Aiden's voice had lost its smooth composure. A scowl marred his features, and as he glared down at the man on the floor, Tamara saw that, he too, was dirt splattered. His formerly cream blazer was torn at the shoulder, a dark red stain visible under where his pale hand clutched the area. Things obviously hadn't gone according to plan, but if Aiden was here, then that must mean the man—

"Yes, that's Oliver," Nathaniel confirmed her guess with dismay.

"He looks terrible."

Oliver rolled up onto his knees, a hand supporting his weight, but Aiden kicked it away.

"Leave him alone!" Tamara pushed past Morgan, but a guard blocked her path. She pulled back before they could touch her, body tense and ready.

"I'd be more concerned about your own skin if I were you," Aiden snarled at her. "The only reason he's still alive is because you're more expendable."

"There's nothing you can do," Oliver had pushed himself back up, voice far stronger than his appearance would suggest. "You can't hurt me any more than you already have."

A half smile hovered over Aiden's lips as he looked down. "I look forward to testing that theory. But I never took you to be so naïve. So far I have done nothing other than respond to your uncalled for aggression."

"You killed him!" Oliver rose unsteadily to his feet, and fear spiked through Tamara as she prepared for him to be struck down again. She looked at Aiden, but he appeared unfazed by Oliver's defiance.

"You think I killed Matthew?" His eyes flicked to her own as he spoke. "I wonder how you could have possibly been given that impression."

For the first time, Oliver seemed to care there were other people in the room. Tamara watched as he followed Aiden's gaze, eyes widening as he saw Morgan.

"You're a clever man, Oliver," Aiden continued. "There's only one person here with a history of murdering royalty."

Tamara's stomach dropped. She had hoped to explain; to break it to him slowly, but any remaining colour had drained from Oliver's face.

Aiden winced, sucking air through his teeth, and Tamara saw him clutch once more at his shoulder. That wound looked bad enough to need healing, though why one of his mage guard hadn't done it, she didn't know. "It seems you've bought yourselves some time. Have fun together." He finished. The two guards filed after him as he spun on his heel and the door was closed again, lock turning with a click.

"Are... are you hurt?" Tamara asked. It seemed like a stupid question. Oliver was breathing heavily, and she wondered if she should insist he sit down before he collapsed.

"Tamara, I assume?"

"Yes," she nodded. "I'm so sorry—"

"Is it true?" Oliver cut across her words. She didn't reply, instead glancing over to where Morgan was standing, watching in silence. "Is it true?" Oliver repeated, frustration giving his voice a dangerous edge.

"It wasn't how he made it sound," Tamara forced herself to look him in the eye, hoping she appeared as honest as her words.

"You lied to me."

"It wasn't a lie! I told you, Aiden's trying to work out the Champion spell. He would have killed him for his experiments. That's why he's taken us and—"

"You manipulated me!" Oliver took a step towards her and Tamara stumbled back. "You knew full well I wouldn't meet with you if I knew the truth!"

"I'm sorry!" She hadn't felt like there was another option, but Oliver was glaring at her in disgust. This wasn't how he had been in any of Nathaniel's memories.

"You're pathetic."

The words bit into her conscience, and Tamara had no response to give. *"I won't say I didn't warn you..."* Nathaniel's presence offered little assurance, though at least he seemed pitying rather than mocking.

"That's enough." Morgan moved forward, and Tamara felt his warmth as he came between her and Oliver's rage. "It's not her that you're angry with."

For a second, Oliver seemed stunned into silence at Morgan's intervention, then his voice lowered to barely more than a whisper. "Don't speak to me."

"Please, it wasn't how you think." Tamara found her fingers brushing against Morgan's own, seeking a reassurance that he quickly pulled away.

"You were there," Oliver turned back to her. "How could

you let him do it? Alex trusted you."

Her mouth tasted acid, the memory of the bloodstained floor once again pushing its way into her mind. "I—" Tamara stuttered, but Morgan spoke over her.

"I shot him." His voice was cool and Tamara looked up at his face in horror. "You want to know how it happened? Then yes, I killed him. He was unconscious, and I shot him in cold blood. Because I believed it was a better option than what awaited."

Oliver made a sound of pain. "You bastard."

"Perhaps you can decide whether the alternative was preferable when you experience it," Morgan continued, unrelenting. "As I am certain my nephew has not brought you here for your company, I doubt you will have to wait long to find out."

"I'll never forgive you." Oliver's words were like ice.

"I don't request your forgiveness."

Oliver appeared to sway on his feet, shifting his weight under his battered coat as he steadied himself. Then, before either of them could react, he slammed his fist into Morgan's face.

"*Finally!*" Nathaniel's pleasure only fuelled Tamara's defensiveness as Morgan staggered back.

"Stop it!" she shouted, reaching out towards Morgan, only to pull her hand away as she remembered his earlier rejection. Drawing on her magic instead, Tamara started to form a healing spell before realising it wouldn't work. Useless, she watched him brush his fingers over the reddening mark on his cheekbone. "Hurting each other isn't going to help."

She rounded on Oliver, who stood pale and swaying. He was in no state for a fight, and it looked as though the meagre punch had used more strength than he had left. A warm hand on her shoulder stopped her before she said any more.

"It's fine, Tamara," Morgan said softly. With a nod he released her, then turned his back on them, returning to the window and leaving her and Oliver alone.

Tamara closed her eyes and tried to slow the breaths that were coming too fast and shallow. She hadn't realised how much her hands were shaking and she couldn't afford to break down, not now.

"...Was any of it true?"

She opened her eyes again at Oliver's words and saw that the effort of speaking wasn't helping his condition. The scowl he had worn before now seemed more like a squint, as though he was struggling to focus.

"You should sit down. You look exhausted." She gestured to the couch beside them.

"Just answer me." Oliver snapped back, and Tamara sighed in resignation.

"It is true. I have Nathaniel with me. That's how Aiden knew how to find you. I told Morgan where—"

"You gave us up?"

"No! Aiden bugged Morgan's office. He knows— He knows everything." The idea that she would have betrayed them hurt more than any insult, but Oliver's voice had gone flat, seemingly too exhausted to care anymore even if she had.

"...Everything?" he replied weakly.

"I'm sorry." Tamara hoped he knew she meant it. "Are you sure you don't want to sit down? You really don't look like you're focussing."

Oliver looked over to where Morgan stood. "I can see well enough what's going on."

She considered protesting, but it was unlikely Oliver would want to hear anything about her lack of relationship with Morgan, even if it was to say there was nothing going on. A silence stretched out between them until, to her surprise, it was Oliver who broke it.

"Why haven't you tried to get out of here?" He exhaled heavily and pinched the bridge of his nose. "I guess you fought them; those guards? But you don't appear weakened?"

"Oh," Tamara said, as she understood. "No. I'm not too weak, it's just... Look." She pointed at the dimly glowing marks that encircled the room, and Oliver blinked as he squinted up at them. "It's the symbols. Aiden told me he was studying them before. That's why we've been stuck here. Somehow they block any magic I've tried."

If there had been any hope remaining in Oliver's eyes, it was gone now. "We might be able to think of something though," Tamara continued quickly as she saw his reaction. "Now that you're here. Nathaniel says you're an excellent tactician—" She stopped as Oliver shook his head.

"I'm... I'm going to lie down." He ran a hand over the arm of the sofa and lowered himself down onto the cushions. "Don't bother waking me when they come to kill us. I think I'd rather die in my sleep."

CHAPTER 36

Roy glanced uneasily at his clothes as the palace came into view. The illusion laying there gave him the appearance of wearing a navy raincoat, complete with visibility stripes and logo, overhanging loose fitting, water resistant trousers; as close a replica of as they could manage based on Alex's description of his father's work uniform. A barely perceptible magic radiated from the illusion, but Eira hadn't been bluffing when she'd claimed the skill to weave it. To anyone watching, the three of them would pass as members of a passive spell company. He just hoped that would be enough to pull this off.

The tall surrounding walls of the palace grounds gave

way to a wrought-iron fence, through which the gravel courtyard was clearly visible; as was the uniformed guard eyeing them up carefully from her box-like shelter behind the gates. Only one, which was a surprisingly good sign. She'd be a mage, of course, but if Roy needed to keep checking the illusion was in place when it was this close to his body, the woman wouldn't stand much chance of sensing it. He raised a hand in greeting.

"Hey there. You're expecting us," Roy spoke with a practiced ease. "Joe, Laura, and Andy from SpellCraft. Here to repair a lock that was damaged yesterday."

He'd been through enough staff entrances that the novelty had worn off, but the nerves blatantly written over Alex's face meant he would have stuck out immediately without him. At least it would be easy to pass him off as a newbie, especially as he looked so young. For Eira's part, she had been silent since they began their approach; the concentration of maintaining their disguise absorbing her whole attention.

"A bit late, isn't it?" The guard replied, glancing down at her watch. Reading it upside down, Roy could tell it was approaching six in the evening. "Can I see your identification?"

Their identity cards were thrown together from the various documents Oliver had left in the safe house, but from experience Roy knew it didn't much matter what your ID looked like, just that you had something to show. As suspected, the woman gave a nod when he pulled his card out, then stepped briefly into the shelter, returning with a clipboarded list. A frown appeared on her face as she flipped back and forth between the pages.

"Yeah, we got delayed a good forty-five minutes at the last job. No one could tell us what we were supposed to be there to fix." Roy gave an exaggerated shrug. "You know how it is. Bet you don't have problems like that here though."

"You'd be surprised." The guard brushed a lock of curly blonde hair out of her face but didn't look up.

"*Don't stop talking.*" Julian's presence pushed into his mind, and Alex's elbow in his side informed him that the Champion wasn't the only one with concerns.

"Let me guess," Roy leaned in close to the bars of the gate and this time the guard lifted her head. "We're not on the list, right?" Rolling his eyes, he turned to Alex with an exaggerated sigh. "I knew it! Janice in operations keeps doing this to me. Do you get this too, Andy?"

Alex's expression told him he hadn't been expecting the attention. "N—no... Janice... err—" He fiddled with the straps of his backpack as he fumbled the words.

"Oh, so she only does it to me then?" Roy cut him off. "I knew she had it in for me since I got her that gift for her baby. It was meant to be a joke!" He laughed and glanced at the guard, catching the smile that flickered over her face. "I'm sorry mate, can I see the list? We've had a few mergers recently and maybe the company name is wrong."

"I'm sorry. If you're not on here, then you can't come in." The guard shook her head apologetically as she tilted the clipboard towards them, and Roy got a clear view of the rows of printed names and time slots.

"*Perfect.*" Julian's satisfaction matched Roy's own, and he had to force himself to look frustrated as he stalled.

"Ugh. I know it's not your fault, I just can't believe Janice —"

"Come on Joe, that's enough," Eira piped up from beside him. "Either we're doing the repairs or not, but I've already spent the last hour hearing you rant about Janice." She turned towards the guard. "I'm so sorry, but would you mind just checking the list one more time? Then we can at least tell the office we tried our best."

The guard shrugged and glanced back down at her paper. "Alright, but as I said—" Blinking, she stopped talking and Roy watched her run a finger once more down the clipboard. "I could have sworn I..."

"What is it?" Roy jumped in before the guard was able to dwell too much on her confusion. Any longer, and she might have detected the subtle illusion that now lay over the pad of paper in her hands.

"You're here. I don't know how I missed it. That's so embarrassing, I'm sorry."

"Not as embarrassing as it'll be for me when I next see Janice!" Roy grinned, earning a relieved smile from the guard as she unlocked the gate.

As they slipped through into the grounds, Roy looked across the courtyard to the staff entrance he'd used the day before. Yesterday there had been two guards by that door as well, but now the only security he saw was the woman beside them.

"*Disappointing,*" Julian spoke in his mind. "*This would never have worked when Nathaniel was in charge of defence.*"

"*Let's just count ourselves lucky,*" Roy retorted. If security had dropped under the Velbians, then it could only be a good thing for them right now. "So, shall we head on in or...?"

"You'll have to wait here a moment." The guard locked the gate behind them, then replaced the list and picked up a communicator. "I'll need to radio across to get someone to search you."

Ah crap. It wasn't as though he hadn't expected them to be searched, but given how flustered Alex was, he doubted the kid would be able to blag his machine through security. That was if their illusionary uniforms would hold up to scratch if investigated by a professional.

"Listen. If it comes to it, we'll take them all out." Julian's confidence held a bloodthirsty edge, but even if Roy had been comfortable harming innocents, he was still reluctant. Fighting their way in would only get the whole palace hunting them and they both knew it.

The radio in the guard's hand crackled as she clicked the button. "Hey Beth, it's Amy on the side gate. We've got SpellCraft here to do some repairs. Can you send someone for a search and escort?"

"Hey Amy. Really? Talk about a late one. Are they on the list?"

"Don't get me started. They're on there." Amy's confirmation offered some reassurance; at least they would be unlikely to check again, and it was one less illusion for Eira to be worried about.

"Alright, let me find out who to send over to you guys. Our usual lot were sent home. Will give you an answer quick as."

"Cheers Beth."

The radio clicked into silence, leaving only the sound of traffic passing on the other side of the gate. Interesting that he had been right about the suspicious lack of guards at the building entrance. Something was up.

"Everyone on holiday after the big party?" Roy's voice drew Amy's attention back to him. "Normally when I come here, there's guards everywhere."

She shrugged at him. "Seems so. We're a little short on staff right now. Not sure why."

"This could work out for us." Roy directed the thought at

Julian, but the only response was a wave of apprehension. "*Jules.*" Roy gave him a mental nudge. "*How are we doing?*"

"*Julian.*" The reply came dryly. "*And you're doing fine. Your mother would be proud.*"

"*Oh fuck off.*"

The pause in conversation was starting to make Roy uncomfortable when a click from the radio broke the silence. "We've got someone waiting inside. Just send them across Amy."

Confusion furrowed Amy's brow, and she turned away from where Roy and the others stood. "Isn't anyone gonna escort them over?" She brought the radio close and lowered her voice enough that he had to strain to hear. "That's not protocol..."

"We're short staffed." The crackling reply came, clearly audible. "It's okay, we got it signed off from upstairs, they're good to go."

Relief lifted some of the tension from Roy's body. Now they would only have to lose the guard inside and they'd have free rein of the palace. Even if it meant stuffing them in a closet, it would be a much simpler job than out here in the open.

"Okay guys," Amy turned to them with a smile. "Seems you're all good to go. Just head over to the staff entrance and someone will help you from there." She pointed towards the double doors that stood about thirty paces opposite.

"Thanks, Amy," Roy smiled back. "Hang in there. You're alright!" He turned and strode confidently over the stoney ground, Alex and Eira scuttling close behind. He'd expected to feel accomplished, but couldn't stop a sense of unease nagging at his mind. Julian again was uncharacteristically silent.

"I'm sorry about back there," Alex mumbled, falling into pace beside him. "How did you make all that up on the spot?"

Roy laughed. "Base all your lies on the truth mate."

"Wait, so Janice is an actual person who you work with? And the baby story?"

"I don't like it." Julian finally voiced the same concern that had been plaguing Roy, and he staggered to a halt half way to the staff doors. Eira bumped against his back, and Roy saw his illusioned uniform blur for a moment before snapping back into focus.

"You're thinking this was too easy." A sinking feeling settled in Roy's stomach and he dropped to one knee as though tying his shoelace. That should at least buy them some time if Amy was still watching.

"What are you doing!" Eira hissed from behind him, but Julian's thoughts overrode her protests.

"Not even Velbians are this lax. Someone's in there waiting for us."

"She did say they were short staffed..." Despite his words, Roy wasn't convinced.

"It's not exactly far to walk. Why aren't they coming to get us?"

"You think they're onto us?"

"I've underestimated them before."

Roy grimaced. *"We can't just walk away now."* They'd come this far, there must be some way to get in safely. He bit his lip as he remembered his exit through the library window. No one should have closed it; the window looked like it hadn't been touched in years, but it was on the opposite side of the building.

"We're going to need a distraction."

When he looked up, Eira was standing beside Alex,

wringing her hands in distress. "Roy!" Her words had become a panicked whisper. "You need to get up! I didn't illusion you to have shoelaces!"

"I'm afraid that's going to be the least of your worries," Roy replied as he stood. "We need a distraction for Amy at the gate. Something like a delivery van pulling up ought to do. Can you do it?" It was a big ask and Eira's face paled, but he didn't have time to feel guilty. "Quick as you can."

"But I haven't practiced—" She glanced at Alex.

"I'm sure it doesn't have to be perfect. Just keep it at a distance." Alex's reassurance seemed enough, and Eira nodded. "You can do this."

When he glimpsed over his shoulder, Roy saw Amy looking their way. "We'll walk as slow as we can, but we can't go inside." He was pleasantly surprised when Alex didn't question the change of plan. Together they moved off again, shuffling across the yard at a pace he hoped still looked natural. There was no way to check what was going on behind them without rousing further suspicion, but Eria hadn't let them down so far.

"Your head person thinks it's a trap?" Alex kept his voice low enough that only Roy could hear, and he tilted his head in answer without turning towards him.

"Jules thinks it's too easy and they're onto us," he explained. "I agree. I left a window open around back. Should be able to get in that way."

A fast crunching on the dirt alerted Roy that Eira was catching up with them. She kept looking back over her shoulder and he saw that her uniform had blurred; smudges of colour rather than the clear buttons and logo. Glancing down, he noticed his own disguise was the same. But it didn't matter. A large white van was making a U turn in the short entranceway, and Amy was far too preoccupied with it to look their way.

"Great work! Over here." Roy veered away from the staff doors, sprinting left towards a line of conifers that marked the separation of the gravel courtyard and the palace gardens. There was a path through the trees, but the foliage would hide them as long as they made it before Eira had to stop her illusion. With luck, Amy would just assume they had gone inside.

The grounds were blessedly empty when they reached the shelter of the conifers. Roy pulled Alex flat beside him, keeping them both out of sight while Eira peered back around, finishing up with the van. To his relief, no angry shout came from the gates and after a moment she joined them, letting out a deep breath.

"Can someone explain to me why I had to do that?" She gave Roy a sideways glare.

"We're getting in a different way," Alex spoke before Roy could answer. "Roy's head person agrees it's too suspicious that they were just going to let us through."

"We shall need to have a talk about this new title," Julian commented, and Roy let out a relieved laugh, earning a confused look from the other two. He gestured to his head as an explanation, catching sight of his arm as he did so. The magic engineer uniform had disappeared, leaving the guard's jacket he had stolen the day before visible. The other's outfits had changed too, replaced by a perfect illusionary replica of his own guard's uniform; sharp and flawless, with barely any residual energy detectable.

Roy whistled. "And you said you were going to go into healing?"

Eira's cheeks took on a faint flush at his praise. They'd

hardly had three hours to plan before leaving the safe house, and even though he'd watched her working in preparation, the result was better than he could have anticipated.

"Don't think flattery will work on me." She retorted, though she now wore a grin of her own.

Alex was looking across the gardens, expression distant. When Roy clapped him on the shoulder, he jumped. "Come on then," he said. "Sooner we get in, the sooner we can leave this place behind, right?"

"...Yeah." Alex's eyes seemed to refocus as he nodded. "You're right. Let's go."

* * *

The library window swung open with ease, though they needed to boost each other up to reach it. Their squeezed entrance wasn't as quiet as Roy had hoped, but both his magic sense and his hearing told him that the room was probably empty. He was proved right when they emerged from between the narrow bookshelves. Lit only by the dim light of the fading sun through the stained glass windows, the library was as vacant as he had left it yesterday. Either it was too late for anyone to be using it, or it was suffering the same deficit of staff as the guards outside.

Now that they had space to breathe, the urgency that drove them through the gardens faded to hesitation. Find Oliver and get out; that was the plan, but Roy didn't feel comfortable making the call to move on. He didn't even know where to start looking, and the musty smell of this place was bringing back bad memories from the previous day.

"Where to from here then?" When he turned towards Alex for input, the kid was again staring at nothing, a distant expression in his eyes. Eira reached out to touch his arm and the gesture seemed to pull Alex out of whatever reverie he had found himself in.

"Back with us?" Roy said. Being here again after everything must be tough. It hadn't been much more than a day since Alex had found out about his father, and the grief in his eyes was hauntingly familiar

"Sorry," Alex shook his head as though to clear it. "I was just..."

"It's okay."

"I know this must be really hard," Eira said, but Alex frowned.

"It's not that," he spoke slowly, as though trying to figure out the words. "It's... You know. The ground magic. I'd forgotten how strong the feeling is when I'm here."

"Ground magic?" Roy didn't follow Alex's meaning, but Eira seemed to understand completely. Even Julian was curious, and Roy was surprised that the Spy didn't have an explanation.

"Alex can sense a kind of magical energy, when he's here in the palace. It's something only he—" She cut herself off with a pained look.

"Apparently it's a royal family thing," Alex said with a shrug, but Roy could guess why Eira had stopped. With Matthew gone, it meant Alex was the last. "It's not specifically the palace," Alex continued. "As far as I can tell, it comes from the land it's built on, but I can sense like... disruptions in the energy, when mages are nearby. I guess like an extension of my normal magic sense, but around everywhere the ground magic reaches."

"So what, you're like a mini-map when you're in here?" Roy replied, but was met with blank looks. "You know, like in a game? Ugh, nevermind. Can you tell if there are guards coming then?"

Alex nodded. "Yeah. If they are mages, at least. But there's something else strange." He frowned again, the distant look returning to his eyes, and Roy realised it reminded him of when Oliver or Eira were talking with their Champions. One to keep in mind for himself in future. "There's a bit I can't sense," Alex continued. "Like some kind of void. It was never there before."

"A void," Roy repeated. If it wasn't there before, he'd put money on it being something to do with Aiden.

"I can't really tell how big, but it's not small. If that makes sense?"

It didn't make any sense, but it was the only shot they had. "Could you find it?"

"Yeah, I think so." Alex shrugged his backpack higher on his shoulders, face taking on an expression of determination.

"Do you think this void-room could be where Aiden's holding Oliver?" Eira saying it out loud made it sound a better plan than it been in his head.

"It's a good enough lead." Alex's words were definitive, and he began to descend the steps to the library doors, Eira beside him. Roy followed, wincing at the noise the made in the quiet space. It wouldn't be long before the palace guard noticed they were missing. All he could hope was that they would make it to Oliver in time.

Chapter 37

An ache burned in Oliver's limbs as awareness assaulted his mind. When he opened his eyes, he could see that the room was still lit by the fading natural light outside; the high ceiling fuzzy and shadowed as he blinked up at it. He instinctively reached for the magic that would sharpen his vision, but the action caused his stomach to roll with nausea. Any attempt to lift his head sent a sharp pain through his neck; as much a consequence of his awkward position on the narrow sofa as from the battle he had endured before arriving in this room.

Exhaustion must have won out, dragging him into a dreamless sleep that left only dread and panic in its wake; as though his mind had been working over his situation even without his conscious thought. Being awake was doing nothing to ease the stress. A tinkle of clumsy piano notes came from beyond the sofa, and Oliver realised that this was what had woken him. The distorted tune was familiar, and he got a sense that he had been urgently trying to solve it.

"*It's one of Nathaniel's.*" Ewen answered the question in his mind. A memory accompanied the words, though Oliver didn't need to see the scene to remember it himself. As a requirement of attending to his mentor, he had often been allowed to sit amongst the former Champions, listening as they talked together in the large drawing room while Nathaniel played.

"*That proves he's with her then.*" There were four of them now. All of them. Even in his current circumstance, the thought should have brought some joy, but Oliver only felt numb.

The melody from the piano started again, slow but smoother this time, as Tamara became more familiar with the notes. He'd always been more at home with the adults than with his peers. With no guarantee which of the many noble children would become a Champion, the palace preferred to educate the rest of the potentials alongside each other. Arriving late and parentless, he was an anomaly even before Ewen had taken him on, and that had done nothing to improve his relationship with his rivals. Those potentials who didn't outright resent him simply tried to ignore his presence. Even Matthew, to whom he was closest, had once treated him more like a bossy older sibling than a friend.

"*It was only us for so long...*" His time at the palace was forgotten history; he and Matthew nothing more than the last remnants of a failed legacy. "*I'm still the last.*" The bitter thought came unbidden to his mind, and Oliver realised just why Tamara's existence hurt. These new Champions were Alex's. He was the only product of the old system left; a system that had failed and consequently been wiped out. *"I should have died with Matthew."*

"You should know that won't get you out of your responsibilities." Ewen's criticism was enough to momentarily jerk Oliver from his self-pity. *"If that's what you truly wanted then you would have let us die at Aiden's feet."*

"Maybe I should have!"

"Don't argue with me over something you don't believe. It wastes both our time."

Oliver's anger rose at his mentor's emotionless dismissal. The man could read his feelings and yet still provided no comfort. But when had he ever been different? From the day Ewen chose him to personally train, Oliver had never understood why.

"I chose you precisely because I don't like having my time wasted, Oliver. And neither should you. It's far too valuable."

"I don't understand."

"Why would I train multiple potentials knowing that the majority would amount to nothing? The others might have enjoyed babysitting, but I required a workable assistant."

It was true that Ewen had started giving him tasks from the first moment he took Oliver on; things that looking back seemed far beyond his years or position. That he'd been trusted enough to sit in on meetings with the active Champions was much more than was expected of the other potentials. *"I'd have considered my reasons for choosing you obvious,"* Ewen continued. *"Your test scores were always impeccable, but even from our earliest interactions I could tell you think correctly. None of this frivolous nonsense that seems to occupy most people's minds. This role requires someone logical. Analytical. You are perfectly suited."*

Oliver didn't know how to respond. It didn't feel like a compliment. Ewen talked as though his abilities were fact, but all he'd ever felt was that he was treading water, barely keeping up with the demands piled upon him. He'd failed so many times. Losing Matthew. Alienating Alex. Walking straight into this very situation. Every time, trying to live up to the expectations of a role he wasn't cut out for.

"*You are more than capable,*" Ewen stated firmly. "*It's about time you believed it too.*"

With a groan, Oliver reached up to rub at his blurry eyes. "*Giving up felt better.*"

"*You'd be doing yourself a disservice. Besides, I'm not ready to die just yet.*"

The ache in his limbs was becoming unbearable and, as much as he didn't want to alert the others to the fact he was awake, he pushed himself up until he was half seated, half slumped against the armrest. Still mostly shielded by the sofa, he rolled his neck to loosen the stiffness and stretched out his cramped muscles. The coat he hadn't bothered to remove had left him clammy and hot in the stuffy room, so he shrugged it off, letting it slide down onto the sofa behind him. As he did so, something hard dug into his side from his pocket.

"*My phone!*" Exhilaration at the discovery faded instantly to regret as he remembered he'd left it in the safe house bedroom after the call with Tamara. "*I'm such an idiot.*" He could have called Dory at least and warned her to switch locations. Even Roy —

And with that thought he realised what the item was. With shaking hands, he rummaged through the coat pocket, letting out a breath of relief when he touched fabric rather than wood. It was the wand. The one Roy had taken from Felix Marek. He'd put it in his pocket the day he'd chased after Matthew. The day they'd received the call about Alex. Forever ago. Oliver winced; any memory of Matthew was like touching an open wound. Back then, Felix Marek had seemed enough of a problem. He'd never have dreamed—

Again, realisation interrupted Oliver's rumination. They'd asked Roy for his help getting into the palace. He'd been there with Matthew. But Alex— Alex hadn't seen Roy until he appeared at the safe house.

"Ewen, when did Roy say his awakening happened?" Oliver projected the thought urgently. *"It was when he triggered an alarm, correct? He said he left Matthew behind so he could cause a distraction."*

"I believe so," Ewen confirmed. *"If I am following your thoughts correctly, you're implying that Roy didn't know Alex before his awakening, and the timing—"*

"He awoke before Matthew died." Oliver felt light headed as he reached the inevitable conclusion. *"Roy could never have awoken for Alex. They never met each other. He awoke for Matthew!"*

Matthew wasn't... Matthew wasn't broken. He'd lost all of his potentials, and in the twenty-three years since there'd never been another. They'd both thought there never would be.

"How? Why now?" Oliver asked the question even as he theorised an answer. Who else could it have been? Matthew never let anyone get close; never relied on anyone except Oliver himself. *"How was I so blind? We always knew the potentials were raised alongside the next in line; that they needed to form a bond. It's the connection that's the trigger!"*

"I don't think you could have forced it even if you knew." Ewen's calm thoughts tempered Oliver's agitation. *"Matthew*

never trusted unless he had to, and finding someone to return that trust is no easy feat. Despite my reservations about him, it can't be denied that Roy put himself at risk to aid Matthew's escape."

"*Of all the people.*" For what felt like the first time in days, the ghost of a smile appeared on Oliver's face. Roy may never return to take up his role, but what he stood for was enough. With that, Oliver pulled the wand, still tightly wrapped in green cloth, from his pocket.

Any contact with the wood would cause the magic contained within to discharge through his body, pulling his own magic away with it, and in his current state, he wasn't sure he would survive the experience. Even after everything that had happened, he still didn't know how the wand worked or what kind of magic it was.

"*Magic doesn't work in this room, though...*" Oliver sat up straight as he thought, resting the wrapped wand on his knees. From this position it was possible to see over the back of the sofa to the piano. Tamara had stopped playing and, although his vision wasn't clear enough to make out her features, the sharp jerk of her head turning away told Oliver she had been looking at him. "*However, I can still hear you. And Tamara can clearly hear Nathaniel.*"

"*Not all magic then.*"

Not all magic. The symbols Tamara had pointed out to him before were still glowing along the upper part of the wall. Oliver picked the wand back up and carefully undid some of the binding until a faint glow showed through the material. "*It's the same.*"

Replacing the cloth so he could hold the wand without worry, Oliver forced himself to his feet. Though his legs screamed in protest, he was relieved to find they supported his weight. Across the room, he saw Morgan and Tamara now sat on the floor beside the piano. Whatever murmured conversation they were having stopped as they saw him, and they both stood as he approached.

"What can you tell me about these markings?" Oliver directed the question at Tamara as he gestured to the glowing symbols above them. For once he was grateful for his shoddy vision keeping Morgan a blur at her side. Anger still simmered under his tentative composure, and he wasn't confident he could face him without the storm returning. It was best to pretend Morgan didn't exist for now.

"They're an old form of magic. I think." Tamara's words were rapid, as though she feared Oliver would give up on this conversation as quickly as he had started it. "Aiden told me he's been studying them. I've seen them somewhere else too. On the passageway that Alex opened."

"On the passageway?" Even if Aiden didn't invent them, why would they be on something constructed generations ago within the palace?

Tamara nodded. "He said they were Ardveldian originally. Which actually makes sense when you think about it. The lines and circles are in the same style as the old royal symbol. It must be one as well." She tugged self-consciously at a dark ringlet of hair, as though remembering who she was speaking to. "Though, I'm sure you know that."

Oliver waved the comment away without a reply. Instead, he crouched down to the floor, beckoning Tamara to do the same. "I've seen them before too." He set the wand between them, still covered by the cloth. "Don't touch it. If you touch it, the magic will run straight through you. It's not very pleasant." Tamara inclined her head in confirmation, and satisfied, Oliver pulled aside the material until the glowing symbols on the wood were fully visible.

Morgan moved closer as the wand was revealed. "Where did you get that?" His voice, though soft, held an authoritative edge, and Oliver's anger threatened to spike.

"That's none of your business." At the edge of his vision, he saw Tamara glancing nervously between them.

"You don't have to tell me," Morgan replied. "But you should see the benefit of putting personal feelings aside. It's clear you have no idea what you have."

"And I suppose you do?" Oliver snapped, feeling foolish even as he said it. Despite the tension between them, Morgan didn't seem the type to baselessly gloat.

"It's a weapon. My nephew makes them." Morgan looked at Tamara. "I'm sure you recall the magic attack in the city last week? It is likely one of these was involved."

Oliver couldn't help a scoff of bitter amusement. "I can guarantee it."

A puzzled frown crossed Tamara's face, and she looked as if she were about to comment until Morgan gave her a pointed look. "Perhaps that is something else we won't enquire further about," he said. She nodded in agreement, and Morgan continued, turning back to Oliver. "Though I am baffled as to how you even have it with you. Were you not searched?"

Come to think of it, it was strange that he hadn't been. Aiden and his guards hadn't treated him with any wariness; after his surrender they had scarcely given him a second look until he was thrown in here. But then again, Oliver didn't consider himself a threat either in his current condition.

"Why would they?" It was Tamara who spoke, her words echoing his own reasoning. "A strong mage doesn't need a weapon. You are the weapon. And Oliver's in no state to fight."

"That's ridiculous." Morgan exclaimed in clear disbelief. "Never make assumptions when it comes to your enemies. Just because no threat appears on the surface doesn't mean there isn't one."

Oliver swallowed hard at the words. "Speaking from experience?" If Morgan heard, he didn't acknowledge it.

There was silence until Tamara cleared her throat.

"Well, Aiden's complacency could be lucky for us. Do you know how it works?" She addressed the question to Morgan, who shook his head.

"Only that they started appearing in the past year or so. I believe they are somehow related to the disappearing mages that Aiden worked with, but I have never seen one that still functions."

The glow from the wand seemed to warp in the fading light of the day. Oliver blinked, then rubbed at his eyes again, wishing he could generate a magelight. Beside him, movement from Morgan made him tense, and he kept a wary eye on the man as he walked towards the locked door.

"What are you doing?" Oliver called, just as there was a click and light flooded the room.

"Turning the light on," Morgan replied. "It seems the electricity still works."

Of course it does. Oliver clenched his teeth, though he had to admit the light helped. As Morgan returned, Oliver watched Tamara hover a hand over the wand, its glowing symbols far less disconcerting under the electric bulbs.

"It feels strange," she said. "I can't sense any purpose in whatever spell is there. Almost like there's no passive spell at all. It's just wild."

"From what I've experienced, it reacts badly to a mage's own magic," Oliver explained. "When I tested it before, the power it holds seemed to ground through me. It's exhausting, as though—"

"I know what it reminds me of!" Tamara cut over Oliver excitedly. "It's just like the magic from Aiden's mage guard! Just much weaker."

Oliver bit back a frustrated response to the interruption. She was right. He'd realised the same thing during his battle in the park; the weakness that coursed through his body at their attacks mirrored the sensation he had experienced when he first touched the wand.

Tamara was looking in his direction, rubbing her hands over each other. "I'm sorry. You were speaking."

"It's fine." Oliver replied absently. His mind was running over the information, putting it together with something Morgan had said. Begrudgingly, he turned towards where he was now standing, leaning against the piano. "...You say Aiden made this."

Arms folded, Morgan gave a curt nod.

"And you think it's linked to mages disappearing?"

"I do," Morgan replied. "These weapons emerged shortly after the first reports. It's too unlikely to be coincidence."

Oliver's mouth went dry. "It didn't make sense to me before," he said. "But this wand... I've never put magic into it. None of us have. After discharging its energy, it should have nothing left— and it doesn't. For a time." He hoped his meaning wouldn't be lost on the other mage.

Across from him, Tamara bobbed her head, chewing on her lip as she thought. "You can't just get magic out of nothing," she spoke slowly. "A spell can't re-charge itself. The only thing that can produce magical energy is, well, a mage." As she said it, her eyes met Oliver's own for the first time, widening as he nodded.

"But how!" Tamara exclaimed. "How could he possibly put a mage's life-force into... into this?" She shrunk away from where the wand lay.

"I don't know how he does it." Morgan glanced at the door, posture tense. "As I said before, I've only heard rumours. But I imagine you might find out soon enough."

Oliver tried to suppress a shudder. The wand on the floor now seemed less a dangerous novelty, more a grotesque grave marker. He got unsteadily to his feet to face Morgan. "You knew he was doing this, and you did nothing?"

"What, exactly, would you have had me do? Openly declare my nephew a murderer? With my sister near death? Based entirely off of rumours? You've been out of the game too long if you can't see the ramifications."

"Oh, so you covered it up to save your own skin? Why does that not surprise me," Oliver spat back, and Morgan froze, a dark look crossing his face.

"I don't care who you are; don't ever accuse me of putting my own welfare above that of this country." The calm had left Morgan' voice, replaced by an icy anger, and he crossed the distance between them until he was looking directly into Oliver's eyes. "You can curse me until your last breath, but I was not going to deliver Ardveld's people straight to Aiden."

Oliver stared back, unflinching. "How noble." His body was tense, but this time he restrained the anger that had previously overwhelmed him. Anger wasn't going to help Alex. It wasn't going to get him out of this room. Anger could wait.

With a deep breath, Oliver broke the eye contact that had kept them both fixed. "Whatever you intended, it doesn't make any difference to our current situation." Leaving Tamara and Morgan by the piano, he walked over to the tall windows. Outside, the grounds were empty, bathed golden in the dying light. It was a familiar sight, yet strange, like a half remembered dream. He shook off the feeling before he could dwell on it.

They were on the ground floor; a simple escape if he could break the window, and there were no guards outside that he could see. The one at the door would have to make it through the room to follow, which could buy them some time.

"The protection spells on the glass are likely still there," Ewen said and Oliver was thankful his mentor didn't comment on the altercation with Morgan. *"That means you would need magic to break it."*

The wand was still lying on the silk handkerchief in which Oliver had bound it. He made his way back over, bent down and folded some cloth over the thicker end to create a handle. Then he stood up and held it out.

"Take it." He ordered, holding the unwrapped end of the wand out to Morgan.

"What are you doing?" Tamara stepped between them, eyeing the wand suspiciously.

"I want to see what happens when a non-mage touches it. The last time I faced one of these, it was wielded against me. Aiden wouldn't create something he couldn't use, so take it." He finished.

"You're prepared to hand me a weapon?" Morgan didn't move, and Oliver didn't pull back.

"I know what I'm doing."

With a careful motion, Morgan reached out to clasp the bare wood of the wand, lifting it gently from Oliver's grasp. The makeshift handle fluttered to the floor as he rotated it, the glowing runes casting an eerie light over his pale skin.

Nothing happened.

"Now what?" Morgan cradled the weapon close to his body, and Oliver was relieved to see he kept the tip pointed away from the two mages.

"Can you feel anything?" Tamara said. They were both keeping a safe distance, but so far any effect had been negligible.

Morgan frowned. "Something. A vibration. It feels unbalanced." He looked down at the wand in his hand, tilting it slowly up and down, as though testing the flow of something inside.

"Be careful. I don't know much power it has. Hopefully it will be enough."

"You're assuming I can work out how to use this." Morgan didn't lower his arm, but he stopped the movement.

"If one of Marek's goons can use one, I'm confident you can figure it out." Oliver tore his gaze away and assessed the remaining items in the room. *Sofa, piano, maybe the paintings.*

"Nathaniel won't be pleased about the piano," Ewen commented, and Oliver found a thin smile forming in response.

"Put it down by the window for now," he called back over his shoulder as he moved towards the sofa. "We need to move some furniture."

***

With his body still weak, Oliver hadn't been much help, but between them they had created a reasonable barricade against the room's door. The need to work silently hadn't made the job easier. At one point, when the glossy black of the grand piano bumped hard enough against the door to dent the white paint, Oliver had held his breath, certain they were about to be interrupted. For once though, it seemed luck was on his side.

"Once we're out of the room, the symbols should no longer be able to block our magic." Oliver ran over the plan again as the three of them stood in front of the tall window. "I'm not convinced we'll fare well if the guard makes it after us, but our chances are better than in here."

"If they want a fight, this time I'll make sure they'll regret it." Fire flashed in Tamara's eyes, leaving Oliver taken aback. It seemed there was more of a warrior there than he had given her credit for. "You still won't have recovered much strength," she continued, looking up at him. "If it comes to it, focus on getting away. I'll try to stop them coming after you."

Oliver shook his head. "Getting to Alex isn't going to make much difference in the long run. We can't hide anymore." He looked over Tamara's head at Morgan, who held the wand at his side, mouth pursed into a line of determination.

"I'd suggest you leave Aiden to me, but I know you won't trust it unless you see it with your own eyes." At Oliver's nod, Morgan turned to Tamara, expression softening as he continued. "And I assume you won't leave, even if I order you to?"

"I don't remember following your orders last time," she smiled. "Anyway, I don't work for you anymore, and I don't see you getting far by yourselves."

"You're probably right." As much as Oliver hated to admit it, having another Champion with him wouldn't hurt their chances.

"I suggest you both stand back."

Oliver and Tamara retreated to the centre of the room at

Morgan's command. He brought the wand up and steadied his stance. "Let's hope this works."

With a flick of his wrist, Morgan snapped the wand forwards, and Oliver felt the air crackle with energy as power exploded away from him. For a moment, the glass held. Then the entire window shattered outwards in a rain of shards and dust.

CHAPTER 38

During his time in the palace, the gentle hum of ground magic had become so comfortable Alex was barely aware of it; only noticing the quiet absence once it had gone. Now though, the void nagged at him like a chipped edge in his mind.

They paused after leaving the library; urgency tempered by the knowledge that the guards had likely noticed they were missing. That, and the fact he wasn't sure where to go. Despite telling Roy he could lead the way, Alex had no real idea where the sensation of the void was coming from. It had felt closer once they entered the palace, but it was impossible to tell how large a space it occupied, or how far from them it might be.

"We need to head that way." Alex pointed vaguely downwards and, unfortunately, at the wall.

"Helpful." Roy raised an eyebrow, and Alex sighed.

"I know. I should be able to narrow it done once we get closer though. I'm pretty confident whatever it is, it's below us."

"There are a lot of rooms down there," Roy replied. "A bunch of reception rooms, mirror gallery, music hall. Our nearest staircase is back there, if you think we should go down." He gestured to his right and away from the area Alex had indicated.

"That would take us near the guest wing," Eira said. "I really don't think that's a good idea, since that's probably where Aiden is staying."

"And the other way goes towards the state rooms." Roy shrugged, his red hair catching the glow of the sunset shining through the windows opposite. "Aiden could be anywhere. There's not much point going all over trying to avoid him."

Eira made a discontented noise, and Alex found himself bewildered by their sudden knowledge of the palace layout until he remembered it likely wasn't their own. He leant against the library doors, the sharp angle of his device digging into his back through the fabric of the rucksack. If they did bump into Aiden and his guards, the hastily crafted machine would be the only defence they had.

"Whichever way we go, we should move soon," Alex said. He'd caught sight of a red dot of light emanating from a camera positioned above the window. "Looks like security's watching us."

Both Eira and Roy followed his gaze, and Alex sensed the

faint shift of Eira's magic as she strengthened their illusioned uniforms.

"Can we get rid of the cameras?" She looked to Roy, who shook his head.

"No. That'll draw attention. Best just keep the illusions running and with any luck we'll slip under their radar." He ran a hand through his hair. "Why don't we stay on this floor for now? There's another staircase long before we hit the main entrance and its deep enough into the palace that we're less likely to bump into any guard patrols."

"You guys know this place better than me." Alex smiled to hide a grimace. That he had such close ties to this foreboding building still didn't seem real. "I'll tell you if anything changes with the void."

With that, they started off, away from the direction Roy had first suggested and towards a set of double doors further down the corridor. As they passed through, the hall expanded into a bright, high ceilinged room which seemed to sparkle as they walked over the glossy floor. Paintings covered golden embossed walls, so intricately carved that they were a work of art themselves, and Alex marvelled at them with an awe not lessened by his previous journeys through the palace.

Wonder didn't ease his nerves for long. A multitude of doors exited the space, any of which could burst open with an assault from Aiden's guards.

"You said we can sense them, right? Aiden's mages?" Alex hoped his question didn't betray his uncertainty. He was confident that his connection to the ground magic would warn him of any approaching mages, but Roy had said magic didn't work on Aiden's guard. What if that meant he couldn't see them coming?

"Don't worry. You'll know them when you feel them." Roy clapped him on his shoulder, but Alex didn't miss the glance he sent behind them. "Come on."

Trying to focus on the void rather than his anxieties, Alex followed Roy's lead. Beside him, Eira was quiet too. The illusion she was running would be taking up much of her attention, but he sensed that wasn't the sole reason for her silence. Any conversation would just bring their fears to the surface.

Room led onto room until Alex had no bearing on where they were in relation to the library. It wasn't until they reached a long white corridor with windows overlooking the gardens that Roy's assertion that he would feel the guards was tested. A crackling energy disrupted the flow of ground magic, coming from somewhere above him. Briefly, he released his focus on it, casting out with his normal magic sense instead for the presence of a mage, but if there was someone there, the ceiling blocked any ability to detect them.

"It's still beautiful, isn't it." Eira paused beside him, and Alex realised he had stopped moving.

"No.... I mean— There's something above us. Can you feel anything?"

Roy tilted his head. "Not on another floor, mate. It's not the void?"

"No. It's something else." Alex looked up at the painted ceiling. "It's disrupting the ground magic, kinda like a mage, but not." There was no way to confirm what was giving off the strange energy, but he felt he could hazard a guess.

"Like a mage, but not. Sounds familiar," Roy confirmed Alex's thoughts. "Are they moving?"

Alex nodded. "Slowly. Headed in the same direction we are." He looked between Eira and Roy. "Do we try a different way?"

"Well, we're not far from the stairs. They might not even know we're down here." Eira's nervous glance at the security cameras undermined her optimistic tone.

"Let's test it then." Before they could debate further, Roy moved off, back the way they had come. Alex jogged to catch up, but Roy held up a hand to slow him. "Just act casual. We're place guards patrolling a corridor, remember? As far as anyone watching can tell, anyway."

For a moment, the crackling disruption stayed behind. Then Alex felt it move, keeping pace with them on the floor above. "It's following."

"Right." Roy swung an arm up towards the nearest security camera. A flare of magic followed; a bolt of energy that snapped the camera to the side, leaving its housing scorched and misshapen. "Hopefully that will do it."

"I thought you said not to touch the cameras!" Eira exclaimed as Roy spun on his heel and bolted past her. Alex followed, the device in his rucksack weighing heavily on his back as he ran.

"They're onto us." Roy blasted another camera as the end of the corridor came into sight. "The stairwell's just ahead. We have to get rid of the cameras around the stairs. The floors above and below too. They know we're in the blackout zone, but at least they won't see where."

"You want us to get the machine ready?" Alex called through panting breaths.

"We're going to have to face those guys at some point. Might as well do it now."

The stairwell was large enough to be a room in itself. From the central landing, a staircase spiralled up to his left, another curving down to his right, with the corridor continuing opposite. The bannister was a dark wood, polished until it reflected the light from the chandeliers suspended above, and when he looked over the edge, Alex could see down to the floor below.

"Head down and take out the cameras." Roy called as he bounded up the stairs. "I'll do the halls above and we'll meet back here."

There was no time to worry about whether the guard was coming before Roy had disappeared out of sight. Leaving Eira to finish the central landing, Alex hurried to the lower level.

The ground floor corridor was narrower than the one he had just left, and despite the tall windows of coloured glass that ran the height of the stairwell, the space seemed dark. To his relief, the cameras in the halls were easy to spot. He followed Roy's example, forcing his breathing to slow as he focussed his will on the bolt of magic that would destroy them. They cracked with a sound that made him flinch; until now, he could almost pretend he wasn't committing a crime.

Eira was wringing her hands when he returned to the landing. "The machine— do we get it ready?" Her words came out in a rush, and Alex shrugged off his backpack as Roy joined them.

"Upstairs is done. No sign of the guard," Roy said. "Can you still feel them?"

"Yeah..." Alex had crouched down to open the rucksack, shaking hands struggling with the zip that held it shut. He paused and closed his eyes. With a deep breath, he reached out again towards the ground magic, its heavy energy blanketing his mind as he tuned back in. The void remained as it had been before, somewhere below them, and there was the static energy of the mage guard, unmoving somewhere above. "They've stopped, but they're still there."

"Probably waiting on orders now they've lost visual," Roy replied. "Gives us time to set up."

"Not much chance of taking them by surprise though." Alex was counting on Aiden's mages not running a shield. If they absorbed magic, like Roy said, there would be no need for one against a magic attack. He'd just have to hope they wouldn't see anything non-magical as a threat.

Turning back to the rucksack, Alex pulled out their makeshift weapon. Despite his modifications, the device didn't look much different from when his mother had placed it into his hands at the safe house. Unobtrusive and rectangular, it was less than half the size of the generator he'd used at the concert; more akin to one of his games consoles than its amp-sized counterpart. Its dull metallic surface dug into his palms as he unravelled the long wires that now extended from its body. Sharp barbed tips marked the end of each wire, designed to penetrate through clothing and skin. The flyback transformer he had salvaged from the safe house TV should increase the voltage enough to paralyse, and Alex had filled the passive spell that would turn the generator with as much magic as he had dared sacrifice; all it needed now was to be activated.

The corridor they'd come down would shield them from sight should the guard enter the landing above them. Alex set his device there and activated the spell. Inside, the generator began to whirr, metal surroundings vibrating under his touch as the power charged.

"Come on, where are they." Roy muttered from above him. He was shifting his balance nervously, occasionally poking his head around the wall to look up the stairs, even though Alex hadn't detected the guard move.

"I can tell you when they—" Alex cut himself off as he felt it. The void! The sensation that had been nagging at him since their arrival; it was gone. "Guys—" He spun on his knees to face Eira, mouth dry. "Something's happened. Something's wrong."

"What do you mean?" Eira kept her voice low as her eyes flashed towards the stairwell. "Are they coming?"

"If we need to fire this thing, tell us quick," said Roy. "It's not gonna take them long to get here."

"It's the room— The void. It's gone!" It was as though his lifeline had been cut. Whatever the void had been, it was the only hope he had of finding his uncle. Now that it had vanished, he was lost.

"Alright, but what about the guard?" Roy spoke through clenched teeth.

"Not moved. But we can't wait here anymore." Alex grabbed the wire nearest to him and started to wind it back up before Eira grasped his hand.

"Alex, stop! They could come any moment. It's already charging, we can't just go!"

"We have to!"

"Look," Roy crouched beside him. "Calm down. We didn't even know what that void was anyway. Let's just stick to the plan. Take this guy out, then keep searching. At least that way we won't have as many creepy mages to worry about when we do."

A sore dent had formed on Alex's palm where he was gripping his machine. It made sense but... "If Uncle Oliver was in that room— What if something's happened? It's the only reason we're even here. I can't take that risk!"

An unreadable expression crossed Roy's face, and for a minute he seemed lost in his thoughts. "It wasn't far, right?

Somewhere below us?" He turned back to Alex, who saw a flicker of worry in his eyes, despite his calm manner. "Do you think you can find it alone?"

"What are you talking about?" Eira said, but Roy ignored her. He shrugged off the guard's jacket he was wearing, and Alex realised his own illusioned version had disappeared; Eira clearly having stopped casting it once they'd destroyed the cameras.

"Take this." Roy handed the jacket to Alex, who hardly registered as he took it. "Go down the stairs and see if you can find where the room was. We'll catch up with you as soon as we're done here."

"No!" Eira spoke in a whispered shout. "You can not be suggesting we split up. That's ridiculous."

"If we pack up and that guard follows we'll all be defenceless," Roy replied. "They'd easily spot the three of us on the cameras, and if we take any more out they'll see we're on the move. Alone, Alex can slip by unnoticed, and he can sense anyone coming from much further than we can." He stood up and held out a hand that Alex didn't take.

"If I go, you won't know if the guard moves." He'd be leaving Eira and Roy completely vulnerable. The blackout zone had to be drawing attention, and Alex couldn't shake the notion that Roy was seizing the opportunity to get him out of harm's way.

"The only way they're going to get here is down those stairs, and once they're that close we'll feel them ourselves." Roy's assurance did little to ease his mind. "I'm not saying go far. If you sense anyone, come straight back."

Alex looked down at the machine, still whirring under his hand. Fear for his uncle wrestled with his instinct to protect his friends. Even if he found the former void, there was no guarantee he'd be able to do anything. And if his device failed against the guard...

"We know how to use it." Eira placed a hand on his arm and squeezed. The worry on her face was replaced by determination. "Roy's right. We can distract them here, and hopefully when you come back you'll have Oliver with you."

"Okay," Alex hesitated, then grabbed Roy's outstretched hand and let him hoist him to his feet. "Get Roy to shoot the wires while you activate the shock. It's got to be hard and fast — If the firing spell gets near them it will be absorbed."

"They'll never see it coming." Roy snorted humourlessly, turning towards the stairwell. "Go on then. Quickly."

With a last look at his two Champions, Alex darted out from their hiding place and back down the stairs to the narrow corridors below.

***

Why did everything look the same? His initial hurry had swept him through a winding series of halls, until wide carpeted rooms had given way to a narrow, windowless corridor with a hard dark floor that only added to his sense of confinement. He knew he should turn back, but without the void to anchor him Alex wasn't even sure he could find the right direction. Not for the first time, he wished whoever had created the Champion spell had allowed it to work on him; he could really use his father right now. *Dad would know the way.*

The click of a door behind him caused his heart to leap. He spun around as he strengthened his shield, breath tight in his chest. There had been no disruption in the ground magic to alert him anyone was here.

"Hold your fire." A man stood before him; young and slim, with dark hair that showed a hint of mahogany red where the electric light caught it. He wore a long, pale coat that seemed out of place for indoors, but his empty hands were held out in a gesture of peace.

Not a mage. Alex relaxed slightly, though he kept his guard up. That explained why he hadn't felt his approach.

The man smiled. "You don't recognise me, Alex?"

Hearing his name shattered any sense of relief. He scanned the face of the stranger, seeing a flicker of disappointment disturb his handsome composure. Then the man lowered his arms and Alex finally recognised the familiar features from the news.

"Ah, there we go." Aiden Heliodor's soft smile returned as Alex stumbled backwards. It hadn't crossed his mind that, of course, Aiden had no magic of his own. But why would he be here alone? Somehow, facing him like this was more unsettling than if he hadn't been.

"There's no need to be afraid." Aiden continued in the face of Alex's silence. "You're lucky I understand what's going on. It could have been a rather compromising situation had anyone else found you before I did."

"I'm not afraid," Alex lied. He narrowed his eyes. "What have you done with my uncle?"

"Oliver is perfectly safe." Aiden sighed and flexed his arms, looking at them distastefully, as though pained by his recent gesture of surrender. "It is unfortunate that I had to take him into my custody. You must understand, he attacked me; presumably due to the same misinformation you have been given. It was for his own safety as well as mine."

Alex wasn't sure he did understand. Tamara had told them Aiden was hunting them down. Roy had watched

Aiden and his guards attack Oliver and drag him away. Aiden had killed his father!

"I'm aware of what you've heard, but it isn't true." Aiden looked at him with an expression of pity. "I assure you that no one was more devastated by what happened to your father than I was."

"You're lying."

"Why would I lie to you, Alex? You can see I don't mean you any harm. Rest assured that I have informed my guards not to hurt your two friends either." For a brief moment, Aiden glanced over his shoulder. "Given how you were misled, I'm prepared to overlook the illegal entry and property damage. Quite generous, I hope you appreciate, considering who you are." His eyes seemed to flash as he said it, and Alex flinched.

"I'm not anyone." He replied. There was no use hiding his ancestry, Aiden certainly knew. But Alex didn't care who he was supposed to be. "I only want to get my uncle. Then we'll leave."

Aiden laughed; a light, pleasant sound that sent a shiver down Alex's back. "Unfortunately, things aren't that simple." He moved closer, enough that Alex could catch the perfumed scent of his clothes. There was magic there, too. Little spells woven into the cloth; water resistance, strengthening to prevent wear, even some to purify the air. "Your Uncle already attempted to assassinate me. He has the power of a royal Champion, along with Tamara and, if I'm not mistaken, the two who accompanied you? You must see that each of them will act in their own self-interest."

"They aren't like that."

"The old system is dead, Alex. There's nothing left to bind them to your wishes. If there were, why would Tamara still be working with Morgan after he killed your father?"

Any retort died in Alex's throat, choked by the pain of Aiden's revelation. Morgan had done it? Then Tamara... Had she lied? Tricked Oliver into coming here? He needed to get away; to find some space where he could breathe, but his legs didn't want to move. Nothing seemed like it made sense anymore.

"You really don't know anything about your heritage, do you?" Aiden inclined his head, looking Alex up and down. "I assume he never told your mother, either? I'm not sure how he could claim to love someone he lied to his whole life. Of course, it could have just been shame. Your father would never have been permitted to spend time with a person like her had the royal family lived."

"What?" Alex barely heard his own response. The conversation seemed to be happening away from him, as though he was separated from it by murky water.

Aiden reached his hands into the pockets of his blazer and shrugged. "Those without magic had no status in Ardveld. Not even someone like me."

"It's not like that anymore."

"Isn't it?"

Movement at Aiden's side caught Alex's eye, and he watched him pull a cylindrical metallic object from the pocket of his long coat. Jerking away, Alex strengthened his shield, but Aiden simply tossed the strange object in the air, casually catching it over and over.

"You're as naïve as your uncle," Aiden continued. "I can see why your father never told you the truth." He caught the cylinder again in his hand, knuckles turning white as he clenched it.

"What's tha—"

Alex's question was cut off as Aiden once more closed the distance between them. He reached towards him and Alex's shield quivered, blurring the air as Aiden's fingers brushed against it. "Your ancestors were selfish. They manipulated the Champion spell to keep themselves in power. A secret that could have given magic to everyone, and they took it to their graves." His lips pursed into a thin line, but Alex's head felt light, as though it were his eyes rather than his shield that had muddied his vision.

"Wha— what..." Alex tried to ask again, but his mouth wouldn't obey enough to form the sounds.

"I was so close..." Aiden hissed, and again he looked behind him, down to where the corridor faded into darkness.

Darkness... Why did it suddenly seem so dark?

"I assume you don't even know how they died?"

Aiden's words flowed through Alex's mind, slipping away before he could grasp at them. How they died? He tried to focus, but all he saw was a blur of movement as his legs gave way.

"What about this, Alex?" Crouching down close to his face, Aiden held up the cylinder that was in his hand. "Do you know what this is?"

The light reflecting from the metal left dots across Alex's vision. As he blinked them away, he found his eyes too heavy to open. Hard and cool, he gained a dim awareness of his face resting on the corridor's floor.

"It's almost poetic." Aiden's voice floated down. "You lived your entire life knowing nothing. Seems you're going to die that way too."

CHAPTER 39

Tamara caught the outline of her reflection in the window. She was dishevelled; her curls flying out in disarray, clothes creased from heat and sweat. The others didn't look much better. Walking between Morgan and Oliver, she could sense the fragile peace between them maintained as much by her presence as by their shared mission. Oliver clearly felt a kinship with her, despite his obvious mistrust, and despite what Morgan had said in the room, she didn't believe he didn't care. As for herself, even with Nathaniel's assurance, she felt as close to being a Champion as she did a minister for Morgan; that is, hardly at all.

They'd re-entered the palace through a side door that

opened at her touch, and on to the staff corridor through which they were now walking. Light from the setting sun dyed the navy carpet a blood red, but from what she could make out, the gardens were still empty. No obvious pursuit. She wasn't sure if that should make her relieved or nervous.

Their pace felt more hurried than it was. With Oliver still weak and stumbling, running was out of the question, but they were still on the ground floor. The long hallway would provider a clear line of sight should anyone enter; for both them and their enemies. Morgan had the wand, though none of them knew how much power it might have left. That meant the task of defending the group may well fall to her alone.

The resolve she'd felt since leaving the room with the symbols was quickly dissolving. Fighting guards to protect her life was one thing, but Aiden wasn't a mage. Unless he'd found some other weapon, he would be defenceless if they got to him, and that was another matter entirely. She hadn't dared ask what the plan was. Both Morgan and Oliver held a deadly glint in their eyes, but even in self-defence, Tamara wasn't sure she could kill.

"You could if you need to." Nathaniel's soft voice entered her thoughts.

"That's easy for you to say." Of course he wouldn't worry about it. His role had been known as the Guardian amongst Ardveld's population, the same role she now technically held, but he'd commanded soldiers; she'd lived most of her life in a library!

"It may surprise you to know, I've never killed," Nathaniel replied. *"But I know now that I could."* A memory flickered into her mind; a room full of people and colour and movement. Mouths moved as though they were shouting, but the scene was muted and blurry, with only its emotions sharp. Horror

and panic. Bodies lying still. People she knew and loved, torn from their seats. The metallic smell of blood.

Only, she didn't know them. This was Nathaniel's past. *"To protect those I care about, I would have done. I see the same in you."*

Her legs felt unsteady. To protect those she cared about... Tamara again looked at Morgan, and felt her heart waring with the sting of grief left by the memory. *"Let's hope it doesn't come to that."* She had a feeling that the people she cared about weren't always going to be the ones she was supposed to protect.

Ahead of them, the corridor finally opened into a dimly lit stairwell. She stopped as her magic sense picked up the flicker of mages ahead. *"Not Aiden's."* They couldn't be; the energy wasn't wild enough to be from his mage guard, but that didn't mean bumping into anyone else was good news either.

"There's someone ahead," Tamara turned to Oliver to see if he'd felt them too, but his magic weakness was likely still impairing his senses. "I think they're ordinary mages, but stay behind me, just in case." Whoever they were, they must be reasonably strong for her to sense them at this distance. If they were enemies, she'd just have to count on the fact she was stronger.

"Regular mages could be staff," Morgan whispered as Tamara made to enter the stairwell. "I'd rather no one else get caught up in this."

"In that case I can send them home as well as you could. They can't hurt me."

His grip had tightened on the wand and for a moment he looked as though he was about to argue. Instead, he said nothing. Oliver for his part, simply nodded, and taking

Morgan's silence as acceptance, she turned back to enter the space ahead.

The staircase curved up to her left, with tall, stained glass windows running the height of the three palace floors. The higher levels were brighter, lit by sparkling chandeliers that hung over the staircase on long, golden chains. Somewhere above her, whispered voices floated down from the first landing.

"What if he's dead?" A panicked whisper cracked into a squeak, and when Tamara looked up through the banister that encircled the first floor, she could see a shaded figure crouched on the ground. Another, taller person was leaning against the wall behind them; a slim male, with what looked like deep red hair. Neither looked like they were palace staff, and they were both looking at something on the floor just out of sight.

"To be honest, I'm not sure I care right now." The curt reply from the taller figure came through heavy breaths, and she thought it sounded like he was about to throw up. "They don't look dead to me." He continued in a softer tone, just as Tamara felt someone come up close behind her.

Typical. Tamara turned to see both Oliver and Morgan, neither of whom had clearly been contented to wait. She sighed, but Oliver was already pushing past her.

"Roy?!" he exclaimed, and the tall man seemed to start. His companion lifted their head and Tamara suddenly realised why her voice had seemed so familiar.

"Eira?" It didn't make sense, and for a moment Tamara felt rooted to the spot. "*How is she here? And where is Alex?*" Her anxiety was magnified by Nathaniel's dismay.

"Oliver! Help please!" Eira's panicked call did nothing to ease her worry.

With surprising energy, Oliver bolted up the stairs towards where the girl was crouched. Tamara followed; rounding the stairs until the floor of the landing came into view. A man was lying there and she recoiled as she saw the uniform. *"One of Aiden's guards!"*

Eira was babbling as Oliver crouched beside her. "It was only supposed to stun them! I've been trying to heal, but they might be dead—"

"Eira!" He interrupted. "What are you doing here? Where's Alex?" There was a fear in his eyes that Tamara hadn't seen before, even when Aiden was threatening his life.

Behind them, the man Oliver had called Roy looked pale and shaken. He'd been staring at Oliver since he'd reached Eira's side, but his expression of relief turned to confusion at the words.

"What do you mean? He was supposed to be finding you!"

Oliver looked up. "You brought him here!"

"Yeah, he—" Roy finally looked in Tamara's direction. "What the hell is he doing here?" His words were a snarl, and Tamara flinched back. But he wasn't looking at her at all. Morgan had made it to the top of the stairs.

She instinctively stepped between them, and this time Roy was glaring at her.

"Tamara, right?" He was a strong mage, she could sense it, and now she noticed he was taller than both Morgan and Oliver. "You're supposed to be one of us!"

Tamara looked him up and down. *"Did Oliver say there were other Champions?"*

"Someone like that? I suppose after you, anything's possible."

"Roy!" Oliver's sharp voice cut across the standoff. "I need someone to answer me. Why are you here? What happened?"

"We came to rescue you." Roy turned back to Oliver, expression softening. "We let Alex go looking. To keep him away from this creep." He nudged the man on the floor with his foot; the resulting groan proving, to Tamara's relief, that he was indeed still alive. Something must have caught Roy's eye too, because he knelt down for a moment by their head, before returning to his previous position with a small, dark object pressed to his ear.

"Roy!" Oliver called out, but he ignored him, attention occupied by what Tamara now realised was a communication device.

Eira was still sat on the floor, her body trembling enough to see. Tamara sat down beside her. "Eira, they aren't dead. It's okay." She wasn't sure whether touching her would provide comfort or distress, so she didn't, instead turning her attention to the unconscious guard.

The uniform was definitely that of Aiden's mages, but there was none of the sickening energy that usually accompanied their presence. He had dark, curly hair, not unlike her own, and this close she could see the faint line lines around his eyes and the beads of sweat on a forehead creased with pain. *"She said she was healing him,"* Tamara sent the thought to Nathaniel. *"But wouldn't the magic just be absorbed?"*

"Unless they used all their power?" Nathaniel mused. *"He certainly doesn't feel like a mage of any sort now."*

"Can you tell me what happened?" There was no response, so Tamara placed a gentle hand on Eira's arm. She jumped, as though noticing her presence for the first time. "How did you do this?"

Eira breathed a shuddering sigh. "Roy told us about

Aiden's mages absorbing magic. We didn't know how we could fight them, but Alex said we could use his machine. You fire the wires then press the button. It's just supposed to stun."

"Well, it seems to have worked." Now she knew what to look for, she noticed the two wires loose on the ground, curling back towards a metallic box at Roy's feet. She reached out and picked one up, noting the sharp metal barb on the end.

"Careful!" Eira exclaimed. "I don't know if there's still power."

Roy's voice interrupted her thoughts. "As far as I can tell, Alex is fine. Can't hear anything about him." He lifted a hand to the earpiece that he'd taken from the guard. "Two of them were following you, but they've stopped to regroup with the ones trailing us— Seems we were right about the trap at the staff entrance."

Tamara turned back to Eira. "Are you sure this was one of Aiden's mages? I can't feel any of their magic."

"He doesn't have any magic because it's all gone through me!" It was Roy who answered. "I had a shield running when we fired the machine. Wasn't sure there was any point, but you know, just in case. Anyway, it turns out these guys really don't like electricity. When we hit him with the jolt, he started glowing for a second, then wham! It was like all his magic exploded out. Destroyed my shield and I got the rest of it. Still feel like I'm gonna throw up." He grimaced. "Thankfully, whatever weird magic they've got seems to go through whoever it hits first. As far as we can tell, Eira didn't get any." A strange expression flickered over Roy's face. "Shit, they've switched channels. Look, it might be better Alex isn't here. They know where we are and I hope you've got a plan, because I don't know how we're going to take out four of these."

She saw Oliver nod; a rapid motion that didn't hide his shock. Then he swallowed, moved to the guard's side, and began to rip open the black shirt coving their chest.

"What are you doing?" No matter who this man was, the action seemed disrespectful. The guard stirred and Oliver frowned before looking at her.

"Can you do a sleep spell? I don't want to take any risks."

"Me?" She hesitated. Of course it would be her; Oliver was too weak and presumably the others didn't have the technical ability without relying on their Champions. "Okay." Half expecting an ethical objection from Eira, she reached for her magic and shaped the spell. It was a form of healing, as with all spells that worked on the body, and it settled so easily into the man's mind that she was sure now that, whatever strange energy he used to possess, he wasn't a mage at all.

"How can that be?" Nathaniel voiced her own question, but neither had an answer.

Oliver finish pulling aside the guard's shirt and Tamara winced as she saw the skin, blistered and red around the small dark puncture wounds from the spike-tipped wires. The marks looked a few days old, likely the work of Eira's healing spell, but as she looked closer she saw they weren't the only damage. All over the guards chest were dark shapes; ragged indents that seemed like scars, alongside sharper lines and circles etched in black, drawn or tattooed onto his skin. They were just like the marks on the wand.

"Just as I thought." Oliver gestured towards a fresh blister wound. It cut straight across one of the symbols.

"It's damaged," Tamara replied. The ink mark had bled into the surrounding skin where the burns didn't reach, as though the mark itself had burst. "The symbols must be what gives them their power."

"And when the symbol broke, it released the magic held inside their body," Oliver continued.

Tamara thought back to their discussion in the room. Aiden had been sacrificing mages to make his weapons; using the symbols to hold their magic inside the wood. Wasn't that enough? "It's not just the wands. He's doing it to people." She rocked her body in a soothing motion as she considered it. "Why?"

"Remember why he wanted us." Oliver fixed her with his golden eyes. "Changing a mage's magic level, or giving magic to those who didn't have it before. We are the only way it's ever been done; passed on from one Royal Champion to the next. He told you these are old Ardveldian symbols, and he knows we inherit our power. He's trying to replicate the Champion spell."

"But that isn't how it works." She hadn't forcibly ripped power from Nathaniel. She hadn't even wanted it. And from the looks of the guard's chest, it hadn't been a painless experience. Again, she analysed the faded and misshapen marks.

"Some of these are older," she said. "Why has he done it more than once?"

"Perhaps it breaks down over time?"

"That would explain why Aiden hasn't tried it himself," Morgan commented, and Tamara realised he had come closer to hear them talk. "He wants it perfect."

Silence followed his words.

"...Oliver," Eira's quiet voice was the one to break it. "I'm scared."

Everyone's eyes fell on the dishevelled Tactician as he got

to his feet. "I know," he said. "But we're going to make it out. I have a plan."

CHAPTER 40

He'd been moved. Glimpses of memory rose and fell, the images blurred by his fading vision. Dark rooms. His captor's laboured breathing. The scraping of his body across the bare floor. Now Alex lay still, head spinning even with his eyes closed. Spinning... Falling into black relief.

A jolt of panic snapped him back. How much time had passed? He'd been with Roy and Eira... No. He'd been alone in the corridor. With Aiden.

Bright light sent a stabbing pain through his head as he opened his eyes. He squeezed them shut. Deep breaths. His mind was clearing, and with it came a sense of his situation. The surface he was lying on was hard and uneven; some kind of mesh cutting into the side of his face. At least that meant he could feel something. His limbs were still numb and distant, as though he'd slept awkwardly, and Alex didn't know if his attempt to flex his fingers was moving them at all.

Once more, he opened his eyes; slowly, tensing for pain. But this time, it didn't come. Instead the room swam into focus.

He'd been right about the mesh. Fine copper coloured wires criss-crossed the surface beneath him, anchored to rough wood that made up the rest of the platform he was lying on. They were giving off the faint sensation of magic and Alex pulled his hands closer to push himself up. The movement jarred to a halt as he tried. Something was bound tight around his wrists. Metal cuffs anchoring him to a point in the centre of the platform.

Strength returned in a wave of adrenaline. Forcing himself to his knees, Alex reached for his magic. The metal looked strong. Too strong to bend or break, but maybe he could at least burn the chain free from the wood? He braced himself as he released the spell, but there was no answering rush of heat. Instead, he felt his magic disperse, as though he'd lost focus part way through the cast.

He tried again. Then again; desperation shaking his focus so much that he wasn't confident he was even shaping the spell correctly. Each time the result was the same. Wrists slick with sweat, he twisted wildly, biting back a whimper of pain as the metal cut into his skin. A hiss of frustration answered him and, for the first time, Alex realised he wasn't alone.

Aiden was standing a few paces away, half shielded by a wooden plinth that rose to his chest, almost like a speaker's pulpit. The coat he'd worn was discarded at his feet and his white shirt lay open and shrugged back on his shoulders, leaving the top half of his body bare and pale in the bright light.

Now that he was on his knees, Alex saw that the area on which he sat was raised up from the floor, but the copper mesh didn't reach the edge. Instead, small symbols ringed the platform, glowing faintly where they were carved into the wood. A cluster of wires extended from somewhere below him, winding their way over the shining floor tiles and up the plinth beside Aiden.

Familiar tiles.

Blue and silver, they seemed to glitter under the towering white pillars that rose around him. Alex's heart leapt in horror. He was back in the throne room.

He pulled frantically against the cuffs once more, the need to flee the room as urgent as any desire to escape his captor. It wasn't until Aiden turned on him that he realised he must have cried out.

"Shut up!" he snarled, and Alex shrank back as far as his bindings would let him. There was something shiny in Aiden's hand, catching the light with a metallic glint, and Alex flinched as he watched him flick it up towards his own bare shoulder and draw a red line across his skin. He worked rapidly, sucking air through gritted teeth, and Alex realised that what he had first taken to be ink was blood.

What was he doing?

He daren't voice the question. The last thing he wanted was to draw attention, but any hope of being forgotten died as Aiden dropped his knife to the floor. The small blade rang a clattering echo in the grand hall.

Aiden strode towards him, but rather than meet Alex's eyes, he began to scan the plinth as if he were an engineer assessing a project; the cool calm of his face an unsettling contrast to his blood smeared body.

"I don't want to rule." Alex forced the words out as Aiden knelt close. For a moment he debated striking a kick into his chest, but his position was awkward and his limbs still heavy. Regardless, Aiden made no move to touch him. When he brushed a hand over the glowing symbols on the plinth, Alex saw they were just like the ones he'd carved into his skin. "I only came to get my uncle, then we'll go," he spoke again in the unsettling silence. "I just want to go home. We're not a threat to you!"

This time, Aiden glared at him. "Your uncle is currently on his way to kill me." He spat the words as he got back to his feet, the rest of the sentence a half mumble, as though he was speaking to himself. "This isn't how I planned it."

"Wait!" An urgency seized hold of Alex as he watched Aiden returning to the plinth, as though keeping him talking could forestall whatever he was planning. "What are you doing?"

Without a response, Aiden placed the flat of his hand on top of the plinth. It too had symbols carved into the surface, and as he watched they grew clearer, becoming brighter with every passing moment until they shone a warm gold that spread down alongside the trail of wires to the ground. Around him, the symbols encircling the platform too began to brighten, and Alex had the stark reminder of where he'd seen them before. They were just like the ones his father had shown him when they opened the passageway. He looked in vain towards the wall where it had been; so close and yet completely out of reach.

Soon, the circle was glowing bright enough that he was forced to squint. Then he felt it. It was as though he was casting an active spell. Slowly at first, his magic started to flow away from him, like water seeping through his hands even as he tried to hold it.

"Stop!" He didn't know if he'd shouted or just thought the word. Fear gripped him as the flow increased and he curled up against the mesh, as though tightening his body could somehow prevent his magic being ripped away. His stomach lurched with the familiar nausea that heralded magic exhaustion, followed by a wave of pain that tore through his abdomen. Before he could catch his breath, it came again searing down his limbs with white agony. Alex screamed.

Chapter 41

Metal shelves lined the walls of the storage closet Roy was hiding in. A unit in the centre took up the remaining space, stacked full of toiletries and cleaning products. The fullness of the cramped room seemed to absorb any sound he made, and with the heavy curtains pulled shut over the one tiny window at the back, the place stank of damp and chemicals. He shuffled his feet, resisting the urge to pace like a caged animal.

They'd kept the room in semi-darkness, so as not to let any light through the small hole he'd burned in the door. *"Last time I deliberately damaged government property I was sixteen."* He sent the comment to Julian, as much to distract himself as to break the eerie feeling of being alone.

"Just like old times then," Julian replied. If Roy hadn't been able to sense his emotions, he would have missed the tension underlying his causal tone. *"Focus on what you're doing."*

It wasn't exactly hard, but Roy turned his attention back to his spells anyway. The corridor beyond the door was filled with illusioned smoke, obscuring any view of what was out there. A mage would be able to tell it was an illusion easily enough; he had nowhere near Eira's level of skill and the magic gave off enough energy. But the point wasn't to be believable. A good job too, or he wouldn't be able to run ten of them and still make conversation.

Somewhere below him, Tamara would be casting the same type of smoke illusions he was, each one stacked upon the next until they obscured sight down the whole corridor. Four of Aiden's guards were tracking them, approaching from the central palace; he had picked up enough before they'd switched channels to determine that. Now, all he could do was wait.

He rested a hand on Alex's machine, feeling the generator whirr as it charged. Hopefully the guards would rush his floor. Eira and Oliver had taken the landing above; the best line of sight for the trickier illusions she would need to cast for Oliver's plan, but it left the two of them defenceless.

"None of us are particularly safe. This is a tenuous alliance," Julian commented as Roy toyed with the barbed ends of the machine's wires.

"Yeah, I'm trying not to think about it. At least we know this works."

Tamara and Morgan only had the wand. He didn't much care about their welfare, but if it failed then he and Julian would be the only ones left fighting and this time he would be firing the machine alone.

A tingling against the first of his spells broke Roy from his musing. *"Looks like it's go time."*

In a rush of static, the first of his illusions dispersed. He tensed, counting down in his head as he waited for the next. Aiden's guards absorbed magic. They would destroy his spells as they approached, willingly or not.

Another illusion vanished, then a third; moving at a steady pace, though there was no way to see how many guards had come his way. Roy straightened, wires gripped ready. His mental count told him the next one was coming. But it didn't. *"What do you think they're—"*

A fizzing bolt of energy blasted through his remaining spells, and Roy jerked back from the door. "Shit." He swallowed hard, then peered through the hole. Two of them.

As long as Eira led the others to the central landing, he'd take care of the rest. He strained to pick up the guard's conversation, but it was too quiet to make out. Oh well. He'd have to get out there at some point.

The door opened soundlessly and Roy poked his head out, wires of Alex's machine in hand. To his right the darkened corridor opened onto the landing where the two guards were now standing, looking down at the unconscious body of the man he'd taken out with Eira.

One cocked their head to their collar, speaking in a low voice to the microphone that must be there, while the other crouched to inspect their colleague. The standing one first then.

The machine was charged and ready, he'd just need to hit the button. Roy took a deep breath, focussed his will on his magic, then blew out a sharp whistle. His target spun around to look. A clear line of sight. With a flick of his wrist, he hurled the sharp tipped wires forward and released his crafted spell. A blast of concentrated air formed behind them as they flew, sending the darts speeding, and the guard let out a yelp as they hit him directly in the chest. Roy threw himself back, pulled Alex's machine towards him, and slammed the button on the side.

There was a clicking sound and the guard cried out again as he collapsed to the floor. A glance back showed Roy he struck true. Golden light was shining through the man's clothes, getting brighter by the moment, and knowing what was coming, he swung himself round the doorframe back into the storage room.

Just in time. A blast of static energy, far more powerful than the one that had destroyed his illusions, sparked against his senses. He flattened himself against the wall as his stomach lurched, thanking the bricks and wood that blocked the worst of the undirected magic.

"One down," Julian said.

"Three to go." It would be too lucky for that blast to have taken out both of them, and he still had no idea where the others were. Roy wiped his sweating hands on his trousers and leant around the door... Then swore loudly as his eyes met those of the second guard. He didn't look happy, and Roy scrambled for the wires of the machine, tugging them hard out of the now unconscious body of the first. *"Where's that distraction? Let's hope they really can't cast a shield."*

Undirected magic crackled from the guard's direction as he readied an attack, but Roy was faster. There was a curse as the wire tips hit their target, and he flung himself to the ground beside the machine, a bolt of nauseating energy grazing too close to his head. He jammed a thumb onto the button once more.

Nothing happened.

He jabbed it again, then realised that there was no familiar whirring from inside the metal. A scan with his magic sense confirmed it. The passive spell was gone.

"Damn it!" Roy yelled out loud. "The blast wiped the spell. It's dead!"

So was he if he didn't move. He rolled as another blast of energy shot past him, then pushed himself up to his knees. The guard's face was pale and ghostly on the shadowed landing, and for a moment they stared at each other. Then, the world went bright.

Roy squinted as light assaulted his senses. The guard was silhouetted against the now brightly lit stairwell, but he caught the flash of blue hair as a small figure appeared in the space behind them.

"*Eira!*" She must have cast the light. He leapt to his feet, just as he felt a rush of undirected magic. Wood exploded from the balustrade, followed by the charred smell of burning. The blue haired figure flickered and vanished. Aiden's guard choked out a gargled cry, and Roy watched, bewildered, as they collapsed.

"*She's too good.*" Roy breathed a laugh, heart still racing.

"*An illusion wouldn't have done that damage. What hit them?*"

There was no time to dwell on it. A familiar glow was seeping through the guard's uniform and Roy darted back to the shelter of his storage room, bile rising at the back of his throat as their energy dispersed. "*Two down.*" He rested his head against the wall. "*That was too close.*"

"*That shot came from downstairs. My guess is the rest are on their way up,*" Julian said. "*Assuming Morgan wouldn't fire at Eira.*"

"*Wouldn't he?*" Roy clenched his jaw. Two more guards, and with the machine dead, he had nothing. But neither did

Oliver and Eira. *"We're just going to have to wing it."* Before he could change his mind, Roy forced himself back into the corridor.

It was empty. He sprinted to where he'd seen the second guard fall, and grimaced as he passed them. Their back was caved in; dark liquid beginning to pool on the floor below.

"No chance of healing that one." Julian seemed indifferent, but Roy had to look away. He'd think about it later.

The air in the stairwell was heavy with magic and smoke. A dozen magelights shone near the chandeliers, too bright to look at, and from below he felt the crackling energy of undirected magic. He leant over the blackened bannister, careful to put no weight near the remaining cracked posts.

Morgan was below, wand in hand; one of Aiden's mage guard slumped against the wall ahead of him. No sign of Tamara, but he couldn't stop to wonder. Movement to Roy's right caught his eye; the last guard was making his way up the stairs towards him.

"Oh fuck off!" Roy exclaimed, not caring anymore who heard him. He dropped to his knees, knowing the remaining spindles of the damaged balustrade would provide no defence. Below, he saw Morgan raise the wand again.

He barely felt the energy as the wand fired. The guard stumbled against the wall as Morgan's shot hit, but there was no answering glow. *Too weak*. They were out of weapons, and out of time.

Aiden's guard righted himself, and Roy ducked back down. *"Maybe if I can't see them, they can't see me."* He thought, humourlessly. The handrail obscured most of his view, and he could see nothing of the guard's face when he looked up; only the chandelier, glittering in glassy brilliance above the stairs.

Confusion emanated from Julian as Roy formed his magic into an intent. *"What are you doing?"*

"Improvising." He replied, and released the spell.

The ceiling around the chain holding the chandelier shattered in a rain of plaster, and Roy watched in open mouthed awe as the ornamental light gently rotated. Then it dropped.

"Yes!" Roy threw himself to his feet, exhaustion forgotten, as glass and metal crashed onto the guard below. *"Just like in the cartoons! I cannot believe that worked!"*

His celebration was short lived. Bloodied and scratched, the man snarled as he attempted to drag himself out from underneath the fixture's frame. His eyes met Roy's, then widened as someone pushed past.

It was Eira. Really Eira this time, and she was holding something heavy with both hands.

"Is that a fire extinguisher?" Roy sent the thought to Julian just as Eira swung the object into the side of the guard's head. It impacted with a hollow clunk and the man collapsed to the floor.

Flushed and wild, she turned to shout at him. "I'll heal him later!"

CHAPTER 42

Alex sucked in a breath as the wave of pain eased. Then another wracked his body, forcing out an agonised cry. He grit his teeth, digging his fingers hard into his palms in an attempt to feel anything else.

The next break left him gasping and immobile, and yet his magic was still being dragged away. A distant part of his brain wondered how much more he had. A moment ago, the idea of losing consciousness had brought terror; he doubted he would wake up. Now, the prospect seemed a mercy.

Too weak to even brace himself for what he knew was coming, Alex lay limp. There was cold below him now; a cool, soothing sensation flowing up through his limbs. He must be dying. The thought was more an academic analysis than anything emotional. That explained why he was suddenly so calm...

The cool energy from below nudged at him again. A pale light, felt more than seen, pressing against his mind, as though he just needed to let it in.

Pain once more sharpened his focus, and Alex realised with sudden clarity what the sensation was. Mentally he scrambled for it; clinging to the last dregs of his consciousness through the encroaching darkness.

It was the ground magic.

In the palace he'd trained himself to sense mages moving through it, but it had always been separate from him, as though repelled by his own energy. It hadn't come this close. Not since Golebach.

It was an idea born more of desperation than logic. With no power of his own left to repel it, maybe he could channel the ground magic instead, just like he'd done with his machine.

As though it had been waiting, the light rushed to meet him as he opened his mind, Alex heaved a sob of relief as the new power poured in, washing the pain away. Aiden's spell continued its assault, but now it was drawing the ground magic rather than his own. As long as he stayed connected to it, he was safe.

Relief didn't last long.

What had started as a trickle of energy now began to pick up speed; a bright river of magic passing easily through the passage granted by his physical form. Alex tried to slow it, but the more he fought for control, the faster the ground magic seemed to flow.

It was too much. Fear gripped him as he recalled the

explosion at Golebach and, as though in answer to his racing heart, a barrier seemed to break. Light flooded his body, burning white in his mind and obscuring all thoughts other than the link between the vast pool of energy below him and the relentless pull of Aiden's spell.

Last time the earthquake had shaken him free. This time he was trapped.

CHAPTER 43

The scene before Oliver froze in a snapshot. Debris and dust clouding magic heavy air. The shattered chandelier. Eira, fire extinguisher in hand, standing over the body of the guard beneath it.

And on the ground floor, Aiden's last mage, slowly getting to his feet.

"Roy! Eira! Below you!" Oliver moved without thinking. The man had been unconscious; knocked out by the first attack from Morgan's wand, but it hadn't lasted, and now Eira was directly in his sight. Oliver stumbled past Roy as he descended the stairs, catching himself against the remnants of the still-smoking bannister as he teetered too close to the gap. Then he was on the step in front of Eira, shielding her body with his own.

"*At least it will buy them a moment.*" Too weak to attempt a shield, he could only wait as magic flared from below.

But it wasn't the sickening static of undirected magic. Instead, the small figure of Tamara burst into view as she released the spell she had been crafting. Oliver flinched back from the bannister as a wall of heat assaulted his senses. It was hot enough to leave his skin stinging, but before he could react it was gone, blown away by Tamara's second spell; a gust of wind that hurled the boiling air forward.

The guard screamed as the heat hit him. Skin red and blistering, he staggered across the room, waving his arms in a futile attempt to swat away the attack. Then a bright glow emanated from beneath his dark uniform. There was nowhere to hide.

"Move!" It was Morgan who shouted. Pushing past Tamara, he hurled himself against the glowing guard, dragging them with him down the corridor opposite and out of sight.

"No!" Tamara cried out and made as if to follow, but Oliver was no longer frozen.

Clambering over the metal wreckage of the chandelier, he descended the remaining stairs, grabbed hold of her arm, and with what little strength he had, flattened them both against the wall just as undirected magic exploded from the corridor beyond.

"*An indirect attack,*" he instinctively sent the thought to Ewen as he worked out what Tamara had done. "*Just like the wind in park. Her spell never touched them, only the hot air. There was nothing to absorb.*"

"*It almost backfired,*" Ewen replied, but Oliver didn't have time to wonder what had happened to Morgan.

"Oliver!" Eira's voice came from above. Roy was beside her, the two of them beckoning wildly. "This guard still has power! He's unconscious, but what do we do?"

Glass littered the carpeted stairs, and this time Oliver picked his way past, noting the crunch that indicated some was already buried in his shoes. The metal frame still pinned the guard's body, but as he approached, they gave a moan and he smelt the telltale acidity of vomit.

"Can't heal the guy or send him to sleep while he's still absorbing magic," Roy said. He stood back, clearly keeping a safe distance. "At least they're too out of it for now to try anything. What do you think?"

"I..." Oliver paused, clenching and unclenching his hands as he thought. They needed to act quickly. Alex was out there alone, and regardless of how cognisant the guard was, he wasn't comfortable leaving them unattended while they had magic. His eyes once again caught the shattered glass at his feet, and he bent down and carefully picked up a shard. "Roy, can you help me move him to a room?" If he could damage the symbols holding the spell in place, then that should be enough. He'd probably make it out in time...

"Don't be ridiculous."

Oliver snapped his head up at Morgan's voice.

"That man is a cockroach! Does he never die?" Ewen's scathing comment came as they saw Morgan and Tamara walking up the stairs towards them. Though ruffled, he seemed completely uninjured, and Oliver pretended not to notice the smile of relief on Tamara's face.

"It appears the discharged magic doesn't affect non-mages." Morgan gestured at the piece of glass in Oliver's hand. "Give that to me."

"Don't kill them!" Eira stepped over the guard, raising her fire extinguisher threateningly, but Morgan just sighed.

"They'll provide better evidence alive. I'm going to destroy the symbols." He pressed his fingers into the bridge of his nose, then turned to Oliver. "I assume that was your plan?"

Oliver nodded as an uncomfortable sense of gratitude washed over him.

"I wouldn't dwell on it." Ewen's words provided little comfort.

Eira looked between them, then moved aside, still eyeing Morgan warily as he hauled the chandelier off of the prone guard.

"The rest of you stay back then." Morgan seemed to meet Tamara's eyes for a moment, then he lifted the guard over his shoulder.

"Wasn't going to help him anyway," Roy mumbled, and the four of them stood in silence until a faint burst of static energy came from the corridor below.

CHAPTER 44

"I wouldn't dwell on it." The words were clear enough that they might have been spoken from right beside him, and Alex jolted in panic, still blinded by the light of the ground magic coursing through his body.

"Oh come on. Why are we even waiting for him?"

A second voice joined the first, speaking with the careless manner of teenage impatience, and Alex frantically turned his head. *"Well I wouldn't."* The words were disjointed and didn't seem directed at him at all.

"I'm just suggesting you're wasting an opportunity." This time the voice was smooth and calm; the deeper tones of an adult male. It was as though he'd entered a room of people,

catching fragments of their conversation as they talked amongst each other. But there was no one. There had been no one except himself and Aiden.

His exhausted brain scrambled for answers that wouldn't come. He was floating in energy; could barely detect his limbs or the ground below him, eyes unseeing.

"*Julian?*" The first voice exclaimed in surprise, a sense of shock and confusion accompanying it.

"*Ewen?*"

"*What's going—*"

"*Julian!*" A fourth joined the turmoil. "*What were you thinking, letting Alex go off alone? Have you no integrity!*"

"*Ah. I missed you too, Nathaniel.*"

Alex listened as the conversation happened around him. Then there was a flash of an image; stairs, broken glass. It vanished as he tried to focus on it, and he realised he hadn't been seeing it with his eyes at all.

"*Eira, wait. I can—*"

"*No, Roy, I've not gone mad!*"

"*What's... How can we hear each other? Is this normal?*" The younger voice rose again above the others. Eira... Whoever it was had said Eira's name. He'd heard his own too, and Roy. Alex tried to open his mouth to speak. Call for help. Anything. But he couldn't move.

"*Please.*" Alex begged in his mind. "*Help... Please...*"

"*Alex?*" Confusion again. And panic. A wave of emotion that wasn't his own poured from the voice that had answered him. "*Alex? Where are you? Are you safe?*"

"*Alex is there? How? Can he hear us?*"

"*Does he know what's happening?*"

"*No, I don't know what's going on. Tell the others— Somehow we can hear Alex.*"

The voices tumbled over each other as the strangers all talked at once, and Alex fought vainly against the weakness of his own body as he attempted to respond.

"Alex, listen to me," the person who had noticed him cut through his panic. *"You don't need to speak. I can follow your thoughts. Can you tell us what's happening?"*

"Who are you?"

"My name is Ewen. I'm... I'm with Oliver. Now, you need to tell me where you are."

"I—" Alex was cut off as the ground lurched beneath him. For a second he was falling, then everything steadied.

The others must have felt it, too. Another image flashed into his mind; the earth shifting under his feet, knocking him hard into the wall of a wide corridor. Someone steadying his balance. It was somewhere in the palace, though Alex didn't know the layout well enough to tell how far it was from the throne room.

"He's in the throne room." Ewen must have seen his thoughts, just as he said he could. *"Hold fast. We're coming."*

Another shudder through the earth, but this time he barely noticed it. Sensation seemed far away, as though there was only a fine tether left to his body. *"I can't— Hurry please! I don't know how much longer I can do this."* This was far longer than he'd channelled the ground magic at Golebach.

"You need to break the connection," Ewen spoke urgently in his mind. *"Whatever this magic is, it's too strong for your body to take. You need to let go before it kills you!"*

"I can't do anything!" Fear spiked as he remembered the pain of his own magic being ripped away. Even if he could somehow stop the flow of the ground magic, he would be back where he started. With no magic of his own, Aiden's spell would kill him anyway.

"You can. You can free yourself." This time, it was the man they had called Julian who spoke. *"You're panicking. Calm down and control it."*

"Julian!" Ewen's fear was barely suppressed. *"He can't control it. He needs to stop—"*

"And what else do you suggest?" Julian snapped back. *"You heard him as well as I did. If he stops now, he'll die before we even make it there."*

"But this… It's too much. We know nothing about this magic. We've no idea what could happen— we don't even understand what's happening now! I can't let him take the risk."

"No… No, Julian's right," Nathaniel said softly. *"Alex, you can't run from this; it's part of who you are. You're the only one who can access this magic. It will respond to you if you focus."*

If he focussed? The thought seemed impossible.

"You can do it." The last voice came quietly in his mind, and Alex finally recognised it must be Xander. *"I know you can."*

"Alex…" Ewen hesitated. *"We'll be here with you. You're going to be okay, but I need you to slow your breathing."*

"Together now. Slow and steady." Calm seemed to exude from Nathaniel as he spoke, and Alex's own panic eased as the Champions grew close beside him. *"The magic seems too much, but it's not going to hurt you. It's yours."*

There was so much; an endless cascade. But as Alex stopped fighting it, he realised Nathaniel was right; the magic wasn't hurting him. In fact, there was a familiar coolness still there, under the surface. It soothed his fear as he focussed on it, and the rushing energy began to slow.

"Just like that."

Julian's voice seemed distant now, but the idea was no longer alarming. Power pooled in Alex's mind, flowing down into his limbs, and as his vision cleared, he seemed to see his own body, lying on the mesh covered platform of Aiden's machine. He saw more too; mages running through a vast lake of light, and before him, a blinding figure, glowing bright enough to see with both his eyes and the second sight that the ground magic gave him.

"*Five minutes,*" Ewen said. "*We'll be with you soon.*"

"*I know,*" Alex replied. The earth itself seemed an extension of him now, and he turned towards the space between himself and Aiden, directing his will into the ground below.

A shudder tore through the earth, and Alex saw Aiden stumble back, pulling the pedestal with him. Wires and symbols stretched to breaking as a crack split the floor of the throne room, and at once, the terrible suction of magic ceased.

For a moment, Alex was left floating in a lake of light. Then he let the magic go. Power ebbed from his body as the world dimmed to muted colours; copper wire, ash wood, the cold grey of metal around his chained wrists.

He groaned as he lifted his head, and pain rushed through his limbs; not the sharp agony of Aiden's spell, but the deep ache of worn muscles. Giving in to his exhaustion, he let himself fall, just as, through half-lidded eyes, he saw the glowing figure of Aiden rise up.

CHAPTER 45

The double doors to the throne room yielded instantly to the blast of Tamara's magic. She rushed in, eyes immediately drawn to the location of the horrors of yesterday. Instead, they landed on the prone form of Alex. He was facing away from her, lying in the centre of a circular contraption of wood and wires. There was no sign of life, and the disruption of their entrance hadn't stirred him.

"*I can't hear him anymore. Or the others.*" Nathanial's voice was unsteady. "*Does that mean—*"

"No. He can't be."

Tamara didn't realise she had stopped in the doorway until Oliver pushed against her. "Alex!" He stumbled forward, half supported by Roy and Eira; the battle and dash through the corridors, clearly having taken its toll.

"Aiden! What have you done?!" Morgan's shout was enough to tear her eyes away from the scene. He sprinted past the group, then slammed to a halt. But he wasn't looking at Alex. Instead, he was fixed on a glowing figure, the vague shape of a man. It staggered out from behind a pillar, towards the dais at the back of the room, and the star-scape mural covering the far wall seemed to shimmer as it approached. Reflections? No... The symbols were glowing, getting brighter by the moment, as though feeding off of whatever energy was being produced. A crackling at the edge of her magic sense confirmed her fears, and she finally detected a familiar nausea beneath her pounding heart.

"*Get Alex away from here!*" Nathaniel commanded, and Tamara didn't need to be told twice. The others were crouched beside Alex now, and as she approached, she saw a great crack in the floor between him and where the figure, who must be Aiden, had once stood.

"He absorbed it..." The sound of Alex's voice brought a rush of relief. "The ground magic. Mine..." His head was cradled in Oliver's arms. Weak, but alive.

But why weren't they moving? "Oliver, we need to get him up!" As she said it, Tamara saw why. A metal cuff bound each of Alex's wrists, securing him together to the wooden platform he lay on. Without releasing him, there was no way to get him out of the room, and if Aiden was about to go the route of his mageguard, they didn't have long.

"It's screwed tight!" Eira tugged vainly at where chain met wood, and as she looked up, Tamara saw her eyes were wide. "What do we do?"

"I can try the wand," Morgan's voice came from beside her. "There might be something left—"

"If that magic touches Alex, he'll die!" Oliver's words seemed to send a chill through them all. He was right. With Alex so weak, even a small amount of undirected magic would be disastrous. For Oliver too, she realised.

The glowing shape of Aiden was bright at the corner of her sight, his energy overwhelming her senses. Whatever he'd done to Alex, the power burning through his body was more than they'd seen from any of his mageguard, and she doubted he could contain it much longer.

"If we heat and cool the metal quickly enough times, that might be enough to break it." Oliver looked wildly between them. "But I don't have enough—"

"I might be able to pick it," Roy interrupted as he rummaged in the pocket of his trousers. "Either way, it's going to take some time."

"We don't have time!"

The world seemed to slow as they shouted over each other. The shape that was once Aiden had lost almost any sense of human form; arcing streaks of light towards the symbols on the wall and the fallen remnants of his pedestal.

The discharged magic will ground through whatever mage it hits first.

"Eira!" Tamara called behind her as she stepped over the crack in the floor. "Can you take care of the magic Oliver needs while Roy tries to pick it? There's something I need to try."

"What are you doing?" Morgan grabbed at her arm and she spun to face him. Pain was written across his features, and they looked at each other in silence, neither pulling away. Then, as though winning an internal battle, he stepped back.

"I'll be fine." She gave what she hoped was a reassuring smile, but received no answering change to Morgan's expression. He retreated to where Alex lay, and Tamara drew a deep breath as she turned away from them.

"*I wish we'd had longer.*" Though remorseful, Nathaniel's voice held no hint of fear as they walked towards the blinding shape. "*Still, at least this death will be more purposeful than my last.*"

"*That's sweet of you to say,*" Tamara replied, as she focused her will on her magic. "*But I don't intend for us to die.*"

This close, the static energy burned hot and cold against her own magical aura; a deep sickness that threatened to occupy every thought. But she'd practiced this more times than she could count. With the barest hint of magic, she cast her will outwards into a fine shield that spread wide, enveloping herself and the group behind her with a faint shimmer.

"*You know a shield won't protect us,*" Nathaniel spoke, almost with pity. "*It doesn't matter how strong we are.*"

"*I don't need it to be strong.*" The first shield fixed in her mind, she cast out another, then a third, each as fragile as the first.

"*You can't possibly hold your focus enough for the amount you'd need!*" Nathaniel exclaimed, and Tamara bit her lip as she added another barrier to the growing line of defence.

"*I've been doing them my whole life. Now be quiet, I need to concentrate.*"

The Aiden figure seemed to rotate towards her, as though drawn by the growing layers of magic, and for a second Tamara felt there were eyes on her, hidden somewhere within the burning figure. Then it howled; a screeching sound filled with rage and pain, and exploded in white.

The wave of energy hit her shields like acid through paper. It tore through the first layers fast enough that she gasped in shock, and her own magic flared in response; flinging more out to replace them as it took down each shield.

"*Hold steady!*" Nathaniel's presence rushed close, and Tamara sensed his will join her own. Together, they pushed back against the tide, but her mind could barely keep up. Twenty layers. Fifteen. It seemed no matter how fast they sent them out, they were going to run out of time.

"*It can't go on forever...*" Tamara's focus slipped as the weakness born of magic use seeped through her muscles. Was the light fading, or was it just her eyes blurring? She stumbled backwards, foot catching against the crack in the tiles. It twisted as she fell, pain and exhaustion stealing her ability to stand. The last shield gave way and a jolt of static ripped through her body, pulling her magic away with it. Acid burned up her throat as her stomach heaved.

Tamara blinked the black dots from her eyes, shaking her head to clear the ache pounding through it. There was a bitter metallic taste in her mouth, and when she wiped at it, her hand came away red. She'd bitten her lip hard enough to draw blood.

"Tamara!" Her name brought the world back into sharp focus. She lifted her head, but then there were arms around her; Morgan, pulling her tight against his body, warmth and pressure and the scent of him filling her senses. "You're hurt?" He leant back enough that she could see the panic on his face as he scanned her features. "Wait— I'm sorry. I shouldn't touch—"

"It's okay." Tamara rested her head back against his shoulder and breathed. The once glowing constellations that dominated the far wall were now dull. There was no trace of Aiden. No light. No body. "I'm okay."

She felt the tension release as Morgan's arms relaxed around her, and she nuzzled closer until she remembered the others.

"Is everyone—?"

"They're all fine." Morgan shifted until the platform of Aiden's machine came into view.

Oliver and Eira were hovering anxiously as Roy got to his feet; Alex held in his arms. Free.

"Looks like we survived." Nathaniel's indignation at her proximity to Morgan was barely detectable, tempered so much by his relief, and Tamara smiled.

"Looks like we did."

Chapter 46

Alex jolted upright. He gasped for breath as he fought back the suffocating material that bound him.

"Woah! It's okay! You're safe."

The voice was familiar, but he hardly registered the words. It was warm. Too warm, but as he kicked away the covers, he realised the surface below him wasn't the painful hardness of Aiden's machine.

"Hey, it's alright. Just take it slow. Breathe."

This time, he turned to search for the speaker. The pounding in his heart had slowed to a more reasonable pace, and Roy nodded as Alex met his eyes.

"I'm sorry if I startled you." Roy was sitting on a low

sofa across the bedroom, face lit by the lamp on the tall table beside him, the room's only source of light. "I'd get up, but..." He inclined his head to where Oliver sat against him, head on Roy's shoulder as he slept. "They refused to leave and get some rest. Good job Oliver's got some games on his phone or I'd be bored out my mind. No offense." Alex didn't respond to Roy's grin, instead scanning the rest of the room.

Four posts rose from the corners of the bed he lay on; the dark blue curtains that would have surrounded it tied back with silver ropes, greyed by a mix of age and the soft lighting. Wooden panelling and shimmering wallpaper covered the walls, up to a high ceiling carved with intricate patterns. A palace bedroom? Then he saw his mother.

She sat in a chair beside him, head resting on the end of the bed by his feet. Worry shrouded her sleeping face, but Alex felt his body calm as he watched her steady breathing.

"Eira's all good, too. She went to ask for some food to be brought up," Roy said, clearly sensing the unasked question, and Alex let out a shaky breath as he turned back.

"The others?" His dry throat made his voice come out in a croak.

"They're fine. Everything's okay. Tamara's gone back to Vailberg for now, though. With him." A shadow seemed to darken Roy's face. "Guess they've got to smooth things over, what with Aiden gone."

Gone. The ache he'd been ignoring burned through Alex's limbs as he sunk back against the pillows. "What happened?" It took effort to speak, and his voice seemed so quiet that for a second Alex wasn't sure Roy had heard him.

"We don't really know." Roy looked away towards the curtain covered window. Bright light glinted through a fine break in the centre, and Alex realised it must be daylight outside. "Seems like whatever power he took from you was more than he could handle. Burned him up until there was nothing left."

"Oh."

"It wasn't your fault."

"...Yeah." Alex rolled onto his side, resting his face against a cool area of his pillow. It didn't seem real. Less than a week ago, he'd been preparing for university. His father had been alive. He'd been normal. Now... he didn't know what he was anymore.

The room fell back into soft silence, only interrupted by the steady breathing of its sleeping inhabitants and the click of buttons from the phone in Roy's hand. They were safe. It should have brought him relief, but all Alex felt was emptiness.

"It takes time."

He looked up at Roy's words.

"It's gonna be rough for a bit. I won't lie. But it gets easier." Rather than pity, there was a knowing look in his eyes. "If you ever want to talk about it... Well... You know," Roy fiddled with awkwardly with the phone. "We're a team now, aren't we?"

Alex propped himself up on his arm. "Yeah," he said. "I guess we are."

"Good." Roy's expression softened as he glanced down at where Oliver lay. "Then you know we're here for you." He looked back at Alex. "You just rest for now. Eira will be back soon."

Rest. It sounded easier than it was, but his body was still screaming its exhaustion. Alex let his head drop back to the pillow. They were a team. He could only hope Roy was right about things getting better, too. "Thank you." He meant it.

Printed in Great Britain
by Amazon